DISCIPLINE

Mary Brunton was born in 1778 on the island of Burra in the Orkneys, and was educated primarily by her mother, under whose tuition she became a proficient musician and an excellent French and Italian scholar.

She married Alexander Brunton at the age of 20 and moved to Bolton and then Edinburgh where she formed a close friendship with Mrs Izett who encouraged her literary endeavours. *Self-Control* was published in 1810/11 and was highly praised by Jane Austen who said that she doubted if she could ever reach such a standard. In 1815, Mary Brunton's second novel, *Discipline*, was published, which also influenced Jane Austen. Her third novel, *Emmeline*, was published posthomously in 1819.

Mary Brunton died tragically in childbirth in 1818, yet her slender literary output is a central part of women's literary tradition. Pandora is reprinting *Self Control* and *Discipline* in the *Mothers of the Novel* reprint series.

Fay Weldon was born and brought up in New Zealand and went to St Andrew's University in Scotland where she graduated in Economics and Psychology. After a decade of odd jobs and hard times she started writing and now, although primarily a novelist, she also writes short stories and radio dramas and is a prolific stage and drama writer. Some of her more recent publications include: *Puffball* (1980); *The Life and Loves of a She Devil* (1983); and *Letters to Alice* (1984).

MOTHERS OF THE NOVEL

Reprint fiction from Pandora Press

Pandora is reprinting eighteenth and nineteenth century novels written by women. Each novel is being reset into contemporary typography and reintroduced to readers today by contemporary women novelists. The following titles in this series are currently available:

The History of Miss Betsy Thoughtless by Eliza Haywood (1751)
Introduced by Dale Spender

The Female Quixote by Charlotte Lennox (1752)
Introduced by Sandra Shulman

Belinda by Maria Edgeworth (1801)
Introduced by Eva Figes

Adeline Mowbray by Amelia Opie (1804)
Introduced by Jeanette Winterson

The Wild Irish Girl by Lady Morgan (1806)
Introduced by Brigid Brophy

Self-Control by Mary Brunton (1810/11)
Introduced by Sara Maitland

Patronage by Maria Edgeworth (1814)
Introduced by Eva Figes

The selection for Spring 1987 includes:

Memoirs of Miss Sidney Bidulph by Frances Sheridan (1761)
Introduced by Sue Townsend

A Simple Story by Elizabeth Inchbald (1791)
Introduced by Jeanette Winterson

The Memoirs of Emma Courtney by Mary Hays (1796)
Introduced by Sally Cline

Discipline by Mary Brunton (1814)
Introduced by Fay Weldon

Helen by Maria Edgeworth (1834)
Introduced by Maggie Gee

Forthcoming in Autumn 1987:

Munster Village by Lady Mary Hamilton (1778)
Introduced by Emma Tennant
and
The Old Manor House by Charlotte Smith (1794)
Introduced by Janet Todd

The companion to this exciting series is:

MOTHERS OF THE NOVEL
100 Good Women Writers before Jane Austen
by Dale Spender

In this wonderfully readable survey, Dale Spender reclaims the many women writers who made a significant contribution to the literary tradition. She describes the interconnections among the writers, their approach and the public response to their work.

DISCIPLINE

MARY BRUNTON

Introduced by Fay Weldon

This edition first published in 1986 by
Pandora Press (Routledge & Kegan Paul plc)
11 New Fetter Lane, London EC4P 4EE

Published in the USA by
Pandora Press (Routledge & Kegan Paul Inc.)
in association with Methuen Inc.
29 West 35th Street, New York, NY 10001

Set in Ehrhardt 10/11½pt.
by Columns, Reading
and printed in Great Britain
by The Guernsey Press Co Ltd
Guernsey, Channel Islands

Library of Congress Cataloging in Publication Data
Brunton, Mary, 1778-1818.
Discipline.
(Mothers of the novel)
Reprint.
I. Title. II. Series.
PR4250.B73D57 1986 823'.7 86-1448

British Library CIP Data also available

ISBN 0-86358-105-6

CONTENTS

INTRODUCTION

MARY BRUNTON, born in 1778, dying in 1818, was an almost exact contemporary of Jane Austen. Both women wrote a handful of novels, both were admired and widely read in their lifetime, and both met untimely ends – Mrs Brunton in childbirth, having her first baby, anticipating her death as if she were one of her own improbable heroines; Jane Austen, more discreetly, of Addisons Disease – and both were (according to friends and family) models of piety, conscience and rectitude. Jane Austen, that secret subversive, has of course entered the annals of English Literature. Mary Brunton (and if we are to envisage those annals as a rather pleasant Georgian house) stands rather timorously on the doorstep, offering her improving tales for inspection – *Discipline* (1815), *Self-Control* (1810) and *Emmeline* (1819).

I myself would very much like to see Mary Brunton let in, at least into the kitchen and the bedroom, if not quite into the parlour where High Literature sits and where Jane Austen is so graciously and elegantly at home – and in this I am at one with Dale Spender, that ardent, admirable rescuer of the female past and present, and editor of this series. For improving the Brunton novels may be, but what fun they are to read, rich in invention, ripe with incident, shrewd in comment, and erotic in intention and fact, and how satisfactory it turns out to be, after decades of modernism, post-modernism, expressive realism and so forth, to read these classic tales of seduction averted, virtue rewarded and evil punished.

The actor MacReady observed of the Brunton novels, in 1834, that their aim was far higher than any to be found in, say, Jane Austen's *Emma*; 'they try to make us better,' he wrote with approval, 'and it is an addition to previous faults if they do not. The necessity, the comfort, and the elevating influence of piety is continually inculcated throughout her works.' And Jane Austen herself, having finally managed to lay her hands on a copy of the best-selling *Self-Control*, found it 'an excellently-meant, elegantly-written work, without anything of nature or probability in it. I do not know whether Laura's passage down her American River is not the most natural, possible, everyday thing she ever does.' (Laura has been pursued over continents and through two thick volumes by a seducing villain, and only finally escapes by way of an Indian canoe.) To which charge of 'improbability' in that and her other novels Mrs Brunton could only patiently reply that 'were such small censures pointed at the lessons which the tales were intended to convey, she would have felt it her duty, as well as her earnest desire, to remove them. But as it was – too bad!'

Jane Austen, I do believe, paid lip service to piety and Mary Brunton a good deal more than lip service, at a time when the reading of a novel, let alone the writing of one, was seen as frivolous at best and immoral at worst, and the imagination of people in general and young ladies in particular considered best left undeveloped, lest it lead them to ideas beyond their station and dreams beyond their sex. But it's hard to keep a good novel down, then as now, and a few people *will* write, and many people *will* read, then as now, and to preserve a high moral tone within the novel was no doubt the best compromise that could be reached at the time.

Fiction *is*, of course, both powerful and dangerous, and remains so, though we in our generation are so surfeited with it, via films and TV, that it does seem to have lost some of its power. Moreover we have come to expect the novel to take from real life and feed back into real life; we see its function as nothing to do with piety, but to do with the explaining of ourselves to ourselves, a process started by Jane Austen and developed by her successors ever since. We, the descendants of those earlier readers, frown upon the improbabilities which, leaving prejudice aside, make *Discipline* so enhancing and enchanting: we turn up our noses at the high moral tone which was perfectly appropriate to the time in which Mary Brunton wrote. We must learn better.

The Brunton novels, as her brother wrote rather sadly in his memoir of his deceased sister, 'rose very fast into celebrity, and their popularity seems to have as quickly sunk away.' But it is, as I say, hard to keep a good novel down; *Discipline* has surfaced again after two and a half centuries, thanks to Dale Spender and the Pandora Press, and at the very least can be read out of sheer literary interest, as the kind of novel which pricked Jane Austen into writing that energetic fictional essay on improbabilities, *Northanger Abbey*.

Fay Weldon
February 1986

CHAPTER I

– I was wayward, bold, and wild;
A self-willed imp; a grandame's child;
But, half a plague and half a jest,
Was still endured, beloved, carest.

Walter Scott

I HAVE heard it remarked, that he who writes his own history ought to possess Irish humour, Scotch prudence, and English sincerity; – the first, that his work may be read; the second that it may be read without injury to himself; the third, that the perusal of it may be profitable to others. I might, perhaps, with truth declare, that I possess only the last of these qualifications. But, besides that my readers will probably take the liberty of estimating for themselves my merits as a narrator, I suspect, that professions of humility may possibly deceive the professor himself; and that, while I am honestly confessing my disqualifications, I may be secretly indemnifying my pride, by glorying in the candour of my confession.

Any expression of self-abasement might, indeed, appear peculiarly misplaced as a preface to whole volumes of egotism; the world being generally uncharitable enough to believe, that vanity may somewhat influence him who chooses himself for his theme. Nor can I be certain that this charge is wholly inapplicable to me; since it is notorious to common observation, that, rather than forego their darling subject, the vain will expatiate even on their errors. A better motive, however, mingles with those which impel me to relate my story. It is no unworthy feeling which leads such as are indebted beyond return, to tell of the benefits they have received; or which prompts one who has escaped from eminent peril, to warn others of the danger of their way.

It is, I believe, usual with those who undertake to be their own biographers, to begin with tracing their illustrious descent. I fear this portion of my history must be compiled from very scanty materials; for my father, the only one of the race who was ever known to me, never mentioned his family, except to preface a philippic against all dignities in church and state. Against these he objected, as fostering 'that aristocratical contumely, which flesh and blood cannot endure'; a vice which I have heard him declare to be, above all others, the object of his special antipathy. For this selection, which will probably obtain sympathy only from the base-born, my father was not without reason; for, to the pride of birth it was doubless owing that my grandfather, a cadet of an ancient family, was doomed to starve upon a curacy, in revenge for his contaminating the blood of the Percys by an unequal alliance; and, when disappointment and privation had brought him to an early grave, it was probably the same sentiment which induced his relations to prolong his punishment in the person of his widow and infants, who, with all possible dignity and unconcern, were left to their fate. My father, therefore, began the world with very slender advantages; an accident of which he was so far from being ashamed, that he often triumphantly recorded it, ascribing his subsequent affluence to his own skill and diligence alone.

He was, as I first recollect him, a muscular dark-complexioned man, with a keen black eye, cased in an extraordinary perplexity of wrinkle, and shaded by a heavy beetling eyebrow. The peculiarity of his face was a certain arching near the corner of his upper lip, to which it was probably owing that a smile did not improve his countenance; but this was of the less consequence, as he did not often smile. He had, indeed, arrived at that age when gravity is at least excusable; although no trace of infirmity appeared in his portly figure and strong-sounding tread.

His whole appearance and demeanour were an apt contrast to those of my mother, in whose youthful form and features symmetry gained a charm from that character of fragility which presages untimely decay, and that air of melancholy which seems to welcome decline. I have her figure now before me. I recollect the tender brightness of her eyes, as laying her hand upon my head, she raised them silently to heaven. I love to remember the fine flush that was called to her cheek by the fervour of the half-uttered blessing. She was, in truth, a gentle being; and bore my wayward humour with an angel's patience. But she exercised a control too gentle over a spirit which needed to be reined by a firmer hand than hers. She shrunk from bestowing even merited reproof, and never inflicted pain without suffering much more than she caused. Yet, let not these relentings of nature be called weakness – or if the stern morality refuse to spare, let it disarm his severity, to learn that I was an only child.

I know not whether it was owing to the carelessness of nurses, or the depravity of waiting-maids, or whether, 'to say all, nature herself wrought in me so'; but, from the earliest period of my recollection, I furnished an instance at least, if not a proof, of the corruption of human kind; being proud, petulant, and rebellious. Some will probably think the growth of such propensities no more unaccountable than that of briars and thorns; being prepared, from their own experience and observation, to expect that both should spring without any particular culture. But whoever is dissatisfied with this compendious deduction, may trace my faults to certain accidents in my early education.

I was, of course, a person of infinite importance to my mother. While she was present, her eye followed my every motion, and watched every turn of my countenance. Anxious to anticipate every wish, and vigilant to relieve every difficulty, she never thought of allowing me to pay the natural penalties of impatience or self-indulgence. If one servant was driven away by my caprice, another attended my bidding. If my toys were demolished, new baubles were ready at my call. Even when my mother was reluctantly obliged to testify displeasure, her coldness quickly yielded to my tears; and I early discovered, that I had only to persevere in the demonstrations of obstinate sorrow, in order to obtain all the privileges of the party offended. When she was obliged to consign me to my maid, it was with earnest injunctions that I should be amused, – injunctions which it every day became more difficult to fulfil. Her return was always marked by fond inquiries into my proceedings during her absence; and I must do my attendants the justice to say, that their replies were quite as favourable as truth would permit. They were too politic to hazard, at once, my favour and hers, by being officiously censorious. On the contrary, they knew how to ingratiate themselves, by rehearsing my witticisms, with such additions and improvements as made my original property in them rather doubtful. My mother, pleased with the imposition, usually listened with delight; or, if she suspected the fraud, was too gentle to repulse it with severity, and too partial herself, to blame what she ascribed to a kindred partiality. On my father's return from the counting-house, my double rectified *bon mots* were commonly repeated to him, in accents low enough to draw my attention, as to somewhat not intended for my ear, yet so distinct as not to balk my curiosity. This record of my wit served a triple purpose. It confirmed my opinion of my own consequence, and of the vast importance of whatever I was pleased to say or do: it strengthened the testimony which my mother's visiters bore to my miraculous prematurity; and it established in my mind that association so favourable to feminine character, between repartee and applause!

To own the truth, my mother lay under strong temptation to report my sallies, for my father always listened to them with symptoms of pleasure. They sometimes caused his countenance to relax into a smile; and sometimes, either when they were more particularly brilliant, or his spirits in a more harmonious tone, he would say, 'Come, Fanny, get me something nice for supper, and keep Ellen in good humour, and I won't go to the club to-night.' He generally, however, had reason to repent of this resolution; for though my mother performed her part to perfection, I not unfrequently experienced, in my father's presence, that restraint which has fettered elder wits under a consciousness of being expected to entertain. Or, if my efforts were more successful, he commonly closed his declining eulogiums by saying, 'It is a confounded pity she is a girl. If she had been of the right sort, she might have got into Parliament, and made a figure with the best of them. But now what use is her sense of?' – 'I hope it will contribute to her happiness,' said my mother, sighing as if she had thought the fulfilment of her hope a little doubtful. 'Poh!' quoth my father, 'no fear of her happiness. Won't she have two hundred thousand pounds, and never know the trouble of earning it, nor need to do one thing from morning to night but amuse herself?' My mother made no answer: – so by this and similar conversations, a most just and desirable connection was formed in my mind between the ideas of amusement and happiness, of labour and misery.

If to such culture as this I owed the seeds of my besetting sins, at least, it must be owned that the soil was propitious, for the bitter root spread with disastrous vigour; striking so deep, that the iron grasp of adversity, the giant strength of awakened conscience, have failed to tear it wholly from the heart, though they have crushed its outward luxuriance.

Self-importance was fixed in my mind long before I could examine the grounds of this preposterous sentiment. It could not properly be said to rest on my talents, my beauty, or my prospects. Though these had each its full value in my estimation, they were but the trappings of my idol, which, like other idols, owed its dignity chiefly to the misjudging worship which I saw it receive. Children seldom reflect upon their own sentiments; and their self-conceit may, humanly speaking, be incurable, before they have an idea of its turpitude, or even of its existence. During the many years in which mine influenced every action and every thought, whilst it hourly appeared in the forms of arrogance, of self-will, impatience of reproof, love of flattery, and love of sway, I should have heard of its very existence with an incredulous smile, or with an indignation which proved its power. And when at last I learnt to bestow on one of its modifications a name which the world agrees to treat with some respect, I could own that I was even 'proud of my pride;' representing every instance of a contrary propensity as the badge of a servile and grovelling disposition.

Meanwhile my encroachments upon the peace and liberty of all who approached me, were permitted for the very reason which ought to have made them be repelled, – namely, that I was but a child! I was the dictatrix of my playfellows, the tyrant of the servants, and the idolised despot of both my parents. My father, indeed, sometimes threatened transient rebellion, and announced opposition in the tone of one determined to conquer or die; but, though justice might be on his side, perserverance, a surer omen of success, was upon mine. Hour after hour, nay, day after day, I could whine, pout, or importune, encouraged by the remembrance of former victories. My obstinacy always at length prevailed, and of course gathered strength for future combat. Nor did it signify how trivial might be the matter originally in dispute. Nothing could be unimportant which opposed my sovereign will. That will became every day more imperious; so that, however much it governed others, I was myself still more its slave, knowing no rest or peace but in its gratification. I had often occasion to rue its triumphs, since not even the cares of my fond mother could always shield me from the consequences of my perverseness; and by the time I had reached my eighth year, I was one of the most troublesome, and, in spite of great natural hilarity of temper, at times one of the most unhappy beings, in that great metropolis which contains such variety of annoyance and of misery.

Upon retracing this sketch of the progress and consequences of my early education, I begin to fear, that groundless censure may fall upon the guardians of my infancy; and that defect of understanding or of principle may be imputed to those who so unsuccessfully executed their trust. Let me hasten to remove such a prejudice. My father's understanding was respectable in the line to which he chose to confine its exertions. Indifference to my happiness or my improvement cannot surely be alleged against him, for I was the pride of his heart. I have seen him look up from his newspaper, while reading the 'shipping intelligence,' or the opposition speeches, to listen to the praises of my beauty or my talents; and, except when his temper was irritated by my perverseness, I was the object of his almost exclusive affection. But he was a man of business. His days were spent in the toil and bustle of commerce; and, if the evening brought him to his home, it was not unnatural that he should there seek domestic peace and relaxation, – a purpose wholly incompatible with the correction of a spoiled child. My mother was indeed one of the finer order of spirits. She had an elegant, a tender, a pious mind. Often did she strive to raise my young heart to Him from whom I had so lately received my being. But, alas! her too partial fondness overlooked in her darling the growth of that pernicious weed, whose shade is deadly to every plant of celestial origin. She continued unconsciously to foster in me that spirit of pride, which may indeed admit the transient admiration of excellence, or even the passing fervours of gratitude, but which is manifestly opposite to vital piety; – to that piety which consists in a surrender of self-will, of self-righteousness, of self in every form, to the Divine justice, holiness, and sovereignty. It was, perhaps, for training us to this temper, of such difficult, yet such indispensable attainment, that the discipline of parental authority was intended. I have long seen reason to repent the folly which deprived me of the advantages of this useful apprenticeship, but this conviction has been the fruit of discipline far more painful.

In the mean time, my self-will was preparing for me an immediate punishment, and eventually a heavy, and irremediable misfortune. I had just entered my ninth year, when one evening an acquaintance of my mother's sent me an invitation to her box in the theatre. As I had been for some days confined at home by a cold, and sore throat, my mother judged it proper to refuse. But the message had been unwarily delivered in my hearing, and I was clamorous for permission to go. The danger of compliance being, in this instance, manifest, my mother resisted my entreaties with unwonted firmness. After arguing with me, and soothing me in vain, she took the tone of calm command, and forbade me to urge her further. I then had recourse to a mode of attack which I often found successful, and began to scream with all my might. My mother, though with tears in her eyes, ordered a servant to take me out of the room. But, at the indignity of plebeian coercion, my rage was so nearly convulsive, that, in terror, she consented to let me remain, upon condition of quietness. I was, however, so far from fulfilling my part of this compact, that my father, who returned in the midst of the contest, lost patience; and, turning somewhat testily to my mother, said, 'The child will do herself more harm by roaring there, than by going to fifty plays.'

I observed (for my agonies by no means precluded observation) that my mother only replied by a look, which seemed to say that she could have spared this apostrophe; but my father growing a little more out of humour as he felt himself somewhat in the wrong, chose to answer to that look, by saying, in an angry tone, 'It really becomes you well, Mrs Percy, to pretend that I spoil the child, when you know you can refuse her nothing.'

'That, I fear,' said my mother, with a sigh, 'will be Ellen's great misfortune. Her dispositions seem such as to require restraint.'

'Poh!' quoth my father, 'her dispositions will do well enough. A woman is the better for a spice of the devil!' – an aphorism, which we have owed at first to some gentleman who, like my father, had slender experience in the pungencies of female character.

Gathering hopes from this dialogue, I redoubled my vociferation, till my father, out of all patience, closed the contest, as others had been closed before, by saying, 'Well, well, you perverse, ungovernable brat, do take your own way, and have done with it.' I instantly profited by the permission, was dressed, and departed for the play.

I paid dearly for my triumph. The first consequence of it was a dangerous fever. My mother, – but what words can do justice to the cares which saved my quivering life; what language shall paint the tenderness that watched my restless bed, and pillowed my aching temples on her bosom; that shielded from the light the burning eye, and warded from every sound the morbid ear; that persevered in these cares of love till nature failed beneath the toil, and till, with her own precious life, she had redeemed me from the grave! My mother – first, fondest love of my soul! is this barren, feeble record, the only return I can make for all thy matchless affection?

After hanging for three weeks upon the very brink of the grave, I recovered. But anxiety and fatigue had struck to the gentlest, the kindest of hearts; and she to whom I twice owed my life, was removed from me before I had even a thought of my vast debt of gratitude. For some months her decline was visible to every eye, except that of the poor heedless being who had most reason to dread its progress. Yet even I, when I saw her fatigued with my importunate prattle, or exhausted by my noisy merriment, would check my spirits, soften my voice to a whisper, and steal round her sofa on tiptoe. Ages would not efface from my mind the tenderness with which she received these feeble attributes of an affection, alas! so dearly earned. By degrees, the constant intercourse which had been the blessing of my life was exchanged for short occasional visits to my mother's chamber. Again these were restricted to a few moments, while the morning lent her a short-lived vigour; and a few more, while I received her evening blessing.

At length three days passed, in which I had not seen my mother. I was then summoned to her presence; and, full of the improvident rapture of childhood, I bounded gaily to her apartment. But all gladness fled, when my mother, folding me in her arms, burst into a feeble cry, followed by the big convulsive sob which her weakness was unable to repress. Many a time did she press her pale lips to every feature of my face; and often strove to speak, but found no utterance. An attendant, who was a stranger to me, now approached to remove me, saying, that my mother would injure herself. In the dread of being parted from her child, my fond parent found momentary strength; and, still clinging to me, hid her face on my shoulder, and became more composed. 'Ellen,' said she, in a feeble broken voice, 'lift up thy little hands, and pray that we may meet again.' Unconscious of her full meaning, I knelt down by her; and, resting my lifted hands upon her knees as I was wont to do while she taught me to utter my infant petitions, I said, 'Oh! let mamma see her dear Ellen again!' Once more she made me repeat my simple prayer; then, bending over me, she rested her locked hands upon my head, and the warmth of a last blessing burst into tremulous interrupted whispers. One only of these parting benedictions is imprinted on my mind. Wonder impressed it there at first; and, when nearly effaced by time, the impression was restored with force irresistible. These were the well-remembered words: 'Oh be kinder than her earthly parents, and show thyself a father, though it be in chastising.'

Many a tender wish did she breathe, long since forgotten by her thoughtless child, till at last the accents of love were again lost in the thick struggling sobs of weakness. Again the attendant offered to remove me; and I, half-wearied with the sadness of the scene, was not unwilling to go. Yet I tried to soothe a sorrow which I could not comprehend, by promising that I would soon return. Once more, with the strength of agony, my mother pressed me to her bosom; then, turning away her head, she pushed me gently from her. I was led from her chamber – the door closed – I heard again the feeble melancholy cry, and her voice was silent to my ear for ever.

The next day I pleaded in vain to see my mother. Another came, and every face looked mournfully busy. I saw not my father; but the few domestics who approached me, gazed sadly on my childish pastime, or uttered an expression of pity, and hurried away. Unhappily, I scarcely knew why, I remembered my resort in all my little distresses, and insisted upon being admitted to my mother. My attendant long endeavoured to evade compliance, and when she found me resolute, was forced to tell the melancholy truth. She had so often combated my wilfulness by deceit, that I listened without believing; yet, when I saw her serious countenance, something like alarm added to my impatience, and, bursting from her, I flew to my mother's chamber.

The door which used to fly open at my signal was fastened, and no one answered my summons; but the key remained in the lock, and I soon procured admission. All seemed strangely altered since I saw it last. No trace appeared of my mother's presence. Here reigned the order and the stillness of desolation. The curtains were drawn back, and the bed arranged with more than wonted care: yet it seemed pressed by the semblance of a human form. I drew away the cover, and beheld my mother's face. I thought she slept; yet the stern quietness of her repose was painful to me. 'Wake, dear mamma,' I hastily cried, and wondered when the smile of love answered not my call. I reached my hand to touch her cheek, and started at its coldness; yet, still childishly incredulous of my loss, I sprang upon the bed, and threw my arm round her neck.

A frightful shriek made me turn, and I beheld my attendant stretching her arms towards me, as if fearing to approach. Her looks of horror and alarm, – her incoherent expressions, – the motionless form before me, at last convinced me of the truth; and all the vulgar images of death and sepulture rushing on my mind, I burst into agonies of mingled grief and fear. To be carried hence by strangers, laid in the earth, shut out for ever from the light and from me! – I clung to the senseless clay, resolved, while I had life, to shield my dear mother from such a fate.

My cries assembled the family, who attempted to withdraw me from the scene. In vain they endeavoured to persuade or to terrify me. I continued to hang on the bosom which had nourished me, and to mingle my cries of Mother! mother! with vows that I would never leave her, not though they should hide me with her in the earth. At last my father commanded the servants to remove me by force. In vain I struggled and shrieked in anguish. I was torn from her, – and the tie was severed for ever!

CHAPTER II

Such little wasps, and yet so full of spite;
For bulk mere insects, yet in mischief strong.
Tate's Juvenal

For some hours I was inconsolable; but at length tired nature befriended me, and I wept myself to sleep. The next morning, before I was sufficiently awake for recollection, I again, in a confused sense of pain, began my instinctive wailing. I was, however, somewhat comforted by the examination of my new jet ornaments; and the paroxysms of my grief thenceforth returned at lengthening intervals, and with abating force. Yet when I passed my mother's chamber-door, and remembered that all within was desolate, I would cast myself down at the threshold, and mix with shrieks of agony the oft-repeated cry of Mother! mother! Or, when I was summoned to the parlour, where no one now was concerned to promote my pastimes, or remove my difficulties, or grant my requests, – on the failure of some of my little projects, I would lean my head on her now vacant seat, and vent a quieter sorrow, till reproof swelled it into loud lamentation.

These passing storms my father found to be very hostile to the calm which he had promised himself in a fortnight of decent seclusion from the cares of the counting-house. Besides, I became, in other respects, daily more troublesome. The only influence which could bend my stubborn will being now removed, he was hourly harassed with complaints of my refractory conduct. It was constantly, 'Sir, Miss Ellen won't go to bed,' – 'Sir, Miss Ellen won't get up,' – 'Sir, Miss Ellen won't have her hair combed.' – 'Sir, Miss Ellen won't learn her lesson.' My father having tried his authority some half-a-dozen times in vain, declared, not without reason, that the child was completely spoiled; so, by way of a summary cure for the evil, so far at least as it affected himself, he determined to send me to a fashionable boarding-school.

In pursuance of this determination I was conveyed to —— House, then one of the most polite seminaries of the metropolis, and committed to the tuition of Madame Duprè. My father, who did not pique himself on his acquaintance with the mysteries of education, gave no instructions in regard to mine, except that expense should not be spared on it; and he certainly never found reason to complain that this injunction was neglected. For my own part, I submitted, without opposition, to the change in my situation. The prospect of obtaining companions of my own age reconciled me to quitting the paternal roof, which I had of late found a melancholy abode.

A school, – it has been observed so often, that we are all tired of the observation, – a school is an epitome of the world. I am not even sure that the bad passions are not more conspicuous in the baby commonwealth, than among the 'children of a larger growth;' since, in after-life, experience teaches some the policy of concealing their evil propensities; while others, in a course of virtuous effort, gain strength to subdue them. Be that as it may, I was scarcely domesticated in my new abode ere I began at once to indulge and to excite the most unamiable feelings of our nature.

'What a charming companion Miss Percy will make for Lady Maria,' said one of the teachers to another who was sitting near her. 'Yes,' returned the other in a very audible whisper, 'and a lovely pair they are.' The first speaker, directing to me a disapproving look, lowered her voice, and answered something of which only the words 'not to be compared' reached my ear. The second, with seeming astonishment at the sentiments of her opponent, and a glance of complacency to me, permitted me to hear that the words 'animation,' 'sensibility,' 'intelligence,' formed part of her reply. The first drew up her head, giving her antagonist a disdainful smile; and the emphatical parts of her speech were, 'air of fashion,' 'delicacy,' 'mien of noble birth,' &c. &c. A comparison was next instituted aloud between the respective ages of Lady Maria and myself; and at this point of the controversy, the said Lady Maria happened to enter the room.

I must confess that I had reason to be flattered by any personal comparison between myself and my little rival, who was indeed one of the loveliest children in the world. So dazzling was the fairness of her complexion, so luxuriant her flaxen hair, so bright her large blue eyes, that, in my approbation of her beauty, I forgot to draw from the late conversation an obvious inference in favour of my own. But I was not long permitted to retain this desirable abstraction from self. 'Here is a young companion for you, Lady Maria,' said the teacher: – 'come, and I will introduce you to each other.'

Her little Ladyship, eyeing me askance, answered, 'I can't come now – the dress-maker is waiting to fit on my frock.'

'Come hither at once when you are desired, young lady,' said my champion, in no conciliating tone; and Lady Maria, pouting her pretty under lip, obeyed.

The teacher, who seemed to take pleasure in thwarting her impatience to begone, detained her after the introduction, till it should be ascertained which of us was eldest, and then till we should measure which was tallest. Lady Maria, who had confessed herself to be two years older than I was, reddened with mortification when my champion triumphantly declared me to have the advantage in stature. It was not till the little lady seemed thoroughly out of humour that she was permitted to retire; and I saw her no more till we met in school, where the same lesson was prescribed to both. Desirous that the first impression of my abilities should be favourable, I was diligent in performing my task. Perhaps some remains of ill-humour made Lady Maria neglect hers. Of consequence, I was commended, Lady Maria reproved. Had the reproof and the commendation extended only to our respective degrees of diligence, the equitable sentence would neither have inflamed the conceit of the one, nor the jealousy of the other; but my former champion, whose business it was to examine our proficiency, incautiously turned the spirit of competition into a channel not only unprofitable but mischievous, by making our different success the test of our abilities, not of our industry; and while I cast a triumphant glance upon my fair competitor, I saw her eyes fill with tears not quite 'such as angels shed.'

At length we were all dismissed to our pastimes; and 'every one strolled off his own glad way;' every one but I; who finding myself, for the first time in my life, of consequence to nobody, and restrained partly by pride, partly by bashfulness, from making advances to my new associates, sat down alone, looking wistfully from one merry party to another. My attention was arrested by a group more quiet than the rest; where, however, my new rival seemed to play the orator, speaking very earnestly to two of her companions, and laying one hand on the shoulder of each, as if to enforce attention. Her Ladyship spoke in whispers, for good manners are not hereditary; casting, at intervals, such glances towards me as showed that I was the subject of remarks not over laudatory.

Presently the group began to move; and Lady Maria, leading it, as if by accident, to the place where I sat, accosted me with an air of restrained haughtiness. 'Pray, Miss Percy,' said she, 'are you of the Duke of Northumberland's family?' – 'No,' answered I. – 'What Percys, then, do you belong to?' – 'I belong to my father, Mr. Percy, the great West India merchant, in Bloomsbury Square,' returned I, not doubting that my consequence would be raised by this information. To my great surprise, however, Lady Maria's ideas of my importance did not seem affected by this intelligence; for she said in a familiar tone, 'But who was your grandfather, my dear? I suppose you had a grandfather!' – and she looked round for applause at this sally.

Now it happened that I was then wholly ignorant of the dignity which may be derived from this relative, having never heard whether I had a grandfather or not; but I plainly perceived that the question was not graciously meant; and therefore I answered, with mixed simplicity and ill-humour, 'Oh! I am not a fool, – I know I must have had a grandfather; but I think he could not be a duke, for I have heard papa say he had just five shillings to begin the world with!'

'So, for aught you can tell,' said Lady Maria, shrugging her shoulders and tittering, 'your father may be the son of a blacksmith or a cobbler!'

'No, no,' interrupted one of her Ladyship's abettors, 'don't you hear Miss Percy say that he owed his being to a crown!'

This piece of boarding-school wit seemed to delight Lady Maria, who, looking me full in the face, burst into a most vociferous fit of laughter; an impertinence which I resented with more spirit than elegance, by giving her Ladyship a hearty box on the ear. A moment of dead silence ensued; the by-standers looking at each in consternation, while my pretty antagonist collected her breath for screams of pain and rage.

The superior powers were speedily assembled on the field of conflict; and the grounds of quarrel were investigated. The incivility of mine adversaries was reproved; but my more heinous outrage was judged worthy of imprisonment. In consequence of my being a stranger, it was proposed that this punishment should be remitted, upon condition of my apologising to Lady Maria, and promising future good behavioiur. With these conditions, however, I positively refused to comply; declaring that, if they were necessary to my release, I would remain in confinement till my father removed me from school. In vain did the teachers entreat, and Madame Duprè command. I insisted, with sobs of indignation, that Lady Maria was justly punished for her impertinence; and stoutly asserted my right to defend myself from aggression. The maintenance of order required that I should be subdued; and, finding me altogether inflexible in regard to the terms of capitulation, the governess, in spite of the wildest transports of my rage, committed me to close custody.

Left to itself, my fury, by degrees, subsided into sullen resolution. Conceiving that I had been unjustly treated, I determined not to yield. This humour lasted till the second day of my captivity, when I began to entertain some thoughts of a compromise with my dignity. Yet, when the original terms were again proposed to me without abatement, pride forbade me to accept what I had so often refused; and I remained another day in durance. At last, when I was heartily wearied of solitude and inaction, I received a visit from my champion; and though I had stubbornly withstood higher authority, I was moved by remembrance of the favour she had shown me, to consent, that, provided Lady Maria would humble herself before me for her impertinence, I would apologise for the blow which I had given. It was now her Ladyship's turn to be obstinate. She refused to comply; so after another day's confinement I was liberated unconditionally, as having sufficiently expiated my fault.

From that time an ill-humour prevailed between Lady Maria and myself, which was kept alive by mutual indications of insolence and ill-will. It had too little dignity to bear the name of hatred; and might rather be characterised as a kind of snappishness, watchful to give and to take offence. Our companions enlisted in our quarrels. By degrees almost every girl in the school had been drawn to engage on one side or other; and our mutual bickerings were often carried on with as much rancour as ever envenomed the contests of Whig and Tory.

Of all my adherents, the last to declare in my favour, the most steady when fixed, was Miss Juliet Arnold, the daughter of an insurance-broker lately deceased. Mr Arnold, finding it impossible to derive from himself or his ancestors sufficient consequence to satisfy his desires, was obliged to draw for importance upon posterity, by becoming the founder of a family; therefore, leaving his daughter almost in a state of dependence, he bequeathed the bulk of a considerable fortune to his son. This young gentleman calculated that the most frugal way of providing for his sister would be to aid her in obtaining an establishment. Miss Juliet Arnold, therefore, was educated to be married.

Let no simple reader, trained by an antiquated grandmother in the country, imagine my meaning to be that Miss Arnold was practised in the domestic, the economical, the submissive virtues; that she was skilled in excusing frailty, enlivening solitude, or scattering sunshine upon the passing clouds of life! – I only mean that Miss Arnold was taught accomplishments which were deemed likely to attract notice and admiration; that she knew what to withdraw from the view, and what to prepare for exhibition; that she was properly instructed in the value of settlements; and duly convinced of the degradation and misery of failure in the grand purpose of a lady's existence. For the rest, nature had done much to qualify Juliet for her profession; for she had a pliant temper, and an easy address; she could look undesigning, and flatter fearlessly; her manners were caressing, her passions cool, and her person was generally agreeable, without being handsome enough to awaken the caution of the one sex or the envy of the other. Even when a child, she had an instinctive preference for companions superior to herself in rank and fortune; and though she was far from being a general favourite, was sure to make herself acceptable where she chose to conciliate.

Miss Arnold balanced long between my party and that of Lady Maria de Burgh. She affected to be equally well inclined to both, and even assumed the character of mediatrix. An invitation from Lady Maria to spend the holidays at the seat of her father the Duke of C——, entirely alienated Miss Arnold from my interests for a time; but just as she had finished her preparations for the important journey, the fickle dame of quality transferred her choice of a travelling companion to a young lady of her own rank, whose holiday festivities she was desirous of sharing in her turn.

From this time, Miss Arnold was my firm ally. She praised me much, defended me pertinaciously, and, right or wrong, embraced my opinions. Of course, she convinced me of her ardent affection for me; and I, accustomed almost from my birth to love with my whole heart, seized the first object that promised to fill the place which was now vacant there. Miss Arnold and I, therefore, became inseparable.

We espoused each other's quarrels, abetted each other's frolics, assisted each other's plots, and excused each other's misdemeanours. I smuggled forbidden novels into school for her; and she introduced contraband sweetmeats for me. In short, to use the language often applied to such confederations, we were 'great friends'.

This compact was particularly advantageous to me; for having, partly from nature, partly from habitual confidence of indulgence, a tendency to blunt plain-dealing, I was altogether inadequate to the invention of the hundred sly tricks and convenient excuses which I owed to the superior genius of my confederate. Often when I would have resigned myself, like a simpleton, to merited reproof, did she, with a bold flight of imagination, interpose, and bear me through in triumph. If these efforts of invention had been made in the cause of another, I might have been tempted to brand them with their proper title; as it was, I first learnt to pardon them because of their good nature, and then to admire them for their ingenuity.

Meanwhile our education proceeded *selon les regles*. We were taught the French and Italian languages; but, in as far as was compatible with these acquisitions, we remained in ignorance of the accurate science, or elegant literature to which they might have introduced us. We learnt to draw landscape; but, secluded from the fair originals of nature, we gained not one idea from the art, except such as were purely mechanical. Miss Arnold painted beautiful fans, and I was an adept in the manufacture of card purses and match figures. But had we been restricted to the use of such apparel as we could make, I fear we should have been reduced to even more than fashionable scantiness of attire. The advertisements from —— House protested that 'the utmost attention should be paid to the morals of the pupils;' which promise was performed, by requiring, that, every Sunday afternoon, we should repeat by rote a page of the Catechism, after which we were sent 'forth to meditate, at even tide,' in the Park. We were instructed in the art of wearing our clothes fashionably, and arranging our decorations with grace and effect; but as for 'the ornaments of a meek and quiet spirit,' they were in no higher estimation at —— House than 'wimples and round tires like the moon.'

At the end of seven years of laborious and expensive trifling, the only accomplishment, perhaps, in which I had attained real proficiency, was music. I had naturally a clear voice, a delicate ear, and a strong sensibility to sweet sounds; but I should never have exercised the perseverance necessary to excellence, had it not been from emulation of Lady Maria de Burgh. This stimulant, of doubtful character, even when untainted with the poison of enmity, operated so effectually, that I at last outstripped all my competitors; and my musical powers were pronounced equal to any which the public may command for hire. This acquisition (I blush whilst I write it) cost me the labour of seven hours a day! – full half the time which, after deducting the seasons of rest and refreshment, remained for all the duties of a rational, a social, an immortal being! Wise Providence! was it to be squandered thus, that leisure was bestowed upon a happy few! – leisure, the most precious distinction of wealth! – leisure, the privilege of Eden! for which fallen man must so often sigh and toil in vain!

Not such were the sentiments with which at sixteen I reviewed my acquirements. I considered them as not less creditable to my genius and industry, than suitable to the sphere in which I expected to move; and I earnestly longed to exhibit them in a world which my imagination peopled with admiring friends. I had, besides, an indistinct desire to challenge notice for gifts of more universal attraction. I knew that I was rich; I more than half suspected that I was handsome; and my heart throbbed to taste the pleasures and the pomps of wealth, but much more to claim the respectful homage, the boundless sway, which I imagined to be the prerogative of beauty.

In the summer of my sixteenth year, Lady Maria was removed from school to accompany the duchess her mother, on a tour to the watering places; and the accounts with which she favoured her less fortunate companions, of her dresses, her amusements, and her beaux, stimulated my impatience for release. My father at last yielded to my importunities; and consented, that, at the beginning of the fashionable winter, I should enter a world which looked so alluring from afar; where the objects, like sparks glittering in the distant fallow, flashed with a splendour which they owed only to the position of the eye that gazed on them.

CHAPTER III

Lamented goodness! – Yet I see
The fond affection melting in her eye.
She bends its tearful orb on me,
And heaves the tender sigh;
As thoughtful she the toils surveys,
That crowd in life's perplexing maze.

Langhorne

My father signalised my return from school by a change in his mode of life. He had been accustomed to repair regularly every morning at ten o'clock, to the counting-house; and there, or upon 'Change, he spent the greater part of the day in a routine of business, which twenty years had seen uninterrupted, save by the death of my mother, and a weekly journey to his villa at Richmond, where he always spent Saturday and Sunday. Upon placing me at the head of his establishment, my father, not aware of the difference between possessing leisure and enjoying it, determined to shake off, in part, the cares of business, and to exchange a life of toil for one of recreation, or rather of repose. Upon this account, and tempted by a valuable consideration, he admitted into the house a junior partner, who undertook to perform all the drudgery of superintending one of the most extensive mercantile concerns in London, while my father retained a large share of the profits.

At the Christmas holidays I quitted school, impatient to enter on the delights of womanhood. My father, whose ideas of relaxation were all associated with his villa at Richmond, determined that I should there spend the time which intervened before the commencement of the gay winter. In compliance with my request, he invited

Miss Arnold, whose liberation took place at the same time with my own, to spend a few weeks with me, – an invitation which was gladly accepted.

This indulgence, however, was somewhat balanced by the presence of a very different companion. My mother was a woman of real piety; and to her was accorded that 'medicine of life,' which respectable authority has assigned exclusively to persons of that character. She had a 'faithful friend.' This friend still survived, and in her my father sought a kind and judicious adviser for my inexperience. He pressed her to make his house her permanent abode, and to share with him in the government of my turbulent spirit, until it should be consigned to other authority. Miss Elizabeth Mortimer, therefore, though she refused to relinquish entirely the independence of a home, left her cottage for a while to the care of her only maid-servant; and rejoicing in an occasion of manifesting affection for her departed friend, and pleasing herself with the idea that one bond of sympathy yet remained between them, prepared to revive her friendship to the mother in acts of kindness to the child.

I regret to say that she was received with sentiments much less amicable. Miss Arnold and I considered her as a spy upon our actions, and a restraint upon our pleasures. We called her Argus and duenna; voted her a stick, a bore, a quiz, or, to sum up all reproach in one comprehensive epithet, a Methodist. Not that she really was a sectary. On the contrary, she was an affectionate and dutiful daughter of the establishment, countenancing schismatics no further, than by adopting such of their doctrines and practices as are plainly scriptural, and by testifying towards them, on all occasions, whether of opposition or conformity, a charity which evinced the divinity of its own origin. But Miss Mortimer displayed a practical conviction, that grey hairs ought to be covered with a cap; and that a neck of five-and-forty is the better for a handkerchief; she attended church regularly; was seldom seen in a public place; and, above all, was said to have the preposterous custom of condescending to join her own servants in daily prayer. Miss Arnold and I were persuaded that our duenna would attempt to import this 'pernicious superstition' into her new residence, and we resolved upon a vigorous resistance of her authority.

Our spirit, however, was not put to the proof. Miss Mortimer affected no authority. She seemed indeed anxious to be useful, but afraid to be officious. She was even so sparing of direct advice, that, had she not been the most humble of human beings, I should have said that she trusted to the dignity and grace of her general sentiments, and the beautiful consistency of her example, for effecting the enormous transition from what I was to what I ought to be.

Her gentleness converted the dislike of her charge into feelings somewhat less hostile. My friend and I could find nothing offensive in her singularities; we therefore attempted to make them amusing. We invented dismal cases of calamity, and indited piteous appeals to her charity, making her often trudge miles over the snow in search of fictitious objects of compassion; that we might laugh at the credulity which was never deaf to the cry of want, and at the principle which refused to give without enquiry. We hid her prayer-book; purloined her hoards of baby linen and worsted stockings; and pasted caricatures on the inside of her pew in church.

Much of the zest of these excellent jokes was destroyed by the calm temper and perverse simplicity of Miss Mortimer. If by chance she was betrayed into situations really ludicrous, nobody laughed with more hearty relish than she. Even on the more annoying of these practical jests, she smiled with good-natured contempt; never, even by the slightest glance, directing to Miss Arnold or myself the pity which she expressed for the folly of the contriver. We could never perceive that she suspected us of being her persecutors; and her simplicity, whether real or affected, compelled us to a caution and respect which we would have renounced had we been openly detected. Our jokes, however, such as they were, we carried on with no small industry and perseverance; every day producing some invention more remarkable for mischief than for wit. At last the tragical issue of one of our frolics inclined me to a suspension of hostilities; and had it not been for the superior firmness of my friend Miss Arnold, I believe I should have finally laid down my arms.

We were invited one day to dine with a neighbouring gentleman, a widower; whose family of dissipated boys and giddy girls were the chosen associates of Miss Arnold and myself. My father was otherwise engaged, and could not go; but Miss Mortimer accepted the invitation, very little to the satisfaction of the junior members of the party, who had projected a plan for the evening, with which her presence was likely to interfere. Miss Arnold and I, therefore, exerted all our ingenuity to keep her at home. We spilt a dish of tea upon her best silk gown; we pressed her to eat pine-apple in hopes of exasperating her toothach; and we related to her a horrible robbery and murder which had been committed only the night before, in the very lane through which we were to pass. These and many other contrivances proved ineffectual. As Miss Mortimer could not wear her best gown, she could go in a worse; she would not eat pine-apple; and she insisted that those who had committed the murder only the night before must be bloody-minded indeed if they were ready to commit another. Next I bribed the coachman to say that the barouche could not stir till it was repaired; but my father, who, on this occasion, seemed as determined as Miss Mortimer, insisting that we should go under her auspices or not go at all, settled that Miss Arnold should ride, while I drove Miss Mortimer in the curricle.

Highly displeased with this decision, I resolved that Miss Mortimer, whose forte certainly was not strength of nerve, should rue the mettle of her charioteer. With this good-natured purpose, I privately arranged that a race should be run between my steeds, and those which were mounted by Miss Arnold, and one of the fry which had already begun to swarm round the rich Miss Percy. We set off quietly enough, but we were no sooner out of sight of my father's windows, than the signal was given, and away we flew with the speed of lightning. I saw poor Miss Mortimer look aghast, though she betrayed no other sign of fear, and I had a malicious triumph in the thoughts of compelling her to sue for quarter.

'Is it not better, my dear,' said she at last, 'to drive a little more deliberately? The road is narrow here, and if we were to run over some poor creature, I know you would never forgive yourself.'

There was such irresistible mildness in the manner of this expostulation, that I could not disregard it; and I was checking my horses at the moment, when my beau, who had fallen behind, suddenly passed me. He gave them a triumphant smack with his whip, and the high-mettled animals sprang forward with a vigour that baffled my opposition: At this moment a decent-looking woman, in standing aside to let me pass, unfortunately threw herself into the line of his course; and I felt the horror which I deserved to feel, when my companions, each bounding over her, left her lying senseless within a step of the destruction which I had lost the power to avert.

From the guilt of murder I was saved by the fortitude of a stranger. He boldly seized the rein; and, with British strength of arm turning the horses short round, they reared, backed, and in an instant overturned the carriage. The stranger, alarmed by this consequence of his interference, hastened to extricate Miss Mortimer and myself; while our jockeys, too intent on the race to look back, were already out of sight.

Miss Mortimer looked pale as death, and trembled exceedingly; yet the moment she was at liberty she flew to the poor woman, whom the stranger raised from the ground. They chafed her temples, and administered every little remedy which they could command, while I stood gazing on her in inactive alarm. At length she opened her eyes; and so heavy a weight was lifted from my heart, that I could not refrain from bursting into tears; but unwilling to exhibit these marks of a reproving conscience, I turned proudly away.

It soon appeared that the woman was not materially hurt, – the horses, more sagacious and humane than their riders, having cleared without striking her. Her cottage was not fifty yards distant from, the spot, and Miss Mortimer, with the stranger, conducted her home; whilst I stood biting my glove, and affecting to superintend the people who were raising our overturned vehicle. The charitable pair soon returned. Neither of us being inclined to mount the curricle again, Miss Mortimer proposed that we should walk home, and send an apology to our party. But dreading that the temptation of an evening's *tête-à-tête* might draw something like a lecture from Miss Mortimer, I determined to accomplish my visit; and she consented that we should proceed on foot, giving, at the same time, permission to her companion to attend us.

I felt a sullen disinclination to talk, and therefore had full leisure to examine the stranger, whom Miss Mortimer introduced to me by the name of Maitland, adding that he was her old acquaintance. He was a tall, erect man, of a figure more athletic than graceful. His features were tolerably regular, and his eyes the brightest I have ever seen; but he was deprived of his pretentions to be called handsome, by a certain *bony* squareness of countenance, which we on the south side of the Tweed are accustomed to account a national deformity. His smile was uncommonly pleasing, either from its contrast with the ordinary cast of his countenance, or because it displayed the whitest and most regular teeth in the world; but he smiled so seldom as almost to forfeit these advantages. His accent was certainly provincial; yet I believe that, without the assistance of his name, I could not decidedly have pronounced him to be a Scotchman. His language, however, was that of a gentleman; always correct, often forcible, and sometimes elegant. But he spoke little, and his conversation borrowed neither strength nor grace from his manner, which was singularly calm, motionless, and unimpassioned.

Either from habitual reserve with strangers, or from particular disapprobation of me, he addressed himself almost entirely to Miss Mortimer, paying me no other attentions than bare civility required; and I, who had already begun to expect far other devoirs, from every man who accosted me, rejoiced when the conclusion of our walk separated us from the presumptuous being who had dared to treat me as a secondary person.

As soon as we entered Mr Vancouver's house, my young companions surrounded me, laughing and hallooing, – 'Beaten, beaten, – fairly beaten!' The victors pressed forward before the rest. 'Down with your five guineas, Ellen,' cried Miss Arnold. – 'Oh! faith 'twas a hollow thing!' shouted the other. Real sorrow for my fault would have made me gentle to those of my fellow-transgressors; but the shame of a proud heart had a contrary effect. – 'Take your five guineas,' said I, throwing them my purse with great disdain, 'and you had better help yourself to a little more – *that* will scarcely repay the risk of being tried for murder.' My ill-humour effected an instantaneous change on the countenances of the group. Miss Arnold, quite crest-fallen, picked up the purse, and stood twisting it in her hand, looking very silly, while she tried to excuse herself, and to throw all the blame upon her companion. He retorted, and their mutual recriminations were occasionally renewed during the afternoon; banishing whatever good humour had been spared by the disappointment which Miss Mortimer had undesignedly occasioned. At last, to our mutual satisfaction, the party separated; and Miss Mortimer, with her hopeful charge, returned home.

Never, during the whole day, did a syllable of reproof escape the lips of Miss Mortimer. She seemed willing to leave me to my conscience, and confident that its sentence would be just. But when, on retiring for the night, I could not help exclaiming, 'Thank heaven! this day is done!' – she took my hand, and said, with a look of great kindness, 'Let me dispose of one hour of your time tomorrow, dear Ellen, and I will endeavour to make it pass more agreeably.' I felt no real gratitude for her forbearance, because I had argued myself, with Miss Arnold's assistance, into a conviction that Miss Mortimer had no right to interfere; but I could not withstand the soothing gentleness of her manner, and therefore promised that I should be at her command at any hour she pleased.

Next day, therefore, while Miss Arnold was shopping in town, I became the companion of Miss Mortimer's morning walk; but I own, I began to repent of my complaisance, when I perceived that she was conducting me to the cottage of the poor woman who had so nearly been the victim of my late frolic. 'Is this,' thought I, 'the way that Miss Elizabeth fulfils her promise of making the hour pass agreeably? Such a finesse might do mighty well for a methodist; but what would she have said, had I been the author of it? It is wonderfully delightful to detect the errors of a saint. On first discovering our destination, my feelings had wavered between shame and anger; but the detection of Miss Mortimer's supposed peccadillo restored me to so much self-complacency, that I was able at least to conceal my reluctance, and entered the cottage with a pretty good grace.

The apartment was clean and comfortable. The furniture, though simple, was rather more abundant and more tasteful than is common in the abodes of labour. Two neat shelves on the wall contained a few books; and in the window stood a tambouring frame. On one side of the fire-place our old woman was busy at her spinning-wheel; on the other, in all the ease of a favourite, lay a beautiful Italian greyhound. Miss Mortimer, with the frankness of old acquaintance, accosted our hostess, who received her with respectful kindness. While they were asking and answering questions of courtesy and good-will, the dog, who had started up on our entrance, did the honours to me. He looked up in my face, smelled my clothes, examined me again, and, wagging his tail, seemed to claim acquaintance. I, too, thought I remembered the animal, though I could not recollect where I had seen him; and I own, I was glad to relieve a certain embarrassment which the old woman's presence occasioned me, by returning his caresses with interest.

'Mrs Wells,' said Miss Mortimer, when she had finished her enquiries, 'I have brought Miss Percy to visit you.'

In spite of my affected nonchalance, I was not a little relieved when I discovered, by the old woman's answer, that she had not recognised me as the author of her accident. 'Miss Ellen!' she exclaimed, as if with surprise and pleasure. Then taking my hand with a sort of obsequious affection, she said, 'Dear young lady, I should never have known you again, you are so grown! and I have never seen you since I lost my best friend,' added she, shaking her head mournfully. 'Poor Fido,' resumed she, 'he has more sagacity. He knew you again in a minute.'

'Fido, mamma's Fido!' cried I, and I stooped over the animal to hide the tears that were rushing to my eyes.

'Yes, miss, your papa sent him here, because he said he did not like to have him killed, being that he was but a young thing, and the very last thing that worthy Mrs Percy had ever taken a liking to; and he could not keep him about the house, because you never set eyes on him but you cried fit to break your heart. So he sent him here, where he was very welcome, as he had a good right to be, having belonged to her; for it was owing to her that I had a home to bring him to.'

'How was that?' enquired I, with some eagerness; for, to this day, my heart beats warm when I hear the praises of my mother.

'Why, ma'am,' returned she, 'my husband was a sober, industrious man, but we were unfortunate in working for great people, who never thought of our wants, because they had no wants of their own. So we became bankrupt, and that went to my husband's heart; for he had a high spirit. So he pined and pined away. I sold our little furniture, and then our clothes; and paid for all honestly, as far as it would go. But what with the doctors and what with the funeral, my two poor little girls and I were quite destitute. I believe it was the second night after my Thomas was laid in his grave, that my youngest girl was crying for bread, and I had none to give her. I saw the eldest cry too; but she said it was not for hunger. So, with one thing and another, I was desperate, and told the children I would go and beg for them. The little one bid me go, for she was hungry; but Sally said I should never beg for her, and followed me to the door, holding me back, and crying bitterly. So, just then, Providence sent that good spirit, Mrs Percy, by our house, and she looked so earnestly at us – for it was not in her nature to see any creature in sorrow, and pass by on the other side: – I thought I could take courage to speak to her; but, when I tried it, I had not the heart; for I had never begged before. But when she saw how things were, I did not need to beg; for she had the heart of a Christian, and the hand of a princess. She put us into this house, and gave us whatever was really needful for us. I was a good worker with my needle then, though my eyes are failing me now; and she got me as much work as I could overtake. She came, besides, every forenoon herself, and taught my eldest girl to make gowns, and my youngest to tambour, so that now they can earn their own bread, and the most part of mine. Yes, Miss Ellen,' continued, the woman, perceiving that she had fixed my pleased attention, 'your worthy mother did more than this; she brought heavenly hopes to me when I had few hopes upon earth; she gave pious counsels to my children, and they minded them the more for coming from so great a lady; so that they are good girls, and a real comfort to my old age.'

After some further conversation, Miss Mortimer put an end to our visit. I own I was somewhat struck with the contrast between the cottager's obligations to my mother and to myself; and I had a desire to place this matter on a footing less painful to my feelings, or, to speak more justly, less galling to my pride. For this reason, when we had gone a few steps from the cottage, I returned, pretending that I had forgotten my handkerchief. 'Mrs Wells,' said I, 'I have a great desire to possess Fido, – will you make an exchange with me?' continued I, presenting my purse to her.

The good woman coloured deeply; and, drawing back with a little air of stateliness, said, 'You are welcome to poor Fido, ma'am. Indeed, as for that, your mother's child is welcome to the best I have; but I cannot think of selling the poor dumb animal. No,' said she, her spirit struggling with the sob that was rising in her throat, 'I shall be poorly off indeed, before I sell the least thing that ever was hers.'

I own, I felt myself colour in my turn, as I awkwardly withdrew my purse; and I had not the confidence to look the woman in the face, while I said, 'Give me poor Fido, then, for my mother's sake; and perhaps the time may come when you will allow me the pleasure of assisting you for my own.'

'One of the girls, ma'am, shall take him to the Park this evening. I know Miss Mortimer wished to have him, but you have the best right to him; and I hope you will make him be kindly treated, ma'am; he is used to kindness.'

I thanked the good woman, promised attention to her favourite, and hurried away. Fido arrived at the Park that afternoon, and soon became the most formidable rival of Miss Arnold; nor unjustly, for he was playful, fawning, and seemingly affectionate, – the very qualities to which she owed my favour.

'See, my dear Ellen,' said Miss Mortimer, when I rejoined her, 'see how your mother's mornings were spent.' Had any one but my mother furnished the subject of this apostrophe; or had my friend Miss Arnold been present to witness its application, I should certainly have turned it off, by ridiculing the absurdity of a handsome woman of fashion spending her time in teaching cottage girls mantua-making and morality. But now, tenderness stealing on my self-reproach, I only answered with a sigh, 'Ah! my mother was an angel; I must not pretend to resemble her.'

'My dearest child!' cried Miss Mortimer, catching my hand with more animation than she had ever shown in speaking to me, 'why this ill-timed humility? Born to such splendid advantages, why should you not aspire to make your life a practical thanksgiving to the bestower? I acknowledge, that your own strength is not "sufficient for these things," but He who has called you to be perfect, will ——'

'Oh! pray now, my good Miss Mortimer,' interrupted I, 'give over for to-day, – I am more than half melancholy already. Ten or a dozen years hence, I shall attend to all these matters.'

Before my reader comment on the wisdom of this reply, let him examine, whether there be any more weight in the reasons which delay his own endeavours after Christian perfection.

Our dialogue was interrupted by the appearance of Mr Maitland, who alighted at the wicket of the cottage garden, with the intention of enquiring after the widow; but, upon hearing that she felt no bad effects from her accident, he gave his horse to his servant, and accompanied us, or rather Miss Mortimer, to the Park. A few civil enquiries were indeed, the only notice which he deigned to bestow upon me; and, to own the truth, I was not at all more gracious to him.

At the door of Sedly Park, stood my father as usual with one arm resting in the hollow of his back, the other supported by his gold-headed cane; and he not only discomposed this favourite attitude by offering his hand to Mr Maitland, but advanced some steps to meet him, a mark of regard which I do not recollect having seen him bestow on any other visiter. He followed up this courtesy, by pressing his guest to dine with him, and Mr Maitland was at length induced to comply; while I stood wondering what my father could mean, by expending so much civility upon a person of whom nobody had ever heard before.

I cannot pretend to have made any observations upon Mr Maitland's manners or conversation during this visit, having previously convinced myself, that neither was worth observing. After dinner, while he discoursed with my father and Miss Mortimer, I, agreeably to the polite practice of many young ladies, formed, apart with Miss Arnold and the young Vancouvers, a coterie which, if not the most entertaining, was at least the most noisy part of the company; the sound and form holding due proportion to the shallowness. My father made some ineffectual attempts to reduce us to order; and Miss Mortimer endeavoured to dissolve our combination, by addressing her remarks to me; but I, scarcely answering her, continued to talk and titter apart with my companions till it was time for our visiters to depart.

As soon as they were gone, my father strode gravely to the upper end of the room, planted himself firmly with his back to the fire, and, knitting his brows, addressed me as I stood at the further window; – 'Miss Percy,' said he 'I do not approve of your behaviour this afternoon. I have placed you at the head of a splendid establishment, and I desire you will consider it as your duty to entertain my guests, – all my guests, Miss Percy.'

A few moments of dead silence followed, and my father quitted the room.

Had this well-deserved reproof been given in private, I might have acknowledged its justice, but Miss Mortimer and my friend were present to stimulate my abhorrence of blame; and, as soon as my father disappeared, I began a surly complaint of his ill humour, wondering 'whether he expected me to sit starched by the side of every tiresome old fellow he brought to his house, like the wooden cuts of William and Mary.'

Miss Arnold joined me in ridiculing the absurdity of such an expectation; but Miss Mortimer took part with my father. 'Indeed, my dear,' said she, 'you must allow me to say, that Mr Percy's guests, of whatever age, have an equal right to your attentions. I particularly wish you had distributed them more impartially to-day; for I would have had you appear with advantage to Mr Maitland, whom I imagine you would not have found tiresome and who is certainly not very old.'

'Appear with advantage to Mr Maitland!' exclaimed I: – 'oh! now the murder is out. My father and Miss Mortimer want me to make a conquest of Stiffy.'

Miss Arnold laughed immoderately at the idea. 'You make a conquest of Mr Maitland!' repeated Miss Mortimer in her turn, gazing in my face with grave simplicity; 'no, my dear, that, indeed, surpasses my expectation. Mr Maitland!' exclaimed she again, in a sort of smiling soliloquy over her knitting; – 'no, that would indeed be too absurd.'

I own my pride was piqued by this opinion of Miss Mortimer's; and I felt some inclination to convince her, that there was no such violent absurdity in expecting that a stiff old bachelor should be caught by a handsome heiress of seventeen. I half determined to institute a flirtation.

The idea was too amusing to be abandoned, and Mr Maitland soon gave me an opportunity of commencing my operations. He again visited Sedly Park; and, in spite of several repulses, I contrived to draw him into conversation; and even succeeded in obtaining my full share of his attention. But when he rose to be gone, I recollected with surprise, that I had spent half an hour without talking much nonsense, or hearing any. Our second interview was not more effective. At the end of the third I renounced my attack as utterly hopeless; and should as soon have thought of shaping a dangler out of Cincinnatus. Mr Maitland's heart, too, seemed as impregnable as his dignity; and I was glad to forget that I had ever formed so desperate a project as an attempt upon either.

Our acquaintance, however, continued to make some progress; and if at any luckless hour I happened to be deserted by more animating companions, I could pass the time very tolerably with Mr Maitland. I believe he was a scholar, and to this perhaps he owed that force and variety of language which was often amusing, independently of the sentiment which it conveyed. He possessed, besides, a certain dry sententious humour, of which the effect was heightened by the inflexible gravity of his countenance, and by the low tones of a voice altogether unambitious of emphasis. His stiffness, which was too gentle for hauteur, and too self-possessed for bashfulness, was a constitutional or rather, perhaps, a national reserve; which made some amends for its repulsive effect upon strangers, by gratifying the vanity of those who were able to overcome it. I own that I was selfish enough to be flattered by the distinction which he appeared to make between Miss Arnold and myself; the more so, because there was, I know not what, in Mr Maitland, which impressed me with the idea of a sturdy rectitude that bowed to no extrinsic advantage. This gratification, however, was balanced by the preference which he constantly showed for Miss Mortimer; and such was my craving for adulation, that I was at times absolutely nettled by this preference, although Mr Maitland was some years above thirty.

Towards the end of our stay at Sedly Park, his visits became more frequent; but in spite of his company, and that of many other gentlemen more agreeable to me, I was dying with impatience for our removal to town. My eagerness increased, when I accidentally heard, that Lady Maria de Burgh had already started as the reigning beauty of the winter. When this intelligence was conveyed to me, I was standing opposite to a large mirror. I glanced towards it, recalled with some contempt the miniature charms of my fairy competitor, and sprung away to entreat that my father would immediately remove to town. But my father had already fixed the fourteenth of January for his removal; and Miss Arnold alleged, that nothing short of a fire would have hastened his departure, or reduced him to the degradation of acquainting the family that he had changed his mind.

The fourteenth of January, however, at length arrived, and I was permitted to enter the scene of my imaginary triumphs.

CHAPTER IV

Next in the daunce followit invy,
Fild full of feid and fellony,
Hid malice and dispyte.
For pryvie haterit that traitour trymlit;
Him followit mony freik dissymlit,
With fenyeit wordes quhyte;
And flattereris into menis facis,
And back-bytaris in secreit placis,
To ley that had delyte;
With rownaris of fals lesingis;
Allace! that courtis of noble kingis,
Of thame can nevir be quyte.

Dunbar (Daunce.)

THE Countess of ——'s ball was fixed upon as the occasion of my first appearance. What meditation did it not cost me, to decide upon the style of my costume for that eventful evening! How did my preference fluctuate between the gorgeous and the simple, the airy and the magnificent! The balance was cast in favour of the latter, by the possession of my mother's jewels; which my father ordered to be reset for me, with superb additions. 'He could afford it,' he said, 'as well as Lady —— or any of her company, and he saw no reason why I should not be as fine as the proudest of them.' My heart bounded with delight, when I at last saw the brilliants flash in my dark hair, mark the contour of my neck, and circle a waist slender as the form of a sylph. All that flattery had told, and vanity believed, seemed now to gain confirmation; yet, still some doubts allayed my self-conceit, till it received its consummation from the cold, the stately Mr Maitland.

I overheard Miss Arnold whisper to him, as I entered the drawing-room where he and a large party were waiting to escort me, 'look what lovely diamonds Mr Percy has given Ellen.' – 'They would have been better bestowed elsewhere,' returned Mr Maitland; 'nobody that looks at Miss Percy will observe them.'

Though certain that this compliment was not meant for my ear, I had the hardihood to acknowledge it, by saying, 'Thank you, sir; I shall put that into my memorandum-book, and preserve it like a Queen Anne's farthing, not much worth in itself, but precious, because she never made but one.'

'The farthing was never meant for circulation,' returned he dryly; 'but it unluckily fell into the hands of a child, who could not keep it to herself.'

The word 'child' was particularly offensive on this first night of my womanhood; and, in the intoxication of my spirits, I should have made some some very impertinent rejoinder, if I had not been prevented by Miss Mortimer. 'What, Ellen!' said she, 'quarrelling with Mr Maitland for compliments! Is it not enough to satisfy you, that he who is so seldom seen in places of that sort accompanies you to the ball to-night?'

'Oh! pray,' returned I, 'since Mr Maitland has so few *bienseances* to spare, allow him to dispose of them as he pleases. His attendance to-night is meant as a compliment to my father.'

'Do not make me pay a whole evening's comfort for what is only a farthing's worth, you know,' said Maitland good-humouredly; 'but leave off trying to be disagreeable and witty. Nay, do not frown now; your face will not have time to recover itself. I see the carriage is at the door.'

I did not wait for a second intimation, but bounded down stairs, and I was already seated in the barouche, with Miss Arnold before my deliberate beau made his appearance. I was too full of expectation to talk; and we had proceeded for some time in silence, when I was awakened from a dream of triumph by Mr Maitland's saying, and, as I thought, with a sigh, 'What a pleasing woman is Miss Mortimer! That feminine simplicity and sweetness make the merest common-place delightful!'

I suppose it was my vanity grasping at a monopoly of praise which made me feel myself teazed by this encomium; and I pettishly answered, 'That it was a pity Miss Mortimer did not hear this compliment, for she might keep it to herself, since she at least was no *child.*'

'Within these few years,' said Mr Maitland, 'she was a very enchanting woman.'

'Indeed!' exclaimed I, more and more out of humour at the unusual warmth of his expressions, 'Miss Mortimer has no wit, and she has never been pretty.'

'True,' returned Mr Maitland, 'but I dislike wits. I am not even fond of beauties. It is in bad taste for a woman to "flash on the startled eye." Miss Mortimer did not burst on us like a meteor, – she stole on us like the dawn, cheering and delightful, not dazzling.'

This speech seemed so manifest an attack upon me who dealt with a certain fearless repartee that passed for wit, and who was already a beauty by profession, that my eyes filled with tears of mortification. Of what use is beauty, thought I, if it be thus despised by men of sense, and draw the gaze only of silly boys? Yet men of sense have felt its power; and when people have, like Mr Maitland, outlived human feelings, they should leave the world, and not stay to damp the pleasures of the young and the happy.

The next moment, however, sparkling eyes and skins of alabaster recovered their full value in my estimation, when, as we pressed into Lady ——'s crowded rooms, a hundred whispers met my ear of 'Lovely!' – 'Charming!' and 'Devilish handsome!' My buoyant spirits rose again, and I looked up to take a triumphant survey of my admirers. Yet, when I met the universal gaze which was attracted by the splendour of my dress, or the novelty of my appearance, nature for a moment stirred in me; and though I had indignantly turned from Mr Maitland, and accepted the devoirs of a more obsequious attendant, I now instinctively caught his arm, and shrunk awkwardly behind him.

I quickly, however, recovered my self-possession, and began to enjoy the gaiety of the scene. Not so my companion; who seemed miserably out of place at a ball, and whose manner appeared even more grave and repulsive than usual. I shall never forget the solemn abstracted air with which he sat silently gazing on a chandelier; and then suddenly interrupting my conversation with a half a dozen beaux, resumed the discussion of a plan, to which I had listened with interest a few days before, for bettering the condition of the negroes upon his plantations. But my attention was at once withdrawn from his discourse, and from the titter which it occasioned, when a sudden movement opening the circle which surrounded me, gave to my view the figure of Lady Maria de Burgh.

Never had she looked so lovely. Her Ariel-like form was flying through the dance; her blue eyes sparkling with pleasure; exercise flushing her snowy skin with the hues of life and health. I observed the graceful fall of her white drapery, the unadorned braids of her sunny hair, and distrusted the taste which had loaded me with ornament.

The dance ended; and Lady Maria was going to throw herself upon a seat, when it was suddenly taken possession of by a young man, who withdrew my attention even from Lady Maria. The easy rudeness of this action, his dress, his manner, his whole air, announced him to be of the first fashion. He languidly extended a limb of the most perfect symmetry, viewed it attentively in every direction, drew his fingers through his elegantly dishevelled hair; then, composing himself into an attitude of rest, began to examine the company, through an eye-glass set with brilliants. Lady Maria having, with some difficulty, wedged herself into a place by his side, was beginning to address him, but he turned from her with the most fashionable yawn imaginable. Presently his eyes were directed, or rather fell upon me; and I felt myself inclined to excuse the plebeian vivacity, with which he instantly pointed me out to his fair companion, seeming to enquire who I was. Her Ladyship looked, and a toss of her head seemed to indicate that her reply was not very favourable. An altercation then appeared to ensue; for the gentleman rising offered the lady his hand, as if to lead her forward; the lady frowned, pouted, flounced, and at last, with a very cloudy aspect, rose and suffered him to conduct her towards me. Scarcely relaxing her pretty features, she addressed me with a few words of very stately recognition; introduced me to her brother, Lord Frederick de Burgh; and then turned away. Miss Arnold claimed her acquaintance by a humble courtesy. Her Ladyship, looking her full in the face, passed, 'and gave no sign.' I was instantly possessed with the spirit of patronage; and though I had before forgotten that Miss Arnold was in the room, I now gave her my arm, and all the attention which I could spare from Lord Frederick de Burgh.

For a man of fashion, Lord Frederick was tolerably amusing. He knew the name, and a little of the private history, of every person in the room. He flattered with considerable industry; and it was not difficult to flatter him in return. He asked me to dance. I was engaged for the three next dances; but disappointed one of my partners that I might sit with Lord Frederick. His Lordship next proposed that I should waltze with him. So much native feeling yet remained in me that I shrunk from making such an exhibition, and at first positively refused; but, happening to observe that Lady Maria was watching, with an eye of jealous displeasure, her brother's attentions to me, I could not resist the temptation of provoking her, by exhibiting these attentions to the whole assembly; and therefore consented to dance the waltze.

I own that I bitterly repented this compliance when I found myself standing with Lord Frederick alone, in the midst of the circle which was instantly formed round us. I forgot even the possibility of the admiration of which I had before been so secure. My knees knocked together, and a mist swam before my eyes. But there was now no retreat, and the dance began. My feelings of disquiet, however, did not rise to their height till, towards the close of the dance, I met the eye of Mr Maitland fixed on me in stern disapprobation. I have never yet met with any person whose displeasure was so disagreeably awful as that of Mr Maitland. At that moment it was more than I could bear. Hastily concluding the dance, I darted through the crowd of spectators, regardless of their praise or censure; and, faint and unhappy, I sunk upon a seat.

I was instantly surrounded by persons who offered me every sort of assistance and refreshment. Lord Frederick was particularly assiduous. But I owed the recovery of my spirits chiefly to the sarcastic smile with which I was eyed by Lady Maria de Burgh, whom I overheard say, with a scornful glance at the gentlemen who crowded round me, 'Really the trick takes admirably!' Mr Maitland now making his way towards me, said very coldly, 'Miss Percy, if you are inclined to go home, I shall attend you.' I was provoked at his unconcern for an uneasiness of which he had been the chief cause; and carelessly answering that I should not go home for an hour or two, accepted Lord Frederick's arm, and sauntered round the room.

During the rest of the evening, I paid no further attention to my father's friend. Once or twice I thought of him, and with an indistinct feeling of self-reproach; but I was occupied with the assiduities of my new admirer, and had no leisure to consider of propriety. I saw, too, or fancied that I saw, Lady Maria make some attempts to detach her brother from me, and I had therefore double enjoyment in detaining him by my side. Though she affected indifference, I could easily see that she continued to watch us; and as often as I perceived her eye turned towards us, I laughed, flirted, and redoubled the demonstrations of our mutual good understanding. About five in the morning the party separated; and I, more worn out by the affectation, than exhilarated by the reality of merriment, returned home. Lord Frederick attended me to my carriage; and Mr Maitland having handed in Miss Arnold, bowed without speaking, and retired.

Some very excellent and judicious persons maintain a custom of calling to mind every night the transactions of the day; but even if the habit of self-examination had at all entered into my system, this was manifestly no season for its exercise. Completely exhausted, I dropped asleep even while my poor weary maid was undressing me; and closed a day of folly, pride, and enmity, without one serious, one repentant thought.

But why do I particularise one day? My whole course of life was aptly described in a short dialogue with Mr Maitland. 'Miss Percy,' said he, 'I hope you are not the worse for the fatigues of last night.' – 'Not in the least, sir.' – 'Well, then, are you any thing the better for them? Do you look back on your amusement with pleasure?' – 'No, I must confess, I do not. Besides, I have not leisure to look back, I am so busily looking forward to this evening's opera.'

Mr Maitland, sighing from the very bottom of his heart, gave me a look which said, as intelligibly as a look could speak, 'Unfortunate, misguided girl!' We were alone; and I was half inclined to bid him give utterance to his sentiments, and tell me all the follies which, in his secret soul, he ascribed to me. Pride was struggling with my respect for his opinion, when Lord Frederick de Burgh was admitted; and the voice of candour, and of common sense, was never again allowed to mingle discord with the sounds of the 'harp and the viol.'

I had entered the throng who were in chase of pleasure, and I was not formed for a languid pursuit. It became the employment of every day, of every hour. My mornings were spent at auctions, exhibitions, and milliners' shops; my evenings wherever fashionable folly held her court. Miss Mortimer attempted gently to stem the torrent. She endeavoured to remove my temptation to seek amusement abroad, by providing it for me at home; but I had drunk of the inebriating cup, and the temperate draught was become tasteless to me. She tried to convince my reason; but reason was in a deep sleep, and stirred no further than to repulse the hand which would have roused. She attempted to persuade me; and I, to escape the subject, told her, that when I had fulfilled the engagements which were to occupy every moment of my time for the six succeeding weeks, I would, on some rainy Sunday, stay at home all day, and patiently swallow my whole dose of lecture at a sitting. I look back with astonishment upon her patient endurance of my impertinences. But she saw my follies with the pity of a superior nature; aware, indeed, of the tremendous difference between her state and mine, yet remembering who it was that had 'made her to differ.'

Finding her own efforts fruitless, she endeavoured to obtain my father's interposition. But my father considered all human kind as divided into two classes, those who were to labour for riches, and those who were to enjoy them; and he saw no reason for restricting me in the use of any pleasure for which I could afford to pay. Besides, he secretly regarded with some contempt the confined notions of Miss Mortimer, and was not without his share of elation in the triumphs which I won. He delighted to read, in the Morning Chronicle, that at Lady G——'s ball, the brilliancy of Miss Percy's jewels had never been surpassed, save by the eyes of the lovely wearer. He chuckled over the paragraph which announced my approaching nuptials with the young Duke of——, although he, at the same time, declared with an oath, that 'he would take care how he gave his daughter and his money to a fellow who might be ashamed of his father-in-aw.' Indeed he took great pleasure in bringing my suitors, especially those of noble birth, to the point of explicit proposal, and then overwhelming them with a tremendous preponderance of settlement. He rejected, in this way, some unexceptionable offers; for my splendid prospects outweighed all my folly and extravagance. I left these matters entirely to his arrangement, for I had neither wish nor love that did not centre in amusement. I sometimes wondered, however, what were his intentions in regard of me, and more than half suspected that they pointed towards Mr Maitland; but I never recollected Mr Maitland's manner towards me, without laughing at the absurdity of such a scheme.

In the mean time, along with a few sober suitors, I attracted danglers innumerable; for I was the fashion; admired by fashionable men; envied by fashionable women; and, of course, raved of by their humbler mimics of both sexes. Each had his passing hour of influence, but the lord of the ascendant was Lord Frederick de Burgh. He was handsome, showy, extravagant, and even more the fashion than myself. He danced well, drove four-in-hand, and was a very Œdipus in expounding anagrams and conundrums. Yet it was not to these advantages alone that he owed my preference. These might have won for him the smiles which he shared with fifty others; but he was indebted for my peculiar grace to his relationship with Lady Maria.

The mutual dislike of this lady and myself had been confirmed by seven years interchange of impertinences; nor was it in the least degree mitigated by the new circumstances in which we were placed. The leader of fashion, for the winter, was nearly related to the De Burgh family, and she had perhaps a stronger connection with me – she owed my father 12,000*l.* Thus she naturally became the chaperon, both to Lady Maria and myself; and we often met in circles where a person of my rank is usually considered as an intruder. Lady Maria, proud of an ancient family, resented this intrusion, the more, perhaps, because I trespassed upon rights, still dearer than the privileges of rank. I, too proud myself to tolerate pride in another, lost no opportunity of retort; and my ingenuity in discovering these occasions was probably heightened by the necessity of improving them with due regard to the rules of politeness. Our mutual acquaintance, accustomed to witness genteel indications of hatred, soon learnt to please, by gentle sarcasms against an absent rival; and we were never without some good-natured friend, who could hint to each whatever debt she owed to the malice of the other. I know not how Lady Maria might feel; but I was alternately pleased with these sacrifices to my malevolence, and mortified by perceiving, that it was visible to every common observer. I attempted to conceal what I was ashamed to avow; but the arrogance and irascibility, still more than the natural openness of my temper, unfitted me for caution; and between the fear of exposing my rancour, and my eagerness to give it vent, – between my quick sensibility to civil scorn, and my impatience to repay it in kind, – I endured more pain than it would have cost me to banish from my breast every vindictive thought.

How does one disorderly passion place us at the mercy of every creature who will use it as a tool to serve his purpose! Even my maid endeavoured to make her peace after the destruction of a favourite cap, by telling me that she had quitted Lady Maria's service for mine, because she had no pleasure in dressing her last lady, who, she said, 'was little bigger than a doll, and not much wiser.' Miss Arnold, who, in spite of her obsequious endeavours to please, had one day the misfortune to offend her capricious patroness, was restored to immediate favour, by informing me, that 'the whole town believed Lady Maria's pretended cold to be nothing but a fit of vexation, because her father had permitted Lord Frederick to pay his addresses to me.'

In spite of the belief of the 'whole town,' however, Lord Frederick was still nothing more than a dangler; nor had I the slightest desire to attract his more particular regards. I was even afraid that he should, by a serious proposal, oblige me to dispense with his future attentions, and thereby deprive me of the amusement of witnessing the frowns, and tosses, and fidgetings, with which Lady Maria watched a flirtation always redoubled when she was near.

This amusement, indeed, was obtained at the expense of incurring some animadversion. My competitors for fashion, and of course for the notice of fashionable men, revenged themselves for my superior success by sarcastic comments upon my supposed conquest; each obliquely insinuating, that she might have transferred it to herself, if she could have descended to such means as I employed. These innuendos, however, were softened ere they reached my ear, into gentle raillery, – friendly questions, as to the time when I was to bless Lord Frederick with my hand, – and tender-hearted expostulations on the cruelty of delay. Miss G—— would speak to me in the most compassionate terms, of the envy which my conquest excited in her poor friend Miss L——; and Miss L——, in her turn, would implore me to marry Lord Frederick, were it only to put poor Miss G—— out of suspense. That which should have alarmed my caution, only flattered my vanity. Instead of discountenancing the attacks of my acquaintance by calm and steady opposition, I invited them by feeble defence; or at best, parried them with a playfulness which authorised their repetition.

CHAPTER V

Here eloquence herself might plead in vain,
Nor one of all the heartless crowd could gain.
And thou! O sweeter than the muse's song,
Affection's voice divine! with cold disdain,
Even thou art heard; while mid th' insulting throng
Thy daunted shivering form moves timidly along.

Mrs Tighe.

MARRIAGE is like sin; if we often allow it to be presented to our view, we learn to look without starting. I was supremely indifferent towards Lord Frederick, and never entertained one serious thought of becoming his wife; but I suffered myself to be rallied upon our future connection, till the idea excited no distinct sentiment of disapprobation; and till by degrees I forgot to make up for the faintness of my denials, by the strength of my inward resolutions against the match. Perhaps I should describe my case more correctly, were I to own that I formed no plan for the future; all my serious consideration being reserved for the comparative merits of satin and velvet, or of an assembly and an opera. The reputation of Lord Frederick's attentions gave me much more pleasure than the attentions themselves; and my companions knew how to flatter me, by reminding me of his assiduities.

Of all my remembrancers, the most persevering, if not the most vehement, was Miss Arnold. She had made her calculations on the increased importance which rank might give her patroness; and, with her accustomed shrewdness, chose the means most effectual for promoting her object. She did not, indeed, like others of my acquaintance, rally me upon marriage; on the contrary, she rather affected some delicacy upon that subject; but, in Lord Frederick's absence, she made him her constant theme; and the moment he approached, she resigned to him her place by my side. As she had intimate access to my mind, she knew how to accommodate her attacks to my prevailing sentiments. At first, she confined herself to chronicling the symptoms of Lady Maria's jealousy and spite; amusing me with pictures, half mimic, half descriptive, of the ill-concealed malice of my foe, and instigating me to further irritation. Next, she began to mingle her register with hints of having observed, that the sport was becoming a serious one to Lord Frederick. I was at first little inclined to credit a circumstance which would have added to the impropriety of my favourite amusement; but when at last Miss Arnold's instances, and my own exuberant vanity, convinced me of the fact, some remains of justice and humanity prompted me to a change of conduct.

'If Lord Frederick has really taken it into his wise head to be in love with me,' said I to her one day when we were alone, 'I believe, Juliet, I ought to carry the jest no farther.'

I spoke with great gravity, for I was half afraid that she must be of my opinion. She looked steadily in my face, as if to see whether I were in earnest; and then burst into a hearty fit of laughter. – 'Ridiculous!' cried she: 'what! you expect him to die of it, do you? Really, my dear, I did not think you had been so romantic.'

I believe I blushed for appearing to over-rate a passion which my companion considered as so frivolous; and answered carelessly, 'Oh! I dare say he'll survive it; but one would not wilfully give uneasiness, however trivial, you know.'

'Bagatelle! you, who make a hundred hearts ache every day, to trouble your conscience about one stray thing! Besides, I'll answer for it, that the affair upon the whole will give him more pleasure than pain. How many sighs, such as lordlings breathe, would it require to repay Lord Frederick for that air of yours, as you turned to him last night from young Lord Glendower!'

'Ah! but that pleasure was a free gift, Juliet. I have no right to make him pay for it; besides, Glendower is such a fool, that it was really a relief to get rid of him. But, to be serious, I believe I shall effect my retreat with the better grace, the sooner I begin it.'

Miss Arnold was silent for a few moments, apparently pondering the matter; then, with an air of mature reflection, said, 'Well! perhaps, upon the whole, you may be right. Your indifference will probably cure Lord Frederick; besides, it will be a double charity, – it will be such a relief to Lady Maria, poor girl! I confess, Ellen, I am often sorry for her. Did you observe what a passion she was in last night when Lord Frederick would not quit you to dance with Lady Augusta Loftus?'

'It was provoking to see one's brother show so little taste,' answered I, pulling myself up, and trying to suppress a simper. 'I should have thought I had no chance with Lady Augusta.'

'Not, indeed,' returned Miss Arnold, with a contemptuous smile, 'if every one judged like Lady Maria de Burgh; and estimated a woman, like a carrot, by the length of root she had under ground! Oh! what a passion she will be in when Lord Frederick makes his proposals, and is refused!'

'But if I go much farther, Juliet, how can I refuse him? I can't tell the man that I have been drawing him on merely for the purpose of teasing his sister.'

'Well,' returned Miss Arnold, 'after all, I believe you are right; so just do as you please. Your father, to be sure, might easily manage that matter, – but do as you please.'

She knew that she might safely intrust me with this permission; secure that, even if my resolutions were good, they would be ineffective. To shake off the attentions of a man who has once been encouraged, requires more firmness than usually falls to the lot of woman. Besides, Lord Frederick had habit in his favour; and, with those who are neither guided by reason nor principle, habit is omnipotent. Pride, too, refused to resign the only means of repaying Lady Maria's scorn; and, in spite of the momentary checks of conscience, the flirtation proceeded just as before.

While my soi-disant friend encouraged my follies, no Mentor was at hand to repress them. My father, mingling little in the circles which I frequented, was ignorant of the encouragement which I gave to Lord Frederick. Miss Mortimer, ill calculated to arrest the notice of the gay and the giddy, was almost excluded from the endless invitations which were addressed to me. The public amusements, which consumed so much of my time, were unsuitable to her habits, to her principles, and to the delicacy of her health. Thus she was seldom the witness of my indiscretions. There is, indeed, no want of people who serve all scandalous tales as the monasteries were wont to do poor strangers, dress them out a little, and help them on their way. But these charitable persons care not to consign a calumny to those who will neither welcome nor advance it; and Miss Mortimer's declared aversion to scandal kept her ignorant of some of the real, and much of the fabulous history of her acquaintance. Accordingly, my intimacy with Lord Frederick had, for almost three months, excited the smiles, the envy, or the censure of 'every body one knows,' when Miss Mortimer was surprised into hearing a copious account of my imprudence from a lady, who declared 'that she was quite concerned to see that lovely girl, Miss Percy, give so much occasion for censorious tales!' Who could doubt the kindness of that concern which led her to detail my errors to my friend, while she delicately forbore from hinting them to myself! My entrance happening to interrupt her narrative, I heard her say, with great emphasis, – 'So very ridiculous, that I thought it an act of friendship ——' But, seeing me, she stopped; frowned very significantly at Miss Mortimer; and then, resuming her complacency of countenance, she accosted me in the most affectionate manner, protesting that she rejoiced in being so fortunate as to meet with me. 'I was just telling Miss Mortimer,' said she, 'that I never saw you look so lovely as when you were delighting us all with that divine concerto upon the harp last night.' In the same style she ran on for about three minutes; then declaring, that she always forgot how time went when she was visiting us, she hurried away; first, however, repeating her frown to Miss Mortimer, accompanied with a cautioning shake of the head.

I turned towards my real friend, and observed that she was looking on me through rising tears. We were alone, and I think I was always less indocile, less unamiable, when there were few witnesses of my behaviour. Touched with the affectionate concern that was painted in her face, before I knew what I was doing, I had locked her hand in mine, and had enquired 'what was the matter with my good friend?'

'My dearest Ellen,' returned she, and her mild eyes filled again, 'would you but allow me to be your friend! But I will not talk to you now. That prating woman has discomposed me.'

My conscience at that moment giving warning of a lecture in embryo, I instantly recollected myself. 'Oh!' cried I, 'how can you mind what she says? She is so prodigal of her talk, that her own stores are nothing to her. She must depend upon the public for supply, and you know what the proverb says of "begging and choosing." But I must be gone; I promised to meet Lady Waller at the exhibition. Good-by.'

My reader, especially if he be a male reader, will more easily conceive than I can express, the abhorrence of rebuke which, at this period of my life, was strong upon me. I believe I could with more patience have endured a fit of cramp, than the most gentle reproof that ever friendship administered. By Miss Arnold's help, I for some days escaped the admonitions of Miss Mortimer, till I was unfortunately placed at her mercy, by an indisposition which I caught in striving, for two hours, to make my way through the Duchess of ——'s lobby on the night of a rout. The first day of my illness, Miss Arnold was pretty constantly at my bed-side. The second, she was obliged to dine abroad, and could not return before two o'clock in the morning. The third, while she was gone to the auction to buy some toy which I had intended purchasing, I received permission to leave my chamber; and Miss Mortimer, who had scarcely quitted me by day or night, attended me to my dressing-room.

From mere habit, I approached my glass; but three days of illness had destroyed its power to please. 'Bless me,' cried I, 'what shall I do? I am not fit to be seen! And I am dying to see somebody or other. Do, Grant, tell them to let in Mr Maitland, if he calls. It is ten to one that he will not observe what a haggard wretch I look.'

'I have heard,' said Miss Mortimer, 'that love-lorn damsels sigh for solitude. I hope your inclination for company is a sign that your heart is still safe, in spite of reports to the contrary.' She forced a smile, yet looked in my face with such sad earnestness, as if she had wished, but feared to read my soul.

There is no escape now, thought I, so I must make the best of it. 'Quite safe,' answered I; 'so safe that I scarcely know whether I have one. I rather imagine, that in me, as in certain heroines whom I have read of at school, a deficiency has been made on one side, on purpose that I might wound with greater dexterity and success.'

'I rejoice to hear you say so,' returned Miss Mortimer, 'and still more to see by that candid countenance, that you are not decieving yourself. I knew that you were above deceiving me.'

'Nay,' said I, 'I won't answer for that, if I had any thing serious to conceal; but there is no cause for deceit. I would not give my dear Fido here for all other animals of his sex upon earth, except my father and ——'

'And whom?' asked Miss Mortimer.

'I was going to say Mr Maitland,' answered I, 'because he is so good a man; but Fido is a hundred times more affectionate and amusing.'

Miss Mortimer now smiled without trying it. 'Mr Maitland is, indeed, a good man,' said she; 'and if you would show him half the kindness and attention that you do to Fido ——'

She too, left the sentence unfinished. Now, though I had not, I believe, a thought of finding a lover in Mr Maitland, I often recollected, not without pique, Miss Mortimer's first decision on that subject; and, with a vague idea that she was going to recant, I said, with some quickness, 'Well, what would happen if I did?'

'You would find him quite as amusing,' answered she.

'Is that all?' said I, poutingly; 'then I may as well amuse myself with Lord Frederick, who does not give me the trouble of drawing him out.'

In my momentary pet I had started the very subject which I wished to avoid. Miss Mortimer instantly took advantage of my inadvertence. 'A little more caution,' said she, gravely, 'may be necessary in the one case than in the other; for Mr Maitland, far from wilfully misleading you, would guard the delicacy of your good name with a father's jealousy.'

'In what respect does Lord Frederick mislead me?'

'Nay, I will not assert that he does; but, my dear Ellen, our grandmothers used to warn us against the arts of men. They represented lovers as insidious spoilers, subtle to contrive, and forward to seize every occasion of advantage. I fear the nature of the pursuer remains the same, though the pursuit be transferred from our persons to our fortunes.'

'Gorgons, and hydras, and chimeras dire!' exclaimed I; 'what a train you have conjured up! But I can assure you, Lord Frederick is no insidious spoiler, nor subtle, nor very bold; but a good-natured, giddy-brained fellow, no more a match for me in cunning than I am for him at the small-sword.'

'Take care, Ellen. We all over-rate ourselves where we are deficient. No part of your character is more striking than your perfect singleness of heart.'

'But what need is there of so much caution. I may as well marry Lord Frederick as any body else. He wants fortune, I want rank. The bargain would be very equitable. What objection could there be to it?'

'None,' replied Miss Mortimer, with a deep sigh, 'provided that your father were satisfied; and, which is, if possible, of still more importance, provided you are sure that Lord Frederick is the man whom your sober judgment would approve.'

'What! would you have me marry on mere sober judgment?'

'No, I would not go quite so far; but, at least, I would not have you marry against your sober judgment. Much, very much, will depend upon the character of your husband. Toys cannot always please you, Ellen; for you have warm affections. These affections may meet with neglect, perhaps with unkindness; and have your habits fitted you for patient endurance? You have strong feelings; and have you learnt the blessed art of weakening their power upon your own mind, by diverting them into less selfish channels?'

She spoke with such warmth as flushed her cheek with almost youthful bloom; while I smiled at the solemnity with which she treated a subject so far from serious; and inwardly pitied that ignorance of the world, which could so much mistake the nature of a harmless flirtation. 'Oh!' cried I, 'if I were to marry Lord Frederick, I should support his neglect with great philosophy; and as for unkindness, we could provide against that in the settlements.'

Miss Mortimer's manner grew still more solemn. 'Answer me as gaily as you will,' said she, 'but, by all that you value, my dearest child, I adjure you to be serious with yourself. You have told me that you mean one day to change your plan of life, – to put away childish things, – to begin your education for eternity. Is Lord Frederick well fitted to be your companion, – your assistant in this mighty work?'

This view of the subject was far too awful for sport, far too just for raillery, and far too grave for my taste; so I hastened to dismiss the theme. 'Well, well, my good Miss Mortimer,' said I, 'be under no apprehensions; I have not the slightest intention of marrying Lord Frederick.'

'If that be the case,' returned she, 'suffer me to ask why you encourage his attentions.'

'Merely for the sake of a little amusement,' answered I.

'Ah, Ellen!' said Miss Mortimer, 'how many young women are lured on by the same bait, till they have no honourable means of escape; and marry without even inclination to excuse their folly or mitigate its effects! Let the warning voice of experience ——'

The warning voice was, at that moment, silenced by the entrance of Miss Arnold. 'Here, Ellen,' said she, 'is a packet for you, which I found in the lobby. – What have you got there?' continued she, as I opened it.

'A note from Lord Frederick, and two tickets to Lady St Edmunds' masked ball.'

'Delightful! When is it to be?'

'On Monday, the fifth of May.'

'Oh, we have no engagement; that is charming!'

Miss Arnold skipped about, and seemed quite in ecstasies. Miss Mortimer, on the contrary, looked gravely intent upon her work. Her gravity, and the extravagance of Juliet's raptures, alike restrained my pleasure; and I only expressed it by saying, with tolerable composure, that of all amusements, a masked ball was the one which I most desired to see.

'Oh! it will be enchanting!' cried Miss Arnold. 'What dresses shall we wear, Ellen?'

Miss Mortimer having cut a cap, which she had been shaping, into more than fifty shreds, now leant earnestly towards me; and, timid and faltering, as if she feared my answer, asked, 'if I would accept of Lord Frederick's tickets?'

'To be sure she will,' said Miss Arnold, answering for me.

'Why should I not?' said I.

'I hope you will at least consider the matter,' returned Miss Mortimer, still addressing herself particularly to me. 'This sort of amusement is regarded with suspicion by all sober-minded persons; and I own I could wish that Miss Percy thought this a sufficient reason for refusing it her countenance.'

'I am sure that is a nonsensical prejudice,' cried Miss Arnold. 'At a subscription masquerade, indeed, one might meet with low people, but at Lady St Edmunds' there will be none but the best company in town.'

'The best *born* company, I suppose you mean,' answered Miss Mortimer; 'but I imagine, that the very use of masks is to banish the privileges and the restraints of personal respectability.'

'Nay now, my dear Miss Mortimer!' cried I, playfully laying my hand upon her mouth, 'pray don't throw away that nice lecture; you know I never was at a masquerade in my life, and you would not be so savage as to prose me out of going to one! only one!'

'If I thought there were any chance of success,' said Miss Mortimer, smiling affectionately on me, 'I would make captives of these little hands till I tried all my rhetoric.'

'It would be all lost,' cried I, 'for positively I must and will go.' Miss Mortimer's countenance fell; for she knew that in spite of the sportiveness of my manner, I was inaccessible to conviction; she clearly perceived, though I was unconscious of the association, that my pride connected an idea of rebellious presumption with whatever thwarted my inclination; and she saw that no argument was likely to find admission, where, instead of being welcomed as an honest counsellor, it was guarded against as an insolent mutineer.

After a short silence, she changed her point of attack. 'If,' said she, 'your acceptance of Lord Frederick's tickets implies any obligation to accept his particular attendance, I think, Ellen, you will see the prudence of refusing them.'

Recollecting our late conversation, I felt myself embarrassed, and knew not what to answer. But my companion quickly relieved my dilemma. 'Indeed, Miss Mortimer,' said she, 'you know nothing of these matters. Ellen cannot invite gentlemen to Lady St Edmunds' house, so it is clear that we must allow Lord Frederick to go with us; but when we are there, we shall soon find attendants enough.'

'Yes,' said I, willing to satisfy Miss Mortimer; 'and when we get into the rooms, we shall be under the Countess's protection, and may shake off the gentlemen as soon as we choose.'

Miss Mortimer looked more and more anxious. 'What protection can Lady St Edmunds afford you,' said she, 'where hundreds around her have equal claims; and left in such a place without any guard but your own discretion? – dearest Ellen, I beseech you, return these tickets.'

Though I was far from owning to myself that Miss Mortimer was in the right, I could not entirely suppress the consciousness that my resistance was wrong. The consequence was, that I grew angry with her for making me displeased with myself, and peevishly answered, that I would not return the tickets, nor be debarred from a harmless amusement by any body's unfounded prejudices.

'Call them prejudices, or what you will, Ellen,' said Miss Mortimer, in a voice which I must have been a savage to resist, 'only yield to them!'

My self-condemnation, and of course my ill-humour, were increased by her mildness; and, forgetting all her claims to my respect, all her patient affection, all her saint-like forbearance, I turned upon her with the petulance of a spoiled child, and asked, 'who gave her a right to thwart and importune me?' Tears rushed to her meek eyes. 'It was your mother! Ellen,' cried she; 'when she bade me, in remembrance of our long and faithful friendship, to watch and advise, and restrain her child. Will you not give me up a few short hours of pleasure for her sake?'

I was overpowered and burst into tears; yet tears, I must own, as much of spleen as of tenderness. Such as they were, I was ashamed of them; and dashing them away, snatched the tickets and enclosed them in a short note of apology to Lord Frederick. 'Are you going to return them?' cried Miss Arnold, looking over my shoulder at what I had written, and speaking in a tone of the utmost surprise. 'Certainly!' said I, in a manner so decided, that without the least attempt to oppose my design, she sat down opposite to me, as if taking wistfully her last look of the tickets.

'Pull the bell, Juliet,' said I, somewhat triumphantly, as I sealed the note.

'Give me the note,' said Miss Arnold, 'I am going down stairs, and will give it to a servant. It is a pity the poor creatures should have unnecessary trouble.' She took the packet, and quitted the room.

Miss Mortimer, the big drops still trickling down her cheek, pressed my hand, as if she would have thanked me, had her voice been at her command. Conscious of having made a proper sacrifice, I involuntarily recovered my good humour; but my pride refused to let my kind friend think her victory complete; and, releasing my hand, I turned away with cold stateliness.

But what am I doing? Is the world peopled with Miss Mortimers, that I should expect its forbearance for such a character as mine? – No; but I will endure the shame which I have merited. Detest me, reader. I was worthy of your detestation! Throw aside, if you will, my story in digust. Yet remember, that indignation against vice is not of itself virtue. Your abhorrence of pride and ingratitude is no farther genuine, than, as it operates against your own pride, your own ingratitude.

CHAPTER VI

Yet still thy good and amiable gifts
The sober dignity of virtue wear not.

Joanna Baillie.

As soon as Miss Arnold and I were alone, she renewed the subject of the masked ball. 'Well, Ellen!' cried she, 'I protest, I never was so much astonished as at your simplicity in returning those tickets. That old woman really winds you about just as she pleases.'

'No, I am not quite so pliant,' answered I, somewhat piqued; 'but after the footing upon which Miss Mortimer put her request, I do not see how I could refuse it.'

'She has art enough to know where you are most accessible,' said Miss Arnold, well knowing that nothing was more likely to stir the proud spirit than a suspicion of being duped. 'It is really provoking to see you so managed!' continued she; 'and now to have her trick us out of this ball, where we should have been so happy! You would have looked quite enchanting as a sultana! and your diamond plume would have been divine in the front of your turban, and —'

She ran on describing our dresses and characters, enlarging on the amusement of which my ill-timed facility had deprived us, till I was thoroughly indignant at Miss Mortimer's interference. 'I am sure,' interrupted I, 'I wish I had not allowed myself to be wheedled over like a great baby; but I promise you that she shan't find it so easy to persuade me another time.' Then I proceeded to reproach my own want of spirit; for we can all attack ourselves where we are invulnerable. 'If I had not been the tamest creature in the world,' said I, 'I should not have yielded the matter; but it is in vain to talk of it now.'

'Why in vain?' cried Miss Arnold with vivacity.

'You know,' answered I, 'that now when we have have returned the tickets nothing more can be done.'

'What if we could still have the tickets?' said Miss Arnold.

'Impossible!' said I; 'I would not condescend to ask them again from Lord Frederick.'

'But,' said Miss Arnold, throwing her arm round my neck with an insinuating smile, 'what if I, seeing that my dearest Ellen's heart was set upon this ball, and guessing that she would soon repent of her saint-errantry, had slily put the tickets into my pocket, and could produce them thus' (showing me a corner of them), 'at this very moment?'

I was thunderstruck. In spite of eight years' intimacy, Miss Arnold had miscalculated upon my sentiments, when she expected me to approve of this manœuvre. Confidence in my mother's mildness and affection had instilled into my infant mind habits of sincerity; habits which she had strengthened less by precept than by encouragement and example. The tint had been infused at the fountain head, and it still coloured the stream. A dead silence followed Miss Arnold's discovery; she, waiting to hear my sentiments, I not caring to speak them; she looking intently in my face, I gazing steadfastly on the tickets, without recollecting that I held them in my hand.

'How could we produce them to Miss Mortimer?' said I, at last, pursuing my reflections aloud. 'She confidently believes that they are gone; and she will think this such a piece of –' cunning, I would have said, but I could not utter the ungracious truth to the kind creature, who had erred purely to oblige me. 'She would be so astonished!' continued I: 'and only this morning she praised my ingenuousness! I cannot keep these tickets.'

'Oh! cried Miss Arnold, 'I am sure there is no disingenuousness on your part. It was not you who detained the tickets. I will tell her honestly how the matter stands. I would be chidden for a month rather than that you should lose this ball, – you would be so happy, and so much admired!'

'My dear, kind-hearted Juliet! you cannot suppose that I will take advantage of your good nature! You would not have me buy my pleasure at the expense of injuring you in any one's good opinion? No, no; were I to keep these tickets it should be at my own hazard.'

I think Miss Arnold blushed; and she certainly hesitated a moment before she replied, – 'I assure you I do not care a straw for her good opinion. What signify the whims of people who think like nobody else?'

Of all my acquaintance, Mr Maitland alone joined Miss Mortimer in 'thinking like nobody else;' and a recollection of him glanced across my mind. The association was not over favourable to Miss Arnold's purpose. 'Some of the most sensible men in the kingdom think like Miss Mortimer,' said I.

'The most sensible men in the kingdom often think wrong,' returned Miss Arnold. 'Besides, what signify their thoughts, so long as they dare not tell us them?'

'Some of them do dare,' said I with a sigh.

'Come, come, Ellen,' said Juliet, 'do you keep the tickets, and I shall willingly take the blame. Be satisfied with being afraid of the men and the methodists yourself; you will never make me so.'

'Afraid!' The word jarred upon my spirit. 'Afraid!' repeated I; 'I fear no mortal! but I scorn to do what the coldest, most correct man in England could think dishonourable. I would not be despised for all the pleasures under heaven! I will send back these tickets this moment.'

I turned proudly away, wholly unconscious how much the sense of honour was indebted to the opportune remembrance of Mr Maitland, and as confident in my own integrity as if it had already been seven times tried in the furnace. I rang the bell; delivered, with my own hand, the tickets to a servant; and never in my life felt more conscious of my advantages of stature. I forgot the languor of indisposition. I walked with the springing step of exultation. I forgave Miss Mortimer my disappointment. I was grateful to Juliet for her kind intentions. Every object was pleasing, for it shone with the reflected light of self-approbation. My evening was cheerful, though comparatively lonely; my sleep refreshing, though unbought by exercise. I could have wished that it had been allowable to tell Miss Mortimer all my cause of triumph; and once (such is the selfishness of pride) I entertained a thought of boasting to her my second sacrifice to propriety; but, when I remembered the meanness of betraying my friend to censure, the base suggestion vanished from my mind; and again I inwardly applauded my own rectitude, instead of blushing that such a thought could have found entrance into my soul.

Almost for the first time in my life I wished for Mr Maitland's presence; probably, though I did not shape the idea to myself, in the hope that he would confirm my self-esteem. But he came not to take advantage of my order for excluding all visiters except himsef. The next day, however, he called; and as I was still somewhat indisposed, he was admitted to my *boudoir*. He had not been seated many minutes, when Miss Mortimer adverted to my late sacrifice. 'You must assist me with your invention, Mr Maitland,' said she. I want to make Monday, the 5th of May, the happiest day in the season, and as gay as is consistent with happiness.

'My intention is quite at your service,' said Mr Maitland; 'but why is the 5th of May to be so distinguished?'

'I am deeply in Miss Percy's debt for amusement on that day; for it was fixed for a masked ball, which she has given up at my request.'

I stole a glance at Mr Maitland, and saw his countenance relax pleasantly. 'I dare say,' said he, 'you owe Miss Percy nothing on that account, for she will have more pleasure in complying with your wish than twenty masked balls would have given her.'

'I am not sure of that,' cried I; 'for of all things on earth, I should like to see a masked ball.'

'Must I then, per force, allow you some merit for relinquishing this one?' said Mr Maitland, seating himself by my side, with such a smile of playful kindness as he sometimes bestowed on Miss Mortimer. 'But why,' continued he, 'should you, of all women, desire to appear in masquerade? Come, confess that you believe you may conceal more charms than fall to the lot of half your sex, and still defy competition.

'You may more charitably suppose,' returned I, 'that I am humbly desirous to escape comparisons.'

'Nay,' said Mr Mailtland, with a smile which banished all the severity of truth, 'that would imply too sudden a reformation. Would you have me believe that you have conquered your besetting sin since the last time we met?

'How have you the boldness,' said I, smiling, 'to talk to me of besetting sin?'

'As I would talk to a solider of his scars,' said Mr Maitland. 'You think it an honourable blemish.'

'This is too bad!' cried I, 'not only to call me vain, but to tell me that I pique myself on my vanity!'

'Ay,' returned Mr Maitland, dryly, 'on your vanity, or your pride, or your ——, call it what you will.'

'Well, pride let it be,' said I. 'Surely there is a becoming pride, which every woman ought to have.'

'A becoming pride!' repeated Mr Maitland; 'the phrase sounds well; now tell me what it means.'

'It means – it means – that is, I believe it means – that sort of dignity which keeps your saucy sex from presuming too far.'

'What connection is there, think you, between cautious decency, – that peculiuar endearing instinct of a woman, – and inordinate self-estimation?

'Oh! I would not have my pride inordinate. I would merely have a comfortable respect for myself and my endowments, to keep up my spirit, that I might not be a poor domestic animal to run about tame with the chickens, and cower with them into a corner as oft as lordly man presented his majestic port before me! – No! I hope I shall never lose my spirit. What should I be without it?'

'Far be it from me to reduce you so deplorably!' said Mr Maitland; beginning with a smile, though, before he ceased to speak, the seriousness of strong interest stole over his countenance. 'But what if Miss Percy, intrusted with every gift of nature and of fortune, should remember that still they were only trusts, and should fear to abuse them? What if, like a wise steward, instead of valuing herself upon the extent of her charge, she should study how to render the best account of it? What would you then be? All that your warmest friends could wish you. You would cease to covet – perhaps to receive – the adulation of fools; and gain, in exchange, the respect, the strong affection, of those who can look beyond a set of features.'

The earnestness with which Mr Maitland spoke was so opposite to the cold composure of his general manner; his eyes, which ever seemed to penetrate the soul, flashed with such added brightness, that mine fell before them, and I felt the warm crimson burn on my cheek. I believe no other man upon earth could have quelled my humour for a moment; but I had an habitual awe of Mr Maitland, and felt myself really relieved, when the entrance of my father excused me from replying.

I knew, by my father's face, that he was full of an important something; for he merely paid the customary compliment to Mr Maitland, and then walked silently up and down the room with an air of unusual stateliness and satisfaction. 'What has pleased you so much this morning, papa?' enquired I.

'Pleased, Miss Percy!' returned my father, knitting his brow, and endeavouring to look out of humour; 'I tell you I am not pleased. I am teased out of my life on your account by one fellow or another.' Then, turning to Maitland, he formally apologised for troubling him with family affairs, though I believe he was, on this occasion, not at all sorry to have his friend for a hearer.

'Which of them has been teasing you now, sir?' said I, carelessly.

'The Duke of C——,' said my father, in a fretful tone, though a smile was lurking at the corner of his mouth, 'has been here this morning to make proposals for a match between you and his son Frederick.'

'Well, sir,' said I, with some little interest in the issue of the conference; but my curiosity was instantly diverted into another channel, by a sudden and not very gentle pressure of the hand, which Mr Maitland had still held, and which he now released. The gesture, however inadvertent, attracted my eye towards him; but his face was averted, and my vanity could not extract one particle of food from the careless air with which he began to turn over the pages of a book which lay upon my work-table.

My father proceeded. 'His Grace proposed to settle two thousand pounds a-year upon his son; no great matter he was forced to confess; but then he harangued about supporting the dignity of the title, and the hardship of burdening the representative of the family with extravagant provision for younger children. But, to balance that, Ellen, he hinted that you might be a Duchess; for the Marquis, like most of these sprigs of quality, is of a very weakly constitution. Pity that ancient blood should so often lose strength in the keeping! Eh, Ellen!'

My father made a pause, and looked as if he expected that I should now express some curiosity in regard to his decision, but my pride was concerned to show my total indifference on the subject; so I sat quietly adjusting my bracelet, without offering him the slightest encouragement to proceed. He looked towards Maitland; but Maitland was reading most intently. He turned to Miss Mortimer; and at last found a listener, who was trembling with interest which she had not power to express.

'What think you of the great man's liberality" continued my father. 'Is not two thousand pounds a-year a mighty splendid offer for a girl like my Ellen there, with a hundred thousand pounds down, and perhaps twice as much more before she dies? Eh, Miss Elizabeth? Should not I be a very sensible fellow, to bring a jackanapes into my house to marry my daughter, and spend my money, and be obliged to me for the very coat on his back, and all by way of doing me a great honour forsooth? No, no. I'll never pay for having myself and my girl looked down upon. She's a pretty girl, and a clever girl, and the d——l a De Burgh in England can make his daughter as well worth an honest man's having: eh, Maitland?'

'Not in your opinion and mine, undoubtedly, sir,' said Maitland, with the air of a man who is obliged to pay a compliment.

'I told the old gentleman my mind very distinctly,' said my father, drawing up his head, and advancing his chest. 'I have given his grandee pride something to digest, I warrant you. And now he is ashamed of his repulse, and wants the whole affair kept private forsooth. I am sure it is none of my concern to trumpet the matter. All the world knows I have refused better offers for Miss Percy.'

'If his Grace wishes the affair to be so private,' cried I, 'I am afraid he won't inform his daughters of it.'

'You of course will consider it as quite at an end,' said my father, addressing himself to me.

'Oh certainly, sir,' answered I; 'but how shall I get the news conveyed to Lady Maria?'

'Tell it to a mutual friend as a profound secret,' said Mr Maitland, dryly. 'But why are you so anxious that Lady Maria should hear of her brother's disappointment?'

'Oh because it will provoke her so delightfully,' cried I. 'The descendant of a hundred and fifty De Burghs to be rejected by a city merchant's daughter! It will ruin her in laces and lip-salve.'

I was so enchanted with the prospect of my rival's vexation, that it was some moments ere I observed that Mr Maitland, actually turning pale, had shrunk from me as far as the end of the couch would permit him, and sat leaning his head on his hand with an air of melancholy reflection. Presently afterwards he was rising to take his leave, when a servant came to inform Miss Mortimer that Mrs Wells, the woman whom Mr Maitland had rescued from the effect of my rashness, was below waiting to speak with her. 'Stay a few minutes, Mr Maitland, and see your protegée,' said Miss Mortimer to him, as he was bidding her good morning. He immediately consented; while my father quitted the room, saying, 'If the woman is come for money, Miss Mortimer, you may let me know. I always send these people what they want, and have done with them.'

Mrs Wells, however, was come, not in quest of money, but of a commodity which the poor need almost as often, though they ask it less frequently. She wanted advice. Finding that Miss Mortimer was not alone, she was at first modestly unwilling to intrude upon the attention of the company. But Mr Maitland, who, I believe, possessed some talisman to unlock at his pleasure every heart but mine, engaged her by a few simple expressions of interest to unfold the purpose of her coming. She told us, that her eldest daughter, Sally, had for some time been courted by a young man of decent character, and was inclined to marry him. 'The girl must be a great fool,' thought I, 'for she can neither expect carriages nor jewels, and what else should tempt any woman to marry?' The lover, Mrs Wells said, could earn five-and-twenty or thirty shillings a week by his trade, which was that of a house-carpenter. This, together with Sally's earnings as a mantua-maker, might maintain the young couple in tolerable comfort. But they had no house, and could not furnish one without incurring debts which would be a severe clog on their future industry. The young man, however, being in love, was inclined to despise all prudential considerations; and, in spite of her mother's counsels, had almost inspired his mistress with similar temerity. Mrs Wells therefore begged of Miss Mortimer to fortify Sally with her advice, and to set before her the folly of so desperate a venture. 'Thanks to your excellent mother, Miss Percy,' said she, 'my children have forgotten poverty; and, indeed, no one rightly knows what it is, but they who have striven with it as I have. Any other distress one may now and then forget; but hard creditors, and cold hungry children will not allow one to forget them.' Her proposal was, that Miss Mortimer should prevail with the girl to resist her lover's solicitations for a few years, till the joint savings of the pair might amount to forty or fifty pounds, which she said would enable them to begin the world reputably.

'Forty or fifty pounds,' cried I; 'is that all? – Oh! if you are sure that Sally really wants to be married, I can settle that in a minute. I am sure I must have more than that left of my quarterly allowance.'

'What are you talking of, Ellen?' cried Miss Arnold, who had just entered the room. 'You are not going to give away fifty pounds at once?'

'Why not?' answered I. 'Probably I shall not want the money; or if I do, papa will advance my next quarter.'

I had, I believe, at first offered my gift from a simple emotion of good-will; but now, taught by my friend's resistance, I began to claim some merit for my generosity; and glanced towards Mr Maitland in search of his approving look. But Mr Maitland had no approving look to reward a liberality which sprang from no principle, and called for no labour, and inferred no self-denial. His eye was fixed upon me with an expression of calm compassion, which seemed to say, 'Poor girl! have even thy best actions no solid virtue in them?' Mrs Wells, however, had less discrimination. The poor know not what it is to give without generosity, for they possess nothing which can be spared without self-denial. Tears of gratitude filled her eyes while she praised and thanked me; but she positively refused to deprive me of such a sum. 'No, no,' said she, 'let Robert and Sally work and save for two or three years; and in that time they will get a habit of patience and good management, which will be of as much use to them as money.' The approving look which I had sought was now bestowed upon Mrs Wells. 'You judge very wisely, Mrs Wells,' said Mr Maitland. 'But two or three years will seem endless to them; say one year, that we may not frighten them, and whatever they can both save in that time, I will double to them.'

Mrs Wells thanked him, not with the servility of dependence, but with the warmth of one whom kindness had made bold. Then turning to me, and apologising for the liberty she took, she begged my patronage for Sally in the way of her business. 'I assure you, ma'am,' said she, 'that Sally works very nicely; and if she could get the name of being employed by such as you, she would soon have her hands full.'

I was thoroughly discomposed by this request. I could part with fifty pounds with inconvenience, but to wear a gown not made by Mrs Beetham, was a humiliation to which I could not possibly submit. Unwilling to disappoint, I knew not what to answer; but Miss Arnold instantly relieved my dilemma. 'Bless you, good woman,' cried she, 'how could Miss Percy wear such things as your daughter would make? Before she could have a pattern, it would be hacked about among half the low creatures in town.'

Mrs Wells coloured very deeply. 'I meant no offence,' said she: 'I thought, perhaps, Miss Percy might direct Sally how she wished her gowns to be made, and I am sure Sally would do as she was directed.'

'Indeed, my good friend,' answered I, 'I can no more direct Sally in making a gown, than in making a steam-engine. But I will ask employment for her wherever I think I am likely to be successful. Come, Miss Mortimer, I shall begin with you.'

'Do,' said Mr Maitland, in his dry manner. 'Miss Mortimer can afford to spare the attraction of a fashionable gown.'

It has been since discovered, that Mr Maitland did, that very day, provide for the accomplishment of his promise, in case that death or accident should prevent his fulfilling it in person. Miss Mortimer easily persuaded Sally to pursue the prudent course; and, besides, exerted her influence so successfully, as to procure employment for every hour of the girl's time. My profuse offer passed from my mind, and was forgotten. But their charity, – the charity of Christians, – had at all times little resemblance to the spurious quality which in my breast usurped the name. Theirs was the animated virtue, instinct with life divine! – mine, the mutilated stony image, which even if it had been complete in all its parts, would still have wanted the living principle. Theirs was the blessed beam of Heaven, active, constant, universal! – mine the unprofitable, unsteady flash of the 'troubled sea, which cannot rest.'

CHAPTER VII

'Her reputation?' That was like her wit,
And seemed her manner and her state to fit.
Something there was – what, none presumed to say,
Clouds lightly passing on a smiling day;
Whispers and hints which went from ear to ear,
And mixed reports no judge on earth could clear.
Crabbe.

RECOVERED from my indisposition, I resumed my gay career. But who ever spent a week in retirement, without projecting some reform, however partial, some small restraint upon desire, or some new caution in its gratification? I determined to observe more circumspection in my conduct towards Lord Frederick; though Miss Arnold laboured to convince me, that our flirtation might now be carried on with more safety than ever, since the parties were aware that it could have no serious issue. *Tête-à-tête* with her in my dressing-room, I could detect the fallacy of her arguments, and refused to be misled by them. The most imprudent being upon earth makes many a judicious resolution; and may trace his errors less to the weakness of his judgment, than to the feebleness of his self-command.

The first party which I joined after my convalescence, was at a concert and *petit souper* which Lady G. gave to fifty-eight of her particular friends. As soon as I entered the room, my attention was arrested by a group, consisting of Lady Maria de Burgh, her favourite Lady Augusta Loftus, Lord Frederick, and Lord Glendower. Lady Augusta seemed assiduous to entertain my admirer, who, lounging against a pillar with his eyes half shut, appeared only to study how he might answer her with the slightest possible exertion of mind or muscle. Perceiving me, Lady Maria touched her friend's arm, as if to direct her eye towards me; then whispered behind her fan somewhat which seemed immoderately entertaining to both. A rudeness which ought to have awakened only my pity, roused my resentment, and I piously resolved to seize an early opportunity of retort. The party continued their merriment, and I even observed Lady Augusta endeavouring to engage Lord Frederick to join in it. This was too much; and I resolved to show Lady Augusta that I was no such despicable rival. But I had been accustomed to accept, not to solicit the attentions of Lord Frederick, and I waited till he should accost me. Lord Frederick, however, seemed entirely insensible to my presence. His eye did not once wander towards me; indeed the assiduity of his companion left scarcely even his eyes at liberty. Weary of watching Lady Augusta's advances to my quondam admirer, I at last condescended to claim his notice by passing close to him. A distant bow was the only courtesy which I obtained. I was asked to sing, and chose an elaborate bravura, which Lord Frederick had often declared to be divine. In the midst of it I saw him break from his obsequious fair one and approach me. My heart, I own, bounded with triumph. Premature triumph, alas! He addressed our hostess, who was bending over me; pleaded indispensable business; and leaving the divine bravura to more disengaged hearers, withdrew.

I was disconcerted; for, like other beauties, I liked better to repulse presumption than to endure neglect. My song ended, I had remained for some time sullen and silent, regardless of the lavish commendations which were poured upon me; when, recollecting that my discomposure would afford matter of exultation to my rivals, I suddenly rallied my spirits, and looked round for some new instrument of offence. Lord Glendower, the reputed suitor of Lady Maria, still kept his station by her side. I contrived to engage him during the remainder of the evening. The penalty of my malice was three hours' close attention to the dullest fool in England; for vice, too, requires her self-denials, though her disciples are not, like those of virtue, forewarned of the requisition. Languid, digusted, and out of humour, I fatigued myself with laborious playfulness, till the separation of the party released me from penance.

Lord Frederick's 'indispensable business' was the next day explained by a report, that he had passed the night in a gaming-house, where he had lost five-and-twenty thousand pounds. Miss Arnold spoke with the tenderest compassion of this disaster, 'smoothing my ruffled plumes,' by ascribing it to the desperation occasioned by his late disappointment. Forgetting that she had so lately ridiculed my romantic estimate of the force of his passion, she suddenly appeared convinced that it was strong enough to account for the most frantic actions. Folly itself is not so credulous as self-conceit. I more than half believed, though I affected to disprove her assertion. It approached, indeed, to the truth more nearly than she suspected. Money, however obtained, was absolutely necessary to Lord Frederick; and mine being beyond his reach, he had recourse to fortune. But, in calculating upon the actions of the gay, the liberal Lord Frederick, the narrow motives of interest never once entered into my account. Dazzled by the false spirit, indicated by the magnitude of his loss, and pleased with the cause to which vanity ascribed it, I had half pardoned his late neglect, when I that evening met him at Mrs Clermont's rout.

So crowded were the rooms that I was not aware when he entered; and when I first observed him, he was standing in close conversation with Miss Arnold. Even pride can make concessions where it imagines cause of pity. I condescended to give Lord Frederick another opportunity of renewing his attention, and moved towards him through the crowd. My friend and he were conversing with great earnestness; and, as I approached them from behind, I caught the last words of their dialogue. His Lordship's speech concluded with the expression, 'I should look confoundedly silly;' – Miss Arnold's answer was, 'The thing is impossible: – he has not another relation upon earth, except ——' Seeing me at her side, Miss Arnold stopped abruptly, and, I think, changed colour; but I had no time to make observations, for Lord Frederick, seizing my hand, exclaimed, 'Ah, you cruel creature, have you at last given me an opportunity to speak with you. I thought you had been determined to cut me, since old squaretoes interfered.' I carelessly answered that I had not made up my mind on that subject: – but, had my reply been delayed a few moments, it could not have been uttered with truth; for just then Lady Maria came to request, with no small earnestness, that her brother would go and exhibit to Lady Augusta Loftus a trick with cards, which it seems he could perform with singular dexterity. 'We shall see who will prevail,' thought I, and I seated myself as if to evince my resolution of remaining where I was. Lord Frederick immediately excused himself to his sister; and she at last, in evident vexation, relinquished her attempt.

This little victory raised my spirits; and I enjoyed with double relish, and provoked with double industry, the jealous glances with which I was watched by Lady Maria and her fair friend. Lord Frederick, on his part, had never been so assiduous to entertain. He flattered, made love, spoke scandal, and even threw out some sarcasms upon the jealousy of his sister. How had enmity perverted my mind, when I could tolerate this unnatural assassination! How had it darkened my understanding, when I shrunk not with suspicion from the heart which was dead to the sacred charities of kindred!

In the course of our conversation, Lord Frederick rallied me on the subject of the masked ball, urging me to give my reasons for refusing the tickets. Weakly ashamed to be suspected of submitting to authority, I employed every excuse except the true one; and, among others, alleged, that I was unacquainted with the lady by whom the ball was to be given. Lord Frederick insisted upon introducing his relation, Lady St Edmunds, to me; declaring that he had often heard her express a desire to be of my acquaintance. I could not resist the temptation of this introduction, for Lady St Edmunds was of the highest fashion. I protested, indeed, that my resolution, with regard to the masquerade, was immutable, but I suffered Lord Frederick to go in search of his gay relative.

He soon returned, leading a lady, in whose appearance some half-a-dozen wrinkles alone indicated the approach of the years of discretion. Her cheek glowed with more than youthful roses. Her eye flashed with more than cheerful fires. Her splendid drapery loosely falling from her shoulders, displayed the full contour of a neck whiter than virgin innocence, pure even from the faintest of those varying hues which stain the lilies of nature. She addressed me with much of the grace and all the ease of fashion, loaded me with compliments and caresses, and charmed me with the artful condescension which veils itself in respectful courtesy. She proposed to wait upon me the next day, and entreated that I would allow her the privilege of old acquaintance, by giving orders that she should be admitted. I readily consented, for indeed I was delighted with my new friend. I was dazzled with the freedom of her language, the boldness of her sentiments, and her apparent knowledge of the world. The partial admiration expressed for me, by one so much my superior in years and rank, warmed a heart accessible through every avenue of vanity; and I spent an hour in lively chit-chat with her and Lord Frederick, without once recollecting that her Ladyship's fame was not quite so spotless as her bosom.

Faithful to her appointment, Lady St Edmunds called upon me the next morning; and though she looked less youthful, was as fascinating as ever. No charm of graceful sportiveness, of artful compliment, or of kindly seeming, was wanting to the attraction of her manners. I was accustomed to the adulation of men; and sometimes, when it was less dexterously applied, or when I was in a more rational humour, I could ask myself which the obsequious gentleman admired the most, – Miss Percy, or the pretty things they said to her. But let no one boast of being inaccessible to flattery, till he had withstood that of a superior; and let that superior be highly bred, seemingly disinterested, and a woman. I did not, at the time, perceive that Lady St Edmunds flattered me; I merely was convinced that she had a lively sensibility towards a kindred mind, and a generosity which could bestow unenvying admiration upon superior youth and beauty.

When she was about to retire, she mentioned her masked ball, expressing a strong desire to see me there, and extending the request to Miss Arnold. With one of the deepest sighs I ever breathed, I told her of my unfeigned regret that it was out of my power to accept her invitation. Lady St Edmunds looked as if she read my thoughts. 'I won't be denied,' said she; 'be as late as you will; but surely you may escape from your engagement for an hour or two at least. Come, dear Miss Percy, you would not be so mischievous as to spoil my whole evening's pleasure; and now that I know you, there is no thinking of pleasure without you.'

I was again on the point of declining, though with tears in my eyes, when I was interrupted by Miss Arnold. 'I can assure your Ladyship,' said she, 'that we have no engagement; only, our duenna does not approve of masquerades, and Ellen happens to be in a submissive frame just now.'

I could better endure the weight of my shackles than the exhibition of them; and, the warm blood rushing to my cheek, I answered, 'That I did not suppose Miss Mortimer, or any other person, pretended a right to control me; that I had merely yielded to entreaties, not submitted to authority.

'And why must the duenna's entreaties be more powerful than mine?' said Lady St Edmunds, laying her white hand upon my arm, and looking in my face with a soul-subduing smile.

'Dear Lady St Edmunds!' cried I, kissing her hand, 'do not talk of entreaty. Lay some command upon me less agreeable to my inclination, that I may show how eager I am to obey you. But indeed, I fear – I think – I – after giving my promise to Miss Mortimer, I believe I ought not to retract.'

'Why not, my dear?' said Lady St Edmunds. 'It is only changing your mind, you know, which the whole sex does every day.'

'You know, Ellen,' said Miss Arnold, 'the case is quite altered since you talked of it with Miss Mortimer. She did not object so much to the masked ball, as to your going with ——'

'Juliet!' said I, stopping her with a frown, for I felt shocked that she should tell Lady St Edmunds that her nephew's attendance was objected to by Miss Mortimer.

'Ah!' cried Lady St Edmunds, with the prettiest air of reproach imaginable, 'I see Miss Arnold is more inclined to oblige me than you are; so to her I commit my cause for the present, for now I positively must tear myself away. Good-by, my pretty advocate. Be sure you make me victorious over the duenna. Farewell, my lovely perverse one,' continued she, kissing my cheek. 'I shall send you tickets, however. I issue only three hundred.'

Lady St Edmunds retired, and left my heart divided between her and the masquerade. She was scarcely gone, when Miss Mortimer came in; and, full of my charming visiter, I instantly began to pronounce her eulogium. I thought Miss Mortimer listened with very repulsive coldness; of course, a little heat of a less gentle kind was added to the warmth of my admiration, and my language became more impassioned. 'I have been told that Lady St Edmunds is very insinuating,' said Miss Mortimer; and this was all the answer I could obtain. My praise became more rapturous than ever. Miss Mortimer remained silent for some moments after I had talked myself out of breath. Perhaps she was considering how she might reply without offence. 'Such manners,' said she, 'must indeed be engaging. I see their effect in the eloquence of your praise. I wish it were always safe to yield to their attraction.'

'Bless me! Miss Mortimer,' interrupted I, 'you are the most suspicious being! I see you want me to suspect Lady St Edmunds of every thing that is bad, and for no earthly reason but because she is delightful!'

'Indeed, my dear Ellen,' returned Miss Mortimer, 'you wrong me. I should be the last person to taint your mind with any unfounded suspicion. But it is natural, you know, that years should teach us caution.'

'Oh!' exclaimed I, fervently clasping my hands, 'if age must chill all my affections, and leave me only a dead soul chained to a half-living body, may Heaven grant that my years may be few! May I go to my grave ere my heart cease to love and trust its fellows!'

'Dearest child!' cried Miss Mortimer, 'may many a happy year improve and refine your affections; and may they long survive the enthusiasm which paints their objects as faultless! But is it not better that you should know a little of Lady St Edmunds' character, before intimacy confirm her power over you?'

'Why should I know any thing more of her than I do? I can see that she has the most penetrating understanding, the most affectionate heart!'

'No doubt these are great endowments; but something more may be necessary. The proverb is not the less true for its vulgarity, which tells us, that the world will estimate us by our associates; and, what is still more important, the estimate will prove just. If you form intimacies with the worthless, or even with the suspected ——'

'Worthless! suspected!' exclaimed I, my blood boiling with indignation; 'who dares to use such epithets in speaking of Lady St Edmunds?'

'Be calm, Ellen. I did not, at the moment that I uttered these offensive words, intend any personal application. If I had, my language should have been less severe. But I can inform you, that the world has been less cautious, and that those epithets have been very freely applied to Lady St Edmunds!'

'Yes! perhaps by a set of waspish bigots, envious of her, who is herself so far above the meanness of envy, – or who cannot pardon her for refusing to make Sunday a day of penance!'

Miss Mortimer, though naturally one of the most timid creatures upon earth, was as inflexible in regard to some particular opinions, as if she had had the nerves of a Hercules. 'Indeed, Ellen,' said she, calmly, 'it would be ungrateful in you, or any other woman of fashion, to charge the world with intolerance towards Sabbath-breakers. I fear that Lady St Edmunds would give little offence by her Sunday's parties, if she were circumspect in her more private conduct.'

'Bless my heart, Miss Mortimer!' cried I, 'what have I to do with the private conduct of all my acquaintance? What is it to me, if Lady St Edmunds spoil her children, or rule her husband, or lose a few hundred pounds at cards now and then?'

Miss Mortimer smiled. – 'Even bigots,' said she, 'must acquit her

Ladyship of all these faults, for she takes no concern with her children, – she is separated from her husband, – and certainly does not *lose* at cards.'

'And so you, who pretend to preach charity towards all mankind, can condescend to retail second-hand calumny! You would have me desert an amiable, and, I am persuaded, an injured woman, merely because she has the misfortune to be slandered!'

'When you know me better, Ellen,' said Miss Mortimer, meekly, 'you will find, that it is not my practice to repeat any scandalous tale, without some better reason than my belief that it is true. I shall not at present defend the justice of the censures which have fallen upon Lady St Edmunds. I will merely offer you my opinion, in hopes that, a few hours hence, you may reconsider it. If a friend, whose worth you had proved, whose affection you had secured, were made a mark for the shafts of calumny, – far be it from you to seek a base shelter, leaving her unshielded, to be 'hit by the archers;' but, against the formation of a new acquaintance, the slightest suspicion ought, in my opinion, to be decisive. The frailty of a good name is as proverbial as its value; and virgin fame is far too precious to be ventured upon uncertainty, and far too frail to escape uninjured even from the appearance of hazard.'

This speech was so long that it gave me time to cool, and so incontrovertible, that I found some difficulty in replying. Before I could summon a rejoinder, Miss Mortimer, who never pursued a victory, had quitted the room. She had left me an unpleasant subject of meditation; but she had allowed me to postpone the consideration of it for a few hours; so, in the mean time, I turned my thoughts to the masquerade.

And first, by way of safeguard against temptation, I thought it best to lay down an immutable resolution that I would not go. It was very hard, indeed, to be deprived of such a harmless amusement; but, as I had given an unlucky promise, I purposed magnanimously to adhere to it, resolving, however, to indemnify myself the next opportunity. Thus mortified, I began to indulge my fancy in painting what *might have been* the pleasures of the masquerade. I imagined (there was surely no harm in imagining!) how well I could have personated the fair Fatima, – how happily the turban would have accorded with the Grecian turn of my head, – how softly the transparent sleeves of my caftan would have shaded my rounded arm, – how favourably the Turkish costume would have shown the light limb, and the elastic step. I invented a hundred witticisms which I might have uttered, – a hundred compliments which I might have received. Above all, I dwelt upon the approbation, the endearments of the charming Lady St Edmunds, till my heart bounded with the ideal joy. When I retired to rest, the same gay visions surrounded me; and I gladly awoke to pursue them again in my waking dreams.

How suitable to our nature is that commandment which places upon the thoughts the first restraints of virtue! It was painful to interrupt my delightful reverie, by renewing my resolutions of self-denial, so I passed them over as already fixed, insensible how fatally I was undermining their foundations. The bribe must be poor indeed, which the aids of imagination cannot render irresistible. The longer my fancy dwelt upon my lost pleasure, the more severe seemed my privation, the more unfounded Miss Mortimer's prejudice. From the wish that the thing had been right, the step was easy to the belief that it could not be *very* wrong. Before the morning, my inclination had so far bewildered my judgment, that Miss Arnold found no difficulty in persuading me to refer the matter to my father; and, regardless of my promise, to abide by his decision.

She herself undertook the statement of the case; for it happened, I know not how, that, even when she spoke only truth, her statements always served a purpose better than mine. The effect of her adroit representation was, that my father decided in favour of the masquerade; observing that 'Miss Mortimer, though a very good woman, had some odd notions, which it would not do for every body to adopt.'

Thus it seemed determined that I was to enjoy the amusement upon which I had set my heart. And yet I was not satisfied. My gay visions were no sooner likely to be realised, than they lost half their charms. A slight scrutiny into my own mind would have enabled me to trace the cause of this change to a consciousness of error; but a vague anticipation of the issue was sufficient to prevent me from entering upon the enquiry. I therefore contented myself with attempting to impose upon my own judgment, by asserting that, since my father was satisfied, I was at full liberty to pursue my inclination. 'To be sure,' said Miss Arnold, 'when Mr Percy has given his permission, who else has any right to interfere?'

'And will you, my dear sir, speak of it to Miss Mortimer,' said I, anxious to transfer that task to any one who would undertake it.

'Oh, I'll manage all that,' cried Miss Arnold. 'If Mr Percy were to mention the matter to Miss Mortimer, it would look as if he thought himself accountable to her; and then there would be no end of it; for she fancies already that she should be consulted in every thing that concerns you, – as if Mr Percy, who has so long superintended the greatest concerns in the kingdom, could not direct his own family without her interference!'

I believe my father, as well as myself, might have some latent misgivings of mind, which made him not unwilling to accept of Miss Arnold's offered services. 'I have so many important affairs to mind,' said he, 'that I shall probably think no more of such a trifle; so I commission you, Miss Juliet, to let Miss Mortimer know my opinion; which, I dare say, you will do discreetly, for you seem a civil, judicious young lady. Elizabeth, poor soul, meant all for the best; thinking to save me a few pounds, I suppose. But you may let her know, that what it may be very commendable in her to save is altogether below my notice. When a man has thousands, and tens of thousands passing through his hands every day, it gives him a liberal way of thinking. But as for a woman, who never was mistress of a hundred pounds at a time, what can she know of liberality?'

My father had now entered on a favourite topic, the necessary connection between riches and munificence. Miss Arnold listened respectfully, approving by smiles, nods, and single words of assent; while I stood wrapt in my meditations, if I may give that name to the succession of unsightly images which conscience forced into my mind, and which I as quickly banished. Having triumphantly convinced an antagonist who ventured not upon opposition, my father withdrew; and left my friend and me to consult upon our communication to Miss Mortimer.

'She will be in a fine commotion,' said I, endeavouring to smile, 'when she hears that we are going to this masquerade after all. But since you have undertaken the business, Juliet, you may break it to her to-night, while I am at the opera; and then the fracas will be partly over before I come home.'

'I have been just thinking,' said Miss Arnold, 'all the time that your father was making that fine oration, that it would be wiser not to break it to her at all. Where is the necessity for her knowing any thing of the matter? We shall have other invitations for the same evening; so we may go somewhere else first, and afterwards look in for an hour or two at the ball. Nobody need know that we have been there.'

'What, Juliet! would you have me steal off in that clandestine way, as if I were afraid or ashamed to do what my father approves of? If I am to act in defiance of Miss Mortimer, I will do it openly, and not slavishly pilfer my right, as if I did not dare to assert it.'

'Don't be angry, Ellen,' said Miss Arnold, soothingly; 'I shall most willingly do whatever you think best. But, for my part, I would almost as soon give up the masquerade, as be lectured about it for the next three weeks.'

'But, to give Miss Mortimer her due,' returned I, 'she does not lecture much.'

'That is true,' replied Miss Arnold. 'But then she will look so dolefully at us. I am sure I would rather be scolded heartily at once.'

In this last sentiment, I cordially sympathised; for the silent upbraiding of the eye is the very poetry of reproach – it addresses itself to the imagination. 'I wish,' cried I, sighing from the very bottom of my heart, 'that I had never heard of this ball!'

'In my opinion,' said Miss Arnold, 'it would save both us and Miss Mortimer a great deal of vexation, if she were never to hear more of it.'

'Say no more of that, Juliet,' interrupted I; 'I am determined not to take another step in the business without her knowledge.'

Miss Arnold was silent for a few moments; and when her voice again drew my attention, I perceived tears in her eyes. 'Well, Ellen,' said she, 'since you are so determined, I see only one way of settling the matter quietly. I will give my ticket to Miss Mortimer, – she can have no objection to your going, if she be there herself to watch you.'

'Never name such a thing to me, Juliet! What! leave you moping alone, fancying all the pleasure you might have had, while I am amusing myself abroad. I had rather never see a mask in my life!'

'I should prefer any thing to bringing her ill-humour upon you,' said Miss Arnold; 'and since you persist in telling her, I see no other way of escape. I shall most cheerfully resign the masquerade to give you pleasure.'

'My own dear Juliet!' cried I, locking my arms round her neck, while unbidden tears filled my eyes, 'how can you talk of giving my pleasure by sacrificing your own, when you know that more than half the delight in my life is to share its joys with you.' Nor were these the empty sounds of compliment, nor even the barren expression of a passing fervour. My purse, my ornaments, my amusements, even the assiduities of my admirers, all on which my foolish heart was most fixed, I freely shared with her. Yet, this same Juliet – but is it for me to complain of ingratitude? – for me, who, favoured by an all-bountiful Benefactor, abused his gifts, despised his warnings, neglected his commands, abhorred his intercourse! Let those who are conscious of similar demerit cease to reproach the less flagrant baseness, which repays with evil the feeble benefits that man bestows on man.

On the present occasion, Juliet's influence prevailed with me so far, that, before we separated, I had agreed to a compromise. I persisted, indeed, in refusing to go clandestinely to the masquerade, but I adhered to my purpose of going; and pledged my word, that, in order to avoid all importunity on the subject, I would leave Miss Mortimer in ignorance of my determination, till the very hour of its accomplishment. Miss Arnold undertook to keep my father silent, which she performed in the most dexterous manner; and with the more ease, because, perhaps, he was conscious that the subject furnished materials for confession as well as for narrative.

CHAPTER VIII

– You squander freely,
But have you wherewithal? Have you the fund
For these outgoings? If you have, go on;
If you have not – stop in good time, before
You outrun honesty.

Cumberland (from Diphilus).

In defiance of Miss Mortimer's advice, I returned Lady St Edmunds' visit without delay. I made, indeed, some general enquiries into the character of my new favourite; myself unwilling to hear, I learnt that she was said to play games of chance with extraordinary skill and success; and that she was suspected of impropriety in a point where detection is still more fatal. It is unfortunate that prudence and self-sufficiency are so rarely found together since he who will make no use of the wisdom of others, certainly needs an extraordinary fund of his own. I was predetermined to consider whatever could be advanced against Lady St Edmunds, as the effect of malicious misrepresentation. My self-conceit pointed me out as no improper person to stem the tide of unjustice; and, by an admirable, though in this case an abused, provision in our nature, my kindly feelings towards her were strengthened at once by my intentions to serve her, and by my resentment of her supposed wrongs.

Lady St Edmunds, on her part, more than met my advances. She treated me with a distinction which I ascribed solely to the most flattering partiality; and sought my society with an eagerness in which I suspected no aim beyond its own gratification. Even now, when experience has taught me to look through these fair seemings, I am convinced that her affection was not entirely feigned; for I have seldom met with a heart so callous, as not to be touched with a transient sympathy at least, by the honest enthusiasm of youth. In the mean time, I had the more confidence in the disinterestedness of her regard, because I could detect no sinister motive for her attentions. Once, and only once, she had engaged me in play; but the stake was not large, and I rose a winner.

Miss Mortimer nevertheless continued her opposition to the acquaintance, remonstrating against it with a perseverance and warmth which alternately surprised and provoked me. Regarding her warnings as the voice of that cold ungenerous suspicion which I imagined to be incident to age, I took a perverse delight in extolling the attractions of my new friend, and in magnifying their power over me. One prophecy of my Cassandra was impressed upon my recollection, by its containing the only severe expression that ever my incorrigible wilfulness could exert from the forbearing spirit of the Christian. Among other rapturous epithets, I called Lady St Edmunds my dear enchantress. 'Well may you give her that name,' said Miss Mortimer, 'for she is drawing you into a circle where nothing good or holy must tread; and if you will follow her to the tempter's own ground, you must bid farewell to better spirits. The wise and the virtuous will one by one forsake you, until you have no guide but such as lead to evil, and no companions but such as take advantage of your errors, or share in your ruin.'

It is astonishing, that beings formed to look forward so anxiously to the future, when anxiety can be of no avail, should often treat it with such perverse disregard, when foresight might indeed be useful. Will it be believed, that, from this very conversation, I went to exhibit myself to half the town, as Lady St Edmunds' companion, by attending her to an auction?

The sale was in consequence of an execution in the house of a lady of high fashion; and thither of course came all those of her own rank, who wished to be relieved of their time, their money, or their curiosity. Lord Frederick de Burgh, who seemed the almost constant associate of his fair relative, was of our party. Indeed I could not help observing, upon all occasions, that his attentions to me were infinitely more particular, since my father had announced his decision. But I regarded that decision as final; and merely inferred, that Lord Frederick, like Miss Arnold, perceived the safety of a flirtation, which could lead to no consequence; or that, in the true spirit of his sex, he grew eager in pursuit, when attainment appeared difficult.

As the sale proceeded, a hundred useless toys were exposed, and called forth a hundred vain and unlovely emotions. Curiosity, admiration, desire, impatience, envy, and resentment, chased each other over many a fair face; and the flush of angry disappointment, or of unprofitable victory, stained many a cheek from whence the blush of modesty had faded for ever. I took out my pencil to caricature a group, in which a spare dame, whose face combined no common contrast of projection and concavity, was darting from her sea-green eyes sidelong flames upon a china jar, which was surveyed with complacent smiles by its round and rosy purchaser. But my labours were interrupted, and from an amused spectator of the scene, I was converted into a keen actor, when the auctioneer exposed a tortoise-shell dressing-box, magnificently inlaid with gold. Art had exhausted itself in the elegance of the pattern and the delicacy of the workmanship. It was every way calculated to arrest the regards of fine ladies; for, like them, it was useless and expensive in proportion to its finery. It was put up at fifty guineas; less, as we were assured by the auctioneer, than half its value. Rather than allow such matchless beauty to be absolutely thrown away, I bade for the bauble. It proved equally attractive to others, and my fair opponents soon raised its price to seventy pounds. There for a while it made a pause, and no one seemed inclined to go farther; but this was still far below its value. I hesitated for a few moments; and then, in the conviction that nobody would bid more, increased my offer. It seems I was mistaken. The lady with whom, but for my perseverance, the prize would have remained, measured me with a very contemptuous look, and bade again with a composure which seemed to say, 'Does the girl fancy she can contend with me?' This was attacking me on the weak side. I instantly bade again. The lady coolly did the same. I, growing more warm, went on. The lady proceeded, with smiles not quite of courtesy; till, in exchange for my discretion, my temper, and a hundred and fifteen pounds, I had gained the tortoise-shell dressing-box.

The costly toy was already in my possession, and already every eye was turned upon me with envy, sarcasm, or compassion, before I remembered that it was necessary to pay for my purchase. In some perplexity I began to search for my purse; recollecting, not without dismay, that it did not contain above twenty guineas. I had indeed a further supply at home, but the law of the sale required that every purchase should be paid for upon the spot, and I was obliged to apply to Lady St Edmunds for assistance. This was the first time that ever I had found occasion to borrow money; and I shall never forget the embarrassment which it cost me. With a confusion which would have dearly paid for the possession of ten thousand baubles, I, in a timid, scarcely intelligible whisper, begged Lady St Edmunds to lend me the necessary sum, assuring her that it should be repaid that very day. Her Ladyship at first frankly consented to my request; but suddenly recollecting herself, declared that she had not a guinea about her; and, without waiting for my concurrence, called upon Lord Frederick to relieve my difficulty. Giddy and imprudent as I was, I shrunk from incurring this obligation to Lord Frederick. I at first positively refused his aid; and while, for a few minutes, I sat affecting to examine my purchase, I was cordially wishing that its materials were still in opposite hemispheres, and endeavouring to gain courage for a petition to some other of my acquaintance.

I at last fixed upon a young lady of fortune with whom I had contracted some intimacy; and, under pretence of exhibiting my box, beckoned her towards me, and requested her to lend me the money. With an aspect of profound amazement, she exclaimed, 'La, my dear! how can you think of such a thing? I have not ten pounds in the world. I never have. It is always spent before I can lay a finger on it.' – 'Indeed! I was in hopes you were in cash just now, for I thought I observed you bid for this box.' – 'Oh, one must bid now and then for a little amusement! But I assure you I had no thoughts of buying such a splendid affair. I must leave that to those who have more money than they know what to do with.'

I could perceive a tincture of malice in the smile which accompanied these words; and turning from her, resumed my conversation with Lady St Edmunds. Her Ladyship rallied me unmercifully upon what she called my prudery; asking me, in a very audible whisper, what sort of interest I expected Lord Frederick to exact, which made me so afraid of becoming his debtor. Lord Frederick himself joined in the raillery; and, laughing, offered to recommend me to an honest Jew, if I preferred such a creditor. Their manner of treating the subject made me almost ashamed of having refused Lord Frederick's assistance, especially as I was certain that the obligation might be discharged in an hour. I suspected, indeed, though I was but imperfectly acquainted with the state of my funds, that they were insufficient for this demand; but I knew that Miss Arnold had money, because I had divided my quarterly allowance with her, and had not since observed her to incur any serious expense. Besides, I was convinced that my father would permit me to draw upon him in advance, so that at all events I should be able to discharge my debt on the following day. I therefore half playfully, half in earnest, accepted of Lord Frederick's offered aid; and he instantly delivered the money to me with a gallantry, which showed that a man of fashion can, upon extraordinary occasions, be polite.

When I had received the notes, I jestingly asked him what security I should give him for their repayment? Lord Frederick took my hand, and drawing from my finger a ring of small value, said, with more seriousness than I expected, 'This shall be my pledge; but you must not imagine that I shall restore it for a few paltry guineas. You may have it again as soon as you will, on a fit occasion.' I could have dispensed with this piece of gallantry, which was conducted too seriously for my taste; but a lady, like a member of Parliament, must accept of no favours if she would preserve the right of remonstrance, and I allowed Lord Frederick to keep the ring.

Soon afterwards we returned home, and I proceeded to examine the state of my funds. I was astonished to find that my bureau did not contain above ten pounds. I searched every drawer and concealment, wondering at intervals what could possibly have become of my money, – a wonder, I believe, in which the fugitive nature of guineas involves every fair lady who keeps no exact register of their departure. Thus employed, I was found by Miss Arnold, to whom I immediately unfolded my dilemma; calling upon her to assist me with her recollection, as to the disposal of my funds, and with her purse, in supply of their present deficiency. On the first point, she was tolerably helpful to me, recalling to my mind many expenses which I had utterly forgotten; but, in regard to the second, she protested, with expressions of deep regret, that she could yield me no assistance. 'You may well look astonished, dearest Ellen,' pursued she, 'considering your noble generosity to me. But, indeed, nothing could have happened more unfortunately. It was only yesterday that I visited my brother, and happened to tell him what a princely spirit you had, and how liberal you had been to me. The deuce take my tongue for being so nimble, – but it is all your own fault, Ellen; for you won't let me praise you to your face, and one can't always be silent. So, just then, in came a fellow with a long bill for some vile thing or another, and my brother bid me lend him my money that he might settle with the creature. What could I do, you know? I could not refuse. But if I had once guessed that you could possibly want it, I should as soon have lent him my heart's blood.'

I suffered the tale to conclude without interruption; for indeed I was fully as much astonished as I looked. I had by no means understood that my friend was upon such terms with her brother as to incline her to lend him money; nor that he was in such circumstances as to need to borrow. A doubt of her truth, however, never once darkened my mind. Self-love prevented me, as it daily prevents thousands, from making the very obvious reflection, that one who could be disingenuous with others to serve me, might be disingenuous with me to serve herself. Miss Arnold proceeded to reproach herself in the bitterest manner for her improvidence in parting with the money, and seemed so heartily vexed, that the little spleen which my disappointment had at first excited entirely subsided; and I comforted my friend as well as I was able, by assuring her that my father would advance whatever money I desired.

Miss Arnold now, in her turn, was silent, wearing a look of grave consideration. 'If I were in your place, Ellen,' said she, at last, 'I don't think I would mention this matter to Mr Percy.'

'Not mention it!' said I, 'why not?'

'Because,' returned Miss Arnold, 'I see no end it can serve, except to make him angry. You know his pompous notions; and, after what has passed, I am sure he will think you borrowing money from Lord Frederick an act of downright rebellion.'

'Indeed,' returned I, 'that is very likely; but I promised to repay Lord Frederick to-morrow; and I have no other way of obtaining the money.'

'Poh! my dear, you are so punctilious about trifles! What can it possibly signify to Lord Frederick whether he be repaid to-morrow, or the day after?'

'Why, to be sure, it cannot signify much; only, as I have given my promise, I do not like to break it.'

'Well, really, Ellen, if I were to shut my eyes, I could sometimes fancy you had been brought up with some queer old aunt in the country. What difference can one day make? And I am sure, by the end of the week, at farthest, I could get the money from my brother, and settle the whole matter peaceably. Do take my advice, and say nothing about it to your father; he will be so angry; and you know, at the worst, you can tell him at any time.'

Had my mind been well regulated, or my judgment sound, Miss

Arnold's argument would itself have defeated her purpose; and the very conviction of my father's disliking my debt to Lord Frederick would have determined me that it should, at all hazards, be repaid. But I was fated, in many instances, to suffer the penalty of those perverted habits of mind, which imposed upon me a sort of moral disability of choosing right, as often as a choice was presented to me. Misled by an artful adviser, or rather, perhaps, by my own inveterate abhorrence of reproof, I chose that clandestine path, in which none can tread with peace or safety. In this fatal decision began a long train of evil.

Warned by my example, let him who is entering upon life review, with a suspicious eye, the transactions which he is inclined to conceal from the appointed guardians of his virtue. If the subject be of moment, let him be wisely fearful to rely upon his own judgment; – if it be trivial, let not concealment swell it to disastrous importance. If he have, unfortunately, a tendency to creep through the winding covered path, let him not strengthen by one additional act a habit so fatal to the lofty port of honour. If, like me, he be of a frank and open nature, let him not, to escape a transient evil, sink the light heart, and pervert the simple purpose, and bend the erect dignity of truth. Let him who can tread firm in conscious soundness of mind leave the stealthy course for those to whom nature has given no better means of attaining their end. The low and tangled way, the subtle tortuous progress, suits the base earth-worm; let creatures of a nobler mould advance erect and steady.

Having dissuaded me from using the only means of discharging my debt without delay, Miss Arnold, like a cautious general, contented herself with fortifying the post she had taken; and, for the present, carried her operations no further. But, the next day, she took occasion to ask me, with a careless air, 'whether I had written a note of excuse to Lord Frederick?' I answered that I had not thought of it. 'You intend writing, of course,' said Miss Arnold, with that look of decision which has often served the purpose of argument.

'Don't you think it will be rather awkward?' said I.

'That you should not write, you mean? – Very awkward, indeed. And then I am sure you ought never to lose an opportunity of writing a note, for I know nobody who has such a talent for turning these things neatly.'

The indistinct idea of impropriety which was floating in my mind was put to flight by the nonchâlance of Miss Arnold's manner; for, when reason and conscience are deposed from their rightful authority at home, it is amazing how abjectly they learn to bend, not to the passions only, but to impulse merely external. I wrote the note to Lord Frederick. My lover, for now I may fairly call him so, contrived to reply to my billet in such terms as, with the help of Miss Arnold's counsels, produced a rejoinder. This again occasioned another; and notes, sonnets, epistles in verse, and billet-doux passed between us, till the folly had nearly assumed the form of a regular correspondence. All this was, of course, carried on without the knowledge of my father or Miss Mortimer; and so rapid are the inroads of evil, that I soon began to find a mysterious pleasure in the dexterity which compassed this furtive intercourse.

In the mean time, Miss Arnold was in no haste to perform her promise. Day after day she found some excuse for not going to ask her money, or some pretence for returning without it; and day after day she persuaded me to wait for its restitution; till the uneasy feeling of undischarged obligation subsided by degrees, and the natural disquiet of a debtor was nearly lost in the giddiness of perpetual amusement.

As the masked ball drew near, my eagerness for it had completely revived. It may seem strange, considering the multitude of my frivolous pleasures, that any single one should have awakened such ardour. But a masquerade was now the only amusement which was new to me; and I had already begun to experience that craving for novelty which is incident to all who seek for happiness where it never was and never will be found, – in bubbles which amuse the sense, but cheat the longing soul.

So entirely was I occupied in anticipating my new pleasure, that I should have had neither thought nor observation to bestow upon any other subject, had not conscience sometimes turned my attention to Miss Mortimer. I thought she looked ill and melancholy. Her complexion, always delicate, had faded to a sickly hue. Her eyes were sunk and hollow; and the jealous watchfulness of one who has given cause of complaint, made me remark that they were often fixed sadly upon me. I half suspected that she had discovered my intended breach of faith; and wondered whether it were possible that my misconduct could make such an impression upon her mind. I was relieved from this suspicion by the frankness with which she one day lamented to me that my father, for some reason which she could not divine, refused to permit a party to be formed for the 5th of May. 'I could have wished,' said she, 'to make that evening pass more gaily than I fear it will. Dear Ellen, how like you are to your mother when you blush!'

'Then I am sure,' said I, 'I wish I could blush always, for there is nobody I should like so much to resemble.'

'Well,' said Miss Mortimer, 'were it not for the fear of making you vain, I could tell you, that there is a more substantial resemblance; for she, like you, knew how to resign her strongest inclinations in compliance with the wishes of her friends.'

This was too much. Conscience-struck, and quite thrown off my guard, I exclaimed, 'Like me! Oh! she was no more like me, than an angel of light is to a dark designing ——' Recollecting that I was betraying myself, I stopped.

Miss Mortimer turned upon me a smile so kind, so confiding, that as oft as it rises to my memory I abhor myself. 'Nay, Ellen,' said she, 'if I am to be your confessor lay open the sins which do really beset you; unless, as Mr Maitland would say, you are afraid that I should have a sinecure.

'I have a great mind,' cried I, 'to make a resolution, that I will never do a wrong thing again without confessing it to somebody!'

'The resolution would be a good one,' said Miss Mortimer, 'provided you could rely upon the judgment and integrity of your confessor; and provided you are sure that the pain of exposing your faults to another will not lead you to conceal them more industriously from yourself.'

'Oh! I am sure I could never do wrong without being sensible of it. But the misfortune is, that people have not the right method of talking of my faults. They always contrive to say something provoking. You need not smile. It is not that I am so uncandid that I cannot endure to be blamed; for there's Juliet often finds fault with me, and I never grow angry.'

'Well, Ellen,' said Miss Mortimer, 'if ever you should be inclined to make trial of me, I promise you never intentionally to say any thing provoking. In dexterity I shall not pretend to vie with Miss Arnold, but in affectionate interest I will yield to none. You have a claim upon my indulgence, which your errors can never cancel; especially as I am sure that they will never lean towards artifice or meanness.'

The heart must be callously vile, which can bear to be stabbed with the words of abused confidence. I sprung away in search of Miss Arnold, that I might retract my promise of concealing from Miss

Mortimer the affair of the masquerade. I was met by the dress-maker, who, loaded with parcels and band-boxes, came to fit on the attire of the fair Fatima; and, during the hour which was consumed on this operation, the ardour of my sincerity had cooled so far, that Miss Arnold easily prevailed on me to let matters remain as we had first arranged them.

How often, I may say how invariably, did my better feelings vanish, ere they issued into action! But feeling is, in its very nature, transient. It is at best the meteor's blaze, shedding strong, but momentary day; while principle, the true principle, be it faint at first as the star whose ray hath newly reached our earth is yet the living light of the higher heaven; which never more will leave us in utter darkness, but lend a steady beam to guide our way.

CHAPTER IX

– There we
Solicit pleasure, hopeless of success;
Waste youth in occupations only fit
For second childhood; and devote old age
To sports which only childhood could excuse.
There they are happiest who dissemble best
Their weariness; and they the most polite,
Who squander time and treasure with a smile,
Though at their own destruction.

Cowper.

THE fifth of May arrived; and never did lover, waiting the hour of meeting, suffer more doubts and tremours than I did, lest Mrs Beetham should disappoiont me of my evening's paraphernalia. Although I had ordered the dress to be at my bed-side as soon as I awoke, the faithless mantua-maker detained it till after two o'clock; and the intermediate hours were consumed in fits of anger, suspense, and despondency. At last it came; and I hastened to ascertain its becomingness and effect. I knew that Miss Mortimer was closeted with a medical friend; I had, therefore, no interruption to fear from her. Yet I locked myself into my dressing-room, because I could not, without constraint, allow even Miss Arnold to witness those rehearsals of vanity, which I was not ashamed to exhibit before Him who remembers that we are but dust. Others may smile at this and many other instances of my folly. I look back upon them as on the illusions of delirium, and shudder whilst I smile.

I was practising before a looking-glass the attitudes most favourable to the display of my dress and figure, when my attention was drawn by the sound of bustle in the staircase. I opened my door to discover the cause of the noise, and perceived some of the servants bearing Miss Mortimer, to all appearance lifeless. In horror and alarm I sprung towards her; and in answer to some incoherent questions, I learnt, that she had had a long private conference with Dr ——, and that he had scarcely left the house, when she had fainted away. A servant had hastened to recall the surgeon, but his carriage had driven off too quickly to be overtaken.

The dastardly habits of self-indulgence had so estranged me from the very forms of sickness or of sorrow, that I now stood confounded by their appearance; and if a menial, whose very existence I scarcely deigned to remember, had not far excelled me in considerate presence of mind, the world might then have lost one of its chief ornaments, and I the glorious lesson of a Christian's life – of a Christian's death! By means of the simple prescriptions of this poor girl, Miss Mortimer revived. Her first words were those of thankfulness for all our cares; her next request that she might be left alone. Recollecting my strange attire, which alarm had driven from my mind, I felt no disinclination to obey; but the girl, whose assistance had already been so useful, begged for permission to remain. 'Indeed, ma'am,' said she, 'you ought not to be left alone while you are so weak and ill.'

'Oh I am weaker than a child!' cried Miss Mortimer; 'but go, my dear: I shall not be alone! I know where the weakest shall assuredly find strength!'

The countenance of the person to whom she spoke gave signal of intelligence; the rest stared with vacant wonder. All obeyed Miss Mortimer's command; and I hastened to lay aside my Turkish drapery, which, for some minutes, I had almost unconsciously been screening from observation behind the magnitude of our fat housekeeper.

As soon as I had resumed my ordinary dress, I stole back to the door of Miss Mortimer's apartment. I listened for a while, – but all was still. I entered softly, and beheld Miss Mortimer upon her knees, her hands clasped in supplication; the flush of hope glowing through the tears which yet trembled on her cheek; her eyes raised with meek confidence, as the asking infant looks up in his mother's face. I was not unacquainted with the attitude of devotion. *That* I might have studied even at our theatres, where a mockery of prayer often insults both taste and decency. I had even preserved from my childish days a habit of uttering every morning a short 'form of sound words.' But the spirit of prayer had never touched my heart; and when I beheld the signs of vital warmth attend that which I had considered as altogether lifeless, it seemed like the moving pictures in the gallery of Otranto, portentous of something strange and terrible. 'Good heavens! my dear Miss Mortimer,' exclaimed I, advancing towards her as she rose, and wiped the tears from her eyes, 'surely something very distressing has happened to you.'

'Nothing new has happened,' answered she, holding out her hand kindly towards me; 'only I have an additional proof that I am, by nature, a poor, timid, trustless creature.'

'Ah!' cried I, 'do trust me. I can be as secret as the grave, and there is nothing on earth I won't do to make you comfortable again.'

'I thank you, dear Ellen,' answered Miss Mortimer; 'but I have no secret to tell; and, to make me comfortable, you must minister to both body and mind. I have long been trifling with a dangerous disorder. I have acted in regard to it as we are wont to do in regard to the diseases of our souls, – deceived myself as to its existence, because I feared to encounter the cure, – and now I must submit to an operation so tedious, so painful!' – She stopped, shuddering. I was so much shocked, that I had scarcely power to enquire whether there were danger in the experiment. 'Some danger there must be,' said Miss Mortimer; 'but it is not the danger which I fear. Even such cowards as I can meet that which they are daily accustomed to contemplate. If it had been the will of Heaven, I would rather have died than —— But it is not for me to choose. Shall I presume to reject any means by which my life may be prolonged? Often, often have I vowed,' continued she with strong energy of manner, 'that I would not "live to myself." And was all false and hollow? Was this but the vow of the hypocrite, the self-deceiver?'

'Oh no!' cried I, 'that is impossible. Before I knew you I might be prejudiced. But now I see that you are always good, – always the same. You cannot be a hypocrite.'

This testimony, extorted from me by uniform, consistent uprightness, was answered only by a distrustful shake of the head; for Miss Mortimer habitually lent a suspicious ear to the praise of her own virtues; and was accustomed to judge of her thoughts and actions, not by the opinion of others, but by a careful comparison with the standard of excellence. Tears trickled down her cheeks while she upbraided herself as one who, having pretended to give up all, kept back a part; and even those tears she reproached as symbols of distrust and fear, rather than of repentance. We soon grow weary of witnessing strong feeling in which we cannot fully sympathise. I hinted to Miss Mortimer that a short rest would compose her spirits, and recruit her strength; and, having persuaded her to lie down, I left her.

Only a few months had passed since the fairest dream of pleasure would have vanished from my mind at the thought that the life of the meanest servant of our household was to hang upon the issue of a doubtful, dangerous experiment. Only a few months had passed since the sufferings of a friend would have banished sleep from my pillow, and joy from my chosen delights. But intemperate pleasure is not more fatal to the understanding than to the heart. It is not more adverse to the 'spirit of a sound mind,' than to the 'spirit of love.' Social pleasures, call we them! Let the name no more be prostituted to that which is poison to every social feeling. Four months of dissipation had elapsed; and the distress, the danger of my own friend, and my mother's friend, now made no change in my scheme of pleasure for the evening. I was merely perplexed how to impart that scheme to the poor invalid. Conscience, indeed, did not fail to remind me, that to bestow this night upon amusement was robbery of friendship and humanity; but I was unhappily practised in the art of silencing her whispers. I assured myself that if my presence could have been essentially useful to Miss Mortimer, I should cheerfully have sacrificed my enjoyment to hers; but I was certain that if I remained at home, the sight of her melancholy would depress me so much as to make my company a mere burden. I endeavoured to persuade myself that, after the scene of the morning, my spirits needed a cordial; and a sudden fit of economy represented to me the impropriety of throwing aside as useless, a dress which had cost an incredible sum. At the recollection of this dress, my thoughts at once flew from excusing my folly to anticipating its delights; and, in a moment, I was already in the ball-room, surrounded with every pleasure, but those of reason, taste, and virtue.

This heartless selfishness may well awaken resentment or contempt; but it ought not to excite surprise. The sickly child, whose helplessness needs continual care, whose endless cravings require endless supplies, whose incessant complainings extort incessant consolation, acquires the undeserved partiality of his mother. The very flower which we have cherished in the sunshine, and sheltered from the storm, attains, in our regard, a value not its own; and whoever confines his cares, and his ingenuity, to his own gratification, will find, that self-love is not less rapid, or less vigorous in its progress, than any better affection of the soul.

All my endeavours, however, could not make me satisfied with my determination. I therefore resorted to my convenient friend, with whose honied words I could always qualify my self-upbraidings. I opened the case, by saying, that I believed we should be obliged to give up the masquerade after all; but I should have been terribly disappointed if that opinion had passed uncontroverted. I was, however, in no danger. Miss Arnold knew exactly when she might contradict without offence; and did not fail to employ all her persuasion on the side where it was least necessary. This question, therefore, was quickly settled; but another still remained, – how were we to announce our purpose to Miss Mortimer? With this part of the subject inclination had nothing to do; and therefore we found this point so much more difficult to decide, that when we were dressed, and ready to depart, the matter was still in debate.

It was, however, suddenly brought to an issue, by the appearance of Miss Mortimer. She had remained alone in her apartment during the early part of the evening; and now entered the drawing-room with her wonted aspect of serene benevolence, a little 'sicklied o'er by the pale cast of thought.' I involuntarily retreated behind Miss Arnold, who herself could not help shrinking back. Miss Mortimer advanced towards her with the most unconscious air of kindness. 'You are quite equipped for conquest, Miss Arnold,' said she.'I never saw any thing so gracefully fantastic.' She had now obtained a view of my figure, and the truth seemed to flash upon her at once; for she started, and changed colour.

A dead silence followed, for indeed I did not dare to look up, much less speak. Miss Arnold first recovered herself. 'Mr Percy,' said she, endeavouring to speak carelessly, 'has given Ellen and me permission to go out for an hour.'

'Yes,' rejoined I hesitatingly, 'papa has given us leave, and we shall only stay a very little while.' – Miss Mortimer made no answer. I stole a glance at her, and saw that she was pale as death. I ventured a step nearer to her. 'You are not very angry with us,' said I.

'No, Miss Percy,' said she, in a low constrained voice; 'I never claimed a right to dictate where you should or should not go. There was, therefore, on this occasion, the less necessity for having recourse to ——'

She left the sentence unfinished; but my conscience filled up the pause. 'Indeed, my dear Miss Mortimer,' said I, for at that moment I was thoroughly humbled, 'I never meant to go without your knowledge. Miss Arnold will tell you that we have been all day contriving how we should mention it to you.'

'Your word did not use to need confirmation,' said Miss Mortimer, sighing heavily. 'I did hope,' continued she, 'that you would have spared to me a part of this evening; for I have many things to say, and this is the last ——'

Miss Mortimer stopped, cleared her throat, bit her quivering lip, and began industriously to arrange the drapery upon my shoulder; but all would not do, – she burst into tears. I could not withstand Miss Mortimer's emotion, and, throwing my arms round her neck, – 'My dear, dear friend,' I cried, 'be angry with me, scold me as much as you will, only do not grieve yourself. If I could once have guessed that you were to be ill to-night, I should never have thought of this vile ball; and I am sure, if it will please you, I will send away the carriage, and stay at home still.'

This proposal was perfectly sincere, but not very intelligible; for the thought of such a sacrifice overpowered me so completely, that the last words were choked with sobs. Miss Mortimer seemed at first to hesitate whether she should not accept of my offer; but, after a few moments' reflection, 'No, Ellen,' said she, 'I will not cause you so cruel a disappointment; for surely – surely this masquerade has seized upon a most disproportionate share of your wishes. You must soon be left to your own discretion; and why should I impose an unavailing hardship? Go then, my love, and be as happy as you can.'

My heart leapt light at this concession. 'Dear, good, kind Miss Mortimer,' cried I, kissing her cheek, 'do not be afraid of me. I assure you, I shall be more discreet and prudent this evening than ever I was in my life.'

Miss Mortimer gave me an April smile. 'This is not much like the garb of discretion,' said she, looking at my dress, which indeed approached the utmost limit of fashionable allurement. 'It seems time that I should cease to advise, else I should beg of you to make some little addition to your dress. You may meet with people, even at a masquerade, who think that no charm can atone for any defect of modesty; and I should imagine, that your spirit would scarcely brook the remarks they might make.'

'I am sure,' said I, with a blush which owed its birth as much to pique as to shame, 'I never thought of being immodest, nor of any thing else, except to look as well as I could; but if it will please you, I shall get a tucker, and let you cover me as much as you will.'

Miss Mortimer good-naturedly accepted this little office; saying, while she performed it, 'it is a good principle in dress, that the chief use of clothing is concealment. I am persuaded, that you would never offend in this point, were you to remember, that if ever an exposed figure pleases, it must be in some way in which no modest woman would wish to please.'

Meanwhile Miss Arnold, who was even more impatient than myself to be gone, had ordered the carriage to the door. Miss Mortimer took leave of me with a seriousness of manner approaching to solemnity; and we departed. The moment we were alone, Juliet proposed to undo Miss Mortimer's labours, declaring that 'they had quite made a fright of me.' Fortunately for such a world as this, the most questionable principle may produce insulated acts of propriety. My pride for once espoused the right side. 'Forbear, Juliet!' cried I indignantly. 'Would you have people to look at me as they do at the very outcasts of womankind, – some with pity, some with scorn?'

Miss Arnold's 'hour' had elapsed long before the concourse of carriages would allow us to alight at Lady St Edmunds' door. On my first entrance, I was so bewildered by the confusion of the scene, and the grotesque figures of the masks, that I could scarcely recognise the mistress of the revels, although we had previously concerted the dress which she was to wear. She presently, however, relieved this dilemma, by addressing me in character; though she was, or pretended to be, unable to penetrate my disguise. The tinge of seriousness which Miss Mortimer had left upon my spirits being aided by the alarm created by so many unsightly shapes, I determined not to quit Lady St Edmunds' side during the evening; and was just going to tell her my name in a whisper, when I was accosted by a Grand Signior, whom, in spite of his disguise, I thought I discovered to be Lord Frederick de Burgh. I was somewhat surprised at this coincidence in our characters, as I had kept that in which I intended to appear a profound secret from all but Miss Arnold, who protested that she had never breathed it to any human being. Lord Frederick, however, for I was convinced that it was he, addressed me as a stranger; and, partly from the vanity of pleasing in a new character, I answered in the same strain. We were speedily engaged in a conversation, in the course of which a conviction of our previous acquaintance placed me so much at ease with my Turk, that I felt little disturbance, when, on looking round, I perceived that our matron had mingled with the crowd, leaving Miss Arnold and me to his protection. I supposed, however, to my friend, that we should go in search of Lady St Edmunds; and, still attended by our Grand Signior, we began our round.

And here let me honestly confess, that my pastime very poorly compensated the concealment, anxiety, and remorse which it had already cost me. Even novelty, that idol of spoilt children, could scarcely defend me from weariness and disgust. In the more intellectual part of my anticipated amusement I was completely disappointed; for the attempts made to support character were few and feeble. The whole entertainment, for the sake of which I had broken my promise, implied, if not expressed, – for the sake of which I had given the finishing stroke to the unkindness, ingratitude, and contumacy of my behaviour towards my mother's friend, – amounted to nothing more than looking at a multitude of motley habits, for the most part mean, tawdry, and unbecoming; and listening to disjointed dialogues, consisting of dull questions and unmeaning answers, thinly bestrown with constrained witticisms, and puns half a century old. The easy flow of conversation, which makes even trifles pass agreeably, was destroyed by the supposed necessity of being smart; and the eloquence of the human eye, of the human smile, was wanting to add interest to what was vapid, and kindliness to what was witty. Lord Frederick, indeed, did what he could to enliven the scene. He pointed out the persons whom he knew through their disguises; and desired me to observe how generally each affected the character which he found the least attainable in common life. 'That,' said he, 'is Glendower in the dress of a conjurer. That virgin of the sun is Lady B——, whose divorce-bill is to be before the House tomorrow. That Minerva is Lady Maria de Burgh; and that figure next to her is Miss Sarah Winterfield, who has stuck a flaxen wig upon her grizzled pate that she may for once pass for a Venus.'

'If I am to judge by your rule,' said I, 'you must be content to be taken for some Christian slave, snatching a transitory greatness.'

'You guess well, fair Fatima; I am indeed a slave; and these royal robes are meant to conceal my chains from all but my lovely mistress.'

'Why then do you confess them so freely to me?'

'Because I am persuaded that this envious mask conceals the face of my sultana.'

'No, no; by your rule I must be some stern old gouvernante, who have locked up your sultana, and come to seize the pleasures which I deny to her.'

'Oh! here my rule is useless; for, from what I see, I can guess very correctly what is concealed. For instance, there is first a pair of saucy hazel eyes, sparkling through their long fringes. Cheeks of roses ——'

'Pshaw! commonplace ——'

'Nay, not common vulgar country roses – but living and speaking, like the roses in a poet's fancy.'

'Well, that's better, go on.'

'A sly, mischievous, dimple, that, Parthian-like, kills and is fled.'

'You can guess flatteringly, I see.'

'Yes; and truly too. Nature would never mould a form like this, and leave her work imperfect; therefore there is but one face that can belong to it; and that face is – Miss Percy's.'

'And I think nature would never have bestowed such talents for flattery without giving a corresponding dauntlessness of countenance; and that I am persuaded belongs only to Lord Frederick de Burgh.'

My attention was diverted from the Sultan's reply by a deep low voice, which, seemingly close to my ear, pronounced the words, 'Use caution; you have need of it.' I started, and turned to see who had spoken; but a crowd of masks were round us, and I could not distinguish the speaker. I applied to Miss Arnold and the Turk, but neither of them had observed the circumstance. I was rather inclined to ascribe it to chance, not conceiving that any one present could be interested in advising me; yet the solemn tone in which the words were uttered, uniting with the impression which, almost unknown to myself, Miss Mortimer's averseness to my present situation had left upon my mind, I again grew anxious to find protection with Lady St Edmunds.

Being now a little more in earnest in my search, I soon discovered the object of it, and I immediately made myself known to her. Lady St Edmunds appeared to receive the intelligence with delighted surprise, and reproached me kindly with having concealed myself so long; then suddenly transferred her reproaches to herself for having, even for a moment, overlooked my identity, 'since, however disguised, my figure remained as unique as that of the Medicean Venus.' I can smile now at the simplicity with which I swallowed this and a hundred other absurdities of the same kind. A superior may always apply his flattery with very little caution, secure that it will be gratefully received; and the young are peculiarly liable to its influence, because their estimate of themselves being as yet but imperfectly formed, they are glad of any testimony on the pleasing side.

I kept my station for some time between Lady St Edmunds and Lord Frederick, drinking large draughts of vanity and pleasure, till Miss Mortimer and my unknown adviser were alike forgotten. A group of Spaniards having finished a fandango, the Countess proposed that Lord Frederick and I should succeed them in a Turkish dance. A faint recollection crossed my mind of the disgust with which I had read a description of this Mohametan exhibition, so well suited to those whose prospective sensuality extends even beyond the grave. I refused, therefore, alleging ignorance as my excuse; but, as I had an absolute passion for dancing, I offered to join in any more common kind of my favourite exercise. Lady St Edmunds, however, insisted that, unless in character, it would be awkward to dance at all; and that I might easily copy the Turkish dances which I had seen performed upon the stage. These had, so far as I could see, no resemblance to the licentious spectacles of which I had read, excepting what consisted in the shameless attire of the performers, in which I sincerely believe that the *Christian* dancing-women have pre-eminence. Blessed be the providential arrangements which make the majority of woman-kind bow to the restraints of public opinion! Hardened depravity may despise them, piety may sacrifice them to a sense of duty: but, in the intermediate classes, they hold the place of wisdom and of virtue. They direct many a judgment which ought not to rely on itself; they aid faltering rectitude with the strength of numbers; for, degenerate as we are, numbers are still upon the side of feminine decorum. Had I been unmasked, no earthly inducement would have made me consent to this blamable act of levity; but, in the intoxication of spirits which was caused by the adulation of my companions, the consciousness that I was unknown to all but my tempters induced me to yield, and I suffered Lord Frederick to lead me out. Yet, concealed, as I fancied myself, I performed with a degree of embarrassment which must have precluded all grace; though this embarrassment only served to enhance the praises which were lavished on me by Lord Frederick.

When the dance was ended, and I was going eagerly to rejoin Lady St Edmunds, I looked round for her in vain; but Miss Arnold, with an acquaintance who had joined her, waited for me, and once more we set out in search of our erratic hostess. In the course of our progress, we passed a buffet spread with wines, ices, and sherbets. Exhausted with the heat occasioned by the crowd, my mask, and the exercise I had just taken, I was going to swallow an ice; when Lord Frederick, vehemently dissuading me from so dangerous a refreshment, poured out a large glass of champagne, and insisted upon my drinking it. I had raised it to my lips, when I again heard the same low solemn voice which had before addressed me. 'Drink sparingly,' it said, 'the cup is poisoned.' Looking hastily round, I thought I discovered that the warning came from a person in a black domino; but in his air and figure I could trace nothing which was familiar to my recollection. My thoughts, I know not why, glanced towards Mr Maitland; but there was no affinity whatever between his tall athletic figure, and the spare, bending diminutive form of the black domino.

No metaphorical meaning occurring to my mind, the caution of the mask appeared so manifestly absurd, that I concluded it to be given in jest; and, with a careless smile, drank the liquor off. Through my previous fatigue, it produced an immediate effect upon my spirits, which rose to an almost extravagant height. I rattled, laughed; and, but for the crowd, would have skipped along the chalked floors, as I again passed from room to room in quest of Lady St Edmunds. Our search, however was vain. In none of the crowded apartments was Lady St Edmunds to be found.

In traversing one of the lobbies, we observed a closed door; Lord Frederick threw it open, and we entered, still followed by Miss Arnold and her companion. The room to which it led was splendidly furnished. Like the rest of those we had seen, it was lighted up, and supplied with elegant refreshments. But it was entirely unoccupied, and the fresh coolness of the air formed a delightful contrast to the loaded atmosphere which we had just quitted. Having shut out the crowd, Lord Frederick, throwing himself on the sofa by my side, advised me to lay aside my mask; and the relief was too agreeable to be rejected. He himself unmasked also, and, handsome as he always undoubtedly was, I think never saw him appear to such advantage. While Miss Arnold and her companion busied themselves in examining the drawings which hung round the room, Lord Frederick whispered in my ear a hundred flatteries, seasoned with that degree of passion, which, according to the humour of the hour, destroys all their power to please, or makes them doubly pleasing. If I know myself, I never felt the slightest spark of real affection for Lord Frederick; yet, whether it was that pleased vanity can sometimes take the form of inclination, or whether, to say all in Miss Mortimer's words, 'having ventured upon the tempter's own ground, better spirits had forsaken me,' I listened to my admirer with a favour different from any which I had ever before shown him.

I even carried this folly so far as to suffer him to detain me after Miss Arnold and her companion had quitted the room, although I began to suspect that I could already discern the effects of the wine, which, from time to time, he swallowed freely. Not that it appeared to affect his intellects; on the contrary, it seemed to inspire him with eloquence; for he pleaded his passion with increasing ardour, and pursued every advantage in my sportive opposition, with a subtlety which I had never suspected him of possessing. He came at length to the point of proposing an expedition to Scotland, urging it with a warmth and dexterity which I was puzzled how to evade. In this hour of folly, I mentally disposed of his request among the subjects which might deserve to be reconsidered. Meantime, I opposed the proposal with a playful resistance, which I intended should leave my sentence in suspense, but which I have since learnt to know that lovers prefer to more direct victory. Lord Frederick at first affected the raptures of a successful petitioner; and though I contrived to set him right in this particular, his extravagance increased, till I began to wish for some less elevated companion. He was even in the act of attempting to snatch a kiss, – for a lord in the inspiration of champagne is not many degrees more gentle or respectful than a clown, – when the door flew open, and admitted Lady Maria de Burgh, Mrs Sarah Winterfield, and my black domino.

Our indiscretions never flash more strongly upon our view than when reflected from the eye of an enemy. All the impropriety of my situation bursting upon me at once, the blood rushed in boiling torrents to my face and neck; while Mrs Sarah, with a giggle, in which envy mingled with triumphant detection, exclaimed, 'Bless my heart!' we have interrupted a flirtation!' – 'A flirtation!' repeated Lady Maria, with a toss expressive of ineffable disdain; while I, for the first time, shrinking from her eye, stood burning with shame and anger.

Lord Frederick's spirits were less fugitive: – 'Damn it!' cried he impatiently, 'if either of you had a thousandth part of this lady's charms, you might expect a man sometimes to forget himself; but I'll answer for it, neither of you is in any danger. Forgive me, I beseech you, dear Miss Percy,' continued he, turning to me: 'if you would not make me the most unhappy fellow in England, you must forgive me.' But I was in no humour to be conciliated by a compliment, even at the expense of Lady Maria. 'Oh! certainly, my Lord,' returned I, glancing from him to his sister; 'I can consider impertinence and presumption only as diseases which run in the family.' I tried to laugh as I uttered this sally; but the effort failed, and I burst into tears.

Lord Frederick, now really disconcerted, endeavoured to soothe me by every means in his power; while the two goddesses stood viewing us with shrugs and sneers, and the black domino appeared to contemplate the scene with calm curiosity. More mortified than ever by my own imbecility, I turned from them all, uttering some impatient reflection on the inattention of my hostess. 'She will not be so difficult of discovery *now*,' said the black domino sarcastically; 'you will find her with your convenient friend in the great drawing-room.' I followed the direction of my mysterious inspector, and found Lady St Edmunds, as he had said, in company with Miss Arnold.

Angrily reproaching my friend with her unseasonable desertion, and even betraying some displeasure against the charming Countess, I announced my intention of returning home immediately. Lady St Edmunds endeavoured to dissuade me, but I was inflexible; and at last Lord Frederick, who still obsequiously attended me, offered to go and enquire for my carriage. 'I commit my sultana to you,' said he, with an odd kind of emphasis to his aunt. She seemed fully inclined to accept the trust; for she assailed my ill-humour with such courteous submissions, such winning blandishments, such novel remark, and such amusing repartee, that, in spite of myself, I recovered both temper and spirits.

Such was the fascination which she could exercise at pleasure, that I scarcely observed the extraordinary length of time which Lord Frederick took to execute his mission. I was beginning, however, to wonder that he did not return, when I was once more accosted by the black domino. 'Infatuated girl!' said he, in the low impressive whisper, to which I now began to listen with alarm, 'whither are you going?'

'Home,' returned I, 'where I wish I had been an hour ago.'

'Are you false as well as weak?' rejoined the mask. 'You are not destined to see home this night.'

'Not see home!' repeated I, with amazement. 'What is it you mean, – or have you any meaning beyond a teasing jest?'

'I know,' replied the mask, 'that the carriage waits which conveys you to Scotland.'

I started at the odd coincidence between the stranger's intelligence and my previous conversation with Lord Frederick. Yet a moment's consideration convinced me, that his behaviour either proceeded from waggery or mistake. 'Get better information,' said I, 'before you commence fortune-teller. It is my father's carriage and servants that wait for me.'

The mask shook his head, and retreated without answering. I enquired of Lady St Edmunds whether she knew him, but she was unacquainted with his appearance. I was just going to relate to her the strange conversation which he had carried on with me in an under-voice, when Lord Frederick returned to tell me, that the carriage was at the door; adding, that he feared he must hasten me, lest it should be obliged to drive off. Hastily taking leave of Lady St Edmunds, Miss Arnold and I took each an arm of Lord Frederick, and hurried down stairs.

My foot was already on the step of the carriage, when I suddenly recoiled: –

'This is not our carriage?' cried I.

'It is mine, which is the same thing,' said Lord Frederick.

'No, no! it is not the same,' said I, with quickness; the warning of the black domino flashing on my recollection. 'I should greatly prefer going in my own.'

'I fear,' returned Lord Frederick, 'that it will be impossible for yours to come up in less than an hour or two.'

I own, I felt some pleasure on hearing him interrupted by the voice of my strange adviser. 'If Miss Percy will trust to me,' said he, 'I shall engage to place her in her carriage, in one tenth part of that time.'

'Trust you!' cried Lord Frederick very angrily. – 'And who are you?'

'Miss Percy's guard for the present,' answered the mask dryly.

'Her guard!' exclaimed Lord Frederick. 'From whom?'

'From you, my Lord, if you make it necessary,' retorted the stranger.

'Oh mercy,' interrupted Miss Arnold, 'here will be a quarrel: – do, for heaven's sake, Ellen, let us be gone.'

'Do not alarm yourself, young lady,' said the stranger, in a sarcastic tone; 'the dispute will end very innocently. Miss Percy, let me lead you to your carriage; or, if you prefer remaining here while I go in search of it, for once show yourself firm, and resist every attempt to entice you from this spot.'

I embraced the latter alternative, and the stranger left us. The moment he was gone, Miss Arnold began to wonder who the impudent officious fellow could be, and to enquire whether we were to wait his pleasure in the lobby for the rest of the night. She protested her belief, that I had been infected by that precise old maid Miss Mortimer; and could by no means imagine what was my objection to Lord Frederick's carriage. I coldly persisted in preferring my own, though my suspicions were staggered by the readiness with which Lord Frederick appeared to acquiesce in my decision. Notwithstanding his impatience at the stranger's first interference, he now treated the matter so carelessly, that my doubts were fast giving ground, when the black domino returned, followed by one of my servants, who informed me that my carriage was now easily accessible.

Leaving Lord Frederick to Miss Arnold, I gave my hand to my mysterious guardian; and, curiosity mingling with a desire to show some little return of civility, I enquired, whether he would allow me to set him down. The stranger declined; but, offering to escort me home, took his place by my side; giving orders to a servant in a plain but handsome livery, that his chariot should follow him to Mr Percy's.

During our drive, I was occupied in endeavouring to discover the name of my unknown attendant, and the means by which he had gained his intelligence. Upon the first point he was utterly impracticable. Upon the second, he frankly declared, that having no business at the masquerade, except to watch me and those with whom I appeared connected for the evening, he had, without difficulty, traced all our motions; but why he had chosen such an office he refused to discover. When he again mentioned the intended expedition to Scotland, Miss Arnold averred that she was lost in astonishment, and asserted her utter incredulity. I too expressed my doubts; alleging, that Lord Frederick could not believe me weak enough to acquiesce in such an outrage. 'As I have not the honour of Miss Percy's acquaintance,' returned the stranger dryly, 'I cannot determine, whether a specious flatterer had reason to despair of reconciling her to a breach of propriety.' The glow of offended pride rose to my cheek; but the carriage stopped, and I had no time to reply; for the stranger instantly took his leave.

As soon as he was gone, Miss Arnold grew more fervent in her expressions of wonder at his strange conduct, and his more strange discovery, of which she repeated her entire disbelief. I had no defined suspicion of my friend, nor even any conviction of Lord Frederick's intended treachery; but I perceived that there was something in the events of the night which I could not unravel; and, weary and bewildered, I listened to her without reply.

We were about to separate for the night, when a servant brought me a note which, he said, he had found in the bottom of the carriage. It was not mine; it belonged to the stranger. 'Oh now!' cried Miss Arnold, eagerly advancing to look at it, 'we shall discover the mystery.' But I was not in a communicative humour; so, putting the note in my pocket, I bade her good night more coldly than I had ever done before, and retired to my chamber.

The note was addressed to a person known to me only by character; but one whose name commands the respect of the wise, and the love of the virtuous. The hand-writing, I thought, was that of Mr Maitland. This circumstance strongly excited my curiosity. But, could I take a base advantage of the accident which empowered me to examine a paper never meant for my inspection? The thing was not to be thought of; and I turned my reflections to the events of the evening.

Nothing agreeable attended the retrospect. Conscience, an afterwise counsellor, upbraided me with the futility of that pleasure which I had purchased at the price of offending my own friend, and my mother's friend. The temptation, which in its approach had allured me with the forms of life and joy, had passed by; and to the backward glance, seemed all lifeless and loathsome. Unknown and concealed, I had failed to attract the attention which was now becoming customary to me. Lady St Edmunds, whose society had been my chief attraction to this ill-fated masquerade, had appeared rather to shun than to seek me. Above all, the indecorous situation in which I had been surprised by Lady Maria, and the aspect which her malice might give to my indiscretion, haunted me, like an evil genius, meeting my 'mind's eye' at every turn.

I was glad to revert from these tormenting thoughts, to my

speculations concerning the black domino. I was unable to divine the motive which could induce a stranger to interest himself in my conduct. I fancied, indeed, that I recognised Mr Maitland's handwriting; and thought for a moment that he might have instigated my mysterious protector. But what concern had Mr Maitland in my behaviour? What interest could I possibly have excited in the composed, stately, impracticable Mr Maitland? Besides, I was neither sure that he really was the writer of the note, nor that its contents had any reference to me. I again carefully examined the address, but still I remained in doubt. There could be no *great* harm, I thought, in looking merely at the signature. I threw the cautious glance of guilt round the room, and then ventured to convince myself. Before I could restore the note to its folds, I had undesignedly read a few words which roused my eager curiousity. Almost unconscious of what I was doing, I finished the sentence which contained them.

Those who are accustomed to watch the progress of temptation, will be at no loss to guess the issue of this ominous first step. Had I been earnest in my resolution to pursue the right path, I ought to have put it out of my own power to choose the wrong. As it was, I first wished – then doubted – hesitated – ventured – and ventured farther – till there was nothing left for curiosity to desire, or honour to forego. The note was as follows: –

'My dear sir, – Our worthy friend, Miss Mortimer, has just now sent to beg that I will follow her young charge to Lady St E's masked ball, whither she has been decoyed by that unprincipled woman. I fear there is some sinister purpose against this poor thoughtless girl. But it is impossible for me to go. The great cause which I am engaged to plead to-morrow must not be postponed to any personal consideration. Will you then undertake the office which I must refuse? Will you watch over the safety of this strange being, who needs an excuse every moment, and finds one in every heart? She must not, and shall not, be entrapped by that heartless Lord F. He cannot love her. He may covet her fortune – perhaps her person too, as he would covet any other fashionable gewgaw; but he is safe from the witchery of her *naif* sensibility, her lovely singleness of mind. I enclose the description which has been sent me of her dress. Should another wear one similar, you will distinguish Miss Percy by a peculiar elegance of air and motion. She is certainly the most graceful of women. Or you may know her by the inimitable beauty of her arm. I once saw it thrown round her father's neck. My dear friend, if you are not most particularly engaged, lose not a moment. She is already among these designing people. I have told you that I am interested in her, for the sake of Miss Mortimer; but I did not express half the interest I feel.

'Yours faithfully,

'H. MAITLAND.'

In spite of the checks of conscience, I read this billet with exultation. I skipped before my looking-glass; and, tossing back the long tresses which I had let fall on my shoulders, surveyed with no small complacency the charms which were acknowledged by the stoical Mr Maitland. Then I again glanced over some of his expressions, wondering what kind of interest it was that he had 'left half told.' Was it love? thought I. But when I recollected his general manner towards me, I was, in spite of vanity and the billet, obliged to doubt. I resolved, however, to ascertain the point; 'and if he be readily caught,' thought I, 'what glorious revenge will I take for all his little sly sarcasms.' To play off a fool was nothing; that I could do every day. But the grave, wise Mr Maitland would be so divertingly miserable, that I was in raptures at the prospect of my future amusement.

Along with this inundation of vanity, however, came its faithful attendant, vexation of spirit. I could not doubt, that the domino would report to his employer the events of the evening. I knew that Mr Maitland's notions of feminine decorum were particularly strict; and I felt almost as much chagrined by the thought of his being made acquainted with the real extent of my indiscretion, as by the prospect of the form which it might take in the world's eye under the colouring of Lady Maria's malice. Harassed with fatigue, my mind tossed between self-accusings, disappointment, curiosity, and mortification, I passed a restless night; nor was it till late in the morning that I fell into a feverish unquiet slumber.

CHAPTER X

Think you the soul, when this life's rattles cease,
Has nothing of more manly to succeed!
Contract the taste immortal. Learn e'en now
To relish what alone subsists hereafter

Young

THE next morning, on entering the breakfast-parlour, the first object which met my eye was Miss Mortimer, in a travelling dress. Notwithstanding our conversation on the preceding day, the consciousness of having done amiss made me ascribe her departure, or at least the suddenness of it, to displeasure against me; and, 'soon moved with touch of blame,' I would not deign to notice the circumstance, but took my place at the breakfast-table in surly silence. Our meal passed gloomily enough. I sat trying to convince myself that Miss Mortimer was unreasonably offended; my father wrinkled his dark brows till his eyes were scarcely visible; Miss Arnold fidgeted upon her chair; and Miss Mortimer bent over her untasted chocolate, stealing up her fingers now and then to arrest the tear ere it reached her cheek.

'Truly, Miss Mortimer,' said my father at last, 'I must say I think it a little strange that you should leave us so suddenly, before we have had time to provide a person to be with Ellen.' This speech, or the manner in which it was spoken, roused Miss Mortimer; for she answered with a degree of spirit which broke upon the meekness of her usual manner like summer lightning on the twilight. 'While I had a hope of being useful to Miss Percy,' said she, 'I was willing to doubt of the necessity for leaving her; but every such hope must end since it is judged advisable to use concealment with me. Besides, I am now fully aware of my situation. Dr —— has told me that any delay will be fatal to all chance of success.'

'Well,' said my father, 'every one is the best judge of his own affairs; but my opinion is that you had better have staid where you are. You might have had my family surgeon to attend you when you chose, without expense. I take it your accommodations would have been somewhat different from what you can have in that confined hovel of yours.'

Miss Mortimer shook her head. 'I cannot doubt your liberality, sir,' said she; 'but the very name of home compensates many a want; and I find it is doubly dear to the sick and the dying.'

Miss Mortimer's last words, and the sound of her carriage as it drove to the door, brought our comfortless meal to a close; and, in a mood between sorrow and anger, I retreated to a window, where I stood gazing as steadfastly into the street, as if I had really observed what was passing there. I did not venture to look round while I listened to Miss Mortimer's last farewell to my father; and I averted my face still more when she drew near and took the hand which hung listless by my side. 'Ellen,' said her sweet plaintive voice, 'shall we not part friends?'

I would have given the universe at that moment for the obduracy to utter a careless answer; but it was impossible: – so I stretched my neck as if to watch somewhat at the farther end of the street, though in truth my eyes were dim with tears more bitter than those of sorrow. Miss Mortimer for a while stood by me silent, and when she spoke, her voice was broken with emotion. 'Perhaps we may meet again,' whispered she, 'if I live, perhaps. I know it is in vain to tell you now that you are leaning on a broken reed; but if it should pierce you – if worldly pleasures fail you – if you should ever long for the sympathy of a faithful heart, will you think of me, Ellen? Will you remember your natural, unalienable right over her whom your mother loved and trusted?'

I answered not. Indeed I could not answer. My father and Miss Arnold were present; and, in the cowardice of pride, I could not dare the humiliation of exposing to them the better feeling which swelled my heart to bursting, – I snatched my hand from the grasp of my friend, – my only real friend, – darted from her presence, and shut myself up alone.

By mere accident the place of my refuge was my mother's parlour. All was there as she had left it; for when the other apartments were new modelled to the fashion of the day, I had rescued hers from change. There lay the drawing-case where she had sketched flowers for me. There was the work-box where I had ravelled her silks unchidden. There stood the footstool on which I used to sit at her feet; and there stood the couch on which at last the lovely shadow leaned, when she was wasting away from our sight. 'Oh mother, mother!' I cried aloud; 'mother who loved me so fondly, who succoured me with thy life! is this my gratitude for all thy love! Thou hadst one friend, one dear and true to thee; and I have slighted, abused, driven her from me, sick and dying! Oh why didst thou cast away thy precious life for such a heartless, thankless thing as I am!'

My well-deserved self-reproach was interrupted by something that touched me. It was poor Fido; who, laying his paw upon my knee, looked up in my face, and gave a short low whine, as if enquiring what ailed me? 'Fido! poor Fido!' said I, 'what right have I to you? – you should have been Miss Mortimer's. She would not misuse even a dog of my mother's. Go, go!' I continued, as the poor creature still fawned on me; 'all kindness is lost upon *me*. Miss Mortimer better deserves to have the only living memorial of her friend.'

The parting steps of my neglected monitress now sounded on my ear as she passed to the carriage; and, catching my little favourite up in my arms, I sprang towards the door. 'I will bid her keep him for my mother's sake,' thought I, 'and ask her too, for my mother's sake, to pardon me.' My hand was on the lock, when I heard Miss Arnold's voice, uttering, unmoved, a cold parting compliment; and I was not yet sufficiently humbled to let her witness my humiliation. I did not dare to meet the stoical scrutiny of her eye, and hastily retreated from the door. After a moment's hesitation I pulled the bell, and a servant came, 'Take that dog to Miss Mortimer,' said I, turning away to hide my swollen eyes, 'and tell her I beg as a particular favour that she will carry him away with her – he has grown intolerably troublesome.' The man stood staring in inquisitive surprise; for all the household knew that Fido was my passion. 'Why don't you do as you are desired?' cried I, impatiently. The servant disappeared with my favourite; I listened till I heard the carriage drive off; then threw myself on my mother's couch, and wept bitterly.

But the dispositions which mingled with my sorrow foreboded its transient duration. My faults stood before me as frightful apparitions, – objects of terror, not of examination; and I hastened to shut them from my offended sight. I quickly turned from reproaching my own persevering rejection of Miss Mortimer's counsels, to blame her method of counselling. Why would she always take such a timid, circuitous way of advising me? If she had told me directly that she suspected Lord Frederick of wishing to entrap me at that odious masquerade, I was sure that I should have consented to stay at home; and I repeated to myself again and again, that I was sure I should, – as we sometimes do in our soliloquies, when we are not quite so sure as we wish to be.

Glad to turn my thoughts from a channel in which nothing pleasurable was to be found, I now reverted to the incidents of the former evening. But there, too, all was comfortless or obscure. The situation in which I had been surprised by Lady Maria was gall and wormwood to my recollection. I could neither endure nor forbear to anticipate the form which the ingenuity of hatred might give to the story of my indiscretion; and, while I pictured myself already the object of sly sarcasm, – of direct reproach, – of insulting pity, – every vein throbbed feverishly with proud impatience of disgrace, and redoubled hatred of my enemy. In the tumult of my thoughts, a wish crossed my mind, that I had once sheltered myself from calumny, and inflicted vengeance on my foe, by consenting to accompany Lord Frederick to Scotland; but this was only the thought of a moment; and the next I relieved my mind from the crowd of tormenting images which pressed upon it, by considering whether my lover had really meditated a bold experiment upon my pliability, or whether my masquerade friend had been mistaken in his intellignce. Finding myself unable to solve this question, I went to seek the assistance of Miss Arnold. I was told she was was abroad; and, after wondering a little whither she could have gone without acquainting me, I ordered the carriage, and went to escape from my doubts, and from myself, by a consultation with Lady St Edmunds.

Her Ladyship's servant seemed at first little inclined to admit me; but observing that a hackney coach moved from the door to let my barouche draw up, I concluded that my friend was at home, and resolutely made my way into the house. The servant, seeing me determined, ushered me into a back drawing-room; where, after waiting some time, I was joined by Lady St Edmunds. She never received me with more seeming kindness. She regretted having been detained from me so long; wondered at the stupidity of her domestics in denying her at any time to me; and thanked me most cordially for having made good my entrance. In the course of our conversation, I related, so far as it was known to me, the whole story of the mask; and ended by asking her opinion of the affair. She listened to my tale with every appearance of curiosity and interest; and, when I paused for a reply, declared, without hesitation, that she considered the whole interference and behaviour of my strange protector as a jest. I opposed this opinion, and Lady St Edmunds defended it; till I inadvertently confessed that I had private reasons for believing him to be perfectly serious. Her Ladyship's countenance now expressed a lively curiosity, but I was too much ashamed of my 'private reasons' to acknowledge them; and she was either too polite to urge me, or confident of gaining the desired information by less direct means.

Finding me assured upon this point, she averred that the information given by my black domino, if not meant in jest, must at least have originated in mistake. 'These prying geniuses,' said she, 'will always find a mystery, or make one. But of this I am sure, Frederick has too much of your own open undesigning temper to entrap you; even though,' added she, with a sly smile, 'he were wholly without hopes from persuasion.' I was defending myself in some confusion from this attack, when Lady St Edmunds interrupted me by crying out, 'Oh I can guess now how this mystery of yours has been manufactured! I have this moment recollected that Frederick intended setting out early this morning for Lincolnshire. Probably he might go the first stage in the carriage which took him home from the ball; and your black domino having discovered this circumstance, has knowingly worked it up into a little romance.'

Glad to escape from the uneasiness of suspicion, and perhaps from the necessity of increasing my circumspection, I eagerly laid hold on this explanation, and declared myself perfectly satisfied; but Lady St Edmunds, who seemed anxious to make my conviction as complete as possible, insisted on despatching a messenger to enquire into her nephew's motions.

She left the room for this purpose; and I almost unconsciously began to turn over some visiting cards which were strewed on her table. One of them bore Miss Arnold's name, underneath which this sentence was written in French: 'Admit me for five minutes; I have something particular to say.' These words were pencilled, and so carelessly, that I was not absolutely certain of their being Miss Arnold's hand-writing. I was still examining this point, when Lady St Edmunds returned; and, quite unsuspectingly, I showed her the card; asking her smiling, 'What was this deep mystery of Juliet's?'

'That?' said Lady St Edmunds; – 'oh, that was – a – let me see – upon my word, I have forgotten what it was – a consultation about a cap, or a feather, or some such important affair – I suppose it has lain on that table these six months.'

'Six months!' repeated I simply. 'I did not know that you had been so long acquainted.'

'How amusingly precise you are!' cried Lady St Edmunds, laughing. 'I did not mean to say exactly six times twenty-nine days and six hours, but merely that the story is so old that I have not the least recollection of the matter.'

She then immediately changed the subject. With a countenance full of concern, and with apologies for the liberty she took, she begged that I would enable her to contradict a malicious tale which, she said, Lady Maria de Burgh had, after I left the masquerade, half-hinted, half-told, to almost every member of the company. Ready to weep with vexation, I was obliged to confess that the tale was not wholly unfounded; and I related the affair as it had really happened. Lady St Edmunds lifted her hands and eyes, ejaculating upon the effects of malice and envy in such a manner, as convinced me that my indiscretion had been dreadfully aggravated in the narration; but when I pressed to know the particulars, she drew back, as if unwilling to wound me further, and even affected to make light of the whole affair. She declared that, being now acquainted with the truth, she should find it very easy to defend me: – 'At all events,' added she, 'considering the terms on which you and Frederick stand with each other, nobody, except an old prude or two, will think the matter worth mentioning.' I was going to protest against this ground of acquittal, when the servant came to inform his mistress aloud, that Lord Frederick had set out for Lincolnshire at five o'clock that morning. This confirmation of Lady St Edmunds' conjecture entirely removed my suspicions; and convinced me, that my black domino, having executed his commission with more zeal than discernment, had utterly mistaken Lord Frederick's intentions.

Some other visiters being now admitted, I left Lady St Edmunds, and ordered my carriage home, intending to take up Miss Arnold before I began my usual morning rounds. At the corner of Bond Street, the overturn of a heavy coal-waggon had occasioned considerable interruption; and, while one line of carriages passed cautiously on, another was entirely stopped. My dexterous coachman, experienced in surmounting that sort of difficulty, contrived to dash into the moving line. As we slowly passed along, I thought I heard Miss Arnold's voice. She was urging the driver of a hackney coach to proceed, while he surlily declared, 'that he would not break his line and have his wheels torn off to please anybody.' The coach had in its better days been the property of an acquaintance of mine, whose arms were still blazoned on the panel; and this circumstance made me distinctly remember, that it was the same which I had seen that morning at Lady St Edmund's door.

On observing me, Miss Arnold at first drew back; but presently afterwards looked out, and nodding familiarly, made a sign for me to stop and take her into my barouche. I obeyed the signal; but not, I must own, with the cordial good-will which usually impelled me towards Miss Arnold. My friend's manner, however, did not partake of the restraint of mine. To my cold enquiry, 'where she had been,' she answered, with ready frankness, that she had been looking at spring silks in a shop at the end of the street. In spite of the manner in which this assertion was made, I must own that I was not entirely satisfied of its truth. The incident of the hackney-coach, and the words which I had seen written on the card, recurring together to my mind, I could not help suspecting that Miss Arnold had paid Lady St Edmunds a visit which was intended to be kept secret from me. Already out of humour, and dispirited, I admitted this suspicion with unwonted readiness; and, after conjecturing for some moments of surly silence, what could be the motive of this little circumvention, I bluntly asked my friend, whether she had not been in Grosvenor Square that morning?

Miss Arnold reddened. 'In Grosvenor Square!' repeated she. 'What should make you think so?'

'Because the very carriage from which you have just alighted I saw at Lady St Edmunds' door not half an hour ago.'

'Very likely,' retorted my friend, 'but you did not see me in it, I suppose.'

I owned that I did not, but mentioned the card, which was connected with it in my mind; confessing, however, simply enough, that Lady St Edmunds denied all recollection of it. Miss Arnold now raised her handkerchief to her eyes. 'Unkind Ellen!' said she, 'what is it you suspect? Why should I visit Lady St Edmunds without your knowledge? But, since yesterday, you are entirely changed,– and, after seven years of faithful friendship ——' She stopped, and turned from me as if to weep.

I was uneasy, but not sufficiently so to make concessions. 'If my manner is altered, Juliet,' said I, 'you well know the cause of the change. Was it not owing to you that I was so absurdly committed to the malice of that hateful Lady Maria? And now there is I know not what of mystery in your proceedings that puts me quite out of patience.'

'Yes, well I know the cause,' answered Miss Arnold, as if still in tears. 'Your generous nature would never have punished so severely an error of mere thoughtlessness, if that cruel Miss Mortimer had not prejudiced you against me. She is gone indeed herself; but she has left her sting behind. And I must go too!' continued Miss Arnold, sobbing more violently. 'I could have borne any thing, except to be suspected.'

My ungoverned temper often led me to inflict pain, which, with a selfishness sometimes miscalled good nature, I could not endure to witness. Entirely vanquished by the tears of my friend, I locked my arms round her neck, assured her of my restored confidence; and, as friends of my sex and age are accustomed to do, offered amends for my transient estrangement in a manner more natural than wise, by recanting aloud every suspicion, however momentary, which had formerly crossed my mind. A person of much less forecast than Miss Arnold might have learned from this recantation where to place her guards for the future.

My friend heard me to an end, and then with great candour confessed, what she could not now conceal, that Lord Frederick had her wishes for his success; but she magnanimously forgave my imagining, even for a moment, that she could condescend to assist him; and appealed to myself, what motive she could have for favouring his suit, except the wish of seeing me rise to a rank worthy of me. She then justified herself from any clandestine transaction with Lady St Edmunds, giving me some very unimportant explanation of the card which had perplexed me.

It is so painful to suspect a friend, and I was so accustomed to shun pain by all possible means, that I willingly suffered myself to be convinced; and harmony being restored by Miss Arnold's address, we engaged ourselves in shopping and visiting till it was time to prepare for the pleasures of the night. My spirits were low, and my head ached violently; but I had not the fortitude to venture upon a solitary evening. From the dread of successful malice, – from the recollection of abused friendship, – in a word, from myself, – I fled, vainly fled, to the opera, and three parties; from whence I returned home, more languid and comfortless than ever.

I had just retired to my apartment, when a letter was brought me which Miss Mortimer had left, with orders that it might be delivered when I retired for the night. 'Oh mercy!' cried I, 'was I not wretched enough without this new torment? But give it me. She has some right to make me miserable.' In this spirit of penance I dismissed my maid, and began to read my letter, which ran as follows: –

'When you read this letter, my dear Ellen, one circumstance may perhaps assist its influence. My counsels, however received, whether used or rejected, are now drawing to a close; and you may safely grant them the indulgence we allow to troubles which will soon cease to molest us. I know not how far this consideration may affect you, but I cannot think of it without strong emotion. I have often and deeply regretted that my usefulness to you has been so little answerable to my wishes; yet, with the sympathy which rivets our eyes on danger which we cannot avert, I would fain have lingered with you still; watching, with the same painful solicitude, the approach of evils, which I in vain implored you to avoid. But it must not be. Aware of my situation, I dare not trifle with a life which is not mine to throw away. I must leave you, my dearest child, probably for ever. I must loosen this last hold which the world has on a heart already severed from all its earliest affections. And can I quit you without one last effort for your safety; – without once again earnestly striving to rouse your watchfulness, ere you have cast away your all for trifles without use or value?

'Ellen, your mother was my first friend. We grew up together. We shared in common the sports and the improvements of youth; and common sorrows, in maturer life, formed a still stronger bond. Yet I know not if my friend herself awakened a tenderness so touching, as that which remembrance mingles with my affection for you, when your voice or your smile reminds me of what she was in her short years of youth and joy. Nor is it only in trifles such as these that the resemblance rises to endear you. You have your mother's simplicity and truth, – your mother's warm affections, – your mother's implicit confidence in the objects of her love. This last was indeed the shade, perhaps the only shade of her character. But she possessed that "alchemy divine" which could transform even her dross into gold; and what might have been her weakness became her strength, when she placed her supreme regards upon excellence supreme. The nature of your affections also seems to give their object, whatever it be, implicit influence with you; and thus it becomes doubly important that they be worthily bestowed. It is this which has made me watch, with peculiar anxiety, the channels in which they seemed inclined to flow; and lament, with peculiar bitterness, that a propensity capable of such glorious application should be lost, or worse than lost to you.

'These, however, are subjects upon which you have never permitted me to enter. You have repelled them in anger; evaded them in sport; or barred them at once as points upon which you were determined to act, I must not say to judge, for yourself. If, indeed, you would have used your own judgment, one unpleasing part of this letter might have been spared; for surely your unbiased judgment might show you the danger of some connections into which you have entered. It might remind you, that the shafts of calumny are seldom so accurately directed, as not to glance aside from their chief mark to those who incautiously approach; that those whom it has once justly or unjustly suspected, the world views with an eye so jaundiced as may discolour even the most innocent action of their willing associate. Even upon these grounds I think your judgment, had it been consulted, must have given sentence against your intimacy with Lady St Edmunds. But these are not all. Persons who know her Ladyship better than I pretend to do, represent her as a mixture, more common than amiable, of improvidence in the selection of her ends, with freedom in the choice, and dexterity in the use of the means which she employs; in short (pardon the severity of truth), as a mixture of imprudence and artifice. My dearest girl, what variety of evil may not result to you from such a connection! Whatever may be my suspicions, I am not prepared to assert that Lady St Edmunds has any sinister design against you. Your manifest indifference towards her nephew makes me feel more security on the point where I should otherwise have dreaded her influence the most. But I am convinced, that the mere love of manœuvring becomes in itself a sufficient motive for intrigue, and is of itself sufficient to endanger the safety of all who venture within its sphere. The frank and open usually possess an instinct which, independently of caution, repels them from the designing. I must not name to you that unhappy trait in your character, by which this instinct has been made unavailing to you;

by which the artful wind themselves into your confidence, and the heartless cheat you of your affection. Has not the ceaseless incense which Miss Arnold offers blinded you to faults, which far less talent for observation than you possess might have exposed to your knowledge and to your disdain? Do not throw aside my letter with indignation; but, if the words of truth offend you, consider that from me they will wound you no more; and pardon me, too, when I confess, that, in despair of influencing you upon this point, I have entreated your father not to renew his invitation to Miss Arnold, but rather to discourage, by every gentle and reasonable means, an intimacy so eminently prejudicial to you.

'And now I think I see you raise your indignant head; and, with the lofty scorn of baseness which I have so often seen expressed in your countenance and mien, I hear you exclaim, 'Shall I desert my earliest friend! – repay with cold ingratitude her long-tried, ardent attachment?' Your indignation, Ellen, is virtuous, but mistaken. If Miss Arnold's attachment be real, she has a claim to your gratitude, indeed; but not to your intimacy, your confidence, your imitation. These are due to far other qualifications. But are you sure, Ellen, that the warm return you make to Miss Arnold's supposed affection is itself entirely real? Are you sure, that it is not rather the form under which you choose to conceal from yourself, that her adulation is become necessary to you? Before you indignantly repel this charge, ask your own heart, whether you are, in every instance, thus grateful for disinterested love? Is there not a friend of whose love you are regardless? – whose counsels you neglect? – whose presence you shun? – from whom you withhold your trust, though the highest confidence were here the highest wisdom? – whom you refuse to imitate, though here the most imperfect imitation were glorious? You exchange your affection, and all the influence which your affection bestows, for a mere shadow of good-will. The very dog that fawns upon you, is caressed with childish fondness. Oh, Ellen, does it never strike you with strong amazement to reflect, that you are sensible to every love but that which is boundless? grateful for every kindness but that which is wholly undeserved – wholly beyond return? Is nothing due to an unwearied friend? Is it fitting, that one who lives, who enjoys so much to sweeten life, by the providence, the bounty, the forebearance of a benefactor, should live to herself alone? Yet ask your own conscience, what part of your plan of life, or rather, since

I believe your life is without a plan, which of your habits is inspired by gratitude. Dare to be candid with yourself, and though the odious word will grate upon your ear, enquire whether selfishness be not rather your chosen guide; – whether you be not selfish in your pursuit of pleasure; – selfish in your fondness for the flatterer who soothes your vanity, – selfish in the profuse liberality with which you vainly hope to purchase an affection which it is not in her nature to bestow, – selfish even in the relief which you indiscriminately lavish on every complainer whose cry disturbs you on your bed of roses. Is this the temper of a Christian – of one "who is not her own, but is bought with a price?" Consider this awful price, and how will your own conduct change in your estimation? How will you start as from a fearful dream, when you remember, that of this mighty debt you have hitherto lived regardless? How will you then abhor that pursuit of selfish pleasure which has hitherto alienated your mind from all that best deserves your care, – blasted the very sense by which you should have perceived the excellence of your benefactor, – diverted your regards from the deeper and deeper death which is palsying your soul; and closed your ear against the renovating voice which calls you to arise and live? This voice, once heard, would exalt your confiding temper to the elevations of faith, – ennoble your careless generosity to the self-devotion of saints and martyrs, – your warmth of affection, now squandered on the meanest of objects, to the love of God. The true religion once received, would change the whole current of your hopes and fears; – would ennoble your desires, subdue passion, humble the proud heart, overcome the world. But you will not give her whereon to plant her foot; for where, amidst the multitude of your toys, shall religion find a place? Oh, why should we, by continual sacrifice, confirm our natural idolatry of created things? Why fill, with the veriest baubles of this unsubstantial scene, hearts already too much inclined to exclude their rightful possessor? The pursuit of selfish pleasure is indeed natural, for self is the idol of fallen man; but the great end of his present state of being is to prostrate that idol before the Supreme. The stony Dagon bows unwillingly, but bow he must. Our heavenly Father, though a merciful, is not a fond or partial parent; and the same lot is more or less the portion of us all. He has freely given. He has done more; he has warned us of the real uses of his gifts. Perverse by nature, we abuse his bounty. Again, he exhorts us by the ministry of his servants; and often graciously sweetens his warnings, by conveying them in the voice of partial friendship, or parental love. We reject counsel; and the father unwillingly chastises. He withdraws the gifts which we have perverted, or suffers them to become themselves the punishment of their own abuse. If kindness cannot touch, nor exhortation move, nor warning alarm, nor chastisement reclaim, what other means can be employed with a moral being: What remains but the fearful sentence, "He is joined to his idols; let him alone.' Oh, Ellen, my blood freezes at the thought that such a sentence may ever go forth against you. Rouse you, dear child of my love, – rouse you from your ill-boding security. Tremble, lest you already approach that state where mercy itself assumes the form of punishment. You have hitherto lived to yourself alone. Now venture to examine this god of your idolatry; – for the being whose pleasure and whose honour you seek, is your god, call it by what name you will. See if it be worthy to divide even your least service with Him who, infinite in goodness, accepts the imperfect, – showers his bounty on the unprofitable, – and opens, even to the rebel, the arms of a father! – who meets your offences with undesired pardon, and anticipates your wants with offers of himself! Think you that this generous love could lay on you a galling yoke? I know that, though you should distrust my judgment, you will credit my testimony; and I solemnly protest to you, that I have found his service to be "perfect freedom." He exalts my joys as gifts of his bounty; He blesses my sorrows as tokens of his love; He lightens my duties by honouring them, poor as they are, with his acceptance; and even the pang with which I feel and own myself a lost sinner is sweetened by remembrance of that mercy which came to seek and to save me, *because* I was lost. These are my pleasures; and I know that they can counterbalance poverty, and loneliness, and pain. Your pleasures too I have tried; and I know them to be cold, fleeting, and unsubstantial, as the glories of a winter sky. Oh for the eloquence of angels, that I might persuade you to exchange them for the real treasure! Yet vain were the eloquence of angels, if the "still small voice" be wanting, which alone can speak to the heart. I may plead, and testify, and entreat; but is aught else within my power? – Yes, – I will go and pray for you.

'E. Mortimer.'

CHAPTER XI

He had the skill, when cunning's gaze would seek
To probe his heart, and watch his changing cheek,
At once the observer's purpose to espy,
And on himself roll back his scrutiny.

Lord Byron.

My friend's letter cost me a whole night's repose. I could not read without emotion the expressions of an affection so ill repaid, – an affection now lost to me for ever. A thousand instances of my ingratitude forced themselves upon my recollection; and who can tell the bitterness of that pity which we feel for those whom we have injured, when we know that our pity can no longer avail? The mild form of Miss Mortimer perpetually rose to my fancy. I saw her alone in her solitary dwelling, suffering pain which was unsoothed by the voice of sympathy, and weakness which no friend was at hand to sustain. I saw her weep over the wounds of my unkindness, and bless me, though 'the iron had entered into her soul!' – 'But she shall not weep, – she shall not be alone and comfortless,' I cried, starting like one who has taken a sudden resolution: 'I will go to her. I will show her, that I am not altogether thankless. I will spend whole days with her. I will read to her, – sing to her, – amuse her a thousand ways. To-morrow I will go – no – to-morrow I am engaged at Lady G.'s, – how provoking! and the day after, we must dine with Mrs Sidney, – was ever any thing so unfortunate? However, some day soon I will most certainly go.' So with this opiate I lulled the most painful of my self-upbraidings.

That part of the letter which related to my chosen associates, was not immediately dismissed from my mind. Had no accident awakened my suspicions, I should have indignantly rejected my friend's insinuations, or despised them as the sentiments of a narrow-minded though well-intentioned person; but now, my own observation coming in aid of her remonstrances, I was obliged to own that they were not wholly unfounded. I received them, however, as a *bon vivant* does the advice of his physician. He is told that temperance is necessary; and he assents, reserving the liberty of explaining the term. I was convinced that it was advisable to restrain my intimacy with Lady St Edmunds; I resolved to be less frank in communicating my sentiments, less open in regard to my affairs; and this resolution held, till the next time it was exposed to the blandishments of Lady St Edmunds. As to Miss Arnold, her faults, like my own, I could review only to excuse them; or rather, they entered my mind only to be banished by some affectionate recollection. Whatever has long ministered to our gratification, is at last valued without reference to its worth; and thus I valued Juliet. Nay, perhaps my perverted heart loved her the more for her deficiency in virtues, which must have oppressed me with a painful sense of inferiority. In short, 'I could have better spared a better' person. But, amidst my present 'compunctious visitings,' I thought of atoning for my former rebellions by one heroic act of submission. I resolved that, in compliance with Miss Mortimer's advice, I would refrain from urging my father to detain Miss Arnold as an inmate of the family. I was, however, spared this effort of self-command. The termination of Miss Arnold's visit was never again mentioned, either by herself, or by my father. In fact, she had become almost as necessary to him as to me; and I have reason to believe, that he was very little pleased with Miss Mortimer's interference on the subject.

But the more serious part of my friend's letter was that which disquieted me the most. The darkness of midnight was around me. The glittering baubles which dazzled me withdrawn for a time, I saw, not without alarm, the great realities which she presented to my mind. I could not disguise from myself the uselessness of my past life; and I shrunk under a confused dread of vengeance. In the silence, in the loneliness of night, – without defence against that awful voice which I had so often refused to hear, – I trembled, as conscience loudly reproached me with the bounties of my benefactor, and the ingratitude with which they were repaid. A sense of unworthiness wrung from me some natural tears of remorse; a sense of danger produced some vague desires of reformation; and this, I fancied, was repentance. How many useless or poisonous nostrums of our own compounding do we call by the name of the true restorative!

But though false medicines may assume the appellation, and sometimes even the semblance of the real, they cannot counterfeit its effects. The cures which they perform are at best partial or transient, – the true medicine alone gives permanent and universal health. I passed the night under the scourge of conscience; and the strokes were repeated, though at lengthening intervals, for several days. I was resolved, that I would no longer be an unprofitable servant; that I would devote part of my time and my fortune to the service of the Giver; that I would earn the gratitude of the poor, – the applauses of my own conscience, – the approbation of Heaven! Of the permanence of my resolutions, – of my own ability to put them in practice, – it never entered my imagination to doubt. I remembered having heard my duties summed up in three comprehensive epithets, 'sober, righteous, and godly.' To be 'righteous' was, I thought, an injunction chiefly adapted to the poor. In the limited sense which I affixed to the command, the rich had no temptation to break it; at all events I did not, – for I defrauded no one. 'Godly' I certainly intended one day or other to become; but for the present I deferred fixing upon the particulars of this change. It was better not to attempt too much at once, – so I determined to begin by living 'soberly.' I would withdraw a little from the gay world in which I had of late been so busy. I would pass more of my time at home. I would find out some poor but amiable family, who had perhaps seen better days. I would assist and comfort them; and, confining myself to a simple neatness in my dress, would expend upon them the liberal allowance of my indulgent father. I was presently transported by fancy to a scene of elegant distress, and theatrical gratitude, common enough in her airy regions, but exceedingly scarce upon the face of this vulgar earth. The idea was delightful. 'Who,' cried I, 'would forfeit the pleasures of benevolence for toys which nature and good sense can so well dispense with? And, after all, what shall I lose by retreating a little from a world where envy and malice are watchful to distort the veriest casualties into the hideous forms upon which slander loves to scowl! No doubt, Lady Maria's malice will find food in my new way of life, – but no matter, I will despise it.' It is so easy to despise malice in our closets! 'Mr Maitland,' thought I, 'will approve of my altered conduct;' and then I considered that retirement would allow me to make observations on the 'interest' which I had excited in

Mr Maitland; for, in the present sobered state of my mind, I thought of making observations, rather than experiments.

Circumstances occurred to quicken the ardour with which vanity pursued those observations. Maitland had hitherto been content to perform the duties of a quiet citizen. Secure of respect, and careless of admiration, he had been satisfied to promote by conscientious industry his means of usefulness, and, with conscientious benevolence, to devote those means to their proper end. With characteristic reserve, he had withdrawn even from the gratitude of mankind. He had been the unknown, though liberal benefactor of unfriended genius. He had given liberty to the debtor who scarcely knew of his existence; and had cheered many a heart which throbbed not at the name of Maitland. But now the name of Maitland became the theme of every tongue; for, in the cause of justice, he had put forth the powers of his manly mind; and orators, such as our senates must hope no more to own, had hung with warm applause, or with silent rapture, upon the eloquence of Maitland! Himself a West India merchant, and interested, of course, in the continuation of the slave-trade, he opposed, with all the zeal of honour and humanity, this vilest traffic that ever degraded the name and the character of man. In the senate of his country he lifted up his testimony against this foul blot upon her frame, – this tiger-outrage upon fellow-man, – this daring violation of the image of God. Alas! that a more lasting page than mine must record, that the cry of the oppressed often came up before British senates, ere they would deign to hear! But, amidst the tergiversation of friends, and the virulence of foes, some still maintained the cause of justice. They poured forth the eloquence which makes the wicked tremble, and the good man exult in the strength of virtue. The base ear of interest refused indeed to hear; but the words of truth were not scattered to the winds. All England, all Europe, caught the inspiration; and burnt with an ardour which reason and humanity had failed to kindle, till they borrowed the eloquence of Maitland.

And now his praise burst upon me from every quarter. Those who affected intimacy with the great, retailed it as the private sentiment of ministers and princes. Our political augurs foretold his rise to the highest dignities of the state. Those who love to give advice were eager that he should forsake his humbler profession, and devote his extraordinary talents to the good of his country. The newspapers panegyrised him; and fashion, rank, and beauty, crowded round the happy few who could give information concerning the age, manners, and appearance of Mr Maitland. Not all his wisdom, nor all his worth, could ever have moved my vain mind so much as did these tributes of applause, from persons unqualified to estimate either. When I heard admiration dwell upon his name, my heart bounded at the recollection of the 'interest' which he had expressed in me; and again I wondered whether that interest were love? I would have given a universe to be able to answer 'yes.' To see the eye which could penetrate the soul hang captive on a glance of mine! – to hear the voice which could awe a senate falter when it spoke to me! – to feel the hand which was judged worthy to hold the helm of state tremble at my touch! – the very thought was inspiration. Let not the forgiving smile which belongs to the innocent weakness of nature be lavished on a vice which leads to such cold, such heartless selfishness. Let it rather be remembered that avarice, oppression, cruelty, all the iron vices which harden the heart of man, are not more rigidly selfish, more wantonly regardless of another's feelings, than unrestrained, active vanity.

Meanwhile, Mr Maitland allowed me abundant opportunities for observation. Instead of withdrawing from us after Miss Mortimer's departure, as I feared he would, he visited us more frequently than ever. He sometimes breakfasted with us in his way to the city; often returned when the House adjourned in the evening; and in short seemed inclined to spend with us the greater part of his few abstemious hours of leisure. Yet even my vanity could trace nothing in his behaviour which might explain this constant attendance. On the contrary, his manner, often cold, was sometimes even severe. He was naturally far from being morose; and often casting off the cares of business, he would catch infectious spirits from my lightness of heart; yet even in those moments, somewhat painful would not unfrequently appear to cross his mind, and he would turn from me as if half in sorrow, half in anger. I could perceive that he listened with interest when I spoke; but that interest seemed of no pleasing kind. He often, indeed, looked amused, but seldom approving; and if once or twice I caught a more tender glance, it was one of such mournful kindness as less resembled love than compassion.

All this was provokingly unsatisfactory. I found that it was vain to expect discoveries from observation; I was obliged to have recourse to experiment; and it is not to be imagined what tricks I practised to steal poor Maitland's fancied secret. So mean is vanity! and so little security have they who submit to its power, that they may not stoop to faults the most remote from their natural tendencies. I flourished the arm of which he had praised the beauty, that I might watch whether his gaze followed it in admiration. I was laboriously 'graceful;' and sported my '*naif* sensibility' till it was any thing but *naif*. I obtruded my 'lovely singleness of mind,' till, I believe, I should have become a disgusting mass of affectation, had it not been for the manly plainness of Mr Maitland. He at first appeared to look with surprise upon my altered demeanour; then fairly showed me by his manner that he detected my little arts, and that he was alternately grieved to find me condescending to plot, and angry that I could plot no better. 'That certainly is the finest arm in England,' whispered he one evening when I had been leaning upon it, exactly opposite to him, for five minutes, 'so now you may put on your glove. Nay, instead of frowning, you should thank me for that blush; for though pride and anger may have some share in it, it is not unbecoming, since it is natural.' I was sullen for a little, and muttered something about 'impertinence,' – but I never flourished my arm again.

'Lady Maria de Burgh is certainly the most beautiful girl in London,' said I to Miss Arnold one day when the subject was in debate. This was a fit of artificial candour; for I had observed, that Maitland detested all symptoms of animosity; and I appealed to him, in hopes that he would at least except me from his affirmative. 'Yes,' returned he, directing, by one flash of his eloquent eye, the warning distinctly to me, 'Yes; but she reminds me of the dog in the fable. Nature has given her beauty enough; but she grasps at more, and thus loses all.'

Affectation seemed likely to be as unavailing as watchfulness; yet, the longer my search lasted, the more eager it became. Whatever occupied attention long, will occupy it much; and, in my vain investigation, I often endured the anxiety of the philosopher, who, having sailed to the antipodes to observe the transit of Venus, saw, at the critical hour, a cloud rise to obstruct his observations. 'How shall I fathom the heart of that impenetrable being?' exclaimed I to my confidante one day, when, in pursuance of my new plan of soberness and charity, I sat learning to knit a child's stocking at the rate of a row in the hour.

'Bless me, Ellen,' returned Miss Arnold, 'what signifies the heart of a musty old bachelor?'

'I don't know what you call old, Juliet; but, in my opinion, I should be more than woman, or less, if I could suspect my power over such a man as Maitland, and not wish to ascertain the point.'

'I do not believe,' returned Juliet, 'that any woman upon earth has power over him, – a cold, cynical, sarcastic ——'

'You forget,' interrupted I, 'that he has owned a strong interest in me;' for, in the soft hour of returning confidence, I had showed his billet to my friend.

'Yes,' answered Miss Arnold, 'that is true; but don't you think he may once have been a lover of your mother's, and that on her account ——'

'My mother's!' cried I. 'Ridiculous! impossible! Maitland must have been a mere child when my mother married.'

'Let me see,' said Miss Arnold, with calculating brow, 'your mother, had she been alive, would now have been near forty.'

'And Maitland, I am sure, cannot be more than two-and-thirty.'

'Is he not?' said Miss Arnold, who had ventured as far as she thought prudent. Silence ensued; for I was now in no very complacent frame. Miss Arnold was the first to speak. 'Perhaps,' said she, 'Mr Maitland only wishes to conceal his own sentiments, till he makes sure of yours, – perhaps he would be secure of success before he condescends to sue.'

'If I thought the man were such a coxcomb', cried I, 'I would have no mercy in tormenting. I detest pride.'

'If I have guessed right,' pursued Miss Arnold, 'a little fit of jealousy would do excellently well to prove him, and punish him at the same time; I am sure he deserves it very well, for making so much mystery of nothing.' A by-stander might have indulged a melancholy smile at my detestation of pride, and Miss Arnold's antipathy to mystery. But our abhorrence of evil is never more vehemently, perhaps never more sincerely expressed, than when our own besetting sin thwarts us in the conduct of others.

'But,' said I, for experience had begun to teach me some awe for Maitland's penetration, 'what if he should see through our design, and only laugh at us and our manœuvring?'

'Oh! as for that,' returned Juliet, 'choose his rival well, and there is no sort of danger. A dull, every-day creature, to be sure, would never do: but fix upon something handsome, lively, fashionable, and it must appear the most natural thing in the world. By the by, did he ever seem to suspect any one in particular?'

'What! don't you remember that, in his note, he speaks with

tolerably decent alarm of Lord Frederick?'

'Oh! true,' returned Miss Arnold, 'I had forgotten. – Well, do you think you could pitch upon a better flirt?'

Now my friend knew that I happened at that moment to have no choice of flirts; for, besides that Lord Frederick was the only dangler whom I had ever systematically encouraged, he was the only one of my present admirers who could boast any particular advantages of figure or situation. 'He might answer the purpose well enough,' returned I, 'if we knew how to bring Maitland and him together; but you know he does not visit here since his foolish old father thought fit to interfere.'

'That may be easily managed,' replied Juliet. 'The slightest hint from you would bring him back.'

I had once determined to listen with caution to Miss Arnold's advice, where Lord Frederick was concerned; but now her advice favoured my inclination; and that which ought to have made me doubly suspicious of her counsels, was the cause why I followed them without hesitation. The hint to Lord Frederick was given at the first opportunity, and proved as effectual as its instigator had foretold. Still, however, some contrivance was necessary to bring the rivals together; for the man of fashion and the man of business seldom paid their visits at the same hour. At length I effected an interview; and never was visiter more partially distinguished than Lord Frederick. We placed ourselves together upon a sofa, apart from the rest of the company, and forthwith entered upon all the evolutions of flirtation; for I whispered without a secret, laughed without a joke, frowned without anger, and talked without discretion.

It was Miss Arnold's allotted province to watch the effect of these fooleries upon Maitland; but I could not refrain from sharing her task, by stealing at times a glance towards him. These glances animated my exertions; for I was almost sure that he looked disturbed; and fancied, more than once, that I saw his colour change. But if he was uneasy at witnessing Lord Frederick's success, he did not long subject himself to the pain; for, after having endured my folly for a quarter of an hour, without offering it the least interruption, he took a very frozen leave, and departed. I laughed at his coldness; convinced, as I now was, that it was only the pettishness of jealousy. Miss Arnold, however, gently insinuated a contrary opinion. 'She might, indeed, be mistaken, she could not pretend to my talent for piercing disguise; but she must confess, that Maitland had succeeded in concealing from her every trace of emotion.' It may easily be imagined, that this opinion, however seasoned with flattery, and however cautiously expressed, was not very agreeable to me. To dispel my friend's doubts, rather than my own, I proposed a second trial; but some time elapsed before that trial could be made. In the mean while, Lord Frederick failed not to profit by his recent admission. His visits even became so frequent, that, dreading an altercation with my father, I began to wish that I had been more guarded in my invitation.

But, this did not prevent me from re-acting my coquetry the next time that the supposed rivals met in my presence. After this second interview, Miss Arnold, though with great deference, persisted in her former sentence; and I was unwillingly obliged to soften somewhat the vehemence of my dissent; for if Maitland was wounded by my preference of Lord Frederick, he certainly endured the smart with Spartan fortitude. I was somewhat disconcerted; and should have laid aside all my vain surmises, had not the recollection of Maitland's note constantly returned to strengthen them.

Our experiments, however, were brought to a close by a disclosure of my father's. 'Miss Percy,' said he one day, taking his posture of exhortation, 'I think Lord Frederick de Burgh seems to wait upon you every day. Now, after what has passed, this is indiscreet; and, therefore, it is my desire that you give him no encouragement to frequent my house. I would have put a stop to the thing at once, but I can perceive that you don't care for the puppy; and Maitland, who is a very sharp fellow, makes the very same observation.'

Now, I knew that this was Mr Percy's method of adopting the stray remarks which he judged worthy to be fathered by himself; and I fully understood, that all my laboured favour to Lord Frederick had failed to impose upon Maitland. What could be more vexatious? I had no resource, however; except, like the fox in the fable, to despise what was unattainable. I vowed that I would concern myself no more with a person who was too wise to have the common feelings of humanity. I assured my confidante that his sentiments were a matter of perfect indifference to me. I hope, for my conscience' sake, that this was true, for I repeated it at least ten times every day.

Meanwhile, in the ardour of my investigation, I had, from time to time, deferred my purposed visit to Miss Mortimer. My heart had not failed to reproach me with this delay; but I had constantly soothed it with promises for to-morrow, – to-morrow, that word of evil omen to all purposes of reformation! At last, however, I was resolved to repair my neglect; for the day after Maitland's quick-sightedness happened to be Sunday; and how could the Sabbath be better employed than in a necessary and pious work? It is no new thing to see that day burdened with the necessity of works which might as well have belonged to any other. Instead, therefore, of going to hear a fashionable preacher, I ordered my carriage to ——.

CHAPTER XII

—— Oh my fate!
That never would consent that I should see
How worthy thou wert both of love and duty,
Before I lost you; ——

With justice, therefore, you may cut me off,
And from your memory wash the remembrance
That e'er I was; like to some vicious purpose,
Which in your better judgment you repent of,
And study to forget.

Massinger.

THE morning shone bright with a summer sun. The trees, though now rich in foliage, were still varied with the fresh hues of spring. The river flashed gaily in the sun beam; or rolled foaming from the prows of stately vessels, which now veered as in conscious grace, now moved onward as in power without effort, bearing wealth and plenty from distant lands. What heart, that is not chilled by misery, or hardened by guilt, is insensible to the charms of renovated nature! What human heart exults not in the tokens of human power! Mine rejoiced in the splendid scene before me; but it was the rejoicing of the proud, always akin to boasting. 'How richly,' I exclaimed, 'has the Creator adorned this fair dwelling of his children! A glorious dwelling, worthy of the noble creatures for whom it was designed; – creatures whose courage braves the mighty ocean, – whose power compels the service of the elements, – whose wisdom scales the heavens, and unlocks the springs of a moving universe! And can there be zealots whose gloomy souls behold in this magnificent frame of things, only the scene of a dull and toilsome pilgrimage, for beings wayworn, guilty, wretched?'

In these thoughts, and others of like reasonableness and humility, I reached the dwelling of my friend. It was a low thatched cottage, standing somewhat apart from a few scattered dwellings, which scarcely deserved the name of a village. I had seen it in my childhood, when a holiday had dismissed me from confinement; and it was associated in my mind with images of gaiety and freedom. Alas! those images but ill accorded with its present aspect. It looked deserted and forlorn. She, by whose taste it had been adorned, was now a prisoner within its walls. The flowers which she had planted were blooming in confused luxuriance. The rose-tree, which she had taught to climb the latticed porch, now half-impeded entrance, and the jessamine which she had twined round her casement, now threw back its dishevelled sprays as if to shade her death-bed. The carriage stopped at the wicket of the neglected garden; and I, my lofty thoughts somewhat quelled by the desolateness of the scene, passed thoughtfully towards the cottage, along a walk once kept with a neatness the most precise, now faintly marked with a narrow track which alone repressed the disorderly vegetation.

The door was opened for me by Miss Mortimer's only domestic; a grave and reverend-looking person, with silver grey hair, combed smooth under a neat crimped coif, and with a starched white handkerchief crossed decently upon her breast. Nor were her manners less a contrast to those of the flippant gentlewomen to whose attendance I was accustomed. With abundance of ceremony, she ushered me up stairs; then passing me with a low courtesy, and a few words of respectful apology, she went before me into her mistress's apartment, and announced my arrival in terms in which the familiar kindness of a friend blended oddly with the reverence of an inferior. Miss Mortimer, with an exclamation of joy, stretched her arms fondly towards me. Prepared as I was for an alteration in her appearance, I was shocked at the change which a few weeks had effected. A faint glow flushed her face for a moment, and vanished. Her eyes, that were wont to beam with such dove-like softness, now shed an ominous brilliance. The hand which she extended towards me, scarcely seemed to exclude the light, and every little vein was perceptible in its sickly transparency. Yet her wasted countenance retained its serenity; and her feeble voice still spoke the accents of cheerfulness. 'My dearest Ellen,' said she, 'this is so kind! And yet I expected it too! I knew you would come.'

Blushing at praise which my tardy kindness had so ill deserved, I hastily enquired concerning her health. 'I believe,' said she smiling, though she sighed too, 'that I am still to cumber the ground a little longer. I am told that my immediate danger is past.'

'Heavens be praised,' cried I, with fervent sincerity.

'God's will be done,' said Miss Mortimer: 'I once seemed so near my haven! I little thought to be cast back upon the stormy ocean; but, God's will be done.'

'Nay, call it not the stormy ocean,' said I. 'Say rather, upon a cheerful stream, where you and I shall glide peacefully on together. You will soon be able to come to us at Richmond; and then I will show you all the affection and all the respect which ——' 'I ought always to have shown,' were the words which rose to my lips; but pride stifled the accents of confession. 'Were you once able,' continued I, 'to taste the blessed air that stirs all living things so joyously to-day, and see how all earth and heaven are gladdened with this glorious sunshine, you would gain new life and vigour every moment.'

'Ay, he is shining brightly,' said Miss Mortimer, looking towards her darkened casement. 'And a better sun, too, is gladdening all earth and heaven; but I, confined in a low cottage, see only the faint reflection of his brightness. But I know that He is shining gloriously,' continued she, the flush of rapture mounting to her face, 'and I shall yet see Him and rejoice!'

I made no reply. 'It is fortunate,' thought I, 'that they who have no pleasure in this life can solace themselves with the prospect of another.' Little did I at that moment imagine, that I myself was destined to furnish proof, that the loss of all worldly comfort cannot of itself procure this solace; that the ruin of all our earthly prospects cannot of itself elevate the hope long used to grovel among earthly things.

I spent almost two hours with my friend; during which, though so weak that the slightest exertions seemed oppressive to her, she at intervals conversed cheerfully. She enquired with friendly interest into my employments and recreations; but she knew me too well to hazard more direct interrogation concerning the effect of her monitory letter. In the course of our conversation, she asked, whether I often saw Mr Maitland? The question was a very simple one; but my roused watchfulness upon that subject made me fancy something particular in her manner of asking it. It had occurred to me, that she might possibly be able to solve the difficulty which had of late so much perplexed me; but I could not prevail upon myself to state the case directly. 'I wonder,' said I, 'now that you are gone, what can induce Maitland to visit us so often?' I thought there was meaning in Miss Mortimer's smile; but her reply was prevented by the entrance of the maid with refreshments. I wished Barbara a thousand miles off with her tray, though it contained rich wines, and some of the most costly fruits of the season. Miss Mortimer pressed me to partake of them, telling me, that she was regularly and profusely supplied. 'The giver,' said she, 'withholds nothing except his name, and that, too, I believe I can guess.'

A gentle knock at the house-door now drew Barbara from the room, and I instantly began to contrive how I might revert to the subject of my curiosity. 'Could you have imagined,' said I, 'that my father was the kind of man likely to attract Maitland so much?'

My enemy again made her appearance. 'Mr Maitland is below, madam,' said she: 'I asked him in, because I thought you would not turn his worthy worship away the third time he is come to ask for you.'

'Well, Ellen,' said Miss Mortimer, smiling, 'as your presence may protect my character, I think I may see him to-day.'

As Mr Maitland entered the room, I saw my friend make a feeble effort to rise from her seat; and, bending towards her, I supported her in my arms. The moment Maitland's eye fell upon me, it lightened with satisfaction. After speaking to my friend he turned to me. 'Miss Percy!' said he; and he said no more; but I would not have exchanged these words and the look which accompanied them for all the compliments of all mankind. Yet at that moment the spirit of coquetry slept; I quite forgot to calculate upon his love, and thought only of his approbation.

I believe neither Maitland nor I recollected that he still held the hand he had taken, till Miss Mortimer offered him some fruit, hinting that she suspected him of having a peculiar right to it. A slight change of colour betrayed him; but he only answered carelessly, that fruit came seasonably after a walk of seven miles in a sultry day. 'You never travel otherwise than on foot on Sunday,' said Miss Mortimer. 'I seldom find occasion to travel on Sunday at all,' answered Maitland; 'but I knew that I could spend an hour with you without violating the spirit of the fourth commandment.'

The hour was spent, and spent without weariness even to me; yet I cannot recollect that a single sentence was uttered in reference to worldly business or amusement; except that Maitland once bitterly lamented his disappointed hopes of usefulness to the African cause. 'However,' added he, 'I believe I had need of that lesson. Our Master is the only one whose servants venture to be displeased if they may not direct what service he will accept from them.'

'Nobody is more in want of such a lesson than I,' said Miss Mortimer, 'when my foolish heart is tempted to repine at the prospect of being thus laid aside, perhaps for years; useless as it should seem to myself and to all human kind.'

'My good friend,' returned Maitland (and a tear for a moment quenched the lightning of that eye before which the most untameable spirit must have bowed submissive), 'say not that you are useless, while you can show forth the praise of your Creator. His goodness shines gloriously when he bestows and blesses the gifts of nature and of fortune; but more gloriously when his mercy gladdens life after all these gifts are withdrawn. It is the high privilege of your condition to prove that our Father is of himself alone sufficient for the happiness of his children.'

'I am sure, my friend,' cried I, 'of all people upon earth, you need the least regret being made idle for a little while; for the recollection of the good which you have already done must furnish your mind with a continual feast.'

'Indeed, Ellen,' returned Miss Mortimer, 'you never were more mistaken. I do not recollect one action of my life, not even among those which originated in a sense of duty, that has not been degraded by some mixture of evil, either in the motive or in the performance.'

'Oh but you know perfection is not expected from us.'

Maitland shook his head. 'I fear,' said he, 'we must not trust much to your plea, so long as we are commanded to "be perfect." Miss Mortimer will feel at peace; not because she hopes that her King will, instead of her just tribute, accept of counters; but because she knows that the full tribute has been paid.'

While I saw the truths of religion affect the vigorous mind of Maitland, – while I saw them triumph in a feebler soul over pain, and loneliness, and fear, – how could I remain wholly insensible to their power? Whilst I listened to the conversation of these Christians, how could I suppress a wish that their comforts might one day be mine? 'Pray for me,' I whispered to Miss Mortimer, half-desirous, half-afraid to extend my petition to Maitland, 'pray for me that, when I am sick and dying, your God may bless me as he now blesses you.' I know not how my friend replied; for Maitland laid his hand upon my head, with a look in which all kind and holy feeling was so blended, that raptured saints can image nothing more seraphic. He spoke not – but the language of man is feeble to the eloquence of that pause!

But my mind was as yet unfit to retain any serious impression. The voice of truth played over it as the breeze upon the unstable waters, moving it gently for a moment, and then passing away. My religious humour vanished with the scene by which it was excited; and even Miss Mortimer's parting whisper helped to replace it by a far different spirit. 'I can guess now,' said she, 'what carries Mr Maitland so often to Bloomsbury Square.' Before hearing this remark, I had offered to convey Maitland to town in my carriage; and now the heart which had so lately swelled with better feelings, beat with a little coquettish fluttering, when, having taken leave of my friend, I found myself seated *tête-à-tête* with my supposed admirer. Maitland was, however, the very innocent cause of my flutterings; since for a whole mile he talked of Miss Mortimer, and nothing but Miss Mortimer; then, perceiving that I was little inclined to answer, he was silent, and left me to my reflections.

The softness of evening was beginning to mingle with the cheerfulness of day, and a fresher breeze began to lighten the sultry air. 'What an Arcadian day!' cried I. 'Pity that you and I were not lovers, to enjoy it thus alone together!'

I meant to utter this with the prettiest air of simplicity imaginable, but found it quite impossible to suppress the conscious glow that stole over my face. I was certain that Maitland coloured too, though he answered with great self-possession. 'I make no pretensions to the character of a lover,' said he; 'but you may allow me to converse with you like a friend, which will do as well.'

'Oh the very worst substitute in nature,' cried I; 'for the conversation of lovers is all complaisance; whereas I find that those who beg leave to talk like friends always mean to ask something which I do not wish to tell, or to tell something which I do not wish to hear.'

'Perhaps I may mean to do both,' said Maitland; 'for there is a question which I have often wished to ask you; and when you have answered, I may perhaps undertake the other office too. Are you aware that common report joins your name with that of Lord

Frederick de Burgh?'

'Stop!' cried I; 'positively you must not be my confessor.'

'That must be as you please,' returned Maitland. 'Then I will in charity suppose you ignorant; and when I tell you that every gossip's tongue is busy with his good fortune, I think you will grant him no additional triumph; unless indeed it be possible that ——' He paused, and then added with unusual warmth, – 'but I will not think of such profanation, much less utter it.'

'Now, do Mr Maitland desist, I entreat you,' cried I, half-smiling, half in earnest; 'for I never was lectured in my life without being guilty of some impertinence; and there is nobody living whom I would not rather offend than you.'

'I believe I must venture,' returned Maitland, looking at me with a good-humoured smile. 'I would hazard much for your advantage.'

'Nay, positively you shall not,' said I, playfully laying my hand upon his mouth.

This gesture, which, I protest, originated in mere thoughtlessness, ended in utter confusion; for Maitland, seizing my hand, pressed it to his lips. The whole affair was transacted in far less time than I can tell it; and we both sat looking, I believe, abundantly silly; though neither, I fancy, had the courage to take a view of the other.

The silence was first broken by a splenetic ejaculation from Maitland. 'Pshaw,' said he, 'you will compel me to act the puppy in spite of myself.' Now, whatever colour Maitland might try to throw upon his inadvertence, I plainly perceived that it had not originated in a cool sense of the duty of gallantry; for he was even studiously inattentive to all the common gallantries which I was accustomed to expect from others. My breast swelled with the pride of victory; and yet my situation was embarrassing enough; for Maitland, far from confirming my dreams of conquest, much more from empowering me to pursue my triumph, maintained a frozen silence, and seemed wrapt in a very unlover-like meditation.

The first words which he uttered were these: 'Although Parliament refuses justice to these Africans, much might be done for those already in slavery. Much might be done by a person residing among them, determined to own no interest but their welfare.' I could not at that time follow the chain which had led to this idea. Unfortunately for me, I was soon enabled to trace the connection.

As soon as we entered the town, Maitland expressed a wish to alight, and immediately took a cold and formal leave. I returned home, with every thought full of my new discovery, every affection absorbed in vanity. Convinced of Maitland's attachment, I now only wondered why it was not avowed. The most probable conjecture I could form was, that he wished to save his pride the pain of a repulse; and again I piously resolved to spare no torture within my power. I was determined that, cost what it would, the secret should be explicitly told; after which I should, of course, be entitled to exhibit and sport with my captive at pleasure. Beyond this mean and silly triumph I looked not. I forgot that the lion, even when tamed, will not learn the tricks of a monkey. Weaker souls, I knew, might be led contented in their silken fetters: I forgot that the strongest cords bound Samson only whilst he slept. To reward the expected patience of my lover was not in all my thoughts. I should as soon have dreamt of marrying my father.

Meanwhile Maitland was in no haste to renew my opportunities of coquetting. Business, or, as I then thought, the fear of committing himself, kept him a whole week from visiting us. During that week, I had canvassed the subject with Miss Arnold under every possible aspect, except those in which it would have appeared to a rational mind. I believe my friend began to be, as perhaps the reader is, heartily tired of my confidence. She certainly wished the occasion of our discussion at an end; but she had no desire that it should end favourably to my wishes. She dreaded the increase of Maitland's influence. A mutual dislike, indeed, subsisted between them. He seemed to have an intuitive perception of the dark side of her character; and she to feel a revolting awe of his undeceiving, undeceivable sagacity. I have often seen the artful, though they despise defenceless simplicity, and delight to exert their skill against weapons like their own, yet shrink with instinctive dread from plain, undesigning common sense. Maitland's presence always imposed a visible restraint upon Miss Arnold; but she had more cogent reasons than her dislike of Maitland, for wishing to arrest the progress of an intercourse which threatened to baffle certain schemes of her own. Meaning to interrupt our good understanding, she gave me the advice which appeared most likely to effect her purpose. Of this I have now no doubt; though, at that time, I harboured not a suspicion of any motive less friendly than a desire to forward every purpose of mine.

'If you don't flirt more sentimentally,' said she, 'you will never make any impression upon Maitland. He knows you would never rattle away as you do to De Burgh, with any man you really cared for. You should endeavour to seem in earnest.'

'Oh, I am quite tired of endeavouring to "seem." And then I really can't be sentimental: it is not in my nature. Besides, it would be all in vain. Maitland has found out that I am not in love with Lord Frederick; and it will be impossible to convince him of the contrary.'

'No matter; you may make him believe that you are somehow bound in honour to Lord Frederick, which will quite answer the purpose.'

'No Juliet; that I cannot possibly do, without downright falsehood.'

'Oh, I'll engage to make him believe it, without telling him one word of untruth. Let me manage the matter, and I'll make him as jealous as a very Osmyn; that is, provided he be actually in love.'

The scepticism of my friend upon this point was a continual source of irritation to me; and, to own the truth, furnished one great cause of my eagerness to ascertain my conquest beyond cavil. 'Well!' returned I, already beginning to yield, 'if you could accomplish it honourably: but – no – I should not like to be thought weak enough to entangle myself with a man for whom I had no particular attachment.'

'I am certain,' returned Miss Arnold, more gravely, 'that if Mr Maitland thought your honour concerned, far from considering the fulfilment of even a tacit engagement as a weakness, he would highly admire you for the sacrifice.'

The prospect of being 'highly admired' by Mr Maitland blinded me to the sophistry of this answer; yet I felt myself unwilling that he should actually believe me to be under engagement, and I expressed that unwillingness to my adviser. 'Oh!' cried she, 'we must guard against making him too sure. I would merely hint the thing, as what I feared might happen, and leave you an opening to deny or explain at any time. As I live, there he comes, just at the lucky moment! Now, leave him to me for half an hour, and I will engage to bring him to confession; that is, if he has any thing to confess.'

'Well! I should like to see you convinced for once, if it be possible to convince you; and yet what if he should ——'

'Oh, there's his knock!' interrupted Juliet. 'If we stand here objecting, we shall lose the opportunity. Sure you can trust to my management.'

'Well, Juliet,' said I, with a prophetic sigh, 'do as you please; but, for Heaven's sake, be cautious!' She instantly accepted the permission, and flew down stairs to receive him in the parlour.

Let no woman retain in her confidence the treacherous ally who once persuades or assists her to depart from the plain path of simplicity. Such an ally, whatever partial fondness may allege, must be deficient either in understanding or in integrity. That the associate who incites you to deceive others will in time deceive yourself, is the least evil to be apprehended from such a connection. The young are notoriously liable to the guidance of their intimates; and most women are, in this respect, young all their lives. If I had naturally any good tendency, it was toward sincerity; and yet a false friend, working on my ruling passion, had led me to the brink of actual deceit. So stable are the virtues which are founded only in constitution or humour! Had I been wisely unrelenting to the first artifice of pretended friendship, and honestly abhorrent even of the wile which professed to favour me, the bitterest misfortunes of my life might have been spared; and I might have escaped from sufferings never to be forgotten, from errors never to be cancelled.

My punishment began even during the moments of Miss Arnold's conference with Maitland. I was restless and agitated. My heart throbbed violently, less with the hopes of triumph than with the anxiousness of duplicity, and the dread of detection. I trembled; I breathed painfully; at every noise I started, thinking it betokened the close of the conference, which yet seemed endless. Again and again I approached the parlour door, and as often retreated, fearing to spoil all by a premature interruption. I was once more resolving to join my friend, when I heard some one leave the house. I flew to a window, and saw Maitland walk swiftly along the square, and disappear, without once looking back. This seemed ominous; but as my friend did not come to make her report, I went in search of her.

I found her in an attitude of meditation; and though she instantly advanced towards me with a smile, her countenance bore traces of discomposure. 'Well, I protest,' cried she, 'there is no dealing with these men without a little management.'

This sounded somewhat like a boast; and, my spirits reviving, I enquired 'how her management had succeeded?'

'You shall judge,' returned Miss Arnold. 'I will tell you all exactly and candidly.' People seldom vouch for the candour of their narratives when it is above suspicion. 'I could not be abrupt, you know,' proceeded my *candid* narrator; 'but I contrived to lead dexterously towards the point; and, after smoothing my way a little just hinted a possibility that Lord Frederick might succeed. Signor Maestoso took not the least notice. Then I grew a little more explicit. Still without effect! He only fixed his staring black eyes upon me, as if he would have looked through me, to see what was my purpose in telling him all that. At last I was obliged to say downrightly (Heaven forgive me for the fib!) that I was afraid you might marry De Burgh at last, though I owned you had no serious regard for him. All this while Don Pompous had been walking about the room; but at this he stopped short, just opposite to me, and asked me, with a frown as dark as a thunder cloud, "what reason I had to say so?" – I – I declare, I was quite frightened.'

Miss Arnold stopped, and seemed to hesitate. 'Well!' Go on!' cried I impatiently. – 'You know,' continued she, 'I could not answer his question in any other way, except by giving him some little instances of your – your good understanding with De Burgh; but still I could extort no answer from the impenetrable creature, except now and then a kind of grunt.'

'How tedious you are! Do proceed.'

'At last, when I found nothing else would do, I – I was obliged to have recourse to – to an expedient, which produced an immediate effect. And now, Ellen, I am convinced that Maitland loves you to distraction!'

'Indeed! What? How?'

'Ah, Ellen! you have a thousand times more penetration than I. I would give the world for your faculty of reading the heart.'

'But, dear Juliet! how was it, – how did you discover ——'

'Why, when nothing else seemed likely to avail, I – I thought I might venture to hint, just by way of a trifling instance of your intimacy with Lord Frederick, that – that you had – had borrowed a small sum from him.'

'Good heaven, Juliet! did you tell Maitland this? Oh! he will despise me for ever. Leave me, – treacherous, – you have undone me.'

'Ellen, my dearest Ellen,' said my friend, caressing me with the most humble affection, 'I own I was very wrong; but indeed – indeed, if you had seen how he was affected, you would have been convinced, that nothing else could have been so effectual. If you had seen how pale he grew, and how he trembled, and gasped for breath! You never saw a man in such agitation. Dear Ellen, forgive me! You know I could have no motive except to serve you.'

In spite of my vexation, I was not insensible to this statement, to which my vanity gave full credit; though the slightest comparison of the circumstances with the character of Maitland must have convinced me that they were exaggerated. At length, curiosity so far prevailed over my wrath, that I condescended to enquire what answer he had given to Miss Arnold's information? Miss Arnold replied, that the first words which he was able to utter, announced, that he must see me instantly. 'And why then,' I asked, 'is he gone in such haste?'

My friend made me repeat this question before she could hear it; – an expedient which often serves those whose answer is not quite ready. 'Because he – he afterwards changed his mind, and said he would call upon you in an hour.'

Before the hour had elapsed, my resentment had yielded partly to my friend's representations, partly to a new subject of alarm. I dreaded lest, if Maitland considered my debt to Lord Frederick in so serious a light, he might think it a duty of friendship to apprize my father of my involvement; and, anxious to secure his secrecy, yet too proud to beg it, I suffered him, at his return, to be admitted to my dressing-room, although I had never before been so unwilling to encounter him. Maitland, on his part, seemed little less embarrassed than myself. He began to speak, but his words were inarticulate. He cleared his throat, and seized my attention by a look full of meaning; and the effort ended in some insignificant enquiry, to the answer of which he was evidently insensible. At last, suddenly laying his hand upon my arm, 'Miss Percy,' said he, 'pardon my abruptness, – I really can neither think nor talk of trifles at this moment. Let me speak plainly to you. Allow me for once the privilege of a friend. You cannot have one more sincere than myself; nor,' added he with a deep sigh, 'one more disinterested.'

'Well!' returned I, moved by the kindness of his voice and manner, and willing to shake off my embarrassment; 'use the privilege generously, and I don't care if, for once, I grant it you.'

Maitland instantly, without compliment or apology, availed himself of my concession. 'I presume,' said he, 'that Miss Arnold has acquainted you with her very strange communication to me this morning.' I only bowed in answer, and did not venture again to raise my head. 'Did she tell you, too,' proceeded Maitland, in the tone of strong indignation, 'that she meant to conceal from you this most unprovoked act of teachery, had I not insisted upon warning you against a confidant who could betray your secret, – and such a secret!'

Abashed and humbled, conscious that since my friend had been partly licensed by myself, she was less blamable than she appeared, yet unable, without exposing myself still farther, to state what little could be alleged in her vindication, I stammered out a few words; implying, that perhaps Miss Arnold did not affix any importance to the secret.

'The inferences she drew,' cried Maitland, 'leave no doubt, that she thought it important; or, granting it were as you say, is the woman fit to be a friend who could regard such a transaction as immaterial? Is there any real friend to whom you could confide it without reluctance? I need not ask if you have intrusted it to your father.'

The tears of mortification and resentment which had been collected in my eyes while Maitland spoke, burst from them when I attempted to answer. But my wounded pride quickly came to my assistance. 'No, sir,' returned I; 'but if you think your own reproofs insufficient you will of course aid them with my father's.'

Maitland could not resist the sight of my uneasiness. His countenance expressed the most gentle compassion; and his voice softened even to tenderness. 'And is the reproof of a father,' said he, 'more formidable to you than all that your delicacy must suffer under obligation to a confident admirer? Dearest Miss Percy, as a friend – a most attached, most anxious friend – I beseech you to ——'

He stopped short, and coloured very deeply, – suddenly aware, I believe, that he was speaking with a warmth which friendship seldom assumes; then taking refuge in a double intrenchment of formality, he begged me to pardon a freedom which he ascribed to his friendship for my father and Miss Mortimer. In spite of my mortifying situation, my heart bounded with triumph as I traced through this disguise the proofs of my power over the affections of Maitland. Recovering my spirits, I told him frankly, that I was determined to make no application to my father, since a few weeks would enable me to escape from my difficulty without the hazard of incensing him. Maitland looked distressed, but made no further attempt to persuade me. 'This is what I feared,' said he; 'but I am sensible that I have no right to urge you.'

He was silent for some moments, and seemed labouring with something which he knew not how to utter. A certain tremour began to steal over me too, and expectation made my breath come short when I again heard his voice. 'There may be an impropriety,' he began, but again he stopped embarrassed. 'There may be objections against your – your condescension to Lord Frederick, which do not apply to all your acquaintance; – and – and I have taken the liberty to – to bring a few hundred pounds in case you would do me the honour to ——' The mainly brown of Maitland's cheek flushed with a warmer tint as he spoke; and the eye which had so often awed my turbulent spirit, now sunk timidly before mine; for he was conferring an obligation, and his generous heart entered by sympathy into the situation of one compelled to accept a pecuniary favour. But I was teazed and disappointed; for here was nothing of the expected declaration; on the contrary, Maitland had wilfully marked the difference between himself and a lover.

He probably read vexation in my face, though he ascribed it to a wrong cause. 'I see,' said he, in a tone of mortification, 'that this is a degree of confidence which I must not expect. Perhaps you will suffer me to mention the matter to Miss Mortimer – she I am sure will allow me to be her banker for any sum you may require.'

Shame on the heartless being who could see in this delicate kindness only a triumph for the most despicable vanity! In vain did Maitland veil his interest under the semblance of friendship. Seeing, and glorying to see, that passion lurked under the disguise, I could not restrain my impatience to force the mask away. I thanked Maitland, but told him that the delay of a few weeks could be of little importance; adding, gaily, that I fancied Lord Frederick was in no haste for payment; and would prefer the right of a creditor over the liberty of his debtor.

Maitland almost shuddered. 'Can you jest upon such a subject?' said he. The expression of uneasiness which crossed his features only encouraged me to proceed. 'No, really,' said I, with affected seriousness, 'I am quite in earnest. One day or other I suppose I must give somebody a right to me, and it may as well be Lord Frederick as another. Marriage will be at best but a heartless business to me – Heigho!'

'I hope it will be otherwise,' said Maitland, with a sigh not quite so audible as mine, but a little more sincere.

'No, no,' said I, sighing again, 'love is out of the question with me. The creatures that dangle after me want either a toy upon which to throw away their money, or money to throw away upon their toys. A heart would be quite lost upon any of them. If, indeed, a man of sense and worth had attached himself to me, – a man with sincerity enough to tell me my faults, – with gentleness to do it kindly, – with –

with something in his character, perhaps in his manners, to secure respect, – he might have – have found me not incapable of – of an animated – I mean of a – a very respectful friendship.'

I could not utter this last sentence without palpable emotion. Nature, which had done much to unfit me for deliberate coquetry, faltered in my voice; and stained my cheek with burning blushes. In the confusion which I had brought upon myself, I should have utterly forgotten to watch the success of my experiment, had not my attention been drawn by the tremor of Maitland's hand. I ventured, thus encouraged, to steal a glance at his countenance.

His eye was fixed upon me with a keenness which seemed to search my very soul. Deep glowing crimson flushed his face. It was only for a moment. His colour instantly fading to more than its natural paleness, he almost threw from him the hand which he had held. 'Oh, Ellen!' he cried in a tone of bitter reproach, 'how can you! suspecting, as I see you do, the power of your witchery over me, how can you! – Others might despise my weakness – I myself despise it – but with you it should have been sacred!'

Where is the spirit of prophecy which can foretell how that, which at a distance seems desirable, will affect us when it meets our grasp? Who could have believed that this avowal, so long expected, so eagerly anticipated, should have been heard only with shame and mortification! Far, indeed, from the elation of conquest were my feelings, while I shrunk from the rebuke of him, whose displeasure had, with me, the power of a reproving angel. Abashed and confounded, I did not even dare to raise my eyes; whilst Maitland, retreating from me, stood for some moments in thoughtful silence. Approaching me again, 'No,' said he, in a low constrained voice, 'I cannot speak to you now. Give me a few minutes to-morrow: – they shall be the last.'

Before I could have articulated a word, had the universe depended upon my utterance, Maitland was gone.

As soon as my recollection returned, I stole, like a culprit, to my own apartment, where, locking myself in, I fell into a reverie; in which stifled self-reproach, resentment against Miss Arnold, and an undefined dread of the consequences of Maitland's displeasure, were but faintly relieved by complacency towards my own victorious charms. Maitland's parting words rung in my ears; and though I endeavoured to persuade myself that they were dictatated by a resentment which could not resist the slightest concession from me, they never recurred to my mind unattended by some degree of alarm. I was determined, however, that no consideration should tempt me to betray the cause of my sex, by humbling myself before a proud lover; 'and, if he be resolved to break my chains, let him do so,' said I, 'if he can.' I justly considered the loss of a lover as no very grievous misfortune. Alas! I could not then estimate the evil of losing such a friend as Maitland.

The next morning he came early to claim his audience; not such as I had seen him the evening before; but calm, self-possessed, and dignified. He entered upon his subject with apparent effort; telling me that he was come to give me, if I had the patience to receive it, the explanation to which he conceived me entitled, after the inadvertencies which had at different times betrayed his secret. Provoked by his composure, I answered, that 'explanation was quite unnecessary, since I did not apprehend that either his conduct or motives could at all affect me.'

'Suffer me then,' said he, mildly, 'to explain them for my own sake, that I may, if I can, escape the imputation of caprice.' I made some light, silly reply; and, affecting the utmost indifference, took my knotting and sat down. 'Have you no curiosity,' said Maitland, 'to know how you won and how you have lost a heart that could have loved you faithfully? Though my affections are of no value to you, you may one day prize those which the same errors might alienate.'

'That is not very likely, sir,' said I. 'I shall probably not approach so near the last stage of celibacy as to catch my advantage of any wandering fancy which may cross a man's mind.'

'This was no wandering fancy,' said Maitland, with calm seriousness. 'You are the first woman I ever loved; and I shall retain the most tender, the most peculiar interest in your welfare, long after what is painful in my present feelings has passed away. But I must fly while I can – before I lose the power to relinquish what I know it would be misery to obtain.'

'Oh, sir, I assure you that this is a misery I should spare you,' cried I; my heart swelling with impatience at a style of profession, for it cannot be called courtship, to which I was so little accustomed.

'Now this is childish,' said Maitland. 'Are you angry at having escaped being teazed with useless importunity? If you would have me feel all the pang of leaving you, call back the candour and sweetness that first bewitched me. For it was not your beauty, Ellen. I had seen you more than once ere I observed that you were beautiful, and twenty times ere I felt it. It was your playful simplicity, your want of all design, your perfect transparency of mind, that won upon me before I was aware; and when I was weary of toil and sick of the heartlessness and duplicity of mankind, I turned to you, and thought –, it matters not what.'

Maitland paused, but I was in no humour to break the silence. My anger gave place to a more gentle feeling. I felt that I had possessed, that I had lost, the approbation of Maitland, and the tears were rising to my eyes; but the fear that he should ascribe them to regret for the loss of his stoic-love, forced them back to the proud heart.

'Yet,' continued Maitland, 'I perceived, pardon my plainness, that your habits and inclinations were such as must be fatal to every plan of domestic comfort; and at four-and-thirty a man begins to foresee, that, after the raptures of the lover are past, the husband has a long life before him; in which he must either share his joys and his sorrows with a friend, or exact the submission of an inferior. To be a restraint upon your pleasure is what I could not endure; yet otherwise they must have interfered with every pursuit of my life, – nay, must every hour have shocked my perceptions of right and wrong. Nor is this all,' continued Maitland, guiding my comprehension by the increased solemnity of his manner. 'Who that seeks a friend would choose one who would consider his employments as irksome, his pleasures as fantastic, his hopes as a dream? – one who would regard the object of his supreme desire as men do a fearful vision, visiting them unwelcome in their hours of darkness, but slighted or forgotten in every happier season? No, Ellen! the wife of a Christian must be more than the toy of his leisure; – she must be his fellow-labourer, his fellow-worshipper.'

'Very well, sir!' interrupted I, my spirit of impatience again beginning to stir. 'Enough of my disqualifications for an office which I really have no ambition to fill.'

'I believe you, Miss Percy,' returned Maitland, 'and that belief is all that reconciles me to my sacrifice; – therefore beware how you weaken it by these affected airs of scorn. I assure you, they were not necessary to convince me that you are not to be won unsought. It was this conviction which made me follow you even when I saw my danger. I flattered myself that I might be useful to you, – or rather, perhaps, this was the only device by which I could excuse my weakness to myself. In a vain trust in the humility of a woman, and a trust yet more vain in the prudence of a lover, I purposed to conceal my feelings till they should be lost amidst the cares of a busy life. Your penetration, or my own imprudence, has defeated that purpose, just as I begin to perceive that you are too powerful for cares and business. Nothing, then, remains but to fly whilst I have the power. In a fortnight hence, I shall sail for the West Indies.'

I started, as if a dart had pierced me. The utmost which I had apprehended from Maitland's threats of desertion, was, that he should withdraw from our family circle. 'For the West Indies!' I faintly repeated.

'Yes. It happens not unfortunately that I have business there. But I have dwelt too long upon myself and my concerns. Since I must "cut off the right hand," better the stroke were past. I have only one request to make, – one earnest request, and then ——' He paused. I would have asked the nature of his request, but a rising in my throat threatened to betray me, and I only ventured an enquiring look. Maitland took my hand: and the demon of coquetry was now so entirely laid, that I suffered him to retain it, without a struggle. 'Dear, ever dear Ellen,' said he, 'many an anxious thought will turn to you when we are far asunder, – repay me for them all, by granting one petition. It is, that you will confide your difficulties, whatever they be, to Miss Mortimer; and, when you do so, give her this packet.'

'No, no,' interrupted I, with quickness. 'The sum I owe Lord Frederick is a trifle compared to what you suppose it. It was the price of a bauble, – a vile bauble. It was no secret, – hundreds saw it, – accident, mere accident made me ——'

Shocked at the emotion I was betraying, and in horror lest Maitland should impute it to a humbling cause, I suddenly changed my manner; haughtily declaring that I would neither distress my friend in her illness nor incur any new obligation. Maitland modestly endeavoured to shake my determination; but, finding me resolute, he rose to be gone. 'Farewell, Ellen,' said he, – 'every blessing ——,' the rest could not reach my ear, but while I have being, I shall remember his look as he turned from me. It was anguish, rendered more touching by a faint struggle for a smile, that came like a watery beam upon the troubled deep, making the sadness more dreary. I turned to a window, and watched till he disappeared.

I have lived to be deserted by all mankind, – to wander houseless in a land of strangers, – to gaze upon the crowds of an unknown city, assured that I should see no friend, – to be secluded, as in a living grave, from human intelligence and human sympathy; but never did I feel so desolately alone, as when I turned to the chamber where Maitland had been and felt that he was gone. Miss Mortimer's words flashed on my mind. 'The good and the wise will one by one forsake you.' – 'They have forsaken me! all forsaken me!' I cried, as, throwing myself upon the ground, I rested my head upon the seat which Maitland had left, hid my face in my arm, and wept.

CHAPTER XIII

In a dull stream, which moving slow,
You hardly see the current flow,
When a small breeze obstructs the course,
It whirls about for want of force;
And in its narrow circle, gathers
Nothing but chaff, and straw, and feathers.
The current of a female mind
Stops thus, and turns with every wind.
Thus whirling round, together draws,
Fools, fops, and rakes, for chaff and straws.

Swift.

I IMAGINE that such of my readers as are still in their teens, and of course expect to find Cupid in ambush at every corner, will now smile sagaciously, and pronounce, 'that poor Ellen was certainly in love.' If so, I must unequivocally assert, that, in this instance, their penetration has failed them. Maitland had piqued my vanity, he had of late interested my curiosity; his conversation often amused me, and the more I was accustomed to it, the more it pleased. It is said, that they who have been restored to sight, find pleasure in the mere exercise of their newly regained faculty, without reference to its usefulness, or even to the beauty of the objects they behold; so I, without a thought of improving by Maitland's conversation, and with feeble perceptions of its excellence, was pleased to find in it occupation for faculties, which, but for him, might have slumbered inactive. I had a sort of filial confidence in his good will, and a respect approaching to reverence for his abilities and character. But this was all; for amidst all my follies, I had escaped that susceptibility which makes so many young women idle, and so many old ones ridiculous.

Lest, however, my assertion seem liable to the suspicion which attaches to the declarations of the accused, I shall mention an irrefragable proof of its truth. In less than twelve hours after Maitland had taken his final leave, I was engaged in an animated flirtation with Lord Frederick de Burgh. It is true, that for some days I used to start when the knocker sounder at the usual hour of Maitland's visit, and to hear with a vague sensation of disappointment some less familiar step approach. It is true, that I loved not to see his seat occupied by others, and that I never again looked towards the spot where he finally disappeared from my sight, without feeling its association with something painful. But I suppose it may be laid down as a maxim, that no woman who is seriously attached to one man, will trifle, *con spirito*, with another; and my flirtations with Lord Frederick were not only continued, but soon began to threaten a decisive termination.

In spite of my father's remonstrance, Lord Frederick's daily visits were continued; for how could I interdict them after his Lordship had said, nay sworn, that I must admit him, or make London a desert to him? We also met often at the house of Lady St Edmunds, where, after Maitland's departure, I became a more frequent guest than ever. Placable as Miss Arnold had hitherto found me, I could not immediately forgive her discovery to Maitland; for, willing to throw from myself the blame of losing him, I more than half ascribed his desertion to her interference. In resentment against one favourite, I betook myself with more ardour to the other; with whom I spent many an hour, more pleasant, it must be owned, than profitable.

Lady St Edmunds had a boudoir to which only her most select associates were admitted. Nothing which taste could approve was wanting to its decoration, – nothing which sense desires could be added to its luxury. The walls glowed with the sultry scenes of Claude, and the luxuriant designs of Titian. The daylight stole mellowed on the eye through a bower of flowering orange trees and myrtles; or alabaster lamps imitated the softness of moonshine. Airy Grecian couches lent grace to the forms which rested on them; and rose-coloured draperies shed on the cheek a becoming bloom. No cumbrous footmen were permitted to invade this retreat of luxury. Their office was here supplied by a fairy-footed smiling girl, whose figure and attire partook the elegance of all around. Had books been needful to kill the time, here were abundance well suited to their place; not works of puzzling science or dull morality; but modern plays, novels enriched with slanderous tales or caricatures of living characters, and fashionable sonnets, guarded to the ear of decency, but deadly to her spirit. In this temple of effeminacy, Lady St Edmunds and I generally passed our morning hours, and it usually happened that Lord Frederick joined the party. Here I often called forth my musical powers to delight my companions, soothed in my turn by the yet sweeter sounds of flattery and love. The easy manners of my hostess banished all restraint. The timidity which had at first admired without venturing to copy, fled before her neat raillery and free example; and high spirits, encouragement, and inconsiderateness, often led me to the utmost limits of discretion.

In such a scene, with such associates, can it be wondered, that I forgot the manly sense, the hardy virtues of Maitland? No longer counteracted by his ascendency, or checked by the warnings of Miss Mortimer, Lady St Edmunds' influence increased every day, and strengthened into an affection which utterly blinded me to every impropriety in her conduct and sentiments; – an awful influence, which almost every girl of seventeen allows more or less to some favourite. Happy the daughter who finds that favourite where nature has secured to her a real friend; – happy the mother who gains support for her authority in the enthusiastic attachments of youth!

As Lady St Edmunds was no restraint upon me, her presence in our coterie was rather advantageous to Lord Frederick, banishing the reserve of a *tête-à-tête*, and allowing him constantly to offer gallantries too indirect to provoke repulse, yet too pointed to be overlooked. Indeed, such attentions from him were now become so habitual to me, that I accepted of them as things of course, without consideration either of motive or consequence. They amused and flattered me; and amusement and flattery were the sum of my desires.

Things were in this train, when, one morning, the usual party being met in the boudoir, Lady St Edmunds was called away to receive a visiter. She went without ceremony; for she never reminded me of our difference of rank, by any of those correct formalities by which the great are accustomed to distance their inferiors. She gaily enjoined Lord Frederick to entertain me; and he accepted of the office with a look which prompted me, I know not why, to move hastily towards a harp, on which I struck some chords. Lord Frederick stopped me; addressing me so much more seriously than he had ever done before, that, in my surprise, I suffered him to proceed without interruption. In the warmest phrase of passion he besought me to tell him how long I meant to continue his lingering probation; and protested, that he was no longer able to endure my delays. The presumptuousness of this language was softened by tones and gestures so humble, that I found it impossible to be angry! but I was not a little confounded at a security which I had been far from intending to authorise. Recovering myself as well as I was able, I affected to receive his protestations in jest, telling him his gallantries were now so hackneyed, that I had already exhausted all my wit in replying to them; and that if he wished to find me at all entertaining, he must positively call a new subject.

His Lordship abated nothing of his solemnity. He fell upon his knees, conjured me to be serious, and talked of as many cruelties, racks, and tortures, as would have furnished the dungeons of the Inquisition; yet still the drift of his rhetoric seemed to be only this, that he had now been for a very competent time the martyr of my charms, and therefore was entitled to claim his reward.

Though somewhat alarmed, I still tried to laugh off the attack; telling him that he had changed his manner much to the worse, since gravity in him seemed the most preposterous thing in nature. 'Was it possible,' Lord Frederick enquired with a tragedy exclamation, 'that I could thus punish him for a disguise of gaiety which he had assumed only to mislead indifferent eyes, but which he was certain had never deceived my penetration?' And then he boldly appealed to my candour, 'whether I had ever for a moment misunderstood him?' Too much startled and confounded to persevere in my levity, I replied in the words of simple truth, 'that I had never bestowed any consideration upon his meaning, since my father had settled the matter.'

Lord Frederick poured forth all the established forms of abuse against parental authority; execrating, in a most lover-like manner, the idea of subjecting the affections to its control, and protesting his belief that I had too much spirit to sacrifice him to such tyranny. Piqued at my lover's implied security, I answered, 'that I had no inclination to resist my father's will; and that so long as he did not require me to marry any man who was particularly disagreeable to me, I should very willingly leave a negative in his power.' Lord Frederick struck his hand upon his forehead, and raised his handkerchief to his eyes, as if to conceal extreme agitation. 'Cruel,

cruel, Miss Percy!' he cried, 'if such are, indeed, your sentiments, – if you are, indeed, determined to submit to the decision of your inhuman father, why – why did you, with such barbarous kindness, restore the hopes which he had destroyed? Why did you, in this very room, allow me to hope that you would reward my faithful love, – that you would fly with me to that happy land where marriage is still free!'

My masquerade folly thus recalled to my recollection, the blood rushed tumultuously to my face and bosom. Unable to repel the charge, and terrified by this glimpse of the shackles which my imprudence had forged for me, I stammered out, that, 'whatever I might have said in a thoughtless moment, I was sure that no friend of Lord Frederick's or mine would advise either of us to so rash a step.'

'No friend of mine,' returned Lord Frederick, using the gestures of drying his fine blue eyes, 'shall ever again be consulted. Could I have foreseen your cruel treatment, never would I have put it in the power, even of my nearest relative, to injure you by publishng the hopes you had given.'

The hint, conveyed in these words, was not lost upon me. I concluded, that Lord Frederick had thought himself authorised to talk of the encouragement he had received. Our sense of impropriety is rarely so just as to gain nothing from anticipating the judgment of our fellow-creatures; and the levity which I had practised as an innocent trifling, took a very different form, when I saw it by sympathy, in the light in which it might soon be seen by hundreds. The folly into which I had been seduced by malice, vanity, and the love of amusement, would stand charactered in the world's sentence, as unjustifiable coquetry. Viewed in its consequences, as ruinous to the peace of a heart that loved me, I myself scarcely bestowed upon it a gentler name.

Confused, perplexed, and distressed, not daring to meet the eye of the man whom I had injured, I sat looking wistfully towards the door, more eager to escape from my present embarrassment than able to provide against the future. Lord Frederick instantly saw his advantage. 'I have wronged you, my heavenly Ellen,' he cried, throwing himself in rapture at my feet. 'I see that, upon reflection, you will yet allow my claim. How could I suspect my dear, generous Miss Percy of trifling with the fondest passion that ever warmed a human breast!'

I involuntarily recoiled, for I had never been less tenderly disposed towards Lord Frederick than at that moment. 'Really, my Lord,' I said, 'even if I could return all this enthusiasm, which indeed I cannot, I should give a poor specimen of my generosity by consenting to involve you in the difficulties which might be the consequence of disobliging my father.'

Lord Frederick cursed wealth in the most disinterested manner imaginable, – swore that 'the possession of his adorable Ellen was all he asked of Heaven,' – and fervently wished, that 'the splendour of his fortune, and the humbleness of mine, had given him an opportunity of proving how lightly he prized the dross when put in balance with my charms.' Though the loftiness of this style was too incongruous with Lord Frederick's general manner to excite no surprise, I must own, that it awakened not one doubt of his sincerity, – for what will not vanity believe? The more credit I gave his generosity, the more did I feel the injustice of my past conduct, yet the more painful it became to enter upon explanation; and I was not yet practised enough in coquetry to suppress the embarrassment which faltered on my tongue, as I told Lord Frederick, that 'I was sorry – very sorry, and much astonished; and that I had never suspected him of allowing such a romantic fancy to take possession of his mind; that my father's determination must excuse me to his Lordship and to the world, for refusing to sanction his hopes.'

Lord Frederick, in answer, vehemently averred, that his hopes had no connection with my father's decision, since, after that decision, he had been permitted to express his passion without repulse. He recalled several thoughtless concessions which I had forgotten as soon as made. Without formal detail, he dexterously contrived to remind me of the ring which I had allowed him to keep; and of the clandestine correspondence which I had begun from folly, and continued from weakness. He again referred to my half consent at the masquerade. Finally, he once more appealed to myself, whether, all these circumstances considered, his hopes deserved to be called presumptuous.

During this almost unanswerable appeal, I had instinctively moved towards the door; but Lord Frederick placed himself so as to intercept my escape. Terrified, and revolting from the bonds which awaited me, yet conscious that I had virtually surrendered my freedom, – eager to escape from an engagement which yet I had not the courage to break, – I began a hesitating, incoherent reply; but I felt like one who is roused from the oppression of nightmare, when it was interrupted by the entrance of Lady St Edmunds. I almost embraced my friend in my gratitude for this fortunate deliverance; but I was too much disconcerted to prolong my visit; and, taking a hasty leave, I returned home.

I had so long been accustomed to find relief from every difficulty in the superior ingenuity of Miss Arnold, that my late resentment, which had already begun to evaporate, entirely gave way to my habitual dependence upon her counsels. Not that I, at the time, acknowledged this motive to myself. Far from it. I placed my renewed confidence solely to the credit of a generous placability of nature; for when any action of mine claimed kindred with virtue, I could not afford to enquire too seriously into its real parentage. However, I took an early opportunity of acquainting Juliet with my dilemma. But my friend's readiness of resource appeared now to have forsaken her. She protested that 'no surprise could exceed hers; that she had never suspected Lord Frederick of carrying the matter so far.' She feared 'that, however unjustly, he might consider himself as aggrieved by a sudden rupture of our intimacy; hinted how much the affair might be misrepresented by the industrious malice of Lady Maria; and lamented that, on such occasions, a censorious world was but too apt to take part with the accuser. But then, to be sure, every thing must be ventured rather than disobey my father: she would be the last person to advise me to a breach of duty, though she had little doubt that it would be speedily forgiven.'

In short, all my skill in cross-examination was insufficient to discover whether Miss Arnold thought I should dismiss Lord Frederick, or fly with him to Scotland; or, taking that middle course so inviting to those who waver between the right and the convenient, endeavour to keep him in suspense till circumstances should guide my decision. Like a prudent counsellor, she gave no direct advice, except that which alone she was certain would be followed: she entreated me to hear the opinion of Lady St Edmunds, and then to judge for myself.

The opinion of Lady St Edmunds was much more explicitly given. She insisted that an overstrained delicacy made me trifle with the man whom I really preferred. She laughed at my denials; asserting that it was impossible I could be such a little actress as to have deceived all my acquaintance, not one of whom entertained a doubt of my partiality for Lord Frederick. One exception to this position I remembered with a sigh; but he who best could have read my heart, and most wisely guided it, was already far on his way to another hemisphere. In vain did I protest my indifference towards all mankind. Lady St Edmunds, kissing my cheek, told me she would save my blushes, by guessing for me what I had not yet confessed to myself.

'Well!' cried I, a little impatiently, 'if I am in love with Lord Frederick, I am sure I don't wish to marry him. I cannot be mistaken upon that point. Some time ago, I should not much have cared; but now, *indeed* I would rather not.'

'Why should you be more reluctant now than formerly,' enquired Lady St Edmunds, looking me intently in the face, 'unless you have begun to prefer another?'

'Oh, not at all,' answered I, with great simplicity; 'I prefer nobody in particular. But of late I have sometimes thought that, if I must marry, I would have a husband whom I could respect, – whom all the world respect; one who could enlighten and convince, ay, and awe other men; one who need only raise his hand to silence an assembled nation; one whose very glance ——'

I stopped, and the glow which warmed my cheek deepened with an altered feeling; for a smile began to play upon the lip of Lady St Edmunds, and where is the enthusiasm that shrinks not from a smile? My friend, laughing, asked which of the heroes of romance I chose to have revived for my mate. 'But,' added she, shaking her head, 'when Oroondates makes his appearance, we must not let Frederick tell tales; for constancy and generosity were indispensable to a heroine in his time.'

Seeing me look disconcerted, she paused; then throwing her white arm round my neck, 'My dearest Ellen,' said she, 'let me candidly own that your treatment of poor De Burgh is not quite what I should have expected from you. But,' continued she, with a tender sigh, 'had you been all that my partiality expected, you must have become too – too dear to me! You would have wiled my heart away from all living beings.'

'Dear Lady St Edmunds,' cried I, clasping her to my breast, 'tell me what you expect from me now, and trust me I will never disappoint you.'

'My charming girl!' exclaimed Lady St Edmunds, 'far be it from me to dictate to you. Let your own excellent heart and understanding be your counsellors.'

'Indeed,' returned I, 'it would be an act of real charity to decide for me. I am so terribly bewildered. I would not for the world act basely to Lord Frederick; and I rather think that before he began to teaze me about marrying him, I liked him better than any body – that is than any man – almost. But then when I think of my father – and I love him so dearly, and he has no other child – no one to love him but only me! Indeed I cannot bear to thwart him.'

'My dear Ellen,' said Lady St Edmunds, 'I believe your father to be a very worthy old gentleman, and I have a great respect for him; but, indeed, his cause could not be committed to worse hands than mine; for I can see no earthly business that he has to interfere in the matter. It is not he who is to be married. For my own part, I married in very spite of my father; and if I live till my children are marriageable, I shall assuredly be reasonable enough to let them be happy in their own way.'

For a while, I defended the parental right, or rather the natural sentiment which still remained to restrain my folly; – but the proper foundation of filial duty, of all duty, was wanting in my mind, and therefore the superstructure was unstable as the vapour curling before the breeze. Even my good propensities had not the healthy nature of real virtue. They were at best but the fevered flush adorning my sickly state in the eyes of others, and fatally disguising it from my own. By frequent argument, by occasional reflections, and by dexterous confounding of truth and falsehood, Lady St Edmunds so far darkened my moral perceptions, that Lord Frederick's claim seemed to outweigh that of my father. Nor was the task hard; for honour and humanity are sounds more soothing to human pride than the harsh name of submission.

Lord Frederick himself meanwhile watched vigilantly over his own interests, and was abundantly importunate and encroaching. Miss Arnold, indeed, continued to affect prudent counsels; but while she offered me such feeble dissuasives as rather served to excite than to deter, she procured or invented intelligence, which, with every expression of indignation, she communicated to me, that Lady Maria had so far misrepresented my indiscretion at the masquerade, as to make my marriage with Lord Frederick a matter of prudence at least, if not of necessity.

Thus goaded on every side, without steadiness to estimate the real extent of my difficulties, or resolution to break through them, having no special dislike to Lord Frederick, nor any conscious preference for another, I sanctioned in weakness the claims which I had conferred in folly. I gave my lover permission to believe that I would soon reward his constancy; if it can be called reward to obtain a wife, whose violation of her early ties gives the strongest pledge that she will disregard those which are new.

Still a lingering reluctance, the constitution of my sex, and the expiring struggles of duty, made me defer, from time to time, the performance of my engagement. But I was hurried at last into its fulfilment, by one of those casualties which are allowed to decide the most important concerns of the thoughtless and unprincipled. My father one day surprised Lord Frederick at my feet; and, glad perhaps of an opportunity to mark his contempt for the artificial distinctions of society, as well as justly indignant at the disregard shown to his injunctions, he dismissed my lover from the house, in terms more decided than courtly.

As my father had four stout footmen to enforce his commands, his Lordship had no choice but acquiescence. He therefore retired; and my father, raising his foot to the panel of the room door, shut it with a force that made the house shake. His sense of dignity for once giving way to indignation, my father, instead of taking his well-known posture of exhortation with his back to the fire, walked up to me, and strongly grasping my hand, exclaimed, 'What the d—l do you mean, Ellen Percy? Did not I tell you, I wouldn't have this puppy of a lord coming here a fortune-hunting? Don't I know the kidney of you all; Don't I know, that if you let a fellow chatter nonsense to you long enough, he is sure of you at last? – Look you, Ellen Percy, let me have no more of this. I can give you three hundred thousand pounds, and I have a scheme in my head that may make it twice as much; – and I'll have your eldest son called John Percy, ay, and his son after him; and you shall marry no proud, saucy, aristocratical beggar, to look down upon the man who was the making of him; d——n me, if you do, Ellen Percy.' Then throwing my arm from him, with a vehemence that made me stagger, he quitted the room.

Even in minds far better regulated than mine, violence is more likely to produce resentment than submission. My surprise quickly gave place to indignation. The unceremonious expulsion of my visiter seemed nothing short of an insult. To place me at the head of a family into which I must admit no guest without permission, was treating me like a baby! – a disgrace scarcely endurable to those who are still a little doubtful of their right to be treated like women.

I earnestly recommend to all ladies who see cause of offence against their rightful governors (an accident which will sometimes happen, notwithstanding the universal meekness of ladies, and the well-known moderation of gentlemen,) never to indulge in meditations upon past injury, much less to exercise their prophetic eye upon future aggression. Ill-humour gives contingent evils such a marvellous appearance of certainty, that we seldom think it unjust to punish them as if already committed.

No inference should have been drawn from my father's hasty words, except that, being spoken in anger, they could not convey his permanent sentiments; but I pondered them until I discovered that they clearly foretold my being sacrificed to some ugly, old, vulgar, ignorant, gouty, purse-proud, blinking-eyed, bandy-legged, stock-jobbing animal, with a snuff-coloured coat, a brown wig, and a pen behind his ear. No wonder if the assured prospect of such outrage redoubled mine ire!

But it had not yet reached its consummation. At dinner, Miss Arnold happened to mention a public breakfast, to which Lady B—— had invited us for the following morning. My father, who was far from affecting privacy in his injunctions or reproofs, informed me, without circumlocution, that I should go neither to Lady B——'s nor any where else, till I gave him my word of honour that I would have no intercourse with Lord Frederick de Burgh. 'I must stay at home, then,' said I, with an air of surly resolution; 'for there is to be a ball after the breakfast, and I have promised to dance with Lord Frederick.'

'Eat your breakfast at home then, Miss Percy,' said my father; 'and no fear but you shall have as good a one as any Lady B—— in the land.'

Great was my disappointment at this sentence; for I had procured for the occasion a dress upon which Lady Maria de Burgh had fixed her heart, when there was no longer time to make another robe with similar embroidery. But my wrath scorned to offer entreaty or compromise; and, leaving the table, I retreated to my chamber, seeking sullen comfort in the thought that I might soon emancipate myself from thraldom. In the course of the evening, however, Miss Arnold, whose influence with my father had of late increased surprizingly, found means to obtain a mitigation of his sentence; but the good humour which might have been restored by this concession, was banished by an angry command to refrain from all such engagements with Lord Frederick for the future.

The next morning, while we were at breakfast (for a public breakfast by no means supersedes the necessity of a private one) my father received a letter, which he read with visible discomposure; and, hastily quitting his unfinished meal, immediately left the house. I was somewhat startled by his manner, and Miss Arnold appeared to sympathise still more deeply in his uneasiness; but the hour of dressing approached, and, in that momentous concern, I forgot my father's disquiet.

The fête passed as fêtes are wont to do. Every one wore the face of pleasure, and a few were really pleased. The dancing began, and I joined in it with Lord Frederick. Among the spectators who crowded round the dancers, were Lady Maria de Burgh and her silly Strephon, Lord Glendower. I at first imagined that she declined dancing, because the lady who was first in the set was one of whom she might have found it difficult to obtain precedence; but, just as it was my turn to begin, she advanced and took her station above me. Provoked by an impertinence which I ought to have despised, I remonstrated against this breach of ball-room laws. Lady Maria answered, with a haughty smile, that she rather conceived she had a right to dance before me. In vain did Lord Frederick interfere. In vain did I angrily represent, that the right claimed by her Ladyship ceased after the dance was begun. How could Lady Maria yield while the disputed dress was full in her eye? At last, seeing that the dance was suspended by our dispute, I proposed to those who stood below me, that, rather than allow such an infringement of our privileges, we should sit down. They, however, had no inclination to punish themselves for the ill-breeding of another; and I, scorning to yield, indignantly retired alone.

Lord Frederick followed me, as usual; and – but why should I dwell upon my folly? Remaining displeasure against my father, a desire to have revenge and precedence of Lady Maria, overcame for an hour my reluctance to the fulfilment of my ill-starred engagement; and in that hour, Lord Frederick had obtained my consent to set out with him the very next morning for Scotland. Such are the amiable motives that sometimes enter into what is called a love match!

To prevent suspicion, and by that means to delay pursuit, it was agreed, that Lady St Edmunds should be made acquainted with our design; that she should call for me early, and convey me in her carriage to Barnet, where she was to resign me to the guardianship of my future lord. Miss Arnold I determined not to trust; because she had of late been accustomed to beg, with a very moral shake of the head, that I would never confide an intended elopement to her, lest she should feel it a duty to acquaint my father with my purpose.

CHAPTER XIV

Fair laughs the morn, and soft the zephyr blows,
While, proudly riding o'er the azure realm,
In gallant trim the gilded vessel goes,
Youth on the prow, and pleasure at the helm;
Regardless of the sweeping whirlwind's sway,
That, hush'd in grim repose, expects his evening prey.

Gray.

NO sooner had I acquiesced in the arrangements for that event which was to seal my destiny, than a confused feeling of regret came upon me. An oppression stole upon my spirits. The sounds of flattery and protestation I heard like a drowsy murmur, reaching the ear without impressing the mind; and the gay forms of my companions flitted before me like their fellow-moths in the sun-beam, which the eye pursues, but not the thoughts. Yet I had not resolution to quit the scene, which had lost its charms for me. To think of meeting my father's eye; or being left to meditate alone in a home which I was so soon to desert; of seeing the objects which had been familiar to my childhood wear the dreary aspect of that which we look upon perhaps for the last time, might have appalled one far better enured than I to dare the assaults of pain. But at last even the haunts of dissipation were forsaken by the throng, and I had no choice but to go.

Late in the night, silently, with the stealthy pace of guilt, I re-entered that threshold which, till now, I had never trod but with the first step of confidence. With breath suppressed, with the half reverted eye of fear, I passed my father's chamber; as superstition passes the haunt of departed spirits. In profound silence I suffered my attendant to do her office; then threw myself upon my bed, with an eager but fruitless wish to escape the tumult of my thoughts in forgetfulness.

Sleep, however, came not at my bidding. Yet, watchful as I was, I might rather be said to dream than to think. A well ordered mind can dare to confront difficulty, – can choose whether patience shall endure, or prudence mitigate, or resolution overcome, the threatened evil. But when was this vigorous frame of soul gained in the lap of self-indulgence? When was the giant foiled by him who is accustomed to shrink even from shadows? The dread of my father's displeasure, – an undefined reluctance to the connection I was forming, – these, and a thousand other feelings which crowded on my mind, were met with the plea, that no choice now remained to me; the stale resort of those who are averse from their fate, but more averse from the exertion which might overcome it. The upbraidings of conscience, I answered with the supposed claims of honour; silencing the inward voice, which might have told me, how culpable was that levity which had set justice and filial duty at unnatural variance. Considerate review of the past, rational plan for the future, had no more place in my thoughts, than in the fevered fancy that sees on every side a thousand unsightly shapes, which, ere it can define one of them, have given place to a thousand more. At last this turmoil yielded to mere bodily exhaustion; and my distressful musings were interrupted by short slumbers, from which I started mid-way in my fall from the precipice, or chilled with struggling in the flood.

I rose long before my usual hour, and sought relief from inaction in preparations for my ill-omened journey. After selecting and packing up some necessary articles of dress, I sat down to write a few lines to be delivered to my father after my departure. But I found it impossible to express my feelings, yet disguise my purpose; and having written nearly twenty billets, and destroyed them all, I determined to defer asking forgiveness till I had consummated my offence.

The hour of breakfast, which my father always insisted upon having punctually observed, was past before I could summon courage to enter the parlour. I approached the door; then, losing resolution, retired; – drew near again, and listened whether my father's voice sounded from within. All was still, and I ventured to proceed, ashamed that a servant, who stood near, should witness my hesitation. I cast a timid glance towards my father's accustomed seat; it was vacant, and I drew a deep breath, as if a mountain had been lifted from my breast. 'Where is Mr Percy?' I enquired. 'He went out early, ma'am,' answered the servant, 'and said he should not breakfast at home.' Miss Arnold and I sat down to a silent and melancholy meal. I could neither speak of the subject which weighed upon my heart, nor force my attention to any other theme.

And now a new distress assailed me. While I had every moment expected the presence of an injured parent, dread of that presence was all powerful. But now when that expectation was withdrawn, my soul recoiled from tearing assunder the bonds of affection, ere they were loosened by one parting word, – one look of farewell. I remembered, that our last intercourse had been chilled by mutual displeasure, and could I go without uttering one kindly expression? – without striving to win one little endearment which I might treasure in my heart, as perhaps a last relic of a father's love? I quitted my scarcely tasted meal, to watch at a window for his coming. My eye accidentally rested on the spot where Maitland had disappeared, and another shade was added to the dark colour of my thoughts. 'He will never know,' thought I, 'how deeply my honour is pledged; and what will he think of me, when he hears that I have left my father? – left him without even one farewell! No! this I will not do.'

The resolution was scarcely formed, when I saw Lady St Edmunds' carriage drive rapidly up to the door. I hastened to receive her; and drawing her apart, informed her of my father's absence, and besought her, either to send or go, and excuse me to Lord Frederick for this one day at least. Lady St Edmunds expostulated against this instance of caprice. She represented my father's absence as a favourable circumstance tending to save me the pain of suppressing, and the danger of betraying my feelings. She protested, that she would never be accessory to inflicting so cruel a disappointment upon a lover of Lord Frederick's passionate temperament. She remonstrated so warmly against the barbarity of such a breach of promise, and expressed such apprehension of its consequences, that, in the blindness of vanity, I suffered myself to imagine it more inhuman to destroy an expectation of yesterday, than to blight the hopes of seventeen years. Lady St Edmunds immediately followed up her victory, and hurried me away.

I sought the companion of my early day, and hastily took such an ambiguous farewell as my fatal secret would allow. 'Juliet,' said I, wringing her hand, 'I must leave you for a while. If my father miss me, you must supply my place. I charge you, dearest Juliet, if you have any regard for me, show him such kindness as – as I ought to have done.' My strange expressions, – my faltering voice, – my strong emotion, could not escape the observation of Miss Arnold; but she was determined not to discover a secret which it was against her interest to know. With an air of the most unconscious carelessness, she dropped the hand which lingered in her hold; and not a shade crossed the last smile that ever she bestowed upon the friend of her youth.

A dark mist spread before my eyes, as I quitted the dwelling of my father; and ere I was again sensible to the objects which surrounded me, all that had been familiar to my sight were left far behind. Lady St Edmunds cheered my failing spirits, – she soothed me with the words of kindness, – pressed me to become her guest immediately on my return from Scotland, – and to call her house my home, until my reconciliation with my father; a reconciliation of which she spoke as of no uncertain event. She interested me by lively characters of my new connections, pointing out, with great acuteness, my probable avenues to the favour of each, although it appeared that she herself had missed the way. Her conversation had its usual effect upon me; and, by the time we reached Barnet, my elastic spirits had in part risen from their depression. Yet, when we stopped at the inn-door, something in the nature of woman made me shrink from the expected sight of my bridegroom; and I drew back into the corner of the carriage, while Lady St Edmunds alighted. But the flush of modesty deepened to that of anger, when I perceived that my lover was not waiting to welcome his bride. 'A good specimen this of the ardour of a secure admirer,' thought I, as in moody silence I followed my companion into a parlour.

The attendant whom Lady St Edmunds had despatched to enquire for Lord Frederick now returned to inform her that his Lordship had not arrived. 'He must be here in five minutes at farthest,' said Lady St Edmunds, in answer to a kind of sarcastic laugh with which I received this intimation; and she stationed herself at a window, to watch for his arrival, while I affected to be wholly occupied with the portraits of the Durham Ox and the Godolphin Arabian. The five minutes, however, were doubly past, and still no Lord Frederick appeared. Lady St Edmunds continued to watch for them, foretelling his approach in every carriage that drove up; but when her prediction had completely failed, she began to lose patience. 'I could have betted a thousand guineas,' said she, 'that he would serve us this trick; for he never kept an appointment in his life.

'His Lordship need not hurry himself,' said I, 'for I mean to beg a place in your Ladyship' carriage to town.'

After another pause, however, Lady St Edmunds declared her opinion, that some accident must have befallen her nephew. 'Only an accident to his memory, madam, I fancy,' said I, and went on humming an opera tune.

After waiting, however, nearly an hour, my spirit could brook the slight no longer; and I impatiently urged Lady St Edmunds to return with me instantly to town. My friend, for a while, endeavoured to obtain some further forbearance towards the tardy bridegroom; but, finding me peremptory, she consented to go. Still, however, she contrived to delay our departure, by calling for refreshments, and ordering her horses to be fed. At length my indignant pride overcoming even the ascendency of Lady St Edmunds, I impatiently declared, that if she would not instantly accompany me, I would order a carriage, and return home alone.

We had now remained almost two hours at the inn; and my companion beginning herself to despair of Lord Frederick's appearance, no longer protracted our stay. She had already ordered her sociable to the door, when a horseman was heard gallopping up with such speed, that, before she could reach the window, he was already dismounted. 'This must be he at last!' cried Lady St Edmunds. 'Now he really deserves that you should torment him a little.'

A man's step approached the door. It opened, and I turned away pouting, yet cast back a look askance, to ascertain whether the intruder was Lord Frederick. I saw only a servant, who delivered a letter to Lady St Edmunds, and retired. The renewed anger and mortification which swelled my breast were soon, however, diverted by an exclamation from my companion, of astonishment not unmixed with dismay. Strong curiosity now mingled with my indignant feelings. I turned to Lady St Edmunds; and thought I gathered from her confused expressions, that she held in her hand a letter of apology from Lord Frederick, which also contained intelligence of disastrous importance.

What this intelligence was, I saw that she hesitated to announce. Her hesitation alarmed me, for I was obliged to infer from it, that she had news to communicate which concerned me yet more nearly than the desertion of Lord Frederick. Already in a state of irritation which admitted not of cool enquiry, I mixed my scornful expressions of indifference as to the conduct of my renegado lover, with breathless, half-uttered questions of its cause. 'Indeed, Miss Percy,' stammered Lady St Edmunds, 'it is a very – very disagreeable office which Lord Frederick has thought fit to lay upon me. To be sure, every one is liable to misfortune, and I dare say you will show that you can bear it with proper spirit. Your father – but you tremble – you had better swallow a little wine.'

'What of my father?' I exclaimed; and with an impatience which burst through all restraints, I snatched the letter from her hands; and, in spite of her endeavours to prevent me, glanced over its contents. I have accidentally preserved this specimen of modern sentiment, and shall here transcribe it: –

> 'My dear St E., – The Percys are blown to the devil. The old one has failed for near a million. By the luckiest chance upon earth, I heard of it not five minutes before I was to set out. See what a narrow escape I have had from blowing out my own brains. I would have despatched Hodson sooner, but waited to make sure of the fact. I shall set about Darnel immediately – a confounded exchange, for the Percy was certainly the finest girl in London. By the by, make the best story you can for me. I know she likes me, for all her wincing; and I shall need some little private comfort, if I marry that ugly thing Darnel.
>
> 'Yours ever,
>
> ' F. De Burgh.
>
> 'You need not quake for your five thousand – Darnel will bite at once.'

The amazement with which I read this letter instantly gave place to doubts of the misfortune which it announced. I had been so accustomed to rest secure in the possession of splendid affluence, that a sudden reverse appeared incredible. It occurred to me that some groundless report must have misled Lord Frederick, who was thus outwitted by his own avarice. But, when I reached the close of his sentimental billet, scorn and indignation overpowered every other feeling. 'The luckiest chance!' I exclaimed. 'Well may he call it so! Oh what a wretch have I escaped! What a complication of all that is basest and vilest! – No!' said I, detaining with a disdainful smile the letter, which Lady St Edmunds reached her hand to receive, 'No!

this I will keep, as a memorial of the disinterestedness of man, and the "passionate temperament" of Lord Frederick de Burgh. Now, I suppose your Ladyship will not object to returning instantly to town.'

Lady St Edmunds, who actually seemed to quail beneath my eye, made no objection to this proposal; but followed in silence, as I haughtily led the way to the carriage. We entered, and it drove rapidly homewards.

My thoughts again recurring to the letter, another light now flashed upn me; and a stronger burst of resentment swelled my heart. 'This epistle,' I suddenly exclaimed, 'is a master-teacher. It shows me the sincerity of friends, as well as the tenderness of lovers. Where was your boasted friendship, Lady St Edmunds? – where was your common humanity, when you took advantage of a foolish pity – a mistaken sense of honour – to lure me into a marriage with that heartless earth-worm? Me, whom you pretended to love, – me, whom in common justice and gratitude ——' The remembrance of all my affection for this treacherous friend choked my voice, and forced bitter – bitter tears to my eyes; but pride, with a strong effort, suppressed the gentler feeling, and I turned scornfully from the futile excuses and denials of my false counsellor.

Resentment, however, at length began to give place to apprehension, when I reflected upon the decisive terms in which Lord Frederick announced my father's ruin, and the certainty which he must have attained of the fact, before he could have determined finally to relinquish his pursuit. Some circumstances tended to confirm his assertion. I now recollected the letter which my father had read with such evident emotion; and his unusual absence in the morning, before the customary hours of business. I vainly endeavoured to balance against these his late boast of his immense possessions, and the improbability of a wreck so sudden.

In spite of myself, an anxious dread fell upon me. My knees trembled; my face now glowed with a hurried flush; and now a cold shudder ran through my limbs. But disdaining to expose my alarm to her who had betrayed my security, I proudly struggled with my anguish, affecting a careless disbelief of my misfortune, and an easy scorn of the summer friendships which had fled from its very name. I even strove to jest upon Lord Frederick's premature desertion, bursting at times into wild hysterical laughter.

The duration of our journey seemed endless; yet when I came within sight of my father's house, I would have given a universe to delay the certainty of what I feared. Every breath became almost a sob, – every movement convulsive, while, in the agony of suppressed emotion, I fixed my straining eyes upon my home, as if they could have penetrated into the souls of its inhabitants. The carriage stopped; and, scarcely hearing Lady St Edmunds' polite excuse for not entering the house of mourning, I sprang towards the door.

It was long ere my repeated summons was answered 'Has my father enquired for me?' I hastily demanded, as I entered.

'No, ma'am, – he never spoke.'

'Is he at home?'

'Mr Percy is – is in the house, ma'am, but ——' The man paused, and his face wore a ghastly expression of horror.

A dark and shapeless dread rushed across my mind; but the cup was already full, and I could bear no more. I sunk down in strong convulsions.

And must I recall those hours of horror? – Must I bare, one by one, the wounds which no time can heal? – Must I retrace, step by step, the fearful way which led me to the very verge of madness?

Could I but escape one horrible picture, I would meet, without recoiling, the remembrance of the rest. But it must not be. To make my melancholy tale intelligible, the arrow must once more enter into my soul, and the truth be told, though it palsy the hand that writes it.

A long forgetfulness was varied only by dim recollections, which came and went like the fitful dreams of delirium. My first distinct impression of the past was formed, when, awaking as if from a deep sleep, I found myself alone in my chamber. My flight, – the humiliation which it had brought upon me, – the treachery of my friend, – the prospect of ruin, all stood at once before me.

My soul, already wounded by affection abused, felt the deserted loneliness in which I was left as a confirmation of the dreaded evil. Juliet Arnold, the companion of my pleasures, came to my thoughts, and her absence stung me like neglect. 'All, all have forsaken me,' thought I. 'Yet there is one heart still open to me. My father will love me still. My father will take me to his breast. And if I must hear the worst, I will hear it from him who has never betrayed me, – who will never cast me off.'

With thoughts like these I quitted my bed, and stole feebly towards my father's apartment. The lights which were wont to blaze cheerfully, – the attendants who used to crowd the halls, – were vanished. A dark twilight faintly showed my way. A strange and dreary silence reigned around me.

I entered my father's chamber. A red glare from the sky gave it a dismal increase of light. Upon a couch lay a form that seemed my father's. The face I saw not. A cloth frightfully stained with blood —— No! – It cannot be told.

CHAPTER XV

—— And yet I breathed!
But not the breath of human life!
A serpent round my heart was wreathed,
And stung my every thought to strife.
Alike all time! Abhorred all place!
Shuddering I shrunk from nature's face,
Where every line that charmed before,
The blackness of my bosom wore.

Lord Byron.

FROM long and dangerous faintings, I revived almost to frenzy. I shed no tears. These are the expression of a milder form of suffering. One horrible image filled my soul; one sense of anguish so strong, so terrible, that every other feeling, – every faculty of mind and body was benumbed in its grasp. Vainly did my awful duties summon me to their performance. I was incapable of action, almost of thought. My eye wandered over surrounding objects, but saw them not. The words which were spoken to me conveyed no meaning to my mind.

At length the form of my early friend seemed to flit before me. She spoke; and though I could not follow the meaning of her words, the sounds were those of kindness. The familiar voice, long associated with so many kindly thoughts, reached the heart, waking a milder tone of feeling; and resting my throbbing head upon her breast, I found relief in a passionate burst of tears. Little did I think how small was the share which friendship or compassion could claim in this visit of my friend to the house of mourning! Little did I guess that its chief motive was to rescue the gifts of my prodigality from being confounded with the property of a bankrupt!

She did not long remain with me; for friends more sympathising than she are soon weary of witnessing the unrestrained indulgence of grief. Yet she did not leave me abruptly. She was too much accustomed to follow the smooth path of conciliation, that she continued to pursue it even when it no longer promised advantage; and she satisfied me with some plausible excuse for going, and with a promise of speedy return.

The tears which for many hours I continued to shed relieved my oppressed spirit; and by degrees I awoke to a full sense of my altered state. From the proudest security of affluence, – from a fearless confidence in myself, and in all around me, one fatal stroke had dashed me for ever. A darker storm had burst upon me, and wrought a ruin more deep, more irretrievable. That tie, which not the hardest heart resigns without pain, had been torn from mine with force sudden and terrible; and a pang unutterable had been added to that misfortune which turns love, and reverence, and gratitude into anguish. What could be added to those horrors, except that conscience should rise in her fury to remind me that, when my presence might have soothed my father's sorrows, I had been absent with an injurious purpose; and that the arrows of misfortune had been rendered mortal by the rebellion of his child? This last incurable pang the mercy of Heaven has saved me. I learned that my father died ignorant of my intended flight.

Miss Arnold, I found, had quitted our house for that of her brother, as soon as our last and worst disaster was discovered by the domestics. Of all the summer friends who had amused my prosperity, not one approached to comfort my affliction. Even my servants, chosen without regard to their moral character, and treated with reference to its improvement; corrupted by the example of dissipation; undisciplined and uninstructed, – repaid the neglect of my domestic duties by a hardened carelessness of my wants and will. After the first transports of grief had subsided, I observed this desertion; and I felt it with all the jealousy of misfortune. Not three days were passed since a crowd of obsequious attendants had anticipated my commands; now I could scarcely obtain even the slight service which real necessity required.

The remains of my unfortunate father still lay near me; and, unable to overcome my horror of passing the chamber of death, I remained entirely secluded in my apartment. The first intruder upon this seclusion was the person who came to seal my father's repositories of papers and money. Having performed his office elsewhere, he entered my apartment with little ceremony; and, telling me that he understood my father had intrusted me with jewels of value, informed me, that it was necessary to prevent access to them for the present. Accustomed as I was to receive all outward testimonies of respect, the instrusion of a stranger at such a time appeared to me a savage outrage. I was ignorant of all the forms of business; and his errand assumed the nature of the most insulting suspicion. Had all the jewels of the earth lain at my feet he might have borne them away unresisted by me; but the proud spirit which grief had bowed almost to the dust roused itself at once to repel insult; and, pointing to the casket, I haughtily commanded him to do his office quickly and begone. By this sally of impatience, a few trinkets of value which I might have justly claimed as my own were lost to me, being contained in the casket which I thus suffered to be appropriated.

Insulted as I thought, and persecuted in my only place of refuge, I became desirous to quit my dismal abode. I imagined, that whatever impropriety there might be in the continuance of Juliet's residence in my desolate habitation, there could be no reason to deter me from taking refuge with my friend; – my gentle, my affectionate friend, who had ever rejoiced in my prosperity, and gloried in my accomplishments, and loved even my faults. Checking the tears which gushed from my eyes at the thought that a father's roof must shelter me no more, I announced my intention to my friend in a short billet: – 'Come to me, dearest Juliet,' I said, 'come and take me from this house of misery. I only stipulate, that you will not ask me to join your brother's family circle. I wish to see no human being except yourself, – for who is there left me to love but you? – Your own ELLEN PERCY.'

The servant whom I despatched with this note brought back for answer, that Miss Arnold was not at home. I had been accustomed to find every one, but especially Miss Arnold, ever ready to attend my pleasure; and even the easiest lessons of patience were yet new to the spoiled child of prosperity. My little disappointment was aggravated by the captiousness with which the unfortunate watch for instances of coldness and neglect. 'Not at home! Ah,' thought I, 'what pleasure should I have found in idle visiting or amusement, while she was wretched?' Still I never doubted, that the very hour of her return would bring her to welcome and to comfort her desolate friend. I waited impatiently, – listened to every sound; and started at every footstep which echoed through my dreary dwelling. But the cheerless evening closed in, and brought no friend. I passed the hours, now in framing her excuse, now in reproaching her unkindness, till the night was far spent; then laid my weary head upon my pillow, and wept myself to sleep.

The morning came, and I rose early, that I might be ready to accompany my friend without delay. But I took my comfortless meal alone. Alone I passed the hour in which Juliet and I had been accustomed to plan the pastime of the day. The hour came at which my gay equipage was wont to attend our call. Just then I heard a carriage stop at the door, and my sad heart gave one feeble throb of pleasure; for I doubted not that Juliet was come. It was the hearse which came to bear my father to his grave. – Juliet, and all things but my lost father, were for a time forgotten.

But as the paroxysm of sorrow subsided, I again became sensible to this unkind delay. My billet had now been so long despatched without obtaining a reply even of cold civility, that I began to doubt the faithfulness of my messenger. I refused to believe that my note had ever reached Miss Arnold; and I endeavoured to shut my eyes against the indifference which even in that case was implied in her leaving me so long to solitary affliction. I was going once more to summon the bearer of my melancholy billet, that I might renew my enquiries in regard to its delivery, when the long expected answer was at length brought to me. I impatiently tore it open, anxious to learn what strong necessity had compelled my friend to substitute for her own presence this colder form of welcome. No welcome, even of the coldest form, was there. With many expressions of condolence, and some even of affection, she informed me of her sorrow 'that she could not receive my visit. I must be aware,' she said, 'that one whose good name was her only dowry should guard the frail treasure with double care. Grieved as she was to wound me, she was obliged to say, that the publicity of my elopement appeared to her brother an insuperable bar to the continuance of our intimacy. Resistance to his will,' she said, 'was impossible, even if that will had been less reasonable than, with grief, she confessed it to be. But though she must withhold all outward demonstrations of regard, she would ever remain my grateful and obedient servant.'

I sat motionless as the dead, whilst I deciphered these inhuman words. The icebolt had struck me to the heart. For a time I was stunned by the blow, and a dull stupor overpowered all recollection.

Then, suddenly the anguish of abused affection, – the iron fangs of ingratitude, – entered into my soul; and all that grief, and all that indignation can inflict, burst in bitterness upon the wounded spirit. I gazed wildly on the cruel billet, while, twisting it in the grasp of agony, I wrenched it to atoms; then, raising to heaven an eye of blasphemy, I dared to insult the Father of Mercies with a cry for vengeance.

But the transport of passion quickly subsided into despair. I threw myself upon the ground; longing that the earth would open and shelter me from the baseness of mankind. I closed my eyes, and wished in bitterness of soul that it were for ever. Sometimes, as memory recalled some kinder endearment of my ill-requited affection, I would start as beneath the sudden stab of murder; then bow again my miserable head, and remain in the stillness of the grave.

No ray of consolation cheered me. The world, which had so lately appeared bright with pleasure, – the worthy habitation of beings benevolent and happy, was now involved in the gloom, and peopled with the unsightly shapes of darkness. While my mind glanced towards the selfishness of Lord Frederick, and the treachery of Lady St Edmunds, – while it dwelt upon the desertion of her who, for seven years, had shared my heart and all else that I had to bestow, the human kind appeared to me tainted with the malignity of fiends, and I alone born to be the victim of their craft, – the sport of their cruelty!

How often has the same merciless aspersion been cast upon their fellow-creatures by those who, like me, have repelled the friendship of the virtuous? How often, and how unjustly, do they who choose their associate for the hour of sunshine, complain when he shrinks from the bitter blast? Oh that my severe experience could warn unwary beings like myself! Oh that they would learn from my fate to shun the fellowship of the unprincipled! Even common reason may teach them to despair of awakening real regard in her whom infinite benefits cannot attach, – nor infinite excellence delight, – nor infinite forgiveness constrain. She wants the very stamina of generous affection; and is destined to wind her way through all the heartless schemes and cowardly apostasies of selfishness.

From the stupor of despair, I was roused by the entrance of the stranger who had before intruded. In the jealous reserve of an anguish too mighty to be profaned by exposure, I rose from my dejected posture; and, with frozen steadiness, enquired, 'what new indignity I had now to bear?' The stranger, awed as it seemed by something in my look and manner, informed me, not without respectful hesitation, that he was commissioned by the creditors to tell me I know not what of forms and rights, of willingness to allow me all reasonable accommodation, and such property as I might justly claim, and to remind me of the propriety of appointing a friend to watch over my further interests. One word only of the speech was fitted to arrest my attention. 'Friend!' I repeated, with a smile such as wrings the heart more than floods of womanly tears. 'Any one may do the office of a friend! Ay, even one of those kindly souls who drove my father to desperation, – who refused him the poor boon of delay, when delay might have retrieved all! Any of them can insult and renounce me. This is the modern office of a friend, is it not?'

The stranger, gazing on me with astonishment, proceeded to request, that I would name an early day for removing from my present habitation; since the creditors only waited for my departure, to dismiss the servants, and to bring my father's house, with all that it contained, to public sale. He added, that he was commissioned by them to present me with a small sum for my immediate occasions.

To be thus forcibly expelled from the home, where, till now, I could command; to be offered as an alms a pittance from funds which I had considered as my hereditary right; to be driven forth to the cold world with all my wounds yet bleeding, stung me as instances of severe injustice and oppression. My spirit, sore with recent injury, writhed under the rude touch. Already goaded almost to frenzy, I told the stranger, that 'had I recollected the rights of his employers, I would not have owed the shelter even of a single night to those whose barbarous exactions had destroyed my father; nor would I ever be indebted to their charity, so long as the humanity of the laws would bestow a little earth to cover me.'

I pulled the bell violently, and gave orders that a hackney-coach should be procured for me. It came almost immediately; and, without uttering another word, – without raising my eyes, – without one expression of feeling, except the convulsive shudderings of my frame, and the cold drops that stood upon my forehead, I passed the apartment where my father perished, – the spot where my mother poured upon me her last blessing, – and cast myself upon the wide world without a friend or home.

I ordered the carriage to an obscure street in the city; a narrow, dark, and airless lane. I had once in my life been obliged to pass through it, and it had impressed my mind as a scene of all that is dismal in poverty and confinement. This very impression made me now choose it for my abode; and I felt a strange and dreary satisfaction in adding this consummation to the horrors of my fate. As the carriage proceeded, I became sensible to the extreme disorder of my frame. Noise and motion were torture to nerves already in the highest state of irritation. Fever throbbed in every vein, and red flashes of light seemed to glare before my heavy eyes. A hope stole upon my mind that all was near a close. I felt a gloomy satisfaction in the thought, that surely my death would reach the heart of my false friend; that surely when she knew that I had found refuge in the grave from calumny and unkindness, she would wish that she had spared me the deadly pang; and would lament that she had doubled the burden which weighed me to the earth.

When the carriage reached the place of its destination, the coachman again applied to me for instructions; and I directed him to stop at any house where lodgings could be obtained. After several ineffectual enquiries, he drew up to the door of a miserable shop, where he was told that a single room was to be hired. 'Would you please to look into my little place yourself, madam?' said a decent-looking woman, who advanced to meet me. 'It is clean, though it be small, and I should be very happy that it would suit.'

'Any thing will suit me,' answered I.

'You, ma'am!' cried the woman in a tone of extreme surprise; then placing herself just opposite to me, she seemed hesitating whether or not she should allow me to pass. Indeed the contrast of my appearance with the accommodation which I sought might well have awakened suspicion. My mourning, in the choice of which I had taken no share, was in material the most expensive, and in form of the highest fashion. The wildness of despair was probably impressed on my countenance; and my tall figure, lately so light and so elastic, bent under sickness and dejection. The woman surveyed me with a curiosity, which in better days I would have ill endured; but perceiving me ready to sink to the ground, she relaxed her scrutiny, while she offered me a seat, which I eagerly accepted. She then went to the door, upon pretence of desiring the coachman to wait till I should ascertain whether her lodgings were such as I approved; and they entered on a conversation in which I heard my own name repeated. When she returned to me, she poured forth a torrent of words, the meaning of which I was unable to follow, but which seemed intended to apologise for some suspicion. Never imagining that my character could be the cause of hesitation, I fancied that the poor woman doubted of my ability to pay for my accommodation; and drawing out my purse, I put into her hands all that remained of an affluence which had so lately been the envy of thousands. 'It is but a little,' said I, 'but it will out-last me.'

I now desired to be shown to my apartment; and laboriously followed my landlady up a steep miserable stair, into a chamber, low, close, and gloomy. In a sort of recess, shaded by a patched curtain of faded chintz, stood a bed, which, only a few days before, no degree of fatigue could have induced me to occupy. Worn out, and heartbroken as I was, I yet recoiled from it for a moment. 'But it matters not,' thought I, 'I shall not occupy it long;' so I laid myself down without undressing, and desired that I might be left alone.

I was now, indeed, alone. In the wilfulness of desperation, I had myself severed the few and slender ties which might still have bound me to mankind; and I felt a sullen pleasure in the thought that my retreat was inscrutable alike to feeble compassion and to idle curiosity. The widow, whose roof afforded my humble shelter, and her daughter, a sickly, ignorant, but industrious creature, at first persecuted me with attentions; vainly trying to bribe, with such delicacies as they could procure, the appetite which turned from all with the loathing of disease. They urged me to send for my friends, and for medical advice. They tried, though ignorant of my real distemper, to soothe me with words of rude comfort. All was in vain. I seldom looked up, or returned any other answer than a faint gesture of impatience; and, weary of my obstinate silence, they at last desisted from their assiduities, nor ever intruded on my solitude, except to bring relief to the parching thirst which consumed me.

Day after day passed on in the same dreary quiet. Night, and the twilight of my gloomy habitation, succeeded each other, unnoticed by me. Disease was preying on my constitution, – hopeless and indignant rejection rankled in my mind. My ceaseless brooding over injury and misfortune was only varied by the dreary consolation that all would soon be lost in the forgetfulness of the grave.

And could a rational and immortal creature turn on the grave a hope in which religion had no part? Could a being, formed for hope and for enjoyment, lose all that the earth has to offer, without reaching forward an eager grasp towards joys less transient? When the meteors which I had so fondly pursued were banished for ever, did no ray from the Fountain of Light descend to cheer my dark dwelling? – No. They who have tasted that the Lord is good, return in their adversity with double eagerness to taste his goodness. But I had lived without God in my prosperity, and my sorrow was without consolation. In the sunshine of my day I had refused the guiding cloud; and the pillar of fire was withdrawn from my darkness. I had forgotten Him who filleth heaven and earth, – and the heavens and the earth were become one dreary blank to me. The tumult of feeling, indeed, unavoidably subsided; but it was into a calm, – frozen, stern, and cheerless as the long night-calm of a polar sea.

From the supineness of sickness and despair, I was at last forced to momentary exertion. My landlady renewed her entreaties that I would send for my friends; enforcing her request by informing me that my little fund was nearly exhausted. Disturbed with her importunity, and careless of providing against difficulties from which I expected soon to escape, I commanded her to desist. But my commands were no longer indisputable. The woman probably fearing, from the continuance of my disorder, that my death might soon involve her in trouble and expense, persisted in her importunity. Finding me obstinately determined to persevere in concealment, she proceeded to hint not obscurely, that it would be necessary to consider of some means of supply, or to provide myself with another abode. Only a few days were past since an insinuation like this would have driven me indignant from a palace; but now the depression of sickness was added to that of sorrow, and I only answered, than when I could no longer repay her trouble, I would release her from it.

Dissatisfied, however, with an assurance which she foresaw that I might be unable to fulfil, the widow proceeded to enquire whether I retained any property which could be converted into money; and mentioned a ring which she observed me to wear. Dead as I was to all earthly affection, I firmly refused to part with this ring, for it had been my mother's. I had drawn it a hundred times from her slender hand, and she thought it best employed as a toy for her little Ellen, while yet its quickly shifting rays made its only value to me. 'No!' said I, as the woman urged me to dispose of it, 'this shall go with me to the grave, in memory that one heart had human feeling towards me.' The landlady, however, venturing a tedious remonstrance against this resolution, the dying fire again gave a momentary flash. 'Be silent,' I cried. 'Speak to me no more till I am penniless; then tell me so at once, and I will that instant leave your house, though I die at the threshold!' Highly offended by this haughty command, the woman immediately retired, leaving me for the rest of that day in total solitude.

An evil was now ready to fall upon me, for which I was wholly unprepared either by experience or reflection. Unaccustomed as I was to approach the abodes of poverty, the very form of want was new to me; and since I had myself been numbered with the poor, my thoughts had chiefly dwelt upon my past misfortunes, or taken refuge from the anticipation of future distress in the prospect of dissolution. But, in spite of my wishes and my prophecies, abstinence, and the strength of my constitution, prevailed over my disorder. My heavy eyes were this night visited by a deep and refreshing sleep, from which I awoke not till a mid-day sun glanced through the smoke a dull ray upon the chimney crags that bounded my horizon.

I looked up with a murmur of regret that I was restored to consciousness. 'Why,' thought I, 'must the flaring light revisit those to whom it brings no comfort?' and I closed my eyes in thankless impatience of my prolonged existence. Oh, where is the *human* physician, whose patience would endure to have his every prescription questioned, and vilified, and rejected! whose pitying hand would offer again and again the medicine which in scorn we dash from our lips! – No! Such forbearance dwells with one Being alone; and such perverseness we reserve for the infallible Physician.

I presently became sensible that my fever had abated. With a deep feeling of disappointment I perceived that death had eluded my desires; and that I must return to the thorny and perplexing path where the serpent lurked to sting, and tigers prowled for prey. While my thoughts were thus engaged, a footstep crossed my chamber; but, lost in my gloomy reverie, I suffered it, ere I raised my eyes, to approach close to my bed. I was roused by a cry of strong and mingled feeling. 'Miss Mortimer!' I exclaimed; but she could not speak. She threw herself upon my bed, and wept aloud. The voice of true affection for a moment touched my heart; but I remembered that the words of kindness had soothed only to deceive; and stern recollection of my wrongs steeled me against better thoughts.

'Why are you come hither, Miss Mortimer?' said I, coldly withdrawing myself from her arms.

'Unkind Ellen!' returned my weeping friend; 'could I know that you were in sorrow and not seek you? May I not comfort, – or, if that cannot be, may I not mourn with you?'

'I do not mourn – I want no comfort – leave me.'

'Oh say not so, dearest child. You are not forbidden to feel. Let us weep together under the chastisement, and trust together that there is mercy in it.'

'Mercy! no. I have been dashed without pity to the earth, and there will I lie till it open to receive me.'

Miss Mortimer gazed on me in sorrowful amazement; then, wringing her hands as in sudden anguish, 'Oh, Heaven!' she cried, 'is this my Ellen? – Is this the joyous spirit that brought cheerfulness wherever it came? – Is this the face that was bright with life and pleasure? Loveliest, dearest, how hast thou lost the comfort which belongs even to the lowest of mankind, – the hope which is offered even to the worst of sinners?'

'Leave me, Miss Mortimer!' I cried, impatient of the self-reproach which her sorrow awakened in my breast. 'I wish only to die in peace. Must even this be denied me?'

'Ellen, my beloved Ellen, is that what you call peace? – Oh Thou who alone canst, deign to visit this troubled soul with the peace of thy children!' Miss Mortimer turned from me, and ceased to speak; but I saw her wasted hand lifted as in prayer, and her sobs attested the fervency of the petition. After a short silence, making a visible effort to compose herself, she again addressed me. 'Do not ask me to leave you, Ellen,' said she. 'I came hither, resolved not to return without you. If you are too weak today for our little journey, I will nurse you here. Nay, you must not forbid me. I will sit by you as still as death. Or, make an effort, my love, to reach home with me, and I will not intrude on you for a minute. You shall not even be urged to join my solitary meals. It will be comfort enough for me to feel that you are near.'

I could not be wholly insensible to an invitation so affectionate; but I struggled against my better self, and pronounced a hasty and peremptory refusal. Miss Mortimer looked deeply grieved and disappointed; but hers was that truly Christian spirit whose kindness no ingratitude could discourage, whose meekness no perverseness could provoke. She might have checked the untoward plant in its summer pride; but the lightning had scathed it, and it was become sacred in her eyes.

Sparing the irritability of the wounded spirit, she forebore to fret it by further urging her request. She rather endeavoured to soothe me by every expression of tenderness and respect. She at last submitted so far to my wayward humour, as to quit my apartment; aware, perhaps, that the spirit which roused itself against opposition might yield to solitary reflection. The voice of kindness, which I had expected never more to hear, stirred in my breast a milder nature; and as my eye followed the feeble step of Miss Mortimer, and read her wasted countenance, my heart smote me for my resistance to her love. 'She has risen from a sick-bed to seek me,' thought I; 'me, renounced as I have been by all mankind, – bereft as I am of all that allured the perfidious. Surely *this* is not treachery.'

My reverie was suddenly interrupted by poor Fido, who made good his entrance as Miss Mortimer left the room; and instantly began to express, as he could, his recognition of his altered mistress. The sight of him awakened at once a thousand recollections. It recalled to my mind my former petulant treatment of my mother's friend, her invariable patience and affection, and the remorse excited by our separation. My mother herself rose to my view, such as she was when Fido and I had gamboled together by her side, – such as she was when sinking in untimely decay. I felt again the caress which memory shall ever hold dear and holy. I saw again the ominous flush brighten her sunken cheek; knelt once more at her feet to pray that we might meet again; and heard once more the melancholy cry which spoke the pang of a last farewell. The stubborn spirit failed. I threw my arms round my mother's poor old favourite, and melted into tears. These tears were the first which I had shed since the unkindness of my altered friend had turned my gentler affections into gall; – and let those who would know the real luxury of grief turn from the stern anguish of a proud heart to the mild regrets which follow those who are gone beyond the reach of our gratitude and our love.

Miss Mortimer did not leave me long alone. She returned to bring me refreshment better suited to my past habits and present weakness than to her own very limited finances. As she entered, I hastily concealed my tears; but when her accents of heartfelt affection mingled in my soul with the recollections which were already there, the claim of my mother's friend grew irresistible. A half confession of my late ingratitude rose to my lips; but that to which Ellen, the favoured child of fortune, might have condescended as an instance of graceful candour, seemed an act of meanness in Ellen fallen and dependent. I pressed Miss Mortimer's hand between mine. 'My best, my only friend!' said I; and Miss Mortimer asked no more. It was sufficient for the generous heart that its kindness was at last felt and accepted.

CHAPTER XVI

—— Fruit —— some harsh, 'tis true,
Pick'd from the thorns and briars of reproof;
But wholesome, well-digested; grateful some
To palates that can taste immortal truth;
Insipid else, and sure to be despised.

Cowper.

THE news of my father's misfortune no sooner reached Miss Mortimer's retirement, than she made an exertion beyond her strength, that she might visit and comfort me. At my father's house, she learnt that I was gone no one knew whither; but the conveyance which I had chosen enabled her at last to trace my retreat, and she lost not a moment in following me thither. There, with all the tenderness of love, and all the perseverance of duty, she watched over my returning health; nor ever quitted me by night or by day, till I was able to accompany her home.

It was on a golden summer morning that we together left my dreary lurking-place. The sun shone forth as brightly as on the last day that I had visited Miss Mortimer's abode; the trees were in yet fuller foliage; and the hues of spring were ripening to the richer tints of autumn. The river flashed as gaily in the beam, and the vessels veered as proudly to the breeze. My friend sought to cheer my mind by calling my attention to the bright and busy scene. But the smile which I called up to answer her cares, came not from the heart. Cold and undelighted I turned from the view. 'To what end,' thought I, 'should this prison-house be so adorned? this den of the wretched and the base!' So dismal a change had a few weeks wrought upon this goodly frame of things to me. But thus it ever fares with those who refuse to contemplate the world with the eye of reason and of religion. In the day of prosperity, this foreign land is their chosen rest, for which they willingly forget their Father's house; but when the hours of darkness come, they refuse to find in it even accommodations fitted for the pilgrim 'that tarries but a night.'

When we had reached the cottage, and Miss Mortimer, with every testimony of affection had welcomed me home, she led me to the apartment which was thenceforth to be called my own. It was the gayest in my friend's simple mansion. Its green walls, snowy curtains, and light furniture, were models of neatness and order; and though the jessamine had been lately pruned from the casement to enlarge my view, enough still remained to adorn the projecting thatch with a little starry wreath.

On one side of my window were placed some shelves containing a few volumes of history, and the best works of our British essayists and poets; on the other was a chest of drawers, in which I found all the more useful part of my own wardrobe, secured to me by the considerate attention of Miss Mortimer. My friend rigidly performed her promise of leaving my time wholly at my own command. As soon as she had established me in my apartment, she resigned it solely to me: nor ever reminded me, by officious attentions, that I was a guest rather than an inmate. She told me the hours at which her meals were punctually served, giving me to understand that when I did not choose to join them, no warning or apology was necessary; since, if I did not appear in the family-room, I should be waited upon in my own. These arrangements being made, she advised me to repose myself after the fatigue of my journey, and left me alone. Wearied out by an exertion to which my strength was yet scarcely equal, I laid myself on a bed more inviting than the last which I had pressed, and soon dropped asleep.

The evening was closing, when I was awakened by a strain of music so soft, so low, that it seemed at first like a dream of the songs of spirits. I listened, and distinguished the sounds of the evening hymn. It was sung by Miss Mortimer; and never did humble praise, – never did filial gratitude, – find a voice more suited to their expression. The touching sweetness of her notes, heightened by the stillness of the hour, roused an attention little used of late to fix on outward things. 'These are the sounds of thankfulness,' thought I. 'I saw her this morning thank God, as if from the heart, for the light of a new day; and now, having been spent in deeds of kindness, it is closed as it began in an act of thanksgiving. What does she possess above all women, to call forth such gratitude? She is poor, lonely, neglected. She knows that she has obtained but a short reprieve from a disease which will waste away her life in lingering torture. Good Heaven! What is there in all this to cause that prevailing temper of her mind; that principle as it would appear, of all her actions? – She must have been born with this happy turn of thought. And, besides, she has never known a better fate; – blest, that poverty and solitude have kept her ignorant of the treachery and selfishness of man!

The strain had ceased, and my thoughts returned to my own melancholy fate. To escape from tormenting recollection, or rather in the mere restlessness of pain, I opened a book which lay upon my table. It was my mother's Bible. The first page was inscribed with her name, and the date of my birth, written with her own hand. Below, my baptism was recorded in the following words: –

'This eleventh of January, 1775, I dedicated my dearest child to God. May He accept and purify the offering, though it be with fire!'

As I read these lines, the half prophetic words of my mother's parting blessing flashed on my recollection. 'Oh, my mother!' I cried, 'couldst thou have forseen how bitter would be my "chastisement," couldst thou have known, that the "fire" would consume all, would not thy love have framed a far different prayer? Yes! for thou hadst a fellow-feeling in every suffering, and how much above all in mine!'

I proceeded to look for some further traces of a hand so dear. The book opened of itself at a passage to which a natural feeling had often led the parent who was soon to forget even her child in the unconsciousness of the grave; and a slight mark in the margin directed my eye to this sentence: 'Can a mother forget her sucking babe, that she should not have compassion upon the son of her womb? Yea, she may forget, yet will not I forget thee.'

These words had often been read in my hearing, when my wandering mind scarcely affixed a meaning to them; or when their touching condescension was lost upon the proud child of prosperity. But now their coincidence with the previous current of my thoughts seized at once my whole attention. I started as if some strange and new discovery had burst upon my understanding. Again I read the passage, and with a care which I had never before bestowed on any part of the book which contains it. 'Is this,' I enquired, 'an expression of the divine concern in each individual of human kind? – No. It seems merely a national promise. Yet, my mother has regarded it in another light; else why has she marked it so carefully?'

It was in vain that I debated this question with myself. Such was my miserable ignorance of all which it most behoved me to know, that I never thought of explaining the letter of the Scriptures by resorting to their spirit. My habitual propensities resisting every pious impression, my mind revolted from the belief that parental love had adjusted every circumstance of a lot which I accounted so severe as mine. To admit this, was virtually to confess that I had need of correction; that I had, to use Miss Mortimer's words, 'already reached that state when mercy itself assumes the form of punishment.' Yet the soothing beauty of the sentiment, the natural yearning of the friendless after an Almighty friend, made me turn to the same passage again and again, till the darkness closed in, and lulled me to a deep and solemn reverie.

'Does the Great Spirit,' thought I, 'indeed watch over us? Does He work all the changes of this changeful world? Does He rule with ceaseless vigilance, – with irresistible control, whatever can affect my destiny? – Can this be true? – If it be even possible, by what strange infatuation has it been banished from my thoughts till now? But it cannot be so. A man's own actions often mould his destiny; and if his actions be compelled by an extraneous energy, he is no more than a mere machine. The very idea is absurd.' And thus, to escape from a sense of my own past insanity, I entered a labyrinth where human reason might stray for ever,

> And find no end, in wandering mazes lost.

But the subject, perplexing as it was to my darkened understanding, had seized upon my whole mind; and sleep fled my pillow, whilst in spite of myself the question again and again recurred; 'If I be at the mercy of a resistless power, why have I utterly neglected to propitiate this mighty arbitrator? If the success of every purpose even possibly depended upon his will, why was that will forgotten in all my purposes?'

As soon as it was day I arose; and, with the eagerness of one who would escape from suspense, I resorted to the book which had so lately arrested my regard. I no longer glanced over its pages in careless haste; for it offered my only present lights upon the questions, interesting by their novelty as well as by their importance – whether I had been guilty of the worse than childish improvidence, which, in attending to trifles, overlooks the capital circumstance? or whether the Creator, having dismissed us like orphans into a fatherless world, is regardless of our improvement, and deaf to our cry? My impatience of doubt made me forget, for a time, that the very fact which confers upon Scripture its authority, supposes a divine interference in human concerns. The great truth, however, shone forth in every page. All spoke of a vigilant witness, a universal, a ceaseless energy. Nor was this all. I could scarcely open the book without finding somewhat applicable to my own character or situation; I was, therefore, no longer obliged to compel my attention, as to the concerns of a stranger; it was powerfully attracted by interests peculiarly my own. The study, indeed, was often painful; but yet I returned to it, as the heir to the deed which is to make him rich or a beggar.

My search, however, produced nothing to elate. I read of benefits which I had forgotten; of duties which I had neglected; of threatenings which I had despised. The 'first and great commandment,' directed every affection of my soul to Him who had scarcely occupied even the least of my thoughts. The most glorious examples were proposed to my imitation, and my heart sunk when I compared them with myself. A temper of universal forbearance, habits of diligent benevolence, were made the infallible marks of a character which I had no right to claim. The happy few were represented as entering with difficulty, and treading with perseverance, the 'strait and narrow way,' which not even self-deceit could persuade me that I had found. That self-denial, which was enjoined to all as an unremitting habit, was new to me almost even in name. The 'lovers of pleasure,' among whom I had been avowedly enrolled, were ranked, by my new guide, with 'traitors and blasphemers.' The pride which, if I considered it at all as an error, I accounted the 'glorious fault' of noble minds, was reprobated as an impious absurdity. The anguish of repentance, – the raptures of piety, – the 'full assurance of hope,' were poured forth; but, with the restless anxiety of him who obtains an imperfect glimpse of the secret upon which his all depends, I perceived, that their language was to me the language of a foreign land.

By degrees, something of my real self was opened to my sight. The view was terrible; but, once seen, I vainly endeavoured to avert my eye. At midnight, and in the blaze of day, in the midst of every employment, in defiance of every effort, my offences stood before me. With the sense of guilt, came the fear before which the boldest spirit fails. I saw the decree already executed which took from me the 'talent buried in the earth;' but, the stroke which had deprived me of all, seemed only a prelude to that more awful sentence which consigns the unprofitable servant to 'outer darkness.' As one who starts from sleep beneath the uplifted sword, – as he to whom the lightning's flash reveals the precipice, – as the mother waked by the struggles of her half-smothered babe, – so I – but what material images of horror can shadow forth the terrors of him who feels that he is by his own act undone? In an overwhelming sense of my folly and my danger, I often sunk into the attitude of supplication; but I had now a meaning to unfold not to be expressed in a few formal phrases which I had been accustomed to hurry over. I saw that I had need of mercy which I had not deserved, and which I had no words to ask. How little do they know of repentance who propose to repay with it, at their own 'convenient season,' the pleasures which they are at all hazards determined to seize!

Meanwhile, though my misfortunes could not be banished from my mind, they no longer held their sullen reign alone. New interests had awakened in my breast; new fears; new regrets. I felt that there is an evil greater than the loss of fame, of fortune, or of friends; that there is a pang compared with which sorrow is pleasure. This anguish I endured alone. The proud spirit could pour into no human ear the language of its humiliation and its dread. I suffered Miss Mortimer to attribute to grief the dejection which at times overpowered me; to impatience of deprivation, the anxious disquiet of one who is seeking rest, and finding none. Yet I no longer shunned her society. I sought relief in the converse of a person rich in the knowledge in which I was wanting, impressed with the only subjects which could interest me now. Miss Mortimer was precisely the companion best calculated to be useful to me. She never willingly oppressed me with a sense of her superiority, – never upbraided my cold reception of doctrines which I was not yet fitted to receive, – never expressed surprise at my hesitation, or impatience with my prejudices, – never aggravated my sense of the danger of my state, nor boasted of the security of her own; but answered my questions in terms direct and perspicuous; opposed my doubts and prejudices with meek reason; represented the condition of the worst of mankind as admitting of hope, – that of the best, as implying warfare.

From the first month of my residence with Miss Mortimer I may date a new era of my existence. My mind had received a new impulse, and new views had opened to me of my actions, my situation, and my prospects. An important step had been made towards a change in my character. But still it was only a step. The tendencies of nature, strengthened by the habits of seventeen years, remained to be overcome, and this was not the work of a month, or a year. I was not, however, of a temper long to endure the sense of helpless misery. Encouraged by the promises which are made to the repentant, and guided now by the example which I had once overlooked or ridiculed, I resolved to associate myself as much as possible, in Miss Mortimer's acts of devotion and of charity. I joined in her family worship, – I visited her pensioners, – and industriously assisted her in working for the poor; an employment to which she punctually devoted part of her time. Little did I then suspect how much the value of the same action was varied by our different motives. She laboured to please a Father, – I to propitiate a hard Master. She was humbly offering a token of gratitude, – I was poorly toiling for a hire.

It was now that I began to feel the effects of my former habits of life. While my feelings were in a state of strong excitement, they held the place of the stimulants to which I had been accustomed; and I should have turned in disgust from the trivial interests which had formerly engaged me. But whenever my mind settled into its more natural state, I became sensible of a vacancy, – a wearisome craving for an undefined something to rouse and interest me. The great truths indeed which I had lately discovered, often supplied this want; and I had only to turn my newly acquired powers of sight towards my own character to be awakened into strong emotion. But compared with my new standards, my own heart offered a prospect so little inviting, that I turned from it as often as I dared; endeavouring to 'lay the flattering unction to my soul,' by wilfully mistaking the resolution to be virtuous for virtue itself.

The activity of my mind had hitherto been so unhappily directed, that it now revolted from every impulse, except such as was either pleasurable or of overwhelming force. Besides, although nothing be more sublime than a life of charity and self-denial in the abstract, nothing is less so in the detail. I was unused to difficulty, and therefore submitted with impatience to difficulties which my own inexperience rendered more numerous. Poverty I had known only as she is exhibited in the graceful draperies of tragedy and romance; therefore I met her real form in all its squalor and loathsomeness, with more, I fear, of disgust than of pity. My imaginary poor had all been innocent and grateful. Short experience in realities corrected this belief; and when I found among the real poor the vices common to mankind, added to those which peculiarly belong to a state of dependence, – when I found them selfish, proud, and sensual, as well as cunning and improvident, – I almost forgot that alms were never meant as a tribute to the virtues of man; and that it is absurd to pretend compassion for the bodily necessities of our fellow-creature, while we exercise none towards the more deplorable wants of his mind. Not knowing, however, what spirit I was of, I called my impatience of their defects a virtuous indignation; and witnessed, with something like resentment, the moderation of Miss Mortimer, who always viewed mental debasement as others do bodily decrepitude, with an averseness which inclined her to withdraw her eye, but with a pity which stretched forth her hand to help. Yet when I beheld the ignorance, the miseries, the crimes of beings in whom I had now, in some degree, learnt to reverence the character of immortality, how did I lament, that, with respect to them, I had hitherto lived in vain! How did I reproach myself, that, while thousands of sensitive and accountable creatures were daily within the sphere of my influence, that influence had served only to deepen, with additional shades, the blackness of human misery and of human guilt.

Accident served to heighten this self-upbraiding. One day when Miss Mortimer, with the assistance of my arm, was walking round her garden, she observed a meagre, barefooted little girl; who, reaching her sallow hand through the bars of the wicket, asked alms in a strong Caledonian accent. My friend, who never dismissed any supplicant unheard, patiently enquired into a tale which was rendered almost unintelligible by the uncouth dialect and national bashfulness of the narrator. All that we could understand from the child was, that she was starving, because her father was ill, and her mother prevented from working, by attendance upon an infant who was dying of the small-pox. Miss Mortimer, who always conscientiously endeavoured to ascertain that the alms which she subtracted from her own humble comforts were not squandered in profligacy, accepted of my offer to examine into the truth of this story; and I accompanied the child to the abode of her parents.

After the longest walk which I had ever taken, my conductress ushered me into a low dark apartment in the meanest part of Greenwich. Till my eye was accommodated to the obscurity, I could very imperfectly distinguish the objects which surrounded me; and, for some minutes after leaving the gladdening air of heaven, I could scarcely breathe the vapour stagnant in the abode of disease and wretchedness. The little light which entered through a window half filled with boards fell upon a miserable pallet, where lay the emaciated figure of a man; his face ghastly wan, till the exertion of a hollow cough flushed it with unnatural red; and his eye glittering with the melancholy brightness which indicates hopeless consumption.

Upon a low stool, close by the expiring embers, sat a woman, vainly trying to still the hoarse cry of an infant. On my entrance, she started up to offer me the only seat which her apartment contained; and the poor Scotchman, with national courtesy to a superior, would have risen to receive me, – but he was unable to move without help. His wife, that she might be at liberty to assist him, called upon the little girl to take charge of her brother. Startled at seeing an infant committed to such care, I thoughtlessly offered my services; and held out my arms for the child. The mother, evidently pleased with what she seemed to regard as condescension, and not aware that the being whom she was fondly caressing could be an object of disgust to others, held the child towards me; but at the first glance I recoiled, with an exclamation of horror, from a creature who scarcely retained a trace of human likeness. That dreadful plague, which the most fortunate of discoveries now promises to banish from the earth, had disguised, or rather concealed, every feature; and, deprived of light, of nourishment, and rest, the sufferer scarcely retained the power to express its misery in a hoarse and smothered wailing. The poor woman, sensibly hurt by my expression of disgust, shed tears, while she reminded me of the evanescent nature of beauty, and enumerated all the charms of which a few days had deprived her boy. I had wounded where I came to heal; and all my address could scarcely atone for an error, that incresased the difficulties which my errand already found in the decent reserve of spirits unsubdued to beggary, and in a dialect which I could very imperfectly comprehend.

What I at length learnt of the story of these poor people may be told in a few words; the man was a gardener, who had been allured from his country by the demand in England for Scotchmen of his trade. Unable to procure immediate employment, he and his family had suffered much difficulty; till, encouraged by the name of a countryman, they had applied to Mr Maitland. By his interest, the man had obtained the situation of under-gardener in Mr Percy's villa at Richmond.

I started at the name of my father, but having been often deceived, I was become cautious; and, without betraying myself, asked whether they had ever seen Miss Percy. The woman answered that they had not; having entered on their service the same day that their master's family removed to town. The evil influence of Miss Percy, however, had blasted all their hopes and comforts. She had given peremptory orders that some delicate exotics should be forced into flower to adorn an entertainment. Poor Campbell, deputed to take care of them, watched them all night in the hot-house; then walked two miles to his lodging through a thick drift of snow; breathed ever afterwards with pain; struggled against disease; wrought hard in the sharp mornings and chilly evenings of spring; and, when my father could no longer repay his services, was dismissed to die, unheeded by a mistress equally selfish in the indulgence of her sorrow as in the thoughtlessness of her prosperity.

As I listened to this tale, I found it confirmed by circumstances which admitted not of doubt. While I looked on the death-struck figure of poor Campbell, saw the misery that surrounded me, and felt that it was *my* work, my situation was more pitiable than that of any mortal, except him who can see that he has done irreparable injury, yet see it without a pang. When I recovered utterance, I enquired whether Campbell had any medical assistance? – a needless question; he had not wherewith to purchase food, much less medicine. – 'But if I were once able, madam,' said he, 'to earn what would be our passage home, I should soon be well, – the air in Scotland is so pure, and breathes so pleasantly!' – 'You shall get home, cost what it will,' cried I, and instantly delivered the whole contents of my purse; without considering that it could scarcely be called mine, and that it could be replenished only from the scanty store of her whose generosity would fain, if possible, have made me forget that I was no longer the rich Miss Percy.

Ignorant as I was of Greenwich and its inhabitants, I next undertook to find medical advice. By enquiring at a shop, I obtained the address of a Mr Sidney, to whom I immediately repaired. He was a young man of a very prepossessing appearance, tall and handsome enough for a hero of romance. Will it be believed that, in spite of the humbling sense of guilt which in that hour was strong upon me, my besetting weakness made me observe with pleasure the surprise and admiration with which my appearance seemed to fill this stranger? But vanity, though powerful in me, was no longer unresisted. I pulled my bonnet over my face; nor once again looked up while I conducted Sidney to the abode of his new patient.

I cannot express the horror which I felt, when, after examining the situation of the poor man, Sidney informed me, in a whisper, that no aid could save his life. I turned faint; and, to save myself from sinking to the ground, retreated to the door for air. At that moment, I overheard Sidney ask, 'Who is that angel?' and the term, applied to one who was little less than a murderer, sharpened the stab of conscience. I hastily turned to proclaim my name, and submit myself to the execrations of this injured family; but I wanted courage for the confession, and the words died upon my lips.

The disfigured infant next engaged Sidney's attention. He discovered that the mother had, according to what I have since found to be the custom of her country, aggravated the dreadful disease, by loading her unhappy child with all the clothes she could command, and carefully defending him from the fresh air. She had even deprived herself of food, that she might procure ardent spirits, which she compelled the hapless being to swallow; to drive, as she expressed it, 'the small-pox from his heart.' Yet this poor woman, so ignorant of the treatment of the most common disorder, possessed, as I afterwards found, a knowledge of the principles of religion, and an acquaintance with the scope of its doctrines and precepts, which, at that time, appeared to me very wonderful in a person of her rank. They are, however, less surprising to me since I became a denizen of Scotland.

But to close a tale, on which its strong impression on my mind has perhaps made me dwell too long, the boy, by means of better treatment, recovered; his father's disease was beyond the reach of human skill. One day, while I was in the act of holding a cordial to his lips, he fell back; and, with a momentary struggle, expired. The little ingenious works which I had been taught at school, were, for the first time, employed by me to a useful purpose, when his widow and children were enabled, by the sale of them, to procure a passage to Scotland.

I cannot express the effect which this incident had upon my mind. A new load of guilt seemed to oppress me. I perceived that actions and habits might have tendencies unsuspected by the agent; that the influence of a fault, – venial, perhaps, in the eyes of the transgressor, – might reach the character and fate of those who are not within the compass of his thoughts; and, therefore, that the real evil of sin could be known only to Him, by whom effects which as yet exist not are traced through their eternal course. Thus a fearful addition of 'secret sins' was made to all those with which conscience could distinctly charge me; and my examinations of my past conduct were like the descent into a dismal cavern, where every step discloses some terrifying sight, and all that is imperfectly distinguished in the gloom is imagined to be still more appalling.

It is true, I had resolved upon a better course of life; but my resolutions were very partially kept; nor, had it been otherwise, could present submission atone for past disobedience. Even my best actions, when weighed in the right balance, were 'found wanting', and rather in need of forgiveness than deserving of reward. My best efforts seemed but the sacrifice of the ignorant Indian, who vows to his god an ingot of gold, and then gilds a worthless offering to defraud him. Nor had they, in truth, one vestige of real worth, void as they still were of that which gives a value to things of small account. It is the fire from heaven which distinguishes the acceptable sacrifice.

Who that had seen me under the depression which these convictions occasioned could have imagined that I had entered on 'ways of pleasantness,' and 'paths of peace?' Anxious and fearful, – seeking rest, and finding none, because remaining pride prevented me from seeking it where alone it was to be found, – I struggled hard to escape the convictions which were forced upon my conscience. I opposed to the truths of religion a hundred objections which had never before occurred to me, only because the subject was new to my thoughts; and I recollected an infinity of the silly jests, and ridiculous associations, by which unhappy sinners try to hide from themselves the dignity of that which they are predetermined to despise. I remember, with amazement, Miss Mortimer's patience in replying to the oft-refuted objection; oft-refuted, I say, because I am certain that far more ingenuity than I can boast would be necessary to invent, upon this subject, a cavil which has not been answered again and again. Far from desiring me, however, to rely upon her authority, she recommended to me such books as she thought likely to secure my rational assent to the truth; carefully reminding me, at the same time, that they could do no more, and that mere rational assent fell far short of that faith to which such mighty effects are ascribed. The direct means of obtaining a gift, she said, was to ask it; and faith she considered as a gift.

'To what purpose,' said I to her one day, after I had laboured through Butler's Analogy, and Macknight's Truth of the Gospel History, – 'to what purpose should I perplex myself with these books, when you own that some of the best Christians you have ever known were persons who had never thought of reasoning upon the evidences of their faith?' – 'Because, my dear,' answered Miss Mortimer, 'the exercise of your highest natural faculties upon your religion is calculated to fix it in your mind, and endear it to your affections. It is true, that piety as pure and as efficient as any I ever knew, I have witnessed in persons who had no leisure, and perhaps no capacity for reasoning themselves into a conviction of the historical truth of Christianity. The author of faith is not bound to any particular method of bestowing his gift. He may, and I believe often does, compensate for the means which he withholds; but this gives no ground to suppose that he will make up for those which we neglect.'

Through Miss Mortimer's persuasion, I steadily persevered in this line of study; and, if my understanding possesses any degree of soundness or vigour, it is to be attributed to this discipline. My education, if the word signify learning what is afterwards to be useful, was now properly beginning; and every day added something to my very slender stock of information. My friend, who was herself no mean proficient in general literature, encouraged me to devote many of my leisure hours to books of instruction and harmless entertainment; and our evenings were commonly enlivened by reading history, travels, or criticism.

Leisure, like other treasures, is best husbanded when it is least abundant; and it was no longer entirely at my command. I still retained enough of the spirit of Ellen Percy, to hold dependence in rather more than Christian scorn, – yet to be ashamed of openly contributing to my own subsistence. In how many shapes does our ruling passion assail us! If we resist it in the form of vice, it will even put on the semblance of virtue. I firmly believed at that time, that a virtuous motive alone induced me to escape, by means of my own labour, from all necessity for applying to the funds of Miss Mortimer; and I forgot to enquire into the reason why my work was always privately done, and privately disposed of.

The manufacture of a variety of ingenious trifles now become useful by ministering to my own wants and those of others, – the share I took in Miss Mortimer's charitable employments, – hours of devotion and serious study, reading, and often writing abstracts of what I read, – left no portion of my time for weariness. But had I been deprived of all bodily employment, the very condition of my mind precluded ennui. I was full of one concern of overwhelming importance. At one time, the truth shone upon me, gladdening me to rapture with its brightness; at another, error darkened my sinking soul, and I was eager in my search for light. Alas! our infirmity loads with many a cloud the dawning even of that true light which 'shineth more and more unto the perfect day.' The natural warmth of my temper, and my long-confirmed habit of yielding to all its impulses, often hurried me into little superstitious austerities, needless scruples, and vehement disputes, which, had they been exposed to common eyes, would have drawn upon me the derision of some, and the suspicion of others; but fortunately Miss Mortimer had few visiters, and my foibles were little seen, except by one who could discover errors in religious judgment, without imputing them either to fanaticism or hypocrisy.

My altercations, for discourse in which passion is permitted to mingle cannot deserve the name of argument, were chiefly carried on with Sidney; who, from the time of his assistance to the Campbells, had become a frequent guest at Miss Mortimer's. His dispositions were amiable, his character unblemished; but his opinions upon some lesser points of doctrine differed widely from mine. This he happened one day accidentally to betray; and I, with the rashness which inclines us to fancy all lately-discovered truths to be of equal importance, combated what I considered as his fatal heresy. Sidney, with great good-humour, rather excited me to speak; perhaps for the same reason as he taught his dog to quarrel with him for his glove.

Miss Mortimer never took part in our disputations, not even by a look. 'How can you,' said I to her one day, when he had just left us, 'suffer such opinions to be advanced without contradiction?'

'I am afraid of losing my temper,' answered she with an arch smile; 'and that I am sure is forbidden in terms more explicit than Mr Sidney's heresy.'

'And would you have me,' cried I, instantly sensible of the implied reproof, 'seem to approve what I know to be false?'

'No, my dear,' returned Miss Mortimer; 'but perhaps you might disapprove without disputing; and I think it is not obscurely hinted by the highest authority, that the modest example of a Christian woman is likely to be more convincing than her arguments. Besides, though we are most zealous in our new opinions, we are most steady in our old ones; therefore I believe, that, upon consideration, you will see it best to ensure your steadiness for the present, and to husband your zeal for a time when it will be more likely to fail.'

When I was cool, I perceived that my friend was in the right; and, by a strong effort, I thenceforth forbore my disputes with Sidney; to which forbearance it probably was owing, that he soon after became my declared admirer.

CHAPTER XVII

Shift not thy colour at the sound of death!
For death ——
Seems not a blank to me; a loss of all
Those fond sensations, – those enchanting dreams,
Which cheat a toiling world from day to day,
And form the whole of happiness it knows.
Death is to me perfection, glory, triumph!

Thomson.

SIDNEY'S overtures cost me some hesitation. They were unquestionably disinterested; and they were made with a plainness rather prepossessing to one who had so lately experienced the hollowness of more flowery profession. Nothing could be objected to his person, manners, or reputation. Miss Mortimer's ill health rendered the protection I enjoyed more than precarious. Honourable guardianship, and plain sufficiency, offered me a tempting alternative to labour and dependence. But I was not in love; and as I had no inclination to marry, I had leisure to see the folly of entering upon peculiar and difficult duties, while I was yet a novice in those which are binding upon all mankind. Sidney had, indeed, by that natural and involuntary hypocrisy, which assumes for the time the sentiments of a beloved object, convinced me that he was of a religious turn of mind; and from his avowed heresies I made no doubt of being able to reclaim him; but he wanted a certain masculine dignity of character, which had, I scarcely knew how, become a *sine quâ non* in my matrimonial views. These things considered, I decided against Sidney; and it so happened, that this decision was formed in an hour after I had received a long and friendly letter from Mr Maitland.

Now this letter did not contain one word of Maitland's former avowal; nor one insinuation of affection, which might not, with equal propriety, have been expressed by my grandmother. But it spoke a strong feeling for my misfortunes; a kindly interest in my welfare; it represented the duties and the advantages of my new condition; and reminded me, that, in so far as independence is attainable by man, it belongs to every one who can limit his desires to that which can be purchased by his labour.

'I see no advantage in being married,' said I, rousing myself from a reverie into which I had fallen after the third reading of my letter. 'Mr Maitland can advise me as well as any husband could; and in ten or a dozen years hence, I might make myself very useful to him too. I might manage his household, and amuse him; and there could be nothing absurd in that after we were both so old.'

'Not quite old enough for that sort of life, I am afraid,' said Miss Mortimer, smiling. 'If, indeed, Mr Maitland were to marry, the woman of his choice would probably be an invaluable protector to you.'

'Oh he won't marry. I am sure he will not; and I wonder, Miss Mortimer, what makes you so anxious to dispose of all your favourites? For my part, I hate to hear of people being married.'

I thought there was meaning in Miss Mortimer's half suppressed smile; but she did not raise her eyes, and only answered good humouredly, that, 'indeed, all her matrimonial plans for the last twenty years had been for others.'

Some expressions of curiosity on my part now drew from Miss Mortimer a narrative of her uneventful life; which, as it is connected with the little I knew of Mr Maitland's, and with the story of my mother's early days, I shall give in my own words: –

Miss Mortimer and my mother were hereditary friends. Their fathers fought side by side, – their mothers became widows together. – Together the surviving parents retired to quiet neglect, and mutually devoted themselves to the duties which still remained for them. Those which fell to the lot of Mrs Warburton were the more difficult; for, while a moderate patrimony placed the only child of her friend above dependence, it was her task to reconcile to poverty and toil the high spirit of a youth of genius; and to arm, for the rude encounters of the world, a being to whom gentleness made them terrible, to whom beauty increased their danger.

The splendid progress of young Warburton's education had been the boast of his teachers, – the delight of his parents, – the pride, the only pride of his sister's heart. But his father's death blasted the fair prospect. The widow's pittance could not afford to her son the means of instruction; and from the pursuit of knowledge, – the pleasures of success, – and the hopes of distinction, – poor Warburton unwillingly turned to earn, by the toil of the day, the support which was to fit him for the toil of the morrow. Disgusted and desponding, he yet refrained from aggravating by complaint the sorrows of his mother and his sister. To Miss Mortimer, the companion of his childhood, he mourned his disappointed ambition, and was heard with sympathy; he deplored the failure of hopes more interesting, and won something more than pity.

In the counting-house, which was the scene of his cheerless labour, he found, however, a friend; and Maitland, though nearly seven years younger than he, gained first his respect, and then his affection.

Maitland, while thus in age a boy, was a tall, vigorous, hardy mountaineer. His nerves had been braced by toilsome exercise and inclement skies; his strong mind had gained power under a discipline which allowed no other rest than change of employment. He had left his native land, and renounced his paternal home, in compliance with the will of his parents, and the caprice of his uncle, who, upon these conditions, offered him the reversion of a splendid affluence. His country he remembered with the virtuous partiality which so strongly distinguishes, and so well becomes, her children. Of his paternal home he seldom spoke. Silent and shy, he escaped the smile of vulgar scorn, which would have avenged the confession that the bribes of fortune poorly repaid the endearments of brethren and friends; that all the charms of spectacle and song could not please like the rude verse which first taught him the legends of a gallant ancestry; that all the treasures of art he would have gladly exchanged for permission to bend once more from the precipice which no foot but his had ever dared to climb, or linger once more in the valley whose freshness had rewarded his first infant adventure. Curiosity is feeble in the busy and the gay. No one asked, no one heard the story of Maitland's youth; and Warburton alone knew the full cost of a sacrifice too great and too painful to be made a theme with strangers. Maitland the elder, retaining his national prejudice in favour of a liberal education, permitted his nephew to pursue and enlarge his studies under the inspection of a man of sense and learning; designing to send him at a proper age to the university. Meanwhile he required him to spend a few hours daily in attendance upon his future profession.

In Maitland, young as he was, Warburton found a companion who could task his mind to its full strength. In classical acquirements, Maitland was already little inferior to his friend; and, if he had less imagination, he had more acuteness and sagacity. Enduring in quiet scorn the derision which his provincial accent excited in the sharers of his humbler lessons, he was pleased to find in Warburton manners more congenial with his own habits. The young scholars had subjects of mutual interest in which the others could not sympathise. The few hours which Maitland spent daily in the counting-house, alone broke the dull monotony of Warburton's labour; and Warburton alone listened with the enthusiasm which unlocks the heart, to Maitland's descriptions of his native scenes, of torrents roaring from the precipice, and woods dishevelled by the storm. They became friends, and Warburton confided his lost hopes, and bewailed the untimely close of his attainments. The hardier mind of Maitland suggested a remedy for the evil. He advised his friend to earn by severer toil, and to save by stricter parsimony, a fund which might in time afford the advantage of a college life. From that hour he himself gave the example of the toil and the parsimony which he recommended. He abridged his rest, he renounced his recreations for the drudgery of translating for a bookseller. The allowance which he had been accustomed to spend, he hoarded with a miser's care. He was invited to share the pleasures of his companions, and resolutely refused. He listened to hints of his penurious temper, and deigned no other answer than a smile. But, when he was better known, few were so unprincipled as to find in him the subject of a jest, and fewer still so daring as to betray their scorn; for Maitland possessed, even then, qualities which ensure command, – integrity which no bribe could warp, – decision which feared no difficulty, – penetration which admitted of no disguise. After two years of silent perseverance, he presented to his friend the fruits of his self-denial, and was more than recompensed when Warburton accompanied him to Oxford.

It was a few months before the completion of this arrangement, that Mr Percy, taking shelter from a shower in a parish church at the hour of morning prayer, was captivated by the beauty, the modesty, and the devotion of Frances Warburton. He followed her home; obtained an introduction; and soon made proposals, with little form and much liberality. Frances shrunk from her new lover; for a difference of thirty years in their ages was the least point of their dissimilarity. The lover, sensible of no disparity but such as a settlement might counterbalance, enlarged his offers. He would have scorned to let any expectation outgo his liberality. He promised competence for life to her mother, and Frances faltered in her refusal. Mrs Warburton did not use direct persuasion; but she sometimes lamented to her daughter that poverty should mar the promise of her Edmund's genius. 'Had he but one friend,' said she, 'even one to encourage or assist him, he would yet be the glory of my old age.' – 'He shall have a friend,' returned the weeping Frances; – and she married Mr Percy.

But the sacrifice was unavailing. Young Warburton was not destined to need such aid as riches can give, nor to attain such advancement as riches can buy. His constitution, already broken by confinement, was unequal to his more willing exertions; yet, insensible to his danger, he pursued his enticing bane; rejected the friendly warning which told him that he was labouring his life away; and was one morning found dead in his study; the essay lying before him which was that day to have introduced him to fame and fortune.

Miss Mortimer and her friend suffering together, became the more endeared to each other. My mother, indeed, had found a new object of interest; and she transferred a part, perhaps too large a part, of her widowed affections to her child. Miss Mortimer raised hers to a better world; and recalled them to this fleeting scene no more.

Maitland, defended from the dangers of a university by steady principles and habits of application, passed safely, even at Oxford, the perilous years between boyhood and majority; then turned his attention to studies more peculiarly belonging to his intended profession. He visited the greatest commercial cities upon the Continent; conversed with the most enlightened of their merchants; and, far from limiting his inquiries to the mere means of gain, he embraced in his comprehensive mind all the mutual relations and mutual benefits of trading nations. At the age of twenty-five he returned home, to take a principal share in the direction of one of the greatest mercantile houses in Britain. Before he was thirty, the death of his uncle had put him in possession of a noble independence, and left him chief partner in a concern which promised to realise the wildest dreams of avarice. But the love of wealth had no place in Maitland's soul. A small part of his princely revenue sufficed for one whose habits were frugal, whose pleasures were simple, whose tastes were domestic. The remainder stole forth in many a channel; like unseen rills, betraying its course only by the riches which it brought.

Awake, as he ever was, to the claims of justice and humanity, it was not personal interest that could shield the slave trade from the reprobation of Maitland. He conquered his retiring nature that, in the senate of his country, he might lend his testimony against this foulest of her crimes; and when that senate stilled the general cry with a poor promise of distant reform, he blushed for England and for human kind. Somewhat of the same honest shame he felt at the recollection that he was himself the proprietor of many hundreds of his fellow-creatures; and when he found that his public exertions in their cause did not avail, he braved the danger of a pestilent climate to mitigate the evil which he could not cure, and to gain, by personal investigation, knowledge which might yet be useful in better times.

Such was Maitland. I dwell upon his character with mingled pleasure and regret: pleasure, perhaps, not untainted with womanly vanity; regret, that, when I might have shared the labours, the virtues, the love of his noble soul, a senseless vanity made me cold to his affection, – a mean coquetry wrecked me in his esteem! I might once, indeed, have bound him to me for ever; but it was now plain that he had cast off his inglorious shackles. Although I answered his letter, he showed no intention of continuing our correspondence, and to Miss Mortimer he noticed me only as a common friend; nor did he ever mention his return to Britain as likely to take place before the lapse of many years.

Warned by the consequences of my past folly, and beginning now to act, however imperfectly, by the only rule which will ever lead us to uniform justice, I had no sooner formed my resolution in regard to Sidney, than I gave him an opportunity of learning my sentiments. I will not deny that this cost me an effort, for I was afraid of losing a pleasant acquaintance; and besides, as the young gentleman was sentimentally in love, his little anxieties and tremours were really, in spite of myself, amusing. But vanity, though unconquerably rooted in me by nature and habit, was no longer overlooked as a venial error. I struggled against it, as a part of that selfish, earth-born spirit, which was altogether inconsistent with my new profession, and which except at the moment of temptation, seemed now too despicable to bias the actions even of an infant. Sidney was a man of sense; and therefore, by a very few efforts of firmness I convinced him that he could be nothing more.

Nor did the explanation occasion even a temporary suspension of our intercourse. Unfortunately, his professional visits were become necessary to Miss Mortimer; and with me he had long before started a topic, amply compensating that which I had interdicted. He had an excellent chemical library, and a tolerable apparatus. By means of these, and a degree of patience not to be expected from any man but a lover, he contrived to initiate me into the first rudiments of a science, which has no detriment except its unbounded power of enticing those who pursue it. By informing me what I might read with advantage, he saved me the time which I might have lost in making the discovery myself; and though he had not always leisure to watch my progress, he could direct me what to attempt. After all, it must be confessed that my attainments in chemistry were contemptible; but even this feeble beginning of a habit of patient enquiry was invaluable. Besides, in the course of my experiments, I made a discovery infinitely more important to me than that of latent heat or galvanism; namely, that the prospect of exhibition is not necessary to the interest of study.

Nothing is more important in its issue, nothing more dull in relation, than a life of quiet and regular employment. A narrative of my first year's residence with Miss Mortimer would be a mere detail of feelings and reflections, mixed with confessions of a thousand instances of rashness, impatience, and pride. My original blemishes were still conspicuous enough to establish my identity; yet one momentous change had taken place, for those blemishes were no longer unobserved or wilful. I had become more afraid of erring than of seeing my error, – more anxious to escape from my faults than from my conscience. Not that her rebukes were become more gentle: on the contrary, an unutterable sense of depravity and ingratitude was added to my self-accusings; for, in receiving the forgiveness of a father, I had awakened to the feelings of a child, and in every act of disobedience I sinned against all the affections of my soul. Let it not be objected to religion, if my judgment was disproportioned to the force of sentiments like these; and if, though no devotion can be extravagant in its degree, mine was sometimes indiscreet in its expression. The fault lay in my education, not in my faith. Christianity justly claims for her own the 'spirit of a sound mind;' but that spirit dwells most frequently with those whose devout feelings have been accustomed to find their chief vent in virtuous actions.

My walk happened one day to lead near a dissenting chapel; and the eagerness to hear which characterises recent converts made me join the multitude who thronged the entrance. 'The truth,' thought I, 'is despised by the gay and the giddy; but to me it shall be welcome, come when it will.' Was there nothing pharisaical in the temper of this welcome? In spite, however, of the liberality for which I was applauding myself, my expectations were influenced by my early prejudices; and I presupposed the preacher, zealous indeed, but loud, stern, and inelegant. Surprise, therefore, added force to my impressions. The unadorned pulpit was occupied by a youth not yet in his prime, nor destined, as it seemed, ever to reach that period. The bloom of youth had given place in his countenance to a wandering glow, that came and went with the mind's or the body's fever. His bright blue eyes – now cast down in humility, now flashing with rapturous hope – had never shone with less gentle fires. His manner had the mild seriousness of entreaty, – his composition the careless vigour of genius; or rather the eloquence of one, who, feeling the essential glory of truth, thinks not of decking her with tinsel.

Reasoning must convince the understanding, and a power which neither human reasoning nor human eloquence can boast must bend the will to goodness; but that which comes from the heart will, for a time at least, reach the heart. Mine was strongly moved. The novel simplicity of form, – the fervour of extemporary prayer, – the zeal of the youthful teacher, his faithful descriptions of a debasement which I strongly felt, his unqualifying application of the only medicine which can minister to this mortal disease, – roused me at once to all the energy of passion. I abhorred the coldness of my ordinary convictions; and, compared with what I now felt, disparaged the impression of regular instruction. I forgot, or I had yet to learn, that the genuine spirit of the Gospel is described as the 'spirit of peace,' not of rapture; that the heavenly weapon is not characterised as dazzling us with its lustre, but as 'bringing into captivity every thought.' Feeling an increase of heat, I rashly inferred that I had received an accession of light; and immediately resolved to join the favoured congregation of a pastor so useful.

My recollection of the prejudice which confounds in one undistinguishing charge of fanaticism many thousands of virtuous and sober-minded persons rather strengthened that resolution; for fire and faggot are not the only species of persecution which arms our natural feelings on the side of the suffering cause. I gloried in the thought of sharing contempt for conscience-sake; and longed with more, it must be owned, of zeal than of humility, to enter upon this minor martyrdom.

That very evening I announced my purpose to my friend, in a tone of premature triumph. Miss Mortimer was so habitually averse to contradicting, that I was obliged to interpret into dissent the grave silence in which she received my communication. Dissent I might have borne, but not such dissent as barred all disputation; and I entered on a warm defence of my sentiments, as if they had been attacked. Miss Mortimer waited the subsiding of that part of my warmth which belonged to mere temper; then gave a mild but firm opinion. 'It had been allowed', she told me, 'by an author of equal candour and acuteness, that "there is, perhaps, no establishment so corrupt as not to make the bulk of mankind better than they would be without it." Our countenance, therefore,' she said, 'to the establishment of the country in which we lived was a debt we owed to society; unless, indeed, the higher duty which we owed to God were outraged by the doctrines of the national church. As for mere form, it had always,' she said, 'appeared to her utterly immaterial, except as it served to express or to strengthen devotion; therefore, it seemed unnecessary to forsake a ritual which had been found to answer these purposes. If the ordinances, as administered by our church, were less efficious to me than they had been to others, she would wish me to examine whether this were not owing to some unobserved error in my manner of using them; but if, after diligent attention, humble self-examination, and earnest prayer for guidance, I continued to find the national worship unsuitable to my particular case, she might regret, but she could not condemn, my secession; since I should then be not only privileged, but bound, to forsake her communion.'

The time was not long past, since even this mild resistance would have only confirmed me in a favourite purpose; but I was becoming less confident in my own judgment, and Miss Mortimer's consistent worth had established an influence over me beyond even that to which my obligations entitled her. Though her natural abilities were merely respectable, her opinions upon every point of duty had such precision and good sense that, without being aware of it, I leant upon her judgment of right and wrong, as naturally as the infant trusts his first unsteady steps to his mother's sustaining hand. She prevailed upon me to pause, ere I forsook the forms in which my fathers had worshipped; and though her own principle has since connected me with a church of simpler government and ritual, I have never seen reason to repent of the delay.

And now, deprived as I was of all the baubles which I had once imagined necessary to comfort, almost to existence, I was nearer to happiness than I had ever been while in the full enjoyment of all that pleasure, wealth, and flattery can bestow; for I now possessed all the materials of such happiness as this state of trial admits, – good health, constant employment, the necessaries of this life, and the steady hope of a better. And let the lover of pleasure, the slave of Mammon, the sage who renounces the light of heaven for the spark which himself has kindled, smile in scorn whilst I avow, that I at times felt rapture, compared with which their highest triumph of success is tame. I can bear the smile, for I know that they are compelled to mingle it with a sigh; that they envy the creature whom they affect to scorn; and wish – vainly wish, that they could choose the better part.

The bitter drop which is found in every cup, was infused into mine by the increasing illness of Miss Mortimer; and by a strong suspicion, that poverty aggravated to her the evils of disease. This latter circumstance, however, was conjectural; for Miss Mortimer, though confidingly open with me upon every other subject, was here most guarded. From the restraint visibly laid upon inclinations which I knew to be liberal in the extreme, – from my friend's obstinate refusal to indulge in any of the little luxuries which sickness and debility require, – from many trifles which cannot evade the eye of an inmate, I began to form conjectures which I soon accidentally discovered to be but too well founded. A gentleman happened to make a visit of business to Miss Mortimer one day when she was too much indisposed to receive him; and he incautiously committed to me a message for her, by which I discovered, that her whole patrimony had been involved in the ruin of my father; that, except the income of the current year, which she had fortunately rescued a few weeks before the wreck, she had lost all; that, while she made exertions beyond her strength to seek and to comfort me, while she soothed my sullen despair, she was herself shrinking before the gaunt aspect of poverty; and that, while she contrived for me indulgences which she denied to herself, her generous soul abhorred to divulge what might have rendered my feeling of dependence more painful.

When the certainty of all this burst upon me, I felt as if I had been in some sort responsible for the injury which my father had inflicted; and, overwhelmed with a sense of most undeserved obligation, I almost sunk to the ground. The moment I recovered myself, I flew to my friend, and with floods of tears, and the most passionate expressions of gratitude, I protested that I would no longer be a burden upon her generosity; and besought her to consider of some situation in which I might earn my subsistence. But Miss Mortimer resisted my proposal upon grounds which I felt it impossible to dispute. 'I cannot spare you yet, my dear child,' said she. 'I have been assured, that in a very few months you must be at liberty; but you will not leave me yet! – you will not leave me to die alone.'

This was the first intimation which I had received of the inevitable fate of one whose gentle virtues and unwearied kindness had centered in herself all my widowed affections; and it wholly overpowered the fortitude which not an hour before I had thought invincible. I hurried from human sight, while I mingled with bitter cries a passionate entreaty, that I might suffer any thing rather than the loss of my only friend. We often ask in folly; but we are answered in wisdom. The decree was gone forth; and no selfish entreaties availed to detain the saint from her reward. When the first emotions were past, I saw, and confessed, that a petition such as mine, clothed in whatever language, was wanting in the very nature of prayer; which has the promise of obtaining what we need, not of extorting what we desire.

In the present situation of my friend, it was impossible for me to forsake her; yet I could not endure to feel myself a burden upon the little wreck which the misfortunes or imprudence of my family had left her. Hour after hour I pondered the means of making my labour answer to my subsistence. But there my early habits were doubly against me. Accustomed to seek in trifling pastimes relaxation from employment scarcely less trifling, perseverance in mere manual industry was to me almost impossible. Habituated to confound the needful with the desirable, I had no idea how large a proportion of what we think necessary to the decencies of our station belongs solely to the wants of our fancy. My highest notion of economy in dress went no farther than the relinquishing of ornament; therefore, all my little works of ingenuity were barely sufficient to supply my own wardrobe, and another channel of expense which I had of late learnt to think at least as necessary. I saw no means, therefore, of escaping my dependence upon Miss Mortimer. Yet it made me miserable to think, that, for my sake, she must deny herself the necessaries of decaying life.

My heart gave a bound as my eye chanced to be caught by the sparkle of my mother's ring, and I recollected that its value might relieve my unwilling pressure upon my friend. But when I had looked at it till a thousand kindly recollections rose to my mind, my courage failed; and I thought it impossible to part with the memorial of my first and fondest attachment. Again my obligations to Miss Mortimer, – the rights of my mother's friend, – the dread of subtracting from the few comforts of a life which was so soon to close, upbraided my reluctance to sacrifice a selfish feeling; but a casuistry, which has often aided me against disagreeable duty, made me judge it best to act deliberately; and thus to defer indefinitely what I could neither willingly do, nor peacefully leave undone.

My decision, however, was hastened by one of those accidents which, I am ashamed to say, have determined half the actions of my life. The next morning, as I was reading to Miss Mortimer in her ground parlour, a woman came to the window offering for sale a basket of beautiful fruit. Fruit had been recommended as a medicine to my friend. I fancied, too, though perhaps it was only fancy, that she looked wistfully at it; and when she turned away without buying any, the scalding tears rushed to my eyes. Hastily producing the money which I had privately received for some painted screens, I heaped all the finest fruit before Miss Mortimer; and when, in spite of her mild remonstrances, I had laid out almost my whole fortune, I was seized with a sudden impatience to visit London; and thither I immediately went, promising to return before night.

I began my journey with a heavy heart. A stage-coach, the only conveyance suited to my circumstances, was quite new to me; and I shrunk with some alarm from companions, much like those usually to be met with in such vehicles, vulgar, prying, and communicative. Finding, however, that they offered me no incivility, I re-assured myself; and began to consider what price I was likely to obtain for my ring, and how I might best present my offering to Miss Mortimer. The first of these points I settled more agreeably to my wishes than to truth; the second was still undetermined when the coach stopped. Then I first recollected, that, with my usual inconsiderateness, I had not left myself the means of hiring a conveyance through the town. I had therefore no choice but to walk alone in some of the most crowded streets of the city.

And now I had some cause for the alarm that seized me, for I was more than once boldly accosted; and, ere I reached the shop where I intended to offer my ring, I was so thoroughly discomposed, that I entered without observing an equipage of the De Burghs at the door.

The shop was full of gay company; but one figure alone fixed my attention. It was that of my heartless friend. I recoiled like one who treads upon a serpent. My first impulse was to fly; but ere I had time to retreat, a deadly sickness arrested my steps; and I stood motionless and crouching towards the earth, as if struck by the power of the basilisk. A person belonging to the shop, who came to enquire my commands, seeing me, I suppose, ready to sink, offered me a chair; upon which I unconsciously dropped, still unable to withdraw my gaze from my apostate friend. Presently I almost started from my seat as her eye met mine. Her deepening colour alone told that she recognized me; for she instantly turned away.

Indignation now began to displace the stupor which had seized me. 'Shall I let this unfeeling creature see,' thought I, 'that she has power to move me thus? Or shall I tamely slink away, as if it were I who should dread the glance of reproach? – as if it were I who had stabbed the heart which trusted me?' My breast swelling with pain, pride, and resentment, I arose; and walking across the shop with steps as stately as if I had been about to purchase all the splendours it contained, I began to transact the business which brought me thither. My attention, however, was so much pre-occupied, that I was scarcely sensible of surprise when the jeweller named five-and-twenty pounds as the price of my ring; a sum less than one third of what I had expected.

I now perceived that Miss Arnold accompanied Lady Maria de Burgh. They talked familiarly together, and I was probably their subject; for Lady Maria stared full upon me, though her companion did not venture another glance towards the spot where I stood. Not satisfied with her arrogant scrutiny, Lady Maria, as if curious to know whether I were the buyer or the seller, made some pretence for approaching close to me, though without any sign of recognition. I had a hundred times abjured my enmity to Lady Maria. I had wept over it as ungrateful, unchristian. In cool-blooded solitude I had vowed a hundred times, that, having been forgiven a debt of ten thousand talents, I would never more wrangle for trifles with my fellow-servants. But when I was fretted with the insults of strangers, and sore with the unkindness of my early friend, when perhaps my pride was wounded by the circumstances in which she was about to detect me, her Ladyship's little impertinence, attacking me on the weak side, stirred at once the gall of my temper. Suspending a bargain which, indeed, I did not wish her to witness, 'Pray,' said I to the shopman, 'attend in the first place to that lady's business; if indeed she has any except to pry into mine.'

Lady Maria, who knew by experience that she was no match for me in a war of words, muttered something, and retreated, tossing her pretty head with disdain. Eager to be gone, I closed with the offer which had been made for my ring; and after delays which I thought almost endless, had received my money, and was about to depart, when Miss Arnold, who was in close conversation with her companion, in a distant part of the shop, suddenly advanced, as if with an intention to accost me. I was breathless with agitation and resentment. 'I will be cool, scornfully cool,' thought I; 'I will show her that I can forget all my long-tried affection, and remember only ——' I turned away, and remembrance wrung tears from me. But the formal effrontery with which she addressed me restored in a moment my fortitude and my indignation. She excused herself for not speaking to me sooner, by asserting that she 'really had not observed me.'

Scorning the paltry falsehood, 'That is no wonder, Miss Arnold,' answered I, 'for I am much lessened since you saw me last.'

I was moving away; but Miss Arnold, who had probably received her instructions, detained me. 'Do stay a few minutes,' said she coaxingly, 'I have a great deal to say to you. Lady Maria will be here for an hour, for she and Glendower are choosing their wedding finery; so if you lodge any way hereabouts, I can take the carriage and set you down.'

The days of my credulous inadvertence were past; and, at once perceiving the drift of this proposal, I answered with ineffable scorn, 'If you or Lady Maria have any curiosity to know my present situation, you may be gratified without hazarding your reputation by being seen with a runaway. I live with Miss Mortimer.'

I think Miss Arnold had the grace to blush, but I did not wait to examine. I hurried away; threw myself into the first hackney coach I could find; and returned home, exhausted and dispirited. I was dissatisfied with myself. The time had been when I should have thought the impertinence of a rival, the cool effrontery and paltry cunning of Miss Arnold, sufficient justification of any degree of resentment or contempt; but now I needed only the removal of temptation to remind me how unsuitable were scorn and anger to the circumstances of one who was herself so undeservedly, so lately, and still so imperfectly reclaimed. I firmly resolved, that if ever I should again meet Miss Arnold or her new protectress, I should treat them with that cool, guarded courtesy which is the unalienable right of all human kind. The strength of this resolution was not immediately tried. All my resentments had time to subside before I again saw or heard of my false friend.

Indeed, my seclusion now became more complete than ever; for Miss Mortimer's malady, the increase of which she had hitherto endeavoured to conceal from me, suddenly became so severe as to baffle all disguise. Yet it was no expression of impatience which betrayed her. For four months I scarcely quitted her bed-side, by day or by night. During this long protracted season of suffering, neither cry nor groan escaped her. Often have I wiped the big drops of agony from her forehead; but she never complained. She was more than patient; the settled temper of her mind was thankfulness. The decay of its prison-house seemed only to give the spirit a foretaste for freedom. Timid by nature, beyond the usual fearfulness of her sex, she yet endured pain, not with the iron contumacy of a savage, but with the submission of filial love. The approach of death she watched more in the spirit of the conqueror than the victim; yet she expressed her willingness to linger on till suffering should have extinguished every tendency to self-will, and helplessness should have destroyed every vestige of pride. Her desire was granted. Her trials brought with them an infallible token that they came from a Father's hand; for her character, excellent as it had seemed, was exalted by suffering; and that which in life was lovely, was in death sublime.

At last, the great work was finished. Her education for eternity was completed; and, from the severe lessons of this land of discipline, she was called to the boundless improvement, the intuitive knowledge, the glorious employments of her Father's house. One morning, after more than ordinary suffering, I saw her suddenly relieved from pain; and, grasping at a deceitful hope, I looked forward to no less than years of her prolonged life. But she was not so deceived. With pity she beheld my short-sighted reasoning. 'Dear child,' said she, 'must that sanguine spirit cheat thee to the end? Think not now of wishing for my life, – pray rather that my death may profit thee.' She paused for a moment, and then added emphatically, 'Do you not every morning pray for a blessing on the events which *that day* will produce?'

Long as I had anticipated this sentence, it was more than I could bear. 'This day! this very day!' I cried. 'It cannot, – it shall not be. It is sinful in you thus to limit your days! this very day! oh, I will not believe it;' and I threw myself upon my friend's death-bed in an agony which belied my words.

She gently reproved my vehemence. 'Ellen, my dear Ellen, my friend, my comforter, how can you lament my release? Your affection has been a blessing in my time of trial, – will you let it disturb the hour of my rejoicing? Had I been necessary to you, my child, I hope I could have wished for your sake to linger here; but "one thing" – only one – "is needful." That one you have received, – and when the light of heaven has risen upon you, can you mourn, that one feeble spark is darkened?'

The physicians, whom I sent in haste to summon, came only to confirm her prediction. She forced them to number the hours she had to live; and heard with a placid smile that the morning's sun would rise in vain for her. She bade farewell to them and to her attendants, bestowing, with her own hand, some small memorial upon each; then gently dismissed all, except myself and the hereditary servant who had grown old with her, and who now watched the close of a life which she had witnessed from its beginning. 'I saw her baptism,' said the faithful creature to me, the big tears rolling down her furrowed face, 'and now – but it is as the Lord will.'

By my dying friend's own desire, she was visited by the clergyman upon whose ministry she had attended; and with him she conversed with her accustomed serenity, directing his attention to some of her own poor, who were likely to become more destitute by her loss; and affectionately commending to his care the unfortunate girl whom her death was to cast once more friendless upon the world.

While he read to her the office for the sick, she listened with the steady attention of a mind in its full strength. When he came to the words, 'Thou hast been my hope from my youth!' – 'Yes!' said she; 'He has indeed been my hope from my youth. He blessed the prayers and the labours of my parents, so that I never remember a time when I could rest in any other trust; yet, till now, I never knew that hope in its full strength and brightness.' Then laying her hand, now chill with the damps of death, upon my arm, she said with great energy, 'Ellen, I trust I can triumphantly appeal to you whether our blessed faith brings not comfort unspeakable; – but how strong, how suitable, how glorious its consolations are, you will never know, till, like me, you are bereft of all others, and, like me, find them sufficient, when all others fail.'

Towards evening her voice became feeble, she breathed with pain, and all her bodily powers seemed to decay. But that which was heaven-born was imperishable. The love of God and man remained unshaken. Complaining that her mind was grown too feeble to form a connected prayer, she bade me repeat to her the triumphant strains in which David exults in the care of the Good Shepherd. When I had ended, 'Yes,' said she; 'He knows how to comfort me in the dark valley, for He has trod it before me; – and what am I that I should die amidst the cares of kind friends, and He amidst the taunts of his enemies! Ellen your mind is entire; – thank Him, thank Him fervently for me, that I am mercifully dealt with.'

As I knelt down to obey her, she laid her hand upon my head as if to bless me. At first, she repeated after me the expressions which pleased her, afterwards single words, then, after a long interval, the name of Him in whom she trusted. When I rose from my knees, her eyes were closed, – the hand which had been lifted in prayer was sunk upon her breast. A smile of triumph lingered on her face. It was the beam of a sun that had set. The saint had entered into rest.

CHAPTER XVIII

—— She hath ta'en farewell. ——
Upon her hearth the fire is dead,
The smoke in air hath vanished.
The last long lingering look is given;
The shuddering start! the inward groan!
And the pilgrim on her way is gone.

John Wilson.

As I tore myself from the remains of my friend, I felt that I had nothing more to lose. My soul, which had so obstinately clung to the earth, had no longer whereon to fix her hold. Words cannot describe the moment when, having assisted in the last sad office of woman, I was led from the chamber of death to wander through my desolate dwelling. Man cannot utter what I felt when I left the grave of my friend, and turned me to the solitary wilderness again.

Yet even the agony of my grief had no likeness to the stern horror which had once overwhelmed my soul. I was in sorrow indeed, but not in despair; I was lonely, but not forsaken. My interests in this scene of things were shaken, – were changed, – but not annihilated; for the world can never be a desert while gladdened by the sensible presence of its Maker; nor life be a blank to one who acts for eternity. The mere effort to become resigned, forbade the listlessness of despair; and even partial success gave some relief from uniformity of anguish. But I was new to the lesson of resignation, and as yet faintly imbued with that spirit which accepts with filial thankfulness the chastisements of a father. The accents of submission were choked by those of sorrow; and when I tried to say, 'Thy will be done,' I could only bow my head and weep.

It was not till the first bitterness of grief was past, that I recollected all the cause I had to grieve. My first feeling of desolateness was scarcely heightened by the reflection, that I was once more cast upon the world without refuge or means of subsistence. A few days after the death of my friend, her legal heir arrived to assert his rights; and the will by which she had intended to secure in her cottage a shelter for her old servant and myself was too informal to entitle us to resist his more valid claim. The will was written with Miss Mortimer's own hand, and expressed with all the touching solemnity of a last address to the object of strong affection. To resist it, seemed to me an instance of almost impious hardness of heart; and when the heir, fretted perhaps by finding his inheritance fall so far below his expectations, gave me notice, that I must either purchase the remainder of the lease, or, within a month, seek another habitation, I resolved that I would owe nothing to the forbearance of a being so callous; – that I would instantly resign to him whatever the relentless law made his own.

But whither could I go? I was as friendless as the first outcast that was driven forth a wanderer. I had no claim of gratitude, relationship, or intimacy on any living being. The few friends of my mother who had visited me after my return from school, I had neglected as persons of a character too grave, and of habits too retiring for the circle in which I desired to move. In that circle, a few months had sufficed to procure me some hundreds of acquaintances; ages probably would not have furnished me with one friend. My own labour, therefore, was now become my only means of obtaining shelter or subsistence; and, foreign as the effort was to all my habits, the struggle must be made. But how was I to direct my attempts? What channel had the customs of society left open to the industry of woman? The only one which seemed within my reach was the tuition of youth; and I felt myself less dependent when I recollected my thorough knowledge of music, and my acquaintance with other arts of idleness. When, indeed, I considered how small a part of the education of a rational and accountable being I was after all fitted to undertake, I shrunk from the awful responsibility of the charge, and I fear pride was still more averse to the task than principle; but there seemed no alternative, and my plan was fixed.

To enter on a state of dependence amidst scenes which had witnessed my better fortunes, – to be recognised in a condition little removed from servitude by those who had seen me at the summit of prosperity, – to meet scorn in the glances of once envious rivals, – and pity in the eye of once rejected lovers, would have furnished exercise for more humility than I had yet attained. Almost the first resolution which I formed on the subject was, that the scene of my labours should be far distant from London. Other circumstances in the situation which I was about to seek, I determined not to weigh too fastidiously; for though the most ambiguous praise from a person of fashion is often thought sufficient introduction to the most momentous of trusts, I had seen enough of the world to know, that it would be difficult to obtain the office of a teacher upon the mere strength of my acquaintance with what I pretended to teach; and I was resolved to owe no recommendation to any of those summer friends, by whom I seemed now utterly neglected and forgotten.

To the clergyman, whose compassion my dying friend had claimed for me, I explained my situation and my purpose. He showed me every kindness which genuine benevolence could dictate, – offered to write in my behalf to a married sister settled in a remote part of the kingdom, – and invited me to reside in his family till I found a preferable situation.

Meanwhile, a most unexpected occurrence placed me beyond the reach of immediate want. Among Miss Mortimer's papers was found a sealed packet addressed to me. It enclosed a bank-bill for 300*l.*; and in the envelope these words were written: –

> 'My dear Ellen, use the enclosed sum without scruple and without enquiry; for it is your own. Mine it never was, and none else has any claim upon it. It came into my possession within this hour, from whence you may never know; but I will conceal it till all is over, lest you squander upon the dying that which the living will need.
>
> 'E. MORTIMER.'

I instantly conjectured that this sum was the gift of Mr Maitland. 'And yet,' said I to myself, 'he has no interest in me now, except such as he would take in any one whom he thought unfortunate. Perhaps – if I could see his letters to Miss Mortimer – but I am sure his sentiments are of no consequence to me, – only, if this money be really his, I ought undoubtedly to restore it; and this from no impulse of pride certainly. Is there not a wide difference between humility and meanness?' Persuading myself, that it was quite necessary to ascertain the true owner of the money, I obtained permission to examine the correspondence which my friend had left behind. I found it to contain many letters from Mr Maitland, but only one in which I was mentioned, otherwise than in the words of common courtesy; and of that one, the tantalising caution of my friend had spared only the following fragment: –

'I will not be dazzled by your pictures of your young friend's improvement. I consider, that while you are drawing them, she is before you; turning up her transparent cheek as she used to do, and looking up in your face half sideways through her long black eyelashes, with that air of arch ingenuousness that must tempt you to give her credit for every virtue. I will not allow your partiality to blind me nor yourself to the probability, that all her apparent progress is not real. Ellen has warm passions and a vivid imagination; therefore, it is impossible that she should fail to receive a strong impression from events which have changed the whole colour of her fate. But the passions and the imagination are not the seat of religion. Besides, admitting that she has received a new principle of action, we must recollect, that pride and self-indulgence are not to be cured in an hour; nor can the opposite virtues spring without culture. The principle which guides our habits may be suddenly changed; and perhaps no means is more frequently employed for this change than severe calamity: but our habits themselves are of slow growth; slowly the seeds of evil are eradicated; laboriously the good ground is prepared; watered with the dews of heaven, the good seed, in progress that baffles human observation, advances from the feeble germ that scarcely rears itself from the dust, to the mature plant which bringeth forth an hundred fold. So you see, my good friend, I am determined to be wise; to read your encomiums with allowance; and, having painfully escaped from danger, to be cautious how I tempt it again.

'The execution of my present plans must detain me in exile for years to come; otherwise I could dream of a time when, having vanquished the power of that strange girl over my happiness, I might venture to watch over hers, perhaps be permitted to aid her improvement. I think I had some slight influence over her. If it were fit that a social being should waste feeling and affection in dreams, I could dream delightfully of ——'

'Of what?' thought I, when I reached this provoking interruption, – and I too began to dream. 'Does he still love me?' I asked myself.

'Can the grave, wise Mr Maitland still remember the rosy cheek and the long black eyelashes? Can he do no more than fly from his bane, but long after it still?' In spite of the regulations under which I had laid my heart, – in spite of the sorrow which weighed heavily upon it, the spirit of Ellen Percy fluttered in it for a moment. 'But why should I smile at his weakness, though I am myself exempt from that strange whim called love. Yes, certainly, for ever exempt. I have not withstood Maitland to be won by the monkey tricks and mawkish common-place of ordinary men. "Power over his happiness!" But for this strange coldness of heart, and my own unpardonable folly, I might have made him happy. But that is all over now. Now I can only wish and pray for his happiness. And if it be necessary to his peace that he forget me, I will pray that he may. No one heart on earth will then, indeed, beat warm to me; but the earth and all that it contains will soon pass away.' – And I shed some tears either over the transitory nature of all things here below, or over some reflection not quite so well defined.

Having perused the mutilated letter more than once, and finding my curiosity rather stimulated than gratified by the perusal, I certainly did not relax in the diligence with which I examined my friend's repositories. But I could not discover one line from Mr Maitland of a later date than six months before the death of Miss Mortimer; and I recollected, that though she regularly received his letters, and affected no mystery in regard to them, she never desired me to read them, but often in my presence destroyed them with her own hand. For the preservation of the fragment I seemed indebted to accident alone; and I more than half suspected, that Mr Maitland's later correspondence had purposely been concealed from the one who formed its principal subject. I wondered at my friend's caution. 'Could she know me so little,' thought I, 'as to fear that I should be infected by this folly of Maitland's? – That I should be won by this involuntary second-hand sort of courtship? – That I should be mean enough to like a man who in a manner rejected me?' But whatever was the motive of Miss Mortimer's caution, she had left no indication of Mr Maitland's present sentiments towards me; nor any clue by which I could trace to him the source of my unexpected wealth.

Still I scarcely doubted, that I owed my three hundred pounds to the generosity of Maitland, and I often thought of restoring the money to him; since, considering the terms upon which we had parted, few things could be more humiliating for me than to become a pensioner on his bounty. But I was restrained from writing to him, by the fear that, as possibly he had never intended to offer me such a gift, he might consider my addressing him upon the subject as a mere device, to obtain the renewal of an intercourse which he had voluntarily renounced.

Besides, Miss Mortimer's bequest furnished my only means of discharging another debt which had long occasioned me more mortification than I could have suffered from any obligation to Mr Maitland. My degrading debt to Lord Frederick was still unpaid; and my deliverance from absolute and immediate want was less gratifying to me, than the power of escaping from obligation to a wretch who had given proof of such heartless selfishness. I, therefore, resolved to comply with my friend's injunction to use without further enquiry the money which had so providentially been placed within my reach; and the first purpose to which it was devoted, was the repayment of Lord Frederick's loan, with every shilling of interest to which law could have entitled him. The remainder I could not help dividing with Miss Mortimer's old servant; as the poor creature, who had grown grey in the family of my friend, had been deprived of the bequest by which her mistress had intended to acknowledge her services. The purchase of a few decencies which my own wardrobe required, and the expense of a plain grave-stone to mark the resting-place of the best of women, reduced my possessions to thirty pounds. With this provision, which, small as it was, I owed to most singular good fortune, I was obliged to quit the asylum which had sheltered me from my bitterest sorrow, and had witnessed my most substantial joys; the home which was endeared to me by the kindness of a lost friend, – the birth-place of my better being, – the spot which was hallowed by my first worship.

It was on a stormy winter night, I remember it well, that I turned weeping from the door of my only home. All day I had wandered through the cottage; I had sat by my friend's death-bed, and laid my head upon her pillow. I had placed her chair as she was wont to place it; had realised her presence in every well known spot, and bidden her a thousand and a thousand times farewell. When I left the house, the closing door sounded as drearily as the earth which I had heard rattle on her coffin. It seemed the signal, that I was shut out from all familiar sights and sounds for ever. The storm that was beating on me became, by a natural thought, the type of my after life; and when all there seemed darkness, my mind wandered back to the sorrows of the past. I recalled another time when the wide earth, which lodges and supports her children of every various tribe, and opens at least in her bosom a resting place for them all, contained no home for me. I remembered a time when I had felt myself alone, though in the presence of the universal Father, – destitute, in a world stored with his bounty, – desolate, though Omnipotence was pledged to answer my cry. My deliverance from this orphan state, – from this disastrous darkness, rushed upon my mind. I thought upon the mighty transformation which had gladdened the desert for me, and made the solitary place rejoice. The cry of thanksgiving burst from my lips, although it died amidst the storm. 'Oh Thou!' I exclaimed, 'who from pollution didst reclaim, – from rebellion didst receive, – from despair didst revive me, – let but Thy presence be with me; and let my path lead where it will!'

As I passed the village churchyard, I turned to visit the grave of her whom I had lost. The stone had been placed upon it since I had seen it last; and I felt as if the performance of the last duty had made our separation more complete. 'And is this all that I can do for thee, my friend?' said I. 'Are all the kindly charities cut off between us for ever? Hast thou, who wert so lately alive to the joys and the sorrows of every living thing, no share in all that is done or suffered here? Hast thou, who so lately wert my other soul, no feeling now that owns kindred with any thought of mine? – Yes. On one theme, in one employment we can sympathise still. We can still worship together.' Kneeling upon the grave of my last earthly friend, I commended myself to a heavenly one, and was comforted.

CHAPTER XIX

They hate to mingle in the filthy fray,
Where the soul sours, and gradual rancour grows
Imbittered more from peevish day to day.
Thomson.

THOUGH I was no longer of a temper to reject the means of comfort which still remained within my reach, or scornfully to repulse the mercies both of God and man, I had accepted with reluctance the asylum offered by the clergyman to whom Miss Mortimer had recommended me; for the reserve which shrinks from obligation is one of the most unconquerable forms of pride. Besides, though the Doctor's professional duties had made me somewhat acquainted with him, his family were, even by character, strangers to me. The state of Miss Mortimer's health had long precluded us from paying or receiving visits; and my friend had none of those habits of moral portrait-painting which seduce so many into caricature. My reluctance to accept of the good man's hospitality had, however, yielded partly to necessity, partly to the recollection that I had once heard the 'Doctor's lady' called 'the cleverest woman in the country.' For ability I had always entertained a high regard; which is one of vanity's least bare-faced ways of claiming kindred with it. A residence with persons of education and good manners was irresistible, when the only alternative was an abode in a mean lodging, in which pride or prudence would forbid me to receive even the few who still owned my acquaintance. I had therefore consented to remain with Dr —— till an answer should arrive from the sister to whom he had written on my behalf.

Though I knew that I was expected at the parsonage on the

evening when I left Miss Mortimer's, I lingered long by the way. The spirit which, for a moment, had raised me above my fate, could not tarry; and earthly woes and earthly passions soon resumed their power. A feeling of loneliness and neglect returned to weigh upon my heart; and when I reached the gate within which I was about to seek a shelter, I stopped; leant my head against it; and wept, as if I had never committed myself to a Father's protection, – never exulted in a Father's care. I felt it unkind that no one came to save me the embarrassment of introducing myself; and perhaps even my pride would not have stooped to the effort, had I not at last been accosted by my host; who excused himself for not having come to escort me, by saying that he had been unavoidably engaged in professional duty. He now welcomed me cordially; expressing a hope that I should soon feel myself at home, – 'that is,' continued he, 'as soon as the exertions of my good woman will allow you.'

To this odd proviso I could only answer, 'That I was afraid my visit might put Mrs —— to inconvenience.'

'I wish that were possible, Miss Percy,' returned he; 'for then she would be quite in her element.'

By this time we had reached the door, and Dr —— knocked loudly. No answer came, though the sounds of busy feet were heard within, and lights glanced swiftly across the windows. After another vigorous assault upon the knocker, the door was opened by a panting maid-servant; in time to exhibit the descent of my hostess from a stool which she had mounted, as it appeared, to light a lamp that hung from the ceiling. Snatching off a checked apron, which she threw into a corner, she advanced to receive me. 'Miss Percy!' she cried, 'I am so glad to see you! – Doctor, I had no notion you could have got back so soon; – and indeed ma'am I am quite proud that you will accept of such accommodations as – Lord bless me, girl! did ever any body see such a candlestick? – This way ma'am, if you please, – To bring up a thing like that before strangers!'

During this miscellaneous oration, I had made my way into the parlour, and taken possession of the first seat I could find. But this was too natural an arrangement of things to satisfy my good hostess. 'Oh dear! Miss Percy,' said she, 'you are quite in the way of the door, – pray take this side; Doctor, can't you give Miss Percy that chair?'

At last the turmoil of placing us was over; and the good lady was compelled to be quiet for a little. The scenes which I had lately witnessed, the sense of being a stranger in what was now my only home, depressed my spirits; yet good manners inclined me to enter into conversation with my hostess. I soon found, however, that this was, for the present, out of the question; for though, under a sense of duty, she frequently spoke to her guest, my replies evidently escaped her powers of attention, these being occupied by certain sounds proceeding from the kitchen. For a while she kept fidgeting upon her chair, looking wistfully towards the door; her politeness maintaining doubtful strife with her anxieties. At last a crash of crockery overcame her self-denial, and she ran out of the room.

Our ears were presently invaded by all the discords of wrath and hurry; but the Doctor, who seemed accustomed to such tumults, quietly drew his chair close to mine, and began to discuss the merits of a late publication, repeating his remarks with immovable patience, as often as they were lost in the din. At length, however, he was touched in a tender point; for now an audible kick produced a howl from the old house-dog. The Doctor started up, took three strides across the room, wiped his forehead, and sat down again. 'I thank Heaven,' said he, 'that the children are all in bed,' – and he went on with his criticism.

Late came the supper; and with it mine hostess, looking 'unutterable things.' She forced her mouth, however, into an incongruous smile, while she apologised to me for her absence; but she was too full of her recent disaster long to deny herself the comforts of complaint and condolence. 'I hope, Miss Percy, you will try to eat a little bit of supper; though to be sure it is a pretty supper indeed for one who has been accustomed as you have been!'

The looks of the speaker showed me that this speech was less intended for me than for the poor girl who waited at table. 'I assure you, madam, the supper is much better than any I ever was accustomed to. I never exceed a biscuit or a jelly.'

'Oh you are very good to say so; but I am sure, – and then to have it served upon such mean-looking, nasty old cracked rubbish, – but I hope you'll excuse it, ma'am; for Kitty there has thought fit to break no less than three dozen of our blue china supper-set at one crash.'

'That is a great pity.'

'Pity! I declare my patience is quite worn out.'

'We have reason to be thankful,' said the Doctor, 'that she did the thing at once; it puts you into only one fury, instead of three dozen. The treatise we were talking of, Miss Percy ——'

'Mercy upon me!' interrupted the lady, 'there is no salt in this stuffing!'

'I say the author appears to me to reason upon false premises when ——'

'Hand the sauce to Miss Percy, do, that she may have something to flavour that tasteless mess.'

The poor fluttered girl, in her haste to obey, dropped the sauce-boat into my lap. 'Heaven preserve me!' exclaimed the lady; 'she has finished your new sarcenet gown, I declare. – Well! if you an't enough to drive one distracted!'

In vain did I protest that the gown was very little injured; – in vain did I represent that the poor girl was unavoidably fluttered by her former misdemeanour; peace was not re-established till the close of supper allowed the delinquent to retire. Mrs —— then seemed to collect her thoughts, and to recollect the propriety of conversing with her guest. 'It must have been very hard upon poor Miss Mortimer,' said she, 'to be so long confined, and all the affairs of her family at sixes and sevens all the while. To be sure, I dare say you would spare no trouble; but, after all, there is nothing like the eye of a mistress.'

Shocked as I was at this careless mention of my friend, I forced myself to answer; 'Miss Mortimer's method was so regular that I never could perceive where any trouble was necessary.'

'That might be the case in Miss Mortimer's family. For my part I have hard enough work with mine from morning to night. I really can't conceive how people get on, who take matters so easily. To be sure there must be great waste; but some people can afford that better than others.'

'There was no waste in Miss Mortimer's family, madam,' answered I, my spirit rising at this reflection on my friend, 'not even a waste of power.'

I repented of this taunt almost the moment it was uttered. But it was lost upon my hostess; who went on to demonstrate, that, without her ceaseless intervention, disorder and ruin must ensue. 'Miss Percy', said the Doctor gravely, 'are you satisfied with the order of pins in ordinary paper; or do you purchase the pins wholesale, that you may arrange them more correctly for yourself?'

'Oh, none of your gibes, Dr ——; you know very well I don't spend my time in sticking pins, or any such trifles. I have work enough, and more than enough, in attending to your family.'

'Ay, my dear, – and fortunate it is that all your industry has taken that turn, for you can never be industrious by proxy; you can work with no hands but your own.'

It was now the hour of rest; or, more properly speaking, it was bed-time; for I was disturbed by the bustle of the household long after I had retired to a chamber, finical enough to keep me in mind that it was the 'stranger's room.' With a sigh, I remembered the quiet shelter I had lost, and that true hospitality which never once reminded me, even by officious cares, that I was a stranger. I hoped, however, that the turmoil occasioned by my arrival, and the destruction of the blue supper-set being over, peace might be restored in the family; and the calm of the following morning be the sweeter for the hurricane of the night. But the tumult of the evening was a lulling murmur to the full chorus of busy morn. Ringing, trampling, scraping, knocking, scrubbing, and all the clatter of housewifery, were mingled with the squalls of children, and the clang of chastisement; and above all swelled my landlady's tones, in every variety of exhortation and impatience.

In short, Mrs —— was one of those who could not be satisfied with putting the machine in motion, unless she watched and impelled the action of every wheel and pivot. The interference was of course more productive of derangement than of despatch. Besides, by taking upon herself all the business of the maids, my hostess necessarily neglected that of the mistress; the consequence of which was general confusion and discomfort. Few can be so ignorant of human nature as to wonder that I endured the petty miseries to which I was thus subjected with less patience than I had lately shown under real misfortune. A little religion will suffice to produce acts of resignation, when events have tinctured the mind with their own solemnity, or when, 'by the sadness of the countenance the heart is,' for a time, 'made better;' but Christian patience finds exercise on a thousand occasions, when the dignity of her name would be misapplied; and I had yet much to gain of that heavenly temper, which extends its influence to lesser actions and lesser foibles. A few hours served to make me completely weary of my new abode; and I anxiously wished for the summons which was to transfer me to another. Dr —— assured me that his sister would lose no time in endeavouring to serve me; and I was determined to accept of any situation which she should propose.

Mrs Murray, the lady to whose patronage I had been recommended, was the wife of a naval officer. Captain Murray was then at sea; and she, with her son and daughter, resided in Edinburgh. Far from being averse to follow my fortunes in this distant quarter, I preferred a residence where I was wholly unknown. The friendship of Mr Sidney procured for me the offer of an eligible situation in town; but I was predetermined against hazarding the humiliations to which such a situation must have exposed me. The wisdom of this resolution, I must own, would not bear examination, and therefore I was never examined; for I retained too much adroitness in self-deceit to let prudence fairly contest the point with pride. I was destined to pay the penalty of my choice, and to illustrate the invariable sequence of a 'haughty spirit' and a 'fall.'

The expected letter at length arrived; and I thought myself fortunate beyond my hopes, when I found that Mrs Murray was inclined to receive me into her own family. My knowledge of music, particularly my skill in playing on the harp, had recommended me as a teacher in a country which pays for her fruitfulness in poetry by a singular sterility in the other fine arts. Mrs Murray enquired upon what terms I would undertake the tuition of her daughter; and seemed only fearful that my demands might exceed her powers. After the receipt of her letter I was most eager to depart. To terms I was utterly indifferent. All I wanted was quiet, and an asylum which inferred no obligation to strangers. It is true, that my hostess often assured me of the pleasure she received from my visit; but my presence evidently occasioned such an infinity of trouble, that, if her assurances were sincere, she must have been filled with more than the spirit of martyrdom in my service. I was too impatient to be gone to wait the formal arrangement of my engagement with Mrs Murray. I instantly wrote to commit the terms of it entirely to herself; and then took measures to obtain my immediate conveyance to Scotland.

A journey by land was too expensive to be thought of; I therefore secured my passage in a merchant vessel. It was in vain that Dr —— advised me to wait further instructions from his sister; in hopes that she might suggest a more eligible mode of travelling, or at least give me notice that she was prepared for my reception. My dislike of my present abode, my restlessness under a sense of obligation to such a person as Mrs ——, prevailed against his counsels. In vain did he represent the discomforts of a voyage at such a season of the year. I was not more habitually impatient of present evil than fearless of that which was yet to come. In short, after a little more than a week's residence at the parsonage, I insisted upon making my début as a sailor in the auspicious month of February, and committing myself, at that stormy season, to an element which as yet I knew only from description.

Dr —— and Mr Sidney accompanied me to the vessel; and I own I began to repent of my obstinacy, when they bade me farewell. As I saw their boat glide from the vessel's side, and answered their parting signals, and saw first the known features, then the forms, then the little bark itself, fade from my sight, I wept over the rashness which had exiled me among strangers; and coveted the humblest station cheered by the face of friend or kinsman. The wind blowing strong and cold soon obliged me to leave the deck; and, when I entered the close airless den in which I was to be imprisoned with fourteen fellow-sufferers, I cordially wished myself once more under the restraint imposed by nice arrangement and finical decoration.

I was soon obliged to retreat to a bed, compared with which the worst I had ever occupied was the very couch of luxury. 'It must be owned,' thought I, 'that a sea voyage affords good lessons for a fine lady.' Sleep was out of the question. I was stunned with such variety of noise as made me heartily regret the quiet of the parsonage. The rattling of the cordage, the lashing of the waves, the heavy measured tread, the tuneless song repeated without end, interrupted only by the sudden dissonant call, and then begun again, – these, besides a hundred inexplicable disturbances, continued day and night. To these was soon added another, which attacked my quiet through other mediums than my senses, the ship sprung a leak, and the pumps were worked without intermission.

Meanwhile the wind rose to what I thought a hurricane; and, among us passengers, whose ignorance probably magnified the danger, all was alarm and dismay. A general fit of piety bespoke the general dread; and they who had before been chiefly intent upon establishing their importance with their fellow-travellers, seemed now feelingly convinced of their own dependence and insignificancy. For my part, I prepared for death with much greater resignation than I had found to bestow upon the previous evils of my voyage; – not surely that it is easier to resign life than to submit to a few inconveniences, – but that I had a tendency to treat my religion like one of the fabled divinities, who are not to be called into action except upon worthy occasions; whereas, it is indeed her agency in matters of ordinary occurrence that shows her true power and value. I am much mistaken, if it be not easier to die like a martyr than to live like a Christian; and if the glory of our faith be not better displayed in a life of meekness, humility, and self-denial, than even in a death of triumph. I am sure the question would not bear dispute, if all mankind were unhappily born with feelings as lively, and passions as strong as mine. Whether my faith would have been equal even to what I account the lesser victory, remains to be proved; for, on the second day, the gale abated, and, from our heart-sinking prison we were once more released, to breathe the fresh breeze which now blew from the near coast of Holland.

The bloody conflict was then only beginning which has won for my country such imperishable honours. At Rotterdam we could then find safety, and the means of refitting our crazy vessel, so far as was necessary for the completion of our voyage. It will readily be believed, that those of our company who were least accustomed to brave the ocean were eager to tread the steady earth once more. We all went on shore; and I, wholly ignorant of all methods of economy in a situation so new to me, took up my abode in a comfortable hotel; where I remained during the week which elapsed before we were able to proceed upon our voyage. At the end of that time, I discovered, with surprise and consternation, that my wealth had diminished to little more than ten guineas. I comforted myself, however, by recollecting, that once under the protection of Mrs Murray I should have little occasion for money; and that a few shillings were all the expense which I was likely to incur before I was safely lodged in my new home.

The remainder of the voyage was prosperous; and in little more than a fortnight after my first embarkation, I found myself seated in the hackney-coach which was to convey me from the harbour to Edinburgh. Not even the beauty and singularity of this romantic town could divert my imagination from the person upon whom I expected so much of my future happiness to depend. I anticipated the character, the manners, the appearance, the very attire of Mrs Murray; imagined the circumstances of my introduction, and planned the general form of our future intercourse. 'Oh that she may be one whom I can love, and love safely,' thought I; 'one endowed with somewhat of the spirit of her whom I have lost!' My intercourse with the world, perhaps my examination of my own heart, had destroyed much of my fearless confidence in every thing that bore the human form; and now my spirits sunk, as I recollected how small was my chance of finding another Miss Mortimer.

A sudden twilight was closing as I entered the street of dull magnificence, in which stood the dwelling of my patroness. Though in the midst of a large city, all seemed still and forsaken. The bustle of business or amusement was silent here. Single carriages, passing now and then at long intervals, sounded through the vacant street till the noise died in the distance. The busy multitudes whom I was accustomed to associate with the idea of a city had retired to their homes; and I envied them who could so retire, – who could enter the sanctuary of their own roof, sit in their own accustomed seat, hear the familiar voice, and grasp the hand that had ten thousand times returned the pressure.

All around me strengthened the feelings of loneliness which are so apt to visit the heart of a stranger; and I anxiously looked from the carriage to descry the only spot in which I would claim an interest. The coach stopped at the door of a large house, handsome indeed, but more dark, I thought, and dismal if possible than the rest. I scarcely breathed till my summons was answered; nor was it without an effort that I enquired whether Mrs Murray was at home?

'No, madam,' was the answer; 'she has been gone this fortnight.'

'Gone! Good heavens! Whither?'

'To Portsmouth, madam. As soon as the news came of the Captain's coming in wounded, Mrs Murray and Miss Arabella set our immediately.'

'And did she leave no letter for me? No instructions?'

The servant's answer convinced me that my arrival was even wholly unexpected. Struck with severe disappointment, overwhelmed with a sense of utter desertedness, my spirits failed; and I sunk back into the carriage faint and forlorn.

'Do you alight here ma'am?' enquired the coachman.

'No!' answered I, scarcely knowing what I said.

'Where do you go next?' asked the man.

I replied only by a bitter passion of tears. 'Alas!' thought I, 'I once, in the mere wilfulness of despair, rejected the blessings of a home and a friend. How righteous is the retribution which leaves me now homeless and friendless!'

'Perhaps, ma'am,' said the servant, seemingly touched by my distress, 'Mrs Murray may have left some message with Mr Henry for you.'

'Mr Henry!' cried I; 'is Mrs Murray's son here?'

'Yes, ma'am. Mr Henry staid to finish his classes in the college. He is not at home just now; but I expect him every minute. Will you please to come in and rest a little?'

With this invitation I thought it best to comply; and dismissing the coach, followed the servant into the house. I was shown into a handsome parlour, where the cheerful blaze of a Scotch coal fire gave light enough to show that all was elegance and comfort. My buoyant heart rose again; and, not considering how improbable it was that my patroness should commit a girl of eighteen to the guardianship of a youth little above the same age, I began to hope that Mrs Murray had given her son directions to receive me. In this hope I sat waiting his return; now listening for his approach; now trying to conjecture what instructions he would bring me; now beguiling the time with the books which were scattered round the room.

Though some of these were works of general literature, there was sufficient peculiarity in the selection, to show that the young student was intended for the bar. Indeed, before he arrived, I had formed, from a view of the family apartment, a tolerable guess of the habits and pursuits of its owners. Open upon a sofa was a pocket Tibullus; within a Dictionary of Decisions lay a well-read first volume of the Nouvelle Eloise. Then there were Le Vaillant's Travels; Erskine's Institutes; and a Vindication of Queen Mary. 'If the young lawyer has not disposed of his heart already, I shall be too pretty for my place,' thought I: 'and now for my patroness!' The card-racks contained some twenty visiting tickets, upon which the same matronly names were repeated at least four times. A large work-bag, which hung near the great chair, was too well stuffed to close over a half-knitted stocking, and a prayer-book, which opened of itself at the prayer for those who travel by sea. My imagination instantly pictured a faded, serious countenance, with that air of tender abstraction which belongs to those whose thoughts are fixed upon the absent and the dear. Miss Arabella's magnificent harp stood in a window, and her likeness in the act of dancing a hornpipe hung over the chimney; her music-stand was loaded with easy sonatas and Scotch songs; and her portfolio was bursting with a humble progression of water-colour drawings.

My conjectures were interrupted by a loud larum at the house-door, which announced the return of my young host. My heart beat anxiously. I started from the sofa like one who felt no right to be seated there; and sat down again, because I felt myself awkward when standing. I thought I heard the servant announce my arrival to his master as he passed through the lobby; and after a few questions asked and answered in an under voice, the young man entered the parlour with a countenance which plainly said, 'What in the world am I to do with the creature?' As I rose to receive him, however, I saw this expression give place to another. Strong astonishment was pictured in his face, then yielded again to the glow of youthful complacency and admiration.

On my part I was little less struck with my student's exterior, than he appeared to be with mine. Instead of the awkward, mawkish school-boy whom I had fancied, he was a tall, elegant young man, with large sentimental black eyes, and a clear brown complexion, whose paleness repaid in interest whatever it substracted from the youthfulness of his appearance.

I was the first to speak. Having expressed my regret at Mrs Murray's absence, and the cause of it, I begged to know whether she had left any commands for me. Murray replied, that he believed his mother had written to me before her departure; and that she had hoped her letter might reach me in time to delay my journey to a milder season.

'Unfortunately,' said I, 'most unfortunately, I had set out before that letter arrived.'

'Excuse me,' returned my companion, with polite vivacity, 'if I cannot call any accident unfortunate which has procured me this pleasure.' I could answer this civility only by a gesture, for my heart was full. I saw that I had no claim to my present shelter; and other place of refuge I had none. Oh how did I repent the self-will which had reduced me to so cruel a dilemma! 'In a few weeks at farthest,' continued Mr Murray, 'my father will be able to travel; and then I am certain my mother will bring Arabella home immediately.'

Still I could make no reply. 'A few weeks!' thought I, 'what is to become of me even for one week, even for one night!' Tears were struggling for vent; but to have yielded to my weakness, would have seemed like an appeal to compassion; and the moment this thought occurred, the necessary effort was made. I rose, and requested that Mr Murray would allow his servant to procure a carriage for me, and direct me to some place where I could find respectable accommodation.

To this proposal Murray warmly objected. 'I hope, – I beg Miss Percy,' said he eagerly, 'you will not think of leaving my mother's house to-night. Though she has been obliged to refuse herself the pleasure of receiving you, I know she would be deeply mortified to find that you would not remain, even for one night, under her roof.'

I made my acknowledgments for his invitation; but said, I had neither title nor desire to intrude upon any part of Mrs Murray's family, and renewed my request. Murray persevered in urgent and respectful entreaties. They were so well seconded by the lateness of the hour, for it was now near ten o'clock, and by the contrast of the comfort within doors, with the storm which was raging abroad, that my scruples began to give way; and the first symptom of concession was so eagerly seized, that, before I had leisure to consider of proprieties, my young host had ordered his mother's bedchamber to be prepared for my reception.

This arrangement made, he turned the conversation to general topics, and amused me very agreeably till we separated for the night. I know not if ever I had offered up more hearty thanksgivings for shelter and security than I did in that evening's prayer; so naturally do we reserve our chief gratitude for blessings of precarious tenure. But I omitted my self-examination that night; either because I was worn out and languid, or because I was half conscious of having done what prudence would not justify.

I slept soundly, however, and awoke in revived spirits. My host renewed all his attentions. We conversed, in a manner very interesting to ourselves, of public places, of the last new novel; and this naturally led us into the labyrinths of the human heart, and the mysteries of the tender passion. Then I played on the harp, which threw my young lawyer into raptures; then I sung, which drew tears into the large black eyes. In short, the forenoon was pretty far advanced before my student recollected that he had missed his law-class by two hours.

All this was the effect of mere thoughtlessness; for I was guiltless of all design upon Murray's affections, or even upon his admiration. I now, however, suddenly recollected myself, and renewed my enquiries for some eligible abode; but Murray, with more warmth than ever, objected to my removal. He laboured to convince me that his mother's house, for so he dexterously called it, was the most eligible residence for me, at least till I should learn how Mrs Murray wished me to act. Finding me a little hard of conviction, he proposed a new expedient. He offered to call upon a sister of his father's, and to obtain for me her advice or assistance. Most cordially did I thank him for this proposal, and urged him to execute it instantly. He lingered, however, and endeavoured to escape the subject; and when

I persisted in pressing it, he fairly owned his unwillingness to perform his promise. 'If Mrs St Clare should wile you away from me,' said he with a very Arcadian sigh, 'how will you ever repay me for such self-devotion?'

'With an old song,' answered I gaily; 'payment enough for such a sacrifice.' But I registered the sigh notwithstanding. 'Touched already!' thought I. 'So much for Tibullus and the Nouvelle Eloise!'

At last I drove him away; but he soon returned, and told me he had not found Mrs St Clare at home. I made him promise to renew his attempt in the evening, amd proposed meanwhile to write to Mrs Murray an account of my situation. My companion at first made no objection; but afterwards discovered that it was almost too late to overtake that day's post, and offered to save time, by mentioning the matter in the postscript of a letter which he had already written. I consented; but afterwards obliged him to tell me, rather unwillingly, in what terms he had put his communication.

'From the way in which you have written,' said I, when he had ended, 'Mrs Murray will never discover that I am residing in her house. Were it not better to say distinctly that I am here?'

I looked at my young lawyer as I spoke, and saw him blush very deeply. He hesitated too; and stammered while he answered, 'that it was unnecessary, since his mother could not suppose me to reside anywhere else.'

The full impropriety of my situation flashed upon me at once. Murray evidently felt that there was something in it which he was unwilling to submit to the judgment of his mother. My delicacy, or rather perhaps my pride, thus alarmed, my resolution was taken in a moment; but as I could not well avow the grounds of my determination, I retired in silence to make what little preparation was necessary for my immediate departure.

If my purpose had wanted confirmation, it would have been confirmed by a dialogue which I accidentally overheard, between Murray and a youth who just then called for him. My host seemed pressing his friend to return to supper. 'Do come,' said he, 'and I will show you an angel – the loveliest girl ——' – 'Where? in this house?' – 'Yes, my sister's governess.' – 'Left to keep house for you? Eh? a good judicious arrangement, faith.' – 'Hush – I assure you her manners are as correct as her person is beautiful; – such elegance, – such modest vivacity, – and then she sings! Oh, Harry, if you did but hear her sing!' – 'Well I believe I must come and take a look of this wonder.' – 'The wonder,' thought I, 'shall not be made a spectacle to idle boys, – nor remain in a situation of which even they can see the impropriety.' I rang for the housemaid; and putting half-a-guinea into her hand, requested that she would direct me to reputable lodgings, and procure a hackney-coach to convey me thither. Both of these services she performed without delay; meanwhile, I went to take leave of my young host.

He heard of my intention with manifest discomposure, and exerted all his eloquence to shake my purpose; entreating me at least to remain with him till he had seen Mrs St Clare; but I was more disposed to anger than to acquiescence, when I recollected that all his entreaties were intended to make me do what he himself felt to need disguise or apology. Finding me resolute, he next begged to know where he might bring Mrs St Clare to wait upon me; but suspecting that my apartments might not be such as I chose to exhibit, I declined this favour. I took, however, the lady's address, meaning to avail myself of her assistance in procuring employment.

CHAPTER XX

Lend me thy clarion, goddess! Let me try
To sound the praise of merit ere it dies;
Such as I oft have chanced to espy,
Lost in the dreary shades of dull obscurity.
Shenstone.

WITH a feeling of dignity and independence which had forsaken me in my more splendid abode, I took possession of an apartment contrived to serve the double purposes of parlour and bedchamber. 'I have done right,' thought I, 'whatever be the consequences; and these are in the hands of One who has given me the strongest pledge that he will over-rule them for my advantage.' Yet, alas for my folly! I was almost the next moment visited by the fear, that the advantage might not be palpable to present observation, and that it might belong more to my improvement than to my convenience.

I now felt no reluctance to address Mrs Murray; and to enquire whether it were still her wish to receive me into her family. One circumstance alone embarrassed me; I plainly perceived, that I had already made such an impression upon Henry, as his mother was not likely to approve; and it seemed dishonourable to owe my admission into her family to her ignorance of that which she would probably deem sufficient reason to exclude me. I knew the world, indeed, too well, to expect that the passion of a youth of twenty, for a girl with a fortune of nine pounds three shillings, was itself likely to be either serious or lasting; but its consequences might be both, if it relaxed industry, or destroyed cheerfulness, darkening the sunny morning with untimely shade.

But how could I forewarn my patroness of her danger? Could I tell her, not only that one day's acquaintance with her son had sufficed me to make the conquest, but, which was still less *selon les regles*, to discover that I had made it? I dared not brave the smile which would have avenged such an absurdity. After some consideration, I took my resolution. I determined to introduce myself the next day to Mrs St Clare, who, I imagined, would not long leave her sister-in-law in ignorance of my personal attractions; for I have often observed, that we ladies, while we grudge to a beauty the admiration and praise of the other sex, generally make her amends by the sincerity and profuseness of our own.

'And if her description alarm Mrs Murray,' thought I; 'if it deter her from admitting me under the roof with her son, what then is to become of me? – What will my pretty features do for me then? – What have they ever done for me, except to fill my ears with flatteries, and my mind with conceit, and the hearts of others with envy and malice. Maitland, indeed, – but no – it was not my face that Maitland loved. Rather to the pride of beauty I owe that wretched spirit of coquetry by which I lost him. And now this luckless gift may deprive me of respectable protection and subsistence. Surely I shall at last be cured of my value for a bauble so mischievous – so full of temptation – so incapable of ministering either to the glory of God or the good of man!' Ah, how easy it is to despise baubles while musing by fire-light in a solitary chamber!

The evening passed in solitude, but not in weariness; for I was not idle. I spent the time in writing to Mrs Murray, and in giving to my friend Dr —— an account of my voyage, and of my disappointment. The hour soon came which I now habitually devoted to the invitation of better thoughts, the performance of higher duties; and thanks be to Heaven, that neither human converse, nor human protection, nor ought else that the worldly can enjoy or value, is necessary to the comfort of that hour!

The next day Murray came early, under pretence of enquiring how I was satisfied with my accommodation; and I was pleased that the mission which he had undertaken to Mrs St Clare, gave me a pretext for being glad to see him. I know not what excuse he could make for a visit of three hours long; but my plea for permitting it was the impossibility of ordering him away. He left me, however, at last; and, more convinced than ever that his mother would do well to dispense with my services, I went to present myself to Mrs St Clare.

Arrived at her house, I was ushered into the presence of a tall, elderly, hard-favoured gentlewoman; who, seated most perpendicularly on a great chair, was employed in working open stitches on a French lawn apron. I cannot say that her exterior was much calculated to dispel the reserve of a stranger. Her figure might have served to illustrate all the doctrines of the acute angle. Her countenance was an apt epitome of the face of her native land; – rough with deep furrow and uncouth prominence, and grim with one dusky uniformity of hue. As I entered, this erect personage rose from her seat, and, therefore, almost necessarily advanced one step to meet me. I offered some apology for my intrusion. From a certain rustle of her stiff lutestring gown, I guessed that the lady made some gesture of courtesy, though I cannot pretend that I saw the fact.

'Mr Murray, I believe, has been so good as to mention me,' said I.

The lady looked towards a chair; and this I was obliged to accept as an invitation to sit down.

'I have been particularly unfortunate in missing Mrs Murray,' said I.

'Hum!' returned the lady, with a scarcely perceptible nod; and a pause followed.

'She left Scotland very unexpectedly.'

'Very unexpectedly.'

Another pause.

'I happened unluckily to have begun my journey before I learnt that it was unnecessary.'

'That was a pity.'

'I hope she is not likely to be long absent?'

'Indeed there is no saying.'

'Perhaps she may not choose that I should wait her return?'

'Really I can't tell.'

Until this hour, I had never known what it was to shrink before the repulse of frozen reserve; for the cordiality which had once been obtained for me by the gifts of nature or of fortune had of late been secured to me by partial affection and Christian benevolence. My temper began to rebel; but struggles with my temper were now habitual with me. I drew a long breath, and renewed my animating dialogue. 'May I ask whether, in case Mrs Murray should not want my services, you think I am likely to find employment here as a governess?'

'Indeed I don't know. Few people like to take entire strangers into their families.'

'The same recommendation which introduced me to Mrs Murray, I can still command.'

'Hum.'

A long silence followed, for I had another conflict with my temper; but I was fully victorious before I spoke again.

'I am afraid, madam,' said I, 'that you will not think me entitled to use Mrs Murray's name with you so far as to beg that, upon her account, if you should hear of any situation in which I can be useful, you will have the goodness to recollect me.'

'It is not likely, Miss Percy, that I should hear of any thing to suit you. At any rate, I make it a rule never to interfere in people's domestic arrangements.'

My patience now quite exhausted, I took my leave with an air, I fear, not less ungracious than that of my hostess; and pursued my lonely way homewards, fully inclined to defer the revolting task of soliciting employment, till I should ascertain that Mrs Murray's plans made it indispensable.

How often, as I passed along the street, did I start, as my eye caught some slight resemblance to a known face, and sigh over the futility of my momentary hope! He who in the wildest nook of earth possesses one friend 'to whom he may tell that solitude is sweet,' knows not how cheerless it is to enter a home drearily secure from the intrusion of a friend. Yet, having now abundance of leisure for reflection, I should have been inexcusable, if I had made no use of this advantage; and if, in the single point of conduct which seemed left to my decision, I had acted with imprudence. There was evident impropriety in Murray's visits. To encourage his boyish admiration would have been cruel to him, ungenerous towards Mrs Murray, and incautious with respect to myself. It was hard, indeed, to resign the only social pleasure within my reach; but was pleasure to be deliberately purchased at the hazard of causing disquiet to the parent, and rebellion in the son? and this too by one engaged to exercise self-denial as the mere instrument of self-command? I peremptorily renounced the company of my young admirer; and whoever would know what this effort cost me, must reject earnest entreaty, and resist sorrowful upbraiding, and listen to a farewell which is the known prelude to utter solitude.

A dull unvaried week passed away, during which I never went abroad except to church. My landlady, indeed, insisted, that even women of condition might with safety and decorum traverse her native city unattended; and pointed out from my window persons whom she averred to be of that description; but the assured gait and gaudy attire of these ladies made me suspect that she was rather unfortunate in her choice of instances. At last, in a mere weariness of confinement, I one day consented to accompany her abroad.

We passed the singular bridge which delighted me with the strangely varied prospect of antique grandeur and modern regularity, – of a city cleft into a noble vista towards naked rock and cultivated plain,– seas busy with commerce, and mountains that shelter distant solitudes. I could scarcely be dragged away from this interesting spot; but my landlady, to whom it offered nothing new, was, soon after leaving it, much more attracted by a little scarlet flag, upon which was printed in large letters, 'A rouping in here.' This she told me announced a sale of household furniture, which she expressed much curiosity to see; and I suffered her to conduct me down a lane, or rather passage, so narrow as to afford us scarcely room to walk abreast, or light enough to guide us through the filth that encumbered our way. A second notice directed us to ascend a dark winding staircase; leading, as I afterwards learned, to the abodes of about thirty families. We had climbed, I think, about as high as the whispering gallery of St Paul's, when our progress was arrested by the crowd which the auction had attracted to one of the several compartments into which each floor seemed divided. I recoiled from joining a party apparently composed of the lowest orders of mankind. But my companion averring that in such places she could often make a good bargain, elbowed her way into the scene of action.

While I hesitated whether to follow her, my attention was caught by the beauty of a child, who now half hiding his rosy face on the shoulder of his mother, cast a side-long glance on the strangers, and now ventured to take a more direct view; while she, regardless of the objects of his curiosity, stood leaning her forehead against the wall in an attitude of quiet dejection. I watched her for a few moments, and saw the tears trickle from her face. So venerable is unobtrusive sorrow, that I could with more ease have accosted a duchess than this poor woman, though her dress denoted her to be one of those upon whom has fallen a double portion of the primeval curse. Her distress, however, did not seem so awe-inspiring to her equals; for one of them presently approaching, gave her a smart slap upon the shoulder, and, in a tone between pity and reproach, enquired, 'what ailed her?' The poor woman looked up, wiped the tears from her eyes, and faintly tried to smile. 'There is not much ails me,' said she; but the words were scarcely articulate.

'Many a one has been rouped out before now,' said the other.

The reflection was ill-timed; for my poor woman covered her face with her apron, and burst into a violent fit of sobbing. I had now found a person of whom I could more freely ask questions, which, indeed, all seemed eager to answer; and I quickly discovered that Cecil Graham, for so my mourner was called, was the wife of a soldier, whom the first and firmest sentiment of a Highlander had lured from his native glen to follow the banner of his chieftain; that when his regiment had been ordered abroad, she had unwillingly been left behind; that, in the decent abode which Highland frugality had procured for her, she had, by her labour, supported herself and two children; but that, on the night before her rent became due, she had been robbed of the little deposit which was meant to pay it; and that her landlord, after some months of vain delay, had availed himself of his right over the property of his debtor.

'And will he,' cried I, touched with a fellow-feeling, 'will he drive this poor young woman abroad among strangers! without a home or a friend! God forgive him.'

'I do not want for friends, and good friends, madam,' said the Highlander, in the strong accent of her country, but with far less of its peculiar pronunciation than disguised the language of her companions; 'all the streams of Benarde canna' wash my blood from the laird's himsel'.'

'What laird?' enquired I, smiling at the metaphorical language of my new acquaintance. 'Eredine himsel', lady; his grandfather and my great-grandmother were sister and brother childer:' meaning, as I afterwards found, that these ancestors were cousins.

'And will the laird do nothing for his relation?' said I.

'That's what *he* would, madam, and that indeed would *he*,' returned Cecil, laying an odd emphasis upon the pronoun, and gesticulating with great solemnity. 'He's no' the man to take the child out of the cradle and put out the smoke.'

'Why do you not apply to him then?'

'Indeed lady I'm no' going to trouble the laird. You see he might think that I judged he was like bound to uphold me and mine, because Jemmy was away wi' Mr Kenneth, ye see.'

'What then will you do? Will you allow yourself to be stripped of all?'

'If I could make my way home, lady,' returned the Highlander, 'I should do well enough; – we must not expect to be always full-handed. What I think the most upon is, that they should sell the bit cloth that mysel' span to row us in.'

'To roll you in!' repeated I, utterly unable to guess what constituted the peculiar value of this bit of cloth.

'Ay,' returned Cecil, 'to wind Jemmy and me in, with your leave, when we are at our rest; and a bonnier bit linen ye could na' see. The like of yoursel' might have lain in it, lady, or Miss Graham hersel'.'

I could scarcely help smiling at the tears which poor Cecil was now shedding over the loss of this strange luxury; and looked up to find some trace of folly in the countenance of one who, robbed of all her worldly possessions, bestowed her largest regrets upon a fine winding-sheet. But no trace of folly was there. The cool sagacity, indicated by the clear broad forehead and the distinct low-set eyebrow, was enlivened by the sparkle of a quick black eye; and her firm sharply chiseled face, though disfigured by its national latitude of cheek, presented a strong contrast to the dull vulgarity of feature which surrounded her. When my examination was closed, I enquired how far distant was the home of which she had spoken.

'Did you ever hear of a place they call Glen Eredine?' said Cecil, answering my question by another. 'It is like a hundred miles and a bit, west and north from this.'

'And how do you propose to travel so far at such a season?'

'If it be the will of the Best, I must just ask a morsel, with your leave, upon the way. I'll not have much to carry – only the infant on my breast, and a pickle snuff I have gathered for my mother. This one is a stout lad-bairn – God save him*; he'll walk on's feet a bit now and then.'

Though my English feelings revolted from the ease with which my

* No Highlander praises any living creature without adding this benediction. It is not confined, in its application, to human beings. If the subject of it belong to the speaker, this expression of dependence is intended to exclude boasting; if you commend what is the property of another, the Highland dread of an evil eye obliged you to intimate that you praise without envy. To be vain of a possession is justly considered as provoking Heaven to withdraw it, or to make it an instrument of punishment; and no true Highlander ever expected comfort in what had been envied or greedily desired by another.

Upon the same account, it is not judged polite to ask, nor safe to tell the number of a flock, or of a family. I once asked a countrywoman the number of a fine brood of chickens. 'They're as many as were gi'en,' said she; 'I'm sure I never counted them.'

Highlander condescended to begging, I could not help admiring the fortitude with which this young creature, for she did not seem above two-and-twenty, looked forward to a journey over frozen mountains, and lonely wilds; which she must traverse on foot, encumbered by two infants, and exposed to the rigour of a stormy season. I stood pondering the means of preventing these evils; and at last asked her 'whether the parish would not bestow somewhat towards procuring her a conveyance?'

'What's your will?' said Cecil, as if she did not quite comprehend me; though at the same time I saw her redden deeply.

Thinking she had misunderstood me, I varied the terms of my question.

Cecil's eyes flashed fire. 'The poor's box!' said she, breathing short from the effort to suppress her indignation, 'Good troth, there's nobody needs *even* me to the like. The parish, indeed! No, no, we have come to much; but we have no come to that yet:' she paused, and tears rose to her eyes. 'My dear dog*,' said she, caressing her little boy, 'ye shall want both house and hauld before your mother cast shame upon ye; and your father so far away.'

Confounded at the emotion which I had unwittingly occasioned, I apologised as well as I was able, assuring her that I had not the least intention to offend; and that in my country, persons of the most respectable character accounted it no discredit to accept of parish aid. At last I partly succeeded in pacifying my Highlander. 'To be sure,' said she, 'every place must have its *oun* fashion, and it may come easy enough to the like of *them*; but its no' to be thought that people that's come of respected gentles will go to *demean* themselves and all that belongs them.'

I was acknowledging my mistake, and endeavouring to excuse it upon the plea of a stranger's ignorance, when one of the crowd advanced to inform Cecil that her treasured web was then offering for sale; and, so far as I could understand the barbarous jargon of the speaker, seemed to urge the rightful owner to buy it back. Cecil's answer was rather more intelligible. 'Well, well,' said she, 'if it be ordained, mysel' shall lie in the bare boards; for that pound shall never be broken by me.'

'What pound?' enquired I.

'A note that Jemmy willed to his mother,' answered Cecil; 'and I

* Mo cuilean ghaolach. – *Gaelic.*

never had convenience to send her yet.'

She spoke with perfect simplicity, as if wholly unconscious of the generous fidelity which her words implied.

I had so long been accustomed to riches that I could not always remember my poverty. In five minutes I had glided through the crowd, purchased Cecil's treasure, restored it to its owner, and recollected that, without doing her any real service, I had spent what I could ill afford to spare.

The time had been when I could have mistaken this impulse of constitutional good nature for an act of virtue; but I had learnt to bestow that title with more discrimination. I was more embarrassed than delighted by the blessings which Cecil, half in Gaelic, half in English, uttered with great solemnity. 'Is it enough,' asked conscience, 'to humour the prejudices of this poor creature, and leave her real wants unrelieved?' – 'But can they,' replied selfishness, 'spare relief to the wants of others, who are themselves upon the brink of want?' – 'She is like you, alone in the land of strangers,' whispered sympathy. – 'She is the object,' said piety, 'of the same compassion to which you are indebted for life – life in its highest, noblest sense!' – 'Is it right,' urged worldly-wisdom, 'to part with your only visible means of subsistence?' – 'You have but little to give,' pleaded my better reason; 'seize then the opportunity which converts the mite into a treasure.' The issue of the debate was, that I purchased for poor Cecil the more indispensable articles of her furniture; secured for her a shelter till a milder season might permit her to travel more conveniently; and found my wealth diminished to a sum which, with economy, might support my existence for another week.

Much have I heard of the rewards of an approving conscience, but I am obliged to confess, that my own experience does not warrant my recommending them as motives of conduct. I have uniformly found my best actions, like other fruits of an ungenial climate, less to be admired because they were good, than tolerated because they were no worse. I suspect, indeed, that the comforts of self-approbation are generally least felt when they are most needed; and that no one, who in depressing circumstances enters on a serious examination of his conduct, ever finds his spirits raised by the review. If this suspicion be just, it will obviously follow, that the boasted dignity of conscious worth is not exactly the sentiment which has won so many noble triumphs over adversity. For my part, as I shrunk into my lonely chamber, and sighed over my homely restricted meal, I felt more consolation in remembering the goodness which clothes the unprofitable lily of the field, and feeds the improvident tenants of the air, than in exulting that I could bestow 'half my goods to feed the poor.'

That recollection, and the natural hilarity of temper which has survived all the buffetings of fortune, supported my spirits during the lonely days which passed in waiting Mrs Murray's reply. At length it came; to inform me, that the state of Captain Murray's health would induce my patroness to shun in a milder climate the chilling winds of a Scotch spring; to express her regrets for my unavailing journey, and for her own inability to further my plans; and, as the best substitute for her own presence, to refer me once more to the erect Mrs St Clare. This reference I at first vehemently rejected; for I had not yet digested the courtesies which I already owed to this lady's urbanity. But, moneyless and friendless as I was, what alternative remained? I was at last forced to submit, and that only with the worse grace for my delay.

To Mrs St Clare's then I went; in a humour which will be readily conceived by any one who remembers the time when sobbing under a sense of injury he was forced to kiss his hand and beg pardon. The lady's mien was nothing sweetened since our last interview. While I was taking uninvited possession of a seat, she leisurely folded up her work, pulled on her gloves, and crossing her arms, drew up into the most stony rigidity of aspect. Willing to despatch my business as quickly as possible, I presented Mrs Murray's letter, begging that she would consider it as an apology for my intrusion. 'I have heard from Mrs Murray,' said my gracious hostess, without advancing so much as a finger towards the letter which I offered. I felt myself redden, but I bit my lip and made a new attempt.

'Mrs Murray,' said I, 'gives me reason to hope that I may be favoured with your advice.'

'You are a much better judge of your own concerns, Miss Percy, than I can be.'

'I am so entirely a stranger here, madam, that I should be indebted to any advice which might assist me in procuring respectable employment.'

'I really know nobody just now that wants a person in your line, Miss Percy.' In my line! The phrase was certainly not conciliating. 'Indeed I rather wonder what could make my friend Mrs Murray direct you to me.'

'A confidence in your willingness to oblige her, I presume, madam,' answered I; no longer able to brook the cool insolence of my companion.

'I should be glad to oblige her,' returned the impenetrable Mrs St Clare; without discomposing a muscle except those necessary to articulation; 'so if I happen to hear of any thing in your way I will let you know. In the mean time, it may be prudent to go home to your friends, and remain with them till you find a situation.'

'Had it been possible for me to follow this advice, madam,' cried I, the scalding tears filling my eyes, 'you had never been troubled with this visit.'

'Hum. I suppose you have not money to carry you home. Eh?'

I would have retorted the insolent freedom of this question with a burst of indignant reproof; but my utterance was choked; I had not power to articulate a syllable.

'Though I am not fond of advancing money to people I know nothing about,' continued the lady, 'yet upon Mrs Murray's account here are five pounds, which I suppose will pay your passage to London.'

For more than a year I had maintained a daily struggle with my pride; and I fancied that I had, in no small degree, prevailed. Alas! occasion only was wanting to show me the strength of my enemy. To be thus coarsely offered an alms by a common stranger, roused at once the sleeping serpent. A sense of my destitute state, dependent upon compassion, defenceless from insult; a remembrance of my better fortune; pride, shame, indignation, and a struggle to suppress them all, entirely overcame me. A darkness passed before my eyes; the blood sprang violently from my nostrils; I darted from the room without uttering a word; and, before I was sensible of my actions, found myself in the open air.

I was presently surrounded by persons of all ranks; for the people of Scotland have yet to learn that unity of purpose which carries forward my townsmen without a glance to the right hand or the left; and I know not if ever the indisposition of a court beauty was enquired after in such varied tones of sympathy as now reached my ear. In a few minutes the fresh air had so completely restored me, that the only disagreeable consequence of my indisposition was the notice which it had attracted. I took refuge from the awkwardness of my situation in the only shop which was then within sight; and soon afterwards proceeded unmolested to my lonely home.

There I had full leisure to reconsider my morning's adventure. The time had been when the bare suspicion of a wound would have made my conscience recoil from the probe. The time had been when I would have shaded my eye from the light which threatened to show the full form and stature of my bosom foe; for then, a treacherous will took part against me, and even my short conflicts were enfeebled by relentings towards the enemy. But now the will, though feeble, was honest; and I could bear to look my sin in the face, without fear, that lingering love should forbid its extermination. A review of my feelings and behaviour towards Mrs St Clare brought me to a full sense of the unsubdued and unchristian temper which they betrayed. I saw that whilst I had imagined my 'mountain to stand strong,' it was yet heaving with the wreckful fire. I felt, and shuddered to feel, that I had yet part in the spirit of the arch-rebel; and I wept in bitterness of heart, to see that my reununciation of my former self had spared so much to show that I was still the same.

Yet had this sorrow no connection with the fear of punishment. I had long since exchanged the horror of the culprit who trembles before his judge, for the milder anguish which bewails offence against the father and the friend; and when I considered that my offences would cease but with my life, – that the polluted mansion must be rased ere the incurable taint could be removed, – I breathed from the heart the language in which the patriarch deprecates an earthly immortality; and even at nineteen, when the youthful spirit was yet unbroken, and the warm blood yet bounded cheerily, I rejoiced from the soul that I should 'not live alway.' Nor had my sorrow any resemblance to despair. A sense of my obstinate tendency to evil did but rouse me to resolutions of exertion; for I knew that will and strength to continue the conflict were a pledge of final victory.

Considering that humility, like other habits, was best promoted by its own acts, I that very hour forced my unwilling spirit to submission, by despatching the following billet to Mrs St Clare: –

> 'Madam, – Strong, and I confess blamable, emotion prevented me this morning from acknowledging your bounty, for which I am not certainly the less indebted that I decline availing myself of it. I feel excused for this refusal, by the knowledge that circumstances, with which it is unnecessary to trouble you, preclude the possibility of applying your charity to the purpose for which it was offered.

'I am, &c.

'ELLEN PERCY.'

If others should be of opinion, as I now am, that the language of this billet inclined more to the stately than the conciliating, let them look back to the time when duty, compassion, and gratitude, could not extort from me one word of concession to answer the parting kindness of my mother's friend. And let them learn to judge of the characters of others with a mercy which I do not ask them to bestow upon mine; let them remember that, while men's worst actions are necessarily exposed to their fellow-men, there are few who, like me, unfold their temptations, or record their repentance.

CHAPTER XXI

His years are young, but his experience old.
His head unmellowed, – but his judgment ripe.
And, in a word, (for far behind his worth,
Come all the praises that I now bestow,)
He is complete in feature and in mind,
With all good grace to grace a gentleman.

Shakspeare.

I WAS now in a situation which might have alarmed the fears even of one born to penury and inured to hardship. Every day diminished a pittance which I had no means of replacing; and, in an isolation which debarred me alike from sympathy and protection, I was suffering the penalty of that perverse temper, which had preferred exile among strangers to an imaginary degradation among 'my own people.'

As it became absolutely necessary to discover some means of immediate subsistence, I expended part of my slender finances in advertising my wishes and qualifications; but not one enquiry did the advertisement produce. Perhaps the Scottish mothers in those days insisted upon some acquaintance with the woman to whom they committed the education of their daughters, beyond what was necessary to ascertain her knowledge of the various arts of squandering time. I endeavourd to ward off actual want by such pastime work as had once ministered to my amusement, and afterwards to my convenience; but I soon found that my labours were as useless as they were light; for Edinburgh, at that time, contained no market for the fruits of feminine ingenuity.

In such emergency, it is not to be wondered if my spirits faltered.

My improvident lightness of heart forsook me; and though I often resolved to face the storm bravely, I resolved it with the tears in my eyes. I asked myself a hundred times a day, what better dependence I could wish than on goodness which would never withhold, and power which could never be exhausted? And yet, a hundred times a day I looked forward as anxiously as if my dependence had been upon the vapour tossed by the wind. I felt that, though I had possessed the treasures of the earth, the blessing of Heaven would have been necessary to me; and I knew that it would be sufficient, although that earth should vanish from her place. Yet I often examined my decaying means of support as mournfully as if I had reversed the sentiment of the Roman; and 'to live,' had been the only thing necessary.

I was thus engaged one morning, when I heard the voice of Murray enquiring for me. Longing to meet once more the glance of a friendly eye, I was more than half tempted to retract my general order for his exclusion. I had only a moment to weigh the question, yet the prudent side prevailed; because, if the truth must be told, I chanced just then to look into my glass; and was ill satisfied with the appearance of my swoln eyes and colourless cheeks; so well did the motives of my unpremeditated actions furnish a clue to the original defects of my mind. However, though I dare not say that my decision was wise, I may at least call it fortunate; since it probably saved me from one of those frothy passions which idleness, such as I was condemned to, sometimes engenders in the heads of those whose hearts are by nature placed in unassailable security,. This ordinary form of the passion was certainly the only one in which it could then have affected me; for what woman, educated as I had been, early initiated like me into heartless dissipation, was ever capable of that deep, generous, self-devoting sentiment which, in retirement, springs amid mutual charities and mutual pursuits; links itself with every interest of this life; and twines itself even with the hopes of immortality? My affections and my imagination were yet to receive their culture in the native land of strong attachment, ere I could be capable of such a sentiment.

As I persevered in excluding Murray, the only being with whom I could now exchange sympathies was my new Highland friend, Cecil Graham. I often saw her; and when I had a little conquered my disgust at the filth and disorder of her dwelling, I found my visits there as amusing as many of more 'pomp and circumstance.' She was to me an entirely new specimen of human character; an odd mixture of good sense and superstition, – of minute parsimony and liberal kindness, – of shrewd observation, and a kind of romantic abstraction from sensible objects. Every thing that was said or done, suggested to her memory an adventure of some 'gallant Graham,' or, to her fancy, the agency of some unseen being.

I had heard Maitland praise the variety, grace, and vigour of the Gaelic language. 'If we should ever meet again,' thought I, 'I should like to surprise him pleasantly;' so, in mere dearth of other employment, I obliged Cecil to instruct me in her mother-tongue. The undertaking was no doubt a bold one, for I had no access to Gaelic books; nor if I had, could Cecil have read one page of them, though she could laboriously decipher a little English. But I cannot recollect that I was ever deterred by difficulty. While Cecil was busy at her spinning, I made her translate every name and phrase which occurred to me; tried to imitate the uncouth sounds she uttered; and then wrote them down with vast expense of consonants and labour. My progress would, however, have been impossible, if Cecil's dialect had been as perplexing to me as that of the Lowlanders of her own rank. But though her language was not exactly English, it certainly was not Scotch. It was foreign rather than provincial. It was often odd, but seldom unintelligible. 'I learnt by book,' said she once when I complimented her on this subject; 'and I had a good deal of English; though I have lost some of it now, speaking among this uncultivate' people.'

Cecil, who had no idea that labour could be its own reward, was very desirous to unriddle my perseverance in the study of Gaelic. But she never questioned me directly; for, with all her honesty, Cecil liked to exert her ingenuity in discovering by-ways to her purpose. 'You'll be thinking of going to the North Country?' said she one day, in the tone of interrogation. I told her I had no such expectation. 'You'll may be get a good husband to take you there yet; and that's what I am sure I wish,' said Cecil; as if she thought she had invocated for me the sum of all earthly good.

'Thank you, Cecil; I am afraid I have no great chance.'

'You don't know,' answered Cecil, in a voice of encouragement. 'Lady Eredine hersel' was but a Southron, with your leave.'

I laughed; for I had observed that Cecil always used this latter form of apology when she had occasion to mention any thing mean or offensive. 'How came the laird,' said I, 'to marry one who was but a

Southron?'

'Indeed, she was just his fortune, lady,' said Cecil, 'and he could not go past her. And Mr Kenneth himsel' too is ordained, if he live, save him, to one from your country.'

'Have you the second-sight, Cecil, that you know so well what is ordained for Mr Kenneth?'

'No, no, lady,' said Cecil, shaking her head with great solemnity, 'if you'll believe me, I never saw any thing *by* common. But we have a word that goes in our country, that "a doe will come from the strangers' land to couch in the best den in Glen Eredine." And the wisest man in Killifoildich, and that's Donald MacIan, told me, that "the loveliest of the Saxon flowers would root and spread next the hall hearth of Castle Eredine." '

'A very flattering prophecy indeed, Cecil; and if you can only make it clear that it belongs to me, I must set out for Glen Eredine, and push my fortune.'

'That's not to laugh at, lady,' said Cecil very gravely; 'there's nobody can tell where a blessing may light. You might even get our dear Mr Henry himsel', if he knew but what a good lady you are.'

Now this 'Mr Henry himsel'' was Cecil's hero. She thought Mr Kenneth, indeed, entitled to precedence as the elder brother and heir-apparent; but her affections plainly inclined towards Henry. He was her constant theme. Wherever her tales began, they always ended in the praises of Henry Graham. She told me a hundred anecdotes to illustrate his contempt of danger, his scorn of effeminacy, his condescension and liberality; and twice as many which illustrated nothing but her enthusiasm upon the subject. Her enthusiasm had, indeed, warmth and nature enough to be contagious. Henry Graham soon ceased to be a mere stranger to me. I listened to her tales till I knew how to picture his air and gestures, – till I learned to anticipate his conduct like that of an old acquaintance; and till Cecil herself was not more prepared than I, to expect from him every thing noble, resolute, and kind.

To her inexpressible sorrow, however, this idol of her fancy was only an occasional visiter in Glen Eredine; for which misfortune she accounted as follows: –

'It will be twenty years at Michaelmas*, since some of that Clan Alpine, who, by your leave, were never what they should be, came

* 'The tract of country which has been described appears, however, to have enjoyed a considerable degree of tranquillity, till about the year 1746. At that time it became

and lifted the cattle of Glen Eredine; and no less would serve them but they took Lady Eredine's *oun* cow, that was called Lady Eredine after the lady's *oun* sel'. Well! you may judge, lady, if Eredine was the man to let them keep *that* with peace and pleasure. Good troth, the laird swore that he would have them all back, hoof and horn, if there was a stout heart in Glen Eredine. Mr Kenneth was in the town then at his learning; more was the pity – but it was not his fault that he was not there to fight for's *oun*. So the laird would ha' won the beasts home himsel', and that would *he*. But Mr Henry was just set upon going; and he begged so long and so sore, that the laird just let him take's will. Donald MacIan minds it all; for he was standing next the laird's own chair when he laid's hand upon Mr Henry's head, and says he, "Boy," says he, "I am sure you'll never shame Glen Eredine and come back empty-handed." And then his honour gave a bit nod with's head to Donald, as much as bid him be near Mr Henry; and Donald told me his heart grew great, and it was no gi'en him to say one word; but thinks he, "I shall be *cutted* in inches before he miss me away from him."

'So ye see, there were none went but Donald and three more; for Mr Henry said that he would make no more dispeace than enough; so much forethought had he, although he was but, I may say, a child; and Donald told me that he followed these cattle by the lay of the heather, just as if he had been thirty years of age; for the eagle has not an eye like his; ay, and he travelled the whole day without so much as stopping to break bread, although you may well think, lady, that, in those days, his teeth were longer than's beard. And at night he rolled him in's plaid, and laid him down with the rest, as many other good gentles have done before, when we had no inns, nor coaches, nor such like niceties.

'Well! in the morning he's astir before the roes; and, with grey light, the first sight he sees coming down Bonoghrie is the Glen

---

infested with a lawless band of depredators, whose fortunes had been rendered desperate by the event of 1745, and whose habits had become incompatible with a life of sobriety and honesty. These banditti consisted chiefly of emigrants from Lochaber, and the remoter parts of the Highlands.'

'In convenient spots they erected temporary huts, where they met from time to time, and regaled themselves at the expense of the peaceable and defenceless inhabitants. The ruins of these huts are still to be seen in the woods. They laid the country under contribution; and whenever any individual was so unfortunate as to incur their resentment, he might lay his account with having his cattle carried off before morning.' – *Graham's Sketches of Perthshire.*

Eredine cattle, and Lady Eredine the foremost. And there was Neil Roy Vich Roban, and Callum Dubh, and five or six others little worth, with your leave; and Donald knew not how many more might be in the shealing. Ill days were then; for the red soldier were come in long before that, and they had taken away both dirk and gun; ay, and the very claymore that Ronald Graham wagged in's hand o'er Colin Campbell's neck, was taken and a'. So he that was born to as many good swords, and targes, and dirks, as would have busked all Glen Eredine, had no a weapon to lift but what grew on's *oun* hazels! But the Grahams, lady, will grip to their foe when the death-stound's in their fingers. So Mr Henry he stood foremost, as was well his due; and he bade Neil Roy to give up these beasts with peace. Well! what think you, lady? the fellow, with your leave, had the face to tell the laird's son that he had ta'en, and he would keep. "If you can," quo' Mr Henry, "with your eight men against five." Then Neil he swore that the like should never be said of him; and he bade Mr Henry choose any five of his company to fight the Glen Eredine men. "A bargain!" says Mr Henry, "so Neil I choose you; and shame befa' the Graham that takes no the stoutest foe he finds." Och on! lady, if you did but hear Donald tell of that fight. It would make your very skin creep cold. Well, Mr Henry he held off himsel' so well that Neil at the length flew up in a rage, and out with's dirk to stick her in our sweet lamb's heart; but she was guided to light in's arm. Then Donald he got sight of the blood, and he to Neil like a hawk on a muir-hen, and gripped him with both's hands round the throat, and held him there till the dirk fell out of's fingers; and all the time Callum Dubh was threshing at Donald as had he been corn, but Donald never heeded. Then Mr Henry was so good that he ordered to let Neil go, and helped him up with's *oun* hand; but he flung the dirk as far as he could look at her.

'Well! by this time two of the Macgregors had their backs to the earth; so the Glen Eredine men that had settled them, shouted and hurra'd, and away to the cattle. And one cried Lady Eredine, and the other cried Dubhbhoidheach*; and the poor beasts knew their voices and came to them. But Mr Henry caused save Janet Donelach's cows first, because she was a widow, and had four young mouths to fill. Be's will, one way or other, they took the cattle, as the laird had said, hoof and horn; and the Aberfoyle men durst not lift a hand to hinder

* Black beauty – pronounced tu voiach.

them , because Neil had bound himsel' under promise, that none but five should meddle.'

'But Cecil,' interrupted I, growing weary of this rude story, 'what has all this to do with Henry Graham's exile from Glen Eredine?'

'Yes, lady,' answered Cecil, 'it has to do; for it was the very thing that parted him from's own. For, you see, the Southron sheriffs were set up before that time; and the laird himsel' could not get's will of any body, as he had a good right; for they must meddle, with your leave, in every thing. The thistle's beard must na' flee by, but they must catch and look into. So when the sheriff heard of the Glen Eredine spraith, he sent out the red soldiers, and took Neil Roy, and Callum Dubh, and prisoned them in Stirling Castle; and the word went that they were to be hanged, with your leave, if witness could be had against them; and Donald, and the rest of them that fought the Aberfoyle men, were bidden come and swear again' them. Then the word gaed that the sheriff would have Mr Henry too; but Lady Eredine being a Southron herself, with your leave, was always wishing to send Mr Henry to the strangers, so now she harped upon the laird till he just let her take her will.

'So, rather than spill man's life, Mr Henry left both friend and foster-brother, and them that could have kissed the ground he trode upon. Och hone! Either I mind that day, or else I have been well told of; for it comes like a dream to me, how my mother took me up in her arms, and followed him down the glen. Young and old were there; and the piper he went foremost, playing the lament. Not one spake above their breath. My mother wouldno' make up to bid farewell; but when she had gone till she was no' able for more, she stood and looked, and sent her blessing with him; wishing him well back, and soon. But the babies that were in arms that day ran miles to meet him the next time he saw Glen Eredine.'

'And what became of the two prisoners?' I enquired at the close of this long story.

' 'Deed, lady,' replied Cecil, 'they were just forced to let them out again; for two of our lads hid themselves not to bear witness; and as for Donald MacIan and Duncan Bane, they answered so wisely that nobody could make mischief of what they said. So Neil, that very night he was let out, he lifted four of the sheriff's cows, just for a warning to him; and drave them to Glen Eredine, in a compliment to Mr Henry.'

This tale, and twenty others of the same sort, while they

strengthened my interest in Cecil's hero, awakened some curiosity to witness the singular manners which they described. I was not aware how much the innovations and oppressions of twenty years had defaced the bold peculiarities of Highland character; how, stripped of their national garb, deprived of the weapons which were at once their ornament, amusement, and defence, this hardy race had bent beneath their fate, seeking safety in evasion, and power in deceit. Nor did I at all suspect how much my ignorance of their language disqualified me from observing their remaining characteristics.

But curiosity is seldom very troublesome to the poor; and the vulgar fear of want was soon strong enough to divert my interest from all that Cecil could tell me of the romantic barbarisms of her countrymen; or of the bright eye, the manly port, the primitive hardihood, and the considerate benevolence of Henry Graham.

I was soon obliged to apply to her for information of a different kind. My wretched fund was absolutely exhausted, and still no prospect opened of employment in any form. Having no longer the means of procuring a decent shelter, I seemed inevitably doomed to be destitute and homeless. One resource, indeed, remained to me in the plain but decent wardrobe which I had brought to Scotland. It is true, this could furnish only a short-lived abundance, since principle, no less than convenience, had prescribed to me frugality in my attire: but our ideas accommodate themselves to our fortunes; and I, who once should have thought myself beggared if reduced to spend 500*l.* a year, now rejoiced over a provision for the wants of one week as over treasure inexhaustible.

I found it easier, however, to resolve upon parting with my superfluous apparel, than to execute my resolution. Ignorant of the means of transacting this humbling business, I had not the courage to expose my poverty, by asking instructions. I often argued this point with myself; and proved, to my own entire conviction, that poverty was no disgrace, since it had been the lot of patriots, endured by sages, and preferred by saints. Nevertheless, it is not to be told with what contrivance I obtained from Cecil the information necessary for my purpose, nor with what cautious concealment I carried it into effect. Having once, however, conquered the first difficulties, I went on without hesitation: it was so much more easy to part with a superfluous trifle than to beg the assistance, or sue for the patronage, of strangers.

My last resource, however, proved even more transient than I had expected. I soon found it absolutely necessary to bend my spirit to my fortunes, and to begin a personal search for employment. On a stern wintry morning I set out for this purpose, with that feeling of dreary independence which belongs to those who know that they can claim no favour from any living soul. I applied at every music shop, and made known my qualifications at every boarding-school I could discover. At some I was called, with forward curiosity, to exhibit my talent; and the disgust of my forced compliance was heightened by the coarse applause I received. From some I was dismissed, with a permission to call again; at others I was informed that every department of tuition was already overstocked with teachers of pre-eminent skill.

At last I thought myself most fortunate in obtaining the address of a lady who wanted a governess for six daughters; but having examined me from head to foot, she dismissed me, with a declaration that she saw I would not do. Before I could shut the room-door, I heard the word 'beauty' uttered with most acrimonious emphasis. The eldest of the young ladies squinted piteously, and the second was marked with the small-pox.

All that I gained by a whole day wandering was the opportunity of economising, by remaining abroad till the dinner hour was past. Heroines of romance often show a marvellous contempt for the common necessaries of life; from whence I am obliged to infer that their biographers never knew the real evils of penury. For my part, I must confess that remembrance of my better days, and prospects of the dreary future, were not the only feelings which drew tears down my cheek, as I cowered over the embers of a fire almost as low as my fortunes, and almost as cold as my hopes. We generally make the most accurate estimate of ourselves when we are stripped of all the externals which serve to magnify us in our own eyes. I had often confessed that all my comforts were undeserved, – that I escaped every evil only by the mitigation of a righteous sentence; but I had never so truly felt the justice of this confession as now, when nothing was left me which could, by any latitude of language, be called my own. Yet, though depressed, I was not comfortless; for I knew that my deserts were not the measure of my blessings; and when I remembered that my severest calamities had led to substantial benefit, – that even my presumption and self-will had often been over-ruled to my advantage, – I felt at once a disposition to distrust my own judgment of present appearances, and an irresistible conviction that, however bereaved, I should not be forsaken. I fear it is not peculiar to me to reserve a real trust in Providence for the time which offers nothing else to trust. However, I mingled tears with prayers, and doubtful anticipation with acts of confidence, till, my mind as weary as my frame, I found refuge from all my cares in a sleep more peaceful than had often visited my pillow when every luxury that whim could crave waited my awaking.

I was scarcely dressed, next morning, when my landlady bustled into my apartment with an air of great importance. She seated herself with the freedom which she thought my situation entitled her to use; and abruptly enquired, whether I was not seeking employment as a governess? A sense of the helplessness and desolation which I had brought upon myself had so well subdued my spirit, that I answered this unceremonious question only by a meek affirmative. Mrs Milne then, with all the exultation of a patroness, declared that she would recommend me to an excellent situation; and proceeded to harangue concerning her 'willingness to befriend people, because there was no saying how soon she herself might need a friend.'

I submitted, resignedly enough, to the ostentation of vulgar patronage, while Mrs Milne unfolded her plan. Her sister, she told me, was waiting-maid to a lady who wanted a governess for her only child, – a girl about ten years old. She added, that believing me to have come into Scotland with a view to employment of that kind, she had mentioned me to this sister; who, she hinted, had no small influence with her mistress. Finally, she advised me to lose no time in offering my services; because, as Mrs Boswell's plan of education was now full four-and-twenty hours old, nobody who knew her could expect its continuance, unless circumstances proved peculiarly favourable to its stablity.

Though I could not help smiling at my new channel of introduction, I was in no situation to despise any prospect of employment; and I immediately proceeded to enquire into the particulars of the offered situation, and into my chance of obtaining it. I was informed that Mr Boswell, having, in the course of a long residence in one of the African settlements, realised a competent fortune, had returned home to spend it among his relations; that he was a good-natured, easy man, who kept a handsome establishment, loved quiet, a good dinner, and a large allowance of claret; that in the first of these luxuries he was rather sparingly indulged by his lady, who, nevertheless, was a very endurable sort of person to those who could suit themselves to her way. These, however, were so few, that but for one or two persons made obsequious by necessity, the Boswells would have eaten their ragouts and drunk their claret alone.

All this was not very encouraging; but it was not for me to startle at trifles; and I only expressed my fears that the recommendation of the waiting-maid might not be thought quite sufficient to procure for me such a trust as the education of an only child. 'Oh! for that matter,' said my landlady, 'if you put yourself in luck's way, you have as good a chance as another; for Mrs Boswell will never fash to look after only but them that looks after her.'

Agreeably to this opinion, I had no sooner swallowed my spare breakfast than I walked to George Square, to present myself to Mrs Boswell. I was informed at her door that she was in bed; but that if I returned about one o'clock, I should probably find her stirring. At the hour appointed, I returned accordingly; and, after some demur and consultation between the footman and the housemaid, I was shown into a handsome breakfast parlour, where, upon a fashionable couch, half sat, half lay, Mrs Boswell.

Her thin sharp face, high nose, and dark eyes, gave her at the first glance, an air of intelligence; but when I looked again, her curveless mouth, her wandering eyebrows, and low contracted forehead, obliged me to form a different judgment. The last impression was probably heightened by the employment in which I found her engaged. From a large box of trinkets which stood before her, she was bedizening herself and a pretty little fair-haired girl with every possible variety of bauble. Each was decked with at least half a dozen necklaces, studded all over with *mal-à-propos* clasps and broaches, and shackled with a multitude of rings and bracelets; so that they looked like two princesses of the South Sea Islands. All this was surveyed with such gravity and self-importance, as showed that the elder baby had her full share in the amusement.

Mrs Boswell did not rise to receive me; but she stirred, which was a great deal for Mrs Boswell. I made my obeisance with no very good will; and told her, that hearing she wanted a governess for Miss Boswell, I had taken the liberty to wait upon her.

Mrs Boswell only answered me by something which she intended for a smile. Most smiles express either benevolence or gaiety; but Mrs Boswell's did neither. It was a mere extension of the mouth; she never used any other. 'My pretty love,' said she, addressing herself to the child, 'will you go and tell Campbell to find my – a – my musk-box; and you can help her to seek it, you know.'

'No, I won't!' bawled the child; 'for I know you only want to send me away that you may talk to the lady about that nasty governess.'

'I an't going to talk about any nasty governess. Do go now, there's a dear; and I'll take you out in the carriage, and buy you another new doll, – a large one with blue eyes.'

'No you won't,' retorted miss; 'for you promised me the doll if I would learn to write *O*, and you did not give it me then; no more will you now.'

'A pretty ground-work for my labours!' thought I.

The altercation was carried on long and briskly, mingled with occasional appeals to me. 'Miss Percy, did you ever see such a child?'

'Oh yes, madam, – a great many such.'

'She has, to be sure, such an unmanageable temper! But then' (in a half whisper), 'the wonderfullest clever little creature! Now, do, Jessie, go out of the room when you are bid.'

At last, command and stratagem being found equally unavailing, Mrs Boswell was obliged to take the course which many people would have preferred from the first; and proceeded to her business in spite of the presence of Miss Jessie.

'Can you teach the *piano?*'

'I believe I understand music tolerably well; and though I am a very inexperienced teacher, I would endeavour to show no want of patience or assiduity.'

'And singing?' said Mrs Boswell, yawning.

'I have been taught to sing.'

'And French, and geography, and all the rest of it?'

I was spared the difficulty of answering this comprehensive question by my pupil elect, who by this time had sidled close up to me, and was looking intently in my face. 'You an't the governess your own self? Are you?' said she.

'I hope I shall be so, my dear.'

'I thought you had been an ugly cross old thing! You an't cross. Are you?'

'No. I do not think I am.'

'I dare say you are very funny and good-natured.'

Mrs Boswell gave me a glance which she intended should express sly satisfaction. 'You would like to *larn* music and every thing of that pretty lady, wouldn't you?' said she to her daughter.

'No. I would never like to *larn* nothing at all; but I should like her to stay with me, if she would play with me, and never bother me with that nasty spelling-book.'

'Well, she shan't bother you. Miss Percy, what terms do you expect?'

'These I leave entirely to you and Mr Boswell, madam. Respectable protection is the more important consideration with me.'

'To be sure protection is very important,' said Mrs Boswell, once more elongating her mouth; and she made a pause of at least five minutes, to recruit after such an unusual expense of idea. This time I employed in making my court so effectually to the young lady, that when her mother at last mentioned the time of my removal to George Square, she became clamorous for my returning that evening. A new set of stratagems was vainly tried to quiet my obstreperous inviter; and then mamma, as usual, gave up the point. 'Pray come to-night, if you can,' said she, 'or there will be no peace.'

CHAPTER XXII

Dependence! heavy, heavy, are thy chains,
And happier they who from the dangerous sea,
Or the dark mine, procure with ceaseless pains,
A hard-earned pittance – than who trust to thee.
Charlotte Smith.

By some untoward fate, the government of husbands generally falls into the hands of those who are not likely to bring the art into repute. Women of principle refuse the forbidden office; women of sense steadily shut their eyes against its necessity in their own case; warm affection delights more in submission than in sway; and against the influence of genius an ample guard is provided in the jealousy of man. Mrs Boswell being happily exempt from any of these disqualifications, did her best to govern her husband. There was nothing extraordinary in the attempt, but I was long perplexed to account for its success, for Mr Boswell was not a fool. The only theory I could ever form on the subject was, that being banished during his exile in the colony from all civilised society, having little employment, and none of the endless resource supplied by literary habits, Mr Boswell had found himself dependent for comfort and amusement upon his wife. She, on her part, possessed one qualification for improving this circumstance to the advancement of her authority; she was capable of a perseverance in sullenness, which no entreaties could move, and no submissions could mollify. She had, besides, some share of beauty; and though this was of course a very transient engine of conjugal sway, she gained perhaps as much from the power of habit over an indolent mind, as she lost by the invariable law of wedlock. Finally, where authority failed, Mrs Boswell could have recourse to cunning. A screw will often work where more direct force is useless; and whatever understanding Mrs Boswell possessed was of the tortuous kind. All her talents for rule, however, were exerted upon Mr Boswell. Her child, her servants, any body who would take the trouble, performed the same office for herself. Except when she was capriciously seized with a fit of what she thought firmness, clamour or flattery were all-prevailing with her.

The very first evening which I spent in her house, furnished me with a specimen of her habits. 'Will you begin French with Jessie to-morrow?' said she to me, with one of her most complaisant simpers.

'I should think, my darling,' said Mr Boswell, not much in the tone of a master, 'that, if you please, it may be as well to exercise her a little more in English first.'

'She can learn that at any time,' said Mrs Boswell, dismissing her smiles.

'Don't you think she had better begin with what is most necessary?' said the husband.

'We can't be losing Miss Percy's time with English,' returned the wife, without deigning to turn her eyes or her head.

Mr Boswell paused to recruit his courage; and then said meekly, 'I dare say Miss Percy will not consider her time as lost in teaching any thing you may think for the child's advantage.'

'Certainly not,' answered I; for Mr Boswell spoke with a look of appeal to me.

Mrs Boswell sat silent for five minutes, settling all the rings upon all her fingers. 'Any body can hear the child read,' said she, at last, without altering her tone or a muscle of her face.

'But Miss Percy's language and pronunciation are such admirable models, that ——' Mr Boswell stopped short, arrested by symptoms which I had not yet learned to discern. The lady uttered not another syllable, nor did she once raise her eyes till we were about to retire for the night.

'Shall I then give Miss Jessie a lesson in English grammar to-morrow morning?' said I, addressing myself to Mr Boswell; merely from a feeling that the father had a right to direct the education of his child.

'As – as you think best – as you please,' answered Mr Boswell hesitatingly; and casting towards his spouse a glance of timid enquiry, which she did not answer even by a look.

I attended her to her bedchamber, where to my great surprise she drew me in and hastily locked the door; leaving Mr Boswell, who was following close behind, to amuse himself in the lobby. She then seated herself; and, with all the coolness in the world, began talking to me of negroes, gold dust, and ivory. Presently Mr Boswell came, and gently requested admission. Of this request the lady took no notice whatever. Some time afterwards the summons was repeated, but still without effect. 'I am afraid I exclude Mr Boswell,' said I, rising and wishing her good night. 'Oh never mind,' said the lady, nodding her head, and endeavouring to look arch. Again I offered to go, but she would not allow me to move; and as she had put the key of the room-door into her pocket, I had no means of retreat. At last Mr Boswell, hopeless of effecting a lodgment in his own apartment, retired to another; and as soon as the lady had, by listening, ascertained this fact, she opened the door and permitted me to depart.

For four days Mrs Boswell never honoured her lord with the slightest mark of her notice. When he addressed her, whether in the tone of remark or of conciliation, she gave no sign of hearing. She would not even condescend to account for her behaviour by seeming out of humour; for to me she was all smiles and courtesy; and towards poor Mr Boswell she merely assumed an air of unconquerable nonchâlance. It was in vain that he acceded to his lady's plan for her daughter's studies. The obdurate fair was not so to be mollified. At length, on the fifth morning, she deigned to acknowledge his presence by a short and sullen answer to some trifle which he uttered. His restoration to favour, however, went on with rapid progression; and before evening the pair were upon the most gracious footing imaginable. Being now admitted behind the scenes, I was perfectly aware of the reason of this change. Mrs Boswell wanted money.

Indeed I was early made a sort of confidante; that is to say, Mrs Boswell told me all her likings and dislikes, all her husband's faults, and all her grounds of quarrel with his relations and her own. She unfolded to me, besides, many ingenious devices for managing Miss Jessie, for detecting the servants, and for cajoling Mr Boswell. I must own I never could discover the necessity for these artifices; but there is pleasure in every effort of understanding, and I verily believe these tricks afforded the only exercise of which Mrs Boswell's was capable.

It is not to be told with what disgust I contemplated this poor woman's character. Her uniform selfishness, her pitiful cunning, her feeble stratagems to compass baby ends, filled me with unconquerable contempt; a contempt which, indeed, I scarcely strove to repress. I imagined it to be the natural stirring of an honourable indignation. I often repeated to myself, that 'I would willingly serve the poor creature if I could.' I always behaved to her with such a show of deference as our mutual relation demanded, and thus concealed from myself 'what spirit I was of.' To forgive substantial injury is sometimes less a test of right temper than to turn an eye of Christian compassion upon the dwarfish distortion of a mind crippled in all its nobler parts.

But of all Mrs Boswell's perversions, the most provoking was her mischievous interference with my pupil. Either from jealousy of my influence, or from the mere habit of circumvention, a sort of intriguing was carried on, which the folly of the mother and the simplicity of the child constantly forced upon my notice. Some indulgence was bestowed, which was to be kept profoundly secret from the governess; or some neglected task was to be slily performed by proxy. If the child was depressed by a sense of my disapprobation, she was to be comforted with gingerbread and sugar-plums; and then exhorted to wash her mouth, that Miss Percy might not discover this judicious supply of consolation.

I believe it is a mistake to suppose that we are not liable to be angry with those whom we despise. I know I was often so much irritated by the petty arts of Mrs Boswell, that necessity alone detained me under her roof. I was the more harassed by her folly; because, duty apart, I had become extremely interested in the improvement of my young charge. The *elève* of such a mother was, of course, idle, sly, and self-willed; but Jessie was a pretty, playful creature, with capacity enough to show that talents are not hereditary, and such a strength of natural kindliness as had outlived circumstances the most unfavourable to its culture. This latter quality is always irresistible; and it was more particularly so to an outcast like myself, who had no living thing to love or trust.

But for this child, indeed, Mr Boswell's house would have been to me a perfect solitude. Mrs Boswell was utterly incapable of any thing that deserved the name of conversation. Six pages a week of a novel, or of the Lady's Magazine, were the utmost extent of her reading. She did nothing; therefore we could have no fellowship of employment. She thought nothing; therefore we could have no intercourse of mind. All her subjects of interest were strictly selfish; therefore we could not exchange sympathies. Either her extreme indolence, or a latent consciousness of inferiority, made her averse to the society of her equals in rank. Her ignorance or disregard of all established courtesies had banished from her table every guest, except one old maiden relative, whose circumstances obliged, and whose meanness inclined, her to grasp at the stinted civilities of Mrs Boswell. To extort even the slightest attention from Mr Boswell was, as I soon found, an unpardonable offence. Thus, though once more nominally connected with my fellow-creatures, I was, in fact, as lonely as when I first set foot upon a land where every face was new, and every accent was strange to me.

In the many thoughtful hours I spent, what lessons did not my proud spirit receive! All the comforts which I drew from human converse, or human affection, I owed to a child. For my subsistence I depended upon one of the most despicable of human beings. But my self-knowledge, however imperfect, was now sufficient to render me satisfied with any circumstances which tended to repress my prevailing sin; a temper from which I even then endeavoured to forebode final, though, alas! far-distant, victory.

Almost the only worldly interest or pleasure which remained for me to forego, I found myself obliged to sacrifice to my new situation. I could not introduce my pupil to the lowly habitation of my Highland friend; and I was too completely shackled to go abroad alone. Thus ended my expectations of reading Ossian in the original; and, what was perhaps a greater disappointment, thus perished my hopes of surprising Mr Maitland – if Maitland and I were ever again to meet. That we should meet I believe I entertained an undefined conviction; for I often caught myself referring to his opinions, and anticipating his decision. Unfortunately this belief had no rational foundation. It was merely the work of fancy, which, wandering over a world that to me had been desolated, could find no other resting-place.

Though I had no longer leisure to pursue my Gaelic studies, I could not entirely relinquish my interest in Cecil Graham; and I seized an hour to visit and bid her farewell, one morning while Mrs Boswell and my pupil were gone to purchase toys.

When I entered Cecil's apartment, she was kneading oat cakes upon the only chair which it contained, the litter upon her table not leaving space for such an operation; but on seeing me, she threw aside the dough; and pulling down a ragged stocking from a rope that stretched across the room, she wiped the chair, and very cordially invited me to sit down. 'Don't let me interrupt you, Cecil,' said I.

'Oh it's no interruption, lady,' returned Cecil. 'I'm sure ye have a lucky foot; and I was feared that I was no' to see you again, 'at I was.'

'Why did not you come and visit me then Cecil?'

' 'Deed lady, I was at your lodging one day; and they told me you were away, and where you were gone to; and I went two or three times and sat with the childer' upon the step of the door to see if you would, may be, come out; but I never had luck to see you.'

'Why did you not enquire for me?'

'I'se warrant, lady,' said Cecil, with a smile of proud humility, 'they might have thought a wonder to see the like of me enquiring for you. But much thought have I had about you. They say "cold is the breath of strangers*;" but troth, if you like to believe me, my heart warmed to you whenever I saw you first.

'Truly, Cecil, I like very much to believe you; for there are not many hearts that warm to me.'

'I'se tell you, lady, the last time I saw you, ye were no like yoursel'; ye were a white's canna†; and I just thought that, may be, an ill ee, with your leave, had taken you.'

'Does an evil eye injure the complexion of any body except the owner, think you, Cecil?' said I.

'An eye will split a stone‡, as they'll say in Glen Eredine,' said Cecil, shaking her head very gravely. 'But I have something, if you would please to accept; she hit mysel' just on the coat, with your leave, one night going through under the face of Benarde,' While she spoke she was searching about her bed, and at length produced a small stone shaped somewhat like a gun flint.§ 'Now,' proceeded she, 'ye'll just sew that within the lining of your stays, lady; or, with your leave, in the band of your petticoat; and there'll nobody *can* harm you.'

* Is fuar gaoth nan coimheach.

† The down of a plant.

‡ Sgoltich suil a chlach.

§ Elfin *arrow*; more properly, elfin 'bolt.' The Gaelic term signifies, 'that which can be darted with destructive force;' there is, therefore, no reason to expect, that these weapons should be feathered and barbed like common arrows. These bolts are believed to be discharged by fairies with deadly intent. Nevertheless, when once in the possession of mortals, they are accounted talismans against witchcraft, evil eyes, and elfish attacks. They are especially used in curing all such diseases of cattle as may have been inflicted by the malice of unholy powers.

'Thank you, Cecil. But if I rob you of this treasure, who knows how far your own good fortune may suffer?'

'Oh laogh mo chridhe*,' cried Cecil affectionately, 'its good my part to venture any thing for your sake; and if it just please Providence to keep us till we be at Glen Eredine, I'll, may be, get another.'

I could not help smiling at Cecil's humble substitute for the care of Providence, and inwardly moralising upon the equal inefficacy of others which are in more common repute. But as a casual attempt to correct her superstition would have been more likely to shake her confidence in myself than in the elfin arrow, I quietly accepted of her gift; enquiring when she would be in a situation to replace it.

'I don't know, lady,' answered Cecil with a sigh. 'The weather's clear and bonny, and I am wearying sore for home; but – but I'm half feared that Jemmy might no be easy, ye see, when he heard that I was at Eredine.'

'How should it make your husband uneasy to hear that you were at home?'

'I don't know,' said Cecil, looking down with a faint smile, and stopped; then sighing deeply, she proceeded, relieving her embarrassment by twisting the string of her apron with great industry. 'Ye see, lady, I have a friend in Glen Eredine, – I – I –'

'So much the better, Cecil. That cannot surely be an objection to your going thither.'

'I mean, – I would say, a lad like that – I should have married, if it had been so ordered.' Cecil stopped, and sighed again.

'And do you think your husband would scruple to trust you, Cecil?' said I.

Her embarrassment instantly vanished, and she looked up steadily

---

The author is in possession of one of these talismans; which connoisseurs affirm to be no common elfin arrow, but the weapon of an elf of dignity. It was hurled at a country beauty, whose charms had captivated the Adonis of the district. The elf being enamoured of this swain, projected a deadly attack upon her rival. But these arrows are lethal only when they smite the uncovered skin. This proved the security of the Gaelic Phillis. The weapon struck her petticoat; she instantly possessed herself of the talisman, and was ever afterwards invulnerable to the attacks of fairies.

Within these twenty years, a staunch Highlander contrived to make her way into a bridal chamber; and, slitting the bride's new corsets, introduced an elfin arrow between the folds. The lady, feeling some inconvenience from this unusual addition to her dress, removed the charm; in consequence of which rash act she has proved childless!

* A common term of endearment – literally, 'Calf of my heart.'

in my face. 'No, no, lady!' said she, 'I'll never think such a thought of him. He's no' so ill-hearted. But he would think that I might be dowie* there, and he so far away;; for it's a sore heart to me, that the poor lad has never been rightly himsel', since my father bade marry Jemmy. And he'll no be forbidden to stand and look after me, and to make of little Kenneth there, and fetch hame our cows at night. And ever since my father died, he'll no be hindered to shear† my mother's peats, although I have never spoken one word to him, good or bad, since that day that ——'

Cecil paused, and drew her sleeve across her eyes. 'It was so ordered,' said she, 'and all's for the best.'

'Yes, but, Cecil, were not you a little hard-hearted, to forsake such a faithful lover?'

'Ochone! lady, what could I do? It was well kent he was no fitting for me. His forbeers were but strangers, with your leave; and though I say it, I'm, sib‡ to the best gentles in the land. So you see my father would never be brought in.'

'And you dutifully submitted to your father!' said I, my heart swelling as I contrasted the filial conduct of this untutored being with my own.

'Woe's me, lady, – I was his own; – he had a good right that I should do his bidding. And besides that, I knew that Robert was no ordained for me; – well knew I that, – that I knew well.' And while I was musing upon my ill-fated rebellion, Cecil kept ringing changes upon these words; for she would rather have repeated the same idea twenty times, then have allowed of a long pause in conversation, where she was the entertainer.

'How did you discover,' I enquired at length, 'that there was a decree against your marrying Robert?'

'I'se tell you, lady,' answered Cecil, lowering her voice; 'we have a seer* in Glen Eredine; and he was greatly troubled with me plainly standing at Jemmy's left hand. And first he saw it in the morning, and always farther up in the day, as the time came near. So he had no freedom in his mind but to tell me. Well, when I heard it, I fell down just as I had been shot; for I knew then what would be. But we must all have our fortune, lady. No' that I'm reflecting; for Jemmy's a good

* Low-spirited.
† Cut her turf for firing.
‡ Related.
* One who has the second-sight.

man to me; and an easy life I have had with him.'

'That is no more than you deserve, Cecil. A dutiful daughter deserves to be a happy wife.'

'Well, now, that's the very word that Miss Graham said, when she was that humble as to busk my first curch[†] with her *oun* hand; ay that's what she did; and when she saw me sobbing as my heart would break; hersel' laid her *oun* arm about my neck; and says she, just as had I been her equal, "My dear Cecil," says she. The Lord bless her! I thought more of these two words, than of all the good plenishing[*][‡] she gave me. But for a' that, I had a sorrowful time of it at the first; and a sorrowfuller wedding was never in Glen Eredine, altho' Mr Henry was the best man himsel'; for you see, Jemmy's his foster-brother.'

† Until very lately, no unmarried woman in the Highlands wore any covering on the head; not even at church, or in the open air. A *snood*, or bandeau of riband or worsted tape, was the only head-dress for maidens. On the morning after marriage, the cap or curch was put on with great ceremony, and the matron never again appeared without this badge of subjection.

In some parts of the Highlands it is still customary to delay the wedding for weeks, often for months after the ceremony of marriage has taken place. The interval is spent by the bride in preparing her bed, bedding, &c. which it is always her part to supply. The wedding is, with a coolness of calculation which might satisfy Mr Malthus, generally postponed till the end of harvest, when labour is scarce, and provisions plentiful. About a week before the bride's removal to her new home, the bridegroom and she go separately to invite their acquaintance, sometimes to the number of hundreds, to the wedding. The bride's approach to her future dwelling is preceded by that of her household stuff; which affords the grand occasion of display for Highland vanity. The furniture is carefully exhibited upon a cart; always surmounted by a spinning-wheel, the *rock* loaded with as much lint as it can carry. It is accompanied by the bride's nearest female relative, and attended by a piper to announce its progress. The procession is met and welcomed by the bridegroom and a few select friends.

The ceremonial of the wedding is conducted exactly according to Cecil's statement.

The next morning, the matrons of the neighbourhood commence a visiting acquaintance, by breakfasting with the married pair; each bringing with her a present suited to her means, such as lint, pieces of linen, or dishes of various sorts. Some of these good women generally 'busk the bride's first curch.' The hair, which the day before hung down in tresses mixed with riband, is now rolled tightly up on a wooden bodkin, and fixed on the top of the head. It is then covered with the curch; a square piece of linen doubled diagonally, and passed round the head close to the forehead. Young women fasten the ends behind; the old wear them tied under the chin. The corner behind hangs loosely down. Thus attired, the bride sits in state, without engaging in any occupation whatever, until she be 'kirked.' If, however, it happens that the parish church is vacant, or if it be otherwise inconvenient to attend public worship, this ceremony can be supplied by her walking three times round the church, or any of the consecrated ruins with which the Highlands abound.

‡ Household furniture.

'The best man? Cecil; I do not understand you. I should have thought the bridegroom might be the most important personage for that day at least.'

Cecil soon made me comprehend, that she meant a brideman; whose office, she said, was to accompany the bridegroom when he went to invite guests to his wedding, and to attend him when he conducted his bride to her home. She told me, that, according to the custom of her country, her wedding was not celebrated till some weeks after she had taken the vows of wedlock; the Highland husband, once secure of his prize, prudently postponing the nuptial festivities and the honey-moon, till the close of harvest brought an interval of leisure. Meanwhile, the forsaken lover, whose attachment had become respectable by its constancy, as well as pitiable by its disappointment, was removed from the scene of his rival's success by the humanity of Henry Graham, who contrived to employ him in a distant part of the country. But, in the restlessness of a disordered understanding, poor Robert left his post; wandered unconsciously many a mile; and reached his native glen on the day of Cecil's wedding.

By means of much rhetoric and gesticulation upon Cecil's part, and innumerable questions upon mine, I obtained a tolerably distinct idea of the ceremonial of this wedding. Upon the eventful morning, the reluctant bride presided at a public breakfast, which was attended by all her acquaitnance, and honoured by the presence of 'the laird himsel'.' I will not bring discredit upon the refinement of my Gael, by specifying the materials of this substantial repast, as they were detailed to me with *naïve* vanity by Cecil; but I may venture to tell, that, like more elegant fetes of the same name, it was succeeded by dancing. 'I danced with the rest,' said Cecil, 'tho', with your leave, it made my very heart sick; and many a time I though, oh, if this dancing were but for my lykwake.'* The harbingers of the bridegroom, (or, to use Cecil's phrase, the *send*,) a party of gay young men and women, arrived. Cecil, according to etiquette, met them at the door, welcomed, and offered them refreshments; then turned

* Latewake. Watching a corpse before interment. Dancing on these occasions was once customary, though this practice is now discontinued.

'It was a mournful kind of movement, but still it was dancing. The nearest relation of the deceased often began the ceremony weeping; but did, however, begin it, to give the example of fortitude and resignation.' – *Mrs Grant's Essays on the Superstitions of the Highlanders*, vol. i, p. 188.

from them, as the prisoner from one who brings his death-warrant, struggling to gather decent fortitude from despair.

At last the report of a musket announced the approach of the bridegroom; and it was indispensable that the unwilling bride should go forth to meet him. 'The wind might have blawn me like the withered leaf,' said Cecil, 'I was so powerless; but Miss Graham thought nothing to help me with her *oun* arm. Jemmy and I *may* be lucky,' continued she, with a boding sigh; 'but I am sure it was an unchancy place where we had luck to meet; – just where the road goes low down into Dorch'thalla†; the very place where Kenneth Roy, that was the laird's grandfather, saw something that he followed for's ill; and it beguiled him over the rock, where he would have been dashed in pieces though he had been iron. The sun never shines where he fell, and the water's aye black there. Well, it was just there that Jemmy had luck to get sight of us; so then, ye see, he ran forward to meet me, as the custom is in our country. Oh, I'll never forget that meeting!' Cecil stopped, shuddering with a look of horror, which I dared not ask her to explain. 'He took off his bonnet,' she continued, 'to take, with your leave, what he never took off my mouth before; but, – oh, I'll never forget that cry! It was like something unearthly. "Cecil! Cecil!" it cried; and when I looked up, there's Robert, just where the eagle's nest was wont to be; he was just setting back's foot, as he would that moment spring down.'

'Did you save him?'

'I, lady! I could not have saved him though he had lighted at my foot. I could do nothing but hide my eyes; and my hands closed so hard, that the nails drew the very blood!'

'Dreadful!' I exclaimed, Cecil's infectious horror making the scene present to me, – 'could nobody save him?'

'Nobody had power to do ought,' answered Cecil, 'save Mr Henry, that's always ready for good. He spoke with a voice that made the craigs shake again; and they that saw his eyes, saw the very fire, as he looked steadily upon Robert, and waved him back with's arm. So then the poor lad was not so *un*sensible, but he knew to do *his* bidding, for they're no born that dare gainsay *him*. And then Mr Henry rounded by the foot of the craig, and up the hill as he'd been a roe; and he caused Robert go home with him to the Castle, and caused keep him there, because he could no settle to work. No'

† The Dark Den.

that he's *un*sensible, except when a notion takes him. There's a glen where we were used to make carkets* when we were herds; and he'll no let the childer' pluck so much as a gowan there; and ever since the lightning tore the great oak, he'll sit beside her sometimes the summer's day, and calls her always "Poor Robert." '

* Garlands of flowers for the neck.

CHAPTER XXIII

Not quite an idiot; for her busy brain
Sought, by poor cunning, trifling points to gain;
Success in childish projects her delight.

—— So weak a mind,
No art could lead, and no compulsion bind.
The rudest force would fail such mind to tame,
And she was callous to rebuke and shame.

Crabbe.

CECIL'S tale, which included all the evening festivities, – the ball, – the throwing of the stocking, and the libation of whisky, which was dashed over the married pair, detained me so long, that Mrs Boswell and my pupil were at home an hour before me. Mrs Boswell, however, received me with her usual simper; and suffered the evening to arrive before she began to investigate, with great contrivance and circumlocution, the cause of my unusual absence. Though provoked at her useless cunning, I readily told her where I had been. But, though the lady had taken me into high favour, and made me the depository of fifty needless secrets, I saw that she did not believe a word of my statement; for Mrs Boswell was one of the many whose defects of the head create a craving for a confidant, while those of the heart will never allow them to confide. Perceiving that my word was doubted, I disdained further explanation; and suffered Mrs Boswell to hint and soliloquise without deigning reply.

The little dingy cloud, which scarcely added to their accustomed dulness, was beginning to settle on the features of my hostess, when another attack was made upon her good humour. My pupil, in a romping humour which I could not always restrain, pulled out the comb that confined my hair; which unfortunately extorted from Mr Boswell a compliment on its luxuriance and beauty. Now Mrs Boswell's *chevelure* happened to have an unlucky resemblance to that of a dancing-bear; a circumstance which I verily believe her poor husband had forgotten, when he incautiously expressed admiration of auburn curls. The lady's face was for once intelligible; her lips grew actually livid; and for some moments she seemed speechless. At last she sbroke forth. 'Her hair may well be pretty,' said she; 'I am sure it costs her pains enough.'

With a smile, more I fear of sarcasm than of good-humour, I thanked her for helping me to some merit, where I was ignorant that I could claim any. Mrs Boswell, either fearing to measure her powers of impertinence with mine, or finding sullenness the most natural expression of her displeasure, made no reply; but sat for a full hour twisting the corner of her pocket-handkerchief, without raising her eyes, or uttering a syllable. At last, she suddenly recovered her spirits; and for the rest of the evening was remarkably gracious and entertaining.

I was not yet sufficiently acquainted with Mrs Boswell to perceive any thing ominous in this change. The next day, however, while I was alone with my pupil, the child began to frolic round me with a pair of scissors in her hand; making a feint, as if in sport, to cut off my hair. A little afraid of such a play-thing, I desired her to desist; speaking to her, as I always did, in a tone of kindness. 'Would you be very sorry,' said she, clasping her arms round my neck, and speaking in a half whisper, 'very, very sorry if all your pretty curls were cut off?'

'Indeed, Jessie,' answered I smiling, 'I am afraid I should; more sorry than the matter would deserve.'

'Then,' cried the child, throwing away the scissors, 'I won't never cut off your hair; not though I should be bid a thousand thousand times.'

'Bid!' repeated I, thrown off my guard by astonishment; 'who could bid you do such a thing?'

'Ah! I must not tell you that, unless you were to promise upon your word ——'

'No,' interrupted I. 'Do not tell me. Be honourable in this at least. And another time, if you wish to injure me, do so openly. I will endure all the little evil in your power to inflict, rather than you should grow up in the habits of cunning.'

That a mother should thus lay a snare for the rectitude of her child, must have appeared incredible, could the fact have admitted of a doubt. I had still too many faults myself to look with calmness upon those of others; and I was seriously angry. 'How is it possible,' thought I, 'to form in this child the habits of rectitude, while I am thus provokingly counteracted; and useless as I am compelled to be, how can I endure to receive the bread of dependence from a creature whose mischief has neither bound nor excuse, except in the weakness of her understanding?' In the height of my indignation, I resolved to upbraid Mrs Boswell with her baseness and folly, and then resign my hopeless task. But I had so often and so severely smarted for acting under irritation, that the lesson had at length begun to take effect; and I recollected that it might be wise to defer my remonstrances till I could suppress a temper which was likely to render them both imprudent and useless. I fear my forbearance was somewhat aided by considering the consequences of renouncing my present situation. However, when I was cool, I conducted my reproofs with what I thought great address. I hid my offending ringlets under a cap, and never more exposed them to the admiration of Mr Boswell. It would have been mere waste of oratory to harangue to Mrs Boswell upon the meanness of artifice; and rather uncivil, all things considered, to talk to her of its inseparable connection with folly; but I represented to her, that the time might come when her daughter would turn against her the arts which she had taught. A fool can never divest an argument of its reference to one particular case. 'If she should cut off my hair,' said the impracticable Mrs Boswell, 'I shan't care much, for wigs are coming into fashion.'

'But if even in trifles she learn to betray, how can you be sure that, in the most important concerns of life, she will not play the traitress?'

'Oh no fear,' cried Mrs Boswell, nodding her head as she always did when she meant to look sagacious; 'I shall be too knowing for her, I warrant.'

'A blessed emulation!' thought I.

Our dialogue was interrupted by the entrance of Mr Boswell, whose features seemed animated by some incipient scheme. He took his place beside his mate, and forthwith began to toy and flatter; looking, however, as if he would fain have ventured to change the subject. At length the secret came forth. He had met a college companion, with whom he had a great inclination to dine that day. Mrs Boswell said nothing; but she looked denial. Mr Boswell sat silent for a little, and then renewed his manœuvres. The praises of a favourite cap soothed the lady into quiescence; for good-humour is too lively a term to express the more amiable turns of Mrs Boswell's temper. The petitioner seized the favourite moment. 'I should really like to dine with poor Tom Hamilton to-day.' said he.

'Poor fiddlesticks!' returned the polite wife. 'What have you to do dining with Tom Hamilton?'

'I don't know, my love: we have not met for twenty years; and he pressed me so much to come and talk over old stories, that – that I was obliged to give him a kind of half-promise.'

'Nonsense!' quoth the lady, with a decisive tone and aspect; and poor Mr Boswell, with a sigh of resignation, moved his chair towards the fire-place, and began to draw figures in the ashes.

Whether this operation assisted his courage, I know not; but, in about ten minutes, he told me, in a half whisper, 'that, if I would entertain Mrs Boswell, he rather thought he would dine with Tom Hamilton.'

'And why should you not? For a husband to go out, it is sufficient that he wills it,' said I; parodying a maxim which was at that time the watchword of a more important revolt. I fancy the smile which accompanied my words was, for the moment, more terrific to Mr Boswell than his lady's frown, for he instantly left us; and having secured his retreat beyond the door, put his head back into the room, saying, with a farewell nod, and a voice of constrained ease. '*Au revoir*, my darling! I dine with Hamilton.'

'Why, Mr Boswell!' screamed the wife, in a tone between wrath and amazement; but the rebel was beyond recall.

The lady was forthwith invested with an obstinate fit of the sullens. Considering me as the cause of her husband's misconduct, she suffered dinner and some succeeding hours to pass without deigning me even a look or a word. My forte, certainly, was not submission; therefore, after speaking to her once or twice without receiving an answer, I made no further effort to soothe her, but amused myself with reading, work, or music, exactly as if Mrs Boswell's chair had been vacant. She made several attempts to disturb my amusement: she spilled the ink upon my clothes. But though she made no apology, I assured her, with wicked good-humour, that a farthing's worth of spirit of salt would repair the disaster. She beat poor Fido; yet even this did not provoke me to speak. She could not make me angry; because, by showing me that such was her purpose, she engaged my pride to disappoint her. Left to itself, her temper at last made a tolerable recovery; or, rather, she spared me, that she might discharge its full venom upon Mr Boswell.

At a late hour the culprit returned; fortified, as it appeared, by a double allowance of claret, but in high spirits and good-humour. Forgetting that he was in disgrace, he walked as directly as he could towards his offended fair; and, with a look of stupid kindness, offered her his hand. The lady flounced away with great disdain. 'Come now, my darling,' stammered the husband, coaxingly; 'don't be cross. Be a good girl, and give me a kiss.'

'Brute!' replied the judicious wife, giving him a push, which, with the help of the extra bottle, made him stagger to the other side of the room. There he placed himself beside me; protesting that I was a sweet, lovely, good-humoured creature, and that he was sure I had never been out of temper in my life; with many other equally well-turned compliments. This was the consummation of his misdeeds. Mrs Boswell pulled the bell till the wire broke. 'Put that creature to bed,' said she to the servant; 'don't you see he's not fit to be any where else?' Mr Boswell was not so much intoxicated as to be insensible to this indignity, which he angrily resisted; while, shocked and disgusted beyond expression, I escaped from the scene of this disgraceful altercation.

The next day Mrs Boswell had recourse, as usual, to silent sullenness; to which she added another mode of tormenting. She constantly held her handkerchief to her eyes, and affected to shed tears. All this, however, was reserved for Mr Boswell's presence, as she soon discovered that it was needless to waste either anger or sensibility upon me. Lest her distress should not sufficiently aggravate the culprit's self-reproach, she pretended that her health was affected by her feelings. It was always one of her Lilliputian ambitions to obtain the reputation of a feeble appetite. But now this infirmity increased to such a degree, that Mrs Boswell absolutely could not swallow a morsel; nor, which was much worse, could she see food tasted by another without demonstrations of loathing. Nevertheless, she regularly appeared at table; and, for three days, every meal was disquieted by the landlady's disgust at our voracity.

Poor Mr Boswell, now completely quelled, did what man could do to restore peace and appetite. He coaxed, entreated; and offered her, I believe, all the compounds recorded in all the cookery books; but in vain. Deaf as the coldest damsel of romance to the prayer of offending love was Mrs Boswell. She retained her youthful passion for sweetmeats; and her good-natured husband came one morning into her dressing-room fraught with such variety of confections, that I was surprised at the self-command with which she refused them all. I could not help laughing to see him court the great baby with sugar-plums; she answering, like any other spoilt child, only by twisting her face, and thrusting forward her shoulder; nor was my gravity at all improved when Fido, making his way into some concealment, drew forth the remains of a portly sirloin.

Mr Boswell looked as if he would fain have joined in my laugh; but he foresaw the coming storm, and prudently effected his retreat. Mrs Boswell's face grew livid with rage. She snatched the poker; and would have struck the poor animal dead, had I not arrested her arm. 'Stop, woman!' said I, in a voice at which I myself was almost startled; 'degrade yourself no further.' It is not the rage of such a creature as Mrs Boswell that can resist the voice of stern authority. Her eye fixed by mine as by the gaze of a rattle-snake, she timidly laid aside her weapon; and shrunk back, muttering that she did not mean to hurt my dog.

From that time Mrs Boswell discovered a degree of enmity towards the poor animal, which I could not have imagined even her to feel towards any thing less than a moral agent. Not that she avowed her antipathy; but I now knew her well enough to detect it even in the caresses which she bestowed on him. She was constantly treading on him, scalding him, tormenting him in every possible way, all by mere accident; and if I left him within her reach, I was sure to be recalled by his howlings. The poor animal cowered at the very sight of her. At last he was provoked to avail himself of his natural means of defence; and one evening, when she had risen from her sofa on purpose to stumble over him, he bit her to the bone.

The moment she recovered from the panic and confusion which this accident occasioned, she insisted upon having the animal destroyed, upon the vulgar plea, that, if he should ever go mad, she must immediately be affected with hydrophobia. Pitying her uneasiness, I at first tried to combat this ridiculous idea; but I soon found that she was determined to resist conviction. 'All I said might be true, but she had heard of such things; and, for her part, she should never know rest or peace, while the life of that animal left the possibility of such a horrible catastrophe.' At last I was obliged to tell her peremptorily that nothing should induce me to permit the destruction of my poor old favourite,– the relic of better times, the last of my friends. I humoured her folly, however, so far as to promise that I would find a new abode for him on the following day. Mrs Boswell was relentlessly sullen all the evening; but I was inflexible.

The only way which occurred to me of disposing of poor Fido was to commit him to the care of Cecil Graham, at least till she should leave Edinburgh. In the morning, therefore, I prepared for a walk, intending to convey my favourite to his new protectress. My pupil was, as usual eager to accompany me; and when I refused to permit her, she took the course which had often led her to victory elsewhere, and began to cry bitterly. This, however, was less effectual with me than with her mother. I persisted in my refusal; telling her that her tears only gave me an additional motive for doing so, since I loved her too well to encourage her in fretfulness and self-will. Mrs Boswell, however, moved somewhat by her child's lamentations, but more by rivalry towards me, soothed and caressed the little rebel; and finally insisted that I should yield the point. Angry as I was, I commanded my temper sufficiently to let the mother legislate for her child; and submitted in silence. But when we were about to set out, Fido was no where to be found. After seeking him in vain, I would have given up my expedition; but Mrs Boswell would not suffer Jessie to be disappointed, so we departed.

I found Cecil's apartment vacant, and all its humble furniture removed. I comprehended that she had returned to her native wilds; and I felt that the connection must be slight indeed which we can without pain see broken for ever! She was gone, and had not left among the thousands, whose hum even now broke upon my ear, one being who would bestow upon me a wish or a care. 'Poor feeble Ellen!' said I to myself, as I dashed the tears from my eyes, 'where foundest thou the disastrous daring which could once renounce the charities of nature, and spurn the intercourse of thy kind?'

A natural feeling leading me to enquire into the particulars of Cecil's departure, I made my way to an adjoining apartment, which was occupied by another family.

On my first entrance, the noisome atmosphere almost overcame me; and, unwilling to expose my little charge to its effects, I desired her to remain without, and wait my return; but her morning's lesson of disobedience had not been lost, and I presently found her at my side.

In answer to my enquiries, the people of the house told me that Cecil had been gone for several days; but as to the particulars of her fate, they showed an ignorance and unconcern scarcely credible in persons who had lived under the same roof. Disgusted with all I saw, I was turning away; when a groan, which seemed to issue from a darker part of the room, drew my steps towards a wretched bed, where lay a young woman in the last stage of disease. I had enquired whether she had any medical assistance, and been answered that she had none, – I had bent over her for some minutes, touched the parched skin, and tried to count the fluttering pulse – before, my eye accommodating itself to the obscurity, I perceived the unconscious gaze and flushed cheek which indicate delirious fever. I turned hastily away; but more serious alarm took possession of me, when I observed that my pupil had followed me close to the bedside, and in childish curiosity was inhaling the very breath of infection. I instantly hurried her away, and returned home.

Though expecting that Mrs Boswell would throw upon me the blame which more properly belonged to herself, I did not hesitate to acquaint her with this accident; begging her to advise with the family surgeon whether any antidote could still be applied. But Mrs Boswell was touched with a more lively alarm than poor Jessie's danger could awaken. 'Bless me!' she cried, 'did you touch the woman? Pray don't come near me. Campbell! get me ever so much vinegar. Pray go away, Miss Percy. I would not be near a person that had the fever for the whole world.'

'Were every one of your opinion, madam,' said I, 'a fever would be almost as great a misfortune as infamy itself; but since you are so apprehensive, Jessie and I will remain above stairs for the rest of the day.'

At the door of my apartment I found poor Fido extended, stiff and motionless. Startled by somewhat unnatural in his posture, I called to him. The poor animal looked at me, but did not stir. 'Fido!' I called again, stooping to pat his head. He looked up once more; wagged his tail; gave a short low whine; and died.

Many would smile were I to describe what I felt at that moment; and yet I believe there are none who could unmoved lose the last memorial of friend and parent, or part unmoved with the creature which had sported with their infancy, and grown old beneath their care. Fido was my last earthly possession. Besides him I had nothing. I thank Heaven that the greater part of my kind must look back to the deprivations of early childhood, ere they can know what a melancholy value this single circumstance gives to what is in itself of little worth.

My feelings took a new turn, when it suddenly occurred to me that my poor old favourite owed his death not to disease, but to poison. His apearance, as well as the suddenness of his death, confirmed the suspicion. Strong indignation already working in my breast, I hastened to question the servants. They all denied the deed; but with such reservations, as showed me that they at least guessed at the perpetrator. Breathless with resentment, and with a vain desire to vent it all, yet to vent it calmly, I entered Mrs Boswell's apartment, and steadily questioned her upon the fact. Mrs Boswell forgot her late alarm, or rather my flashing eye was for a moment an over-match for the fever. She changed colour more than once; but she answered me with that forced firmness of gaze, which often indicates determined falsehood. 'She could not imagine who could do such a thing. She could not believe that the animal was poisoned. She did not suppose that any of the servants would venture. In short, she was persuaded that Fido died a natural death.'

'That shall be examined into,' said I, still looking at her in stern enquiry. Again she changed colour, and resumed her denials, but with a more restless and evasive aspect. Presently my glance followed hers to some papers which lay upon the table. I saw her as if by accident cover them with her hand, then dexterously throw them upon the ground; and she was just endeavouring to conceal them with her foot when I snatched up one of them. I observed that it had been the envelope of a small parcel; and turning the reverse, saw that it was marked with the word 'arsenic.'

Dumb for a moment with unutterable scorn, I merely presented the paper to Mrs Boswell, and hearing her stammer out some lying explanation, turned in disgust away. But indignation again supplied me with words. 'Find another instructor for your child, Mrs Boswell,' said I; 'I will no longer tell her to despise treachery, and falsehood, and cruelty, lest I teach her to scorn her mother.'

Then, without waiting reply, I left the room.

'Dost thou well to be angry?' said my conscience, as soon as she had time to speak. I answered, as every angry woman will answer, 'Yes. I do well to be angry. Vile were the spirit that would not stir against such inhuman baseness!' This was well spoken, – perhaps it was well felt. Yet I would advise all lofty spirits to be abstemious in their use of noble indignation. It borders too nearly on their prevailing sin.

I soon recollected, that I had renounced my only means of support; but it is a feeble passion which cannot justify its own acts. 'Better so,' said I, 'than receive the bread of dependence from one whom I ought to despise; or cling to an office in which I can perform nothing.'

I began, however, to look with some uneasiness to the consequences of my rashness. I had neither home, property, nor friends. That which gives independence – the only real independence – to the poorest menial, was wanting to me; for I had neither strength for bodily labour, nor resolution to endure want. Nor could I claim the irresistible consolation of tracing, in the circumstances of my lot, the arrangements of a Father's wisdom. My own temerity had shaped my fate. My own impatience of human wickedness and folly was about to cut me off from human support; and I, who had no forbearance for the weakness of my brethren, was about to try what strength was in myself.

All this might perhaps pass darkly through my mind, but was not permitted to take a determinate form. The sin, whatever it be, which easily besets us, is to each of us the arch-deceiver. It is the first which the Christian renounces in general, the last which he learns to detect in its particulars. I had resolved to call my self-will 'virtuous indignation;' for indeed my ruling frailty has had, in its time, as many styles and titles as any ruler upon earth, though seldom like them designed by its *Christian* name.

It was an obvious escape from examining the past, to anticipate the future. I had some experience of the difficulties which awaited me; and knew how little my merits, such as they were, would avail towards the advancement of an unfriended stranger. Yet the fearless buoyancy of my temper supported me. I had now spent in Mrs Boswell's family three months of weariness and drudgery, for which I had received no remuneration; I concluded, of course, that she was my debtor for some return, however small. Upon this sum I expected to subsist till some favourable change should take place in my situation. How or whence this change should come, I fancy I should have been puzzled to divine; so I was content with assuring myself that come it certainly would.

At the beginning of my connection with Mrs Boswell, I had, with more politeness than prudence, submitted the recompense of my services to her decision. From that time she seemed to have forgotten the subject; and delicacy, or perhaps pride, forbade me to bring it to her recollection. It was now absolutely necessary to surmount this feeling; but it was surmounted in vain. Mrs Boswell reminded me, that I had stipulated for protection only; and declared, that she understood me as engaged to serve her without any other reward. Confounded as I was at her meanness and effrontery, I yet retained sufficient command of temper to address a civil appeal to a faculty which, in Mrs Boswell's mind, was an absolute blank; but argument was vain, and my only resource was an application to Mr Boswell.

Well knowing that his lady's presence would give a fatal bias to the scales of justice, I requested to speak with him in private. Unwilling to shock him by a detail of his wife's baseness, I assigned no reason for the resolution which I announced of quitting his family. I merely submitted to his arbitration the misunderstanding which had arisen in regard to the terms of my servitude. I had reason to be flattered by the regret, perhaps I might rather say dismay, with which the good man heard of my intended removal. With every expression of affectionate and fatherly regard he entreated me to reconsider my purpose. He assured me, that it was the first wish of his heart that his child should resemble me; he said, that he could neither hope nor even desire to see another obtain such influence as I had already gained over her; and that all his prospects of comfort depended on the use of this influence. 'I need not affect to disguise from you, my dear Miss Percy,' said he, 'that Mrs Boswell, however willing, is not likely to assist much in forming Jessie's temper and manners. The variableness of her spirits ——'

'Spirits!' repeated I involuntarily.

'Well,' resumed Mr Boswell with a heavy sigh, 'perhaps I should rather have said temper. But whatever it be, the more useless it makes her to Jessie, and the more vexatious to me, the more have we both need of that delightful gaiety, that blessed sweetness which breathes peace and cheerfulness wherever you come. Dear Miss Percy, say that you will remain with my girl, that you will teach her to be as delightful as yourself, and you will repay me for ten of the most comfortless years that ever a poor creature spent.'

Somewhat embarrassed by this strange sort of confidence, I answered, that were I to accept the trust he offered I should only disappoint his expectations, since all my influence with my pupil was as nothing compared with that which was thrown into the opposite scale. I therefore renewed my request, that he would enable me immediately to relinquish my charge.

Mr Boswell employed all his rhetoric to change my resolution, but I was inflexible. 'Well, well!' said he at last, with a sigh and a shrug, 'I see how it is. The same confounded nonsense that has driven every comfort from my doors for these ten years past is driving you away too. Well, well! Hang me if I can help it. A man must submit to any thing for the sake of peace.'

'Undoubtedly,' said I, suppressing a smile; 'while he finds that he actually reaps that fruit from his submission.'

'Why as to that I can't say much. But bad as matters are, they might be worse if I were as determined to have my own way as my wife is. I have tried it once or twice, indeed; but – really her perseverance is most wonderful!' Mr Boswell pursued the subject at great length; labouring to convince me, or rather to convince himself, that where submission was unattainable on the one side, the defect ought to be supplied by the other; always inferring, from the necessary unhappiness of this situation, that I ought not, by my departure, to deprive him of his only remaining comfort. All he could obtain, however, was my consent to continue in his family for a few days longer. In return, he promised the full discharge of my claim upon Mrs Boswell, as soon as he should find means to dispose of such a sum *peaceably*; that is, as soon as he could by stealth abstract so much of his own property.

I suppose the pleasures of complaint increase in proportion to the folly and impropriety of complaining. I never could otherwise account for the frequent lamentations over the perfidy of lovers and the obduracy of parents; nor imagine any other reason why Mr Boswell, having once entered on the subject of his conjugal distresses, returned to it on every possible occasion. In his wife's presence it was recalled to my recollection by cautious hints, and by significant sighs and looks. In her absence the theme seemed inexhaustible.

The embarrassment inflicted on me by this continual reference to a secret was increased, when I perceived that Mrs Boswell, whose jealousy in this instance supplied her want of penetration, suspected some intelligence between her husband and myself. She was now, indeed, under a stubborn fit of taciturnity; but I had at last learnt to read a countenance which never forsook its stony blank, except to express some modification of malevolence. I alarmed Mr Boswell into more caution; but when the lady's suspicions once were roused, it was not in the most guarded prudence, nor in the most open simplicity of conduct, to lull them.

Unfortunately Mr Boswell and I soon found a more legitimate subject of sympathy. The very day after her ill-fated visit to the abode of disease, poor Jessie showed symptoms of infection; and before the week expired, was pronounced to be in extreme danger. The mother, on this occasion, showed a degree of anxiety, which was wonderful in Mrs Boswell. She sent for nurse after nurse, and for doctors innumerable. She made diligent enquiry after a fortune-teller, to unveil the fate of her child; and she actually shed tears when the fire emitted a splinter which she called a coffin. Stronger minds than Mrs Boswell's become superstitious, when their most important concerns depend upon circumstances over which they have no control. Finally, she questioned every member of the family concerning the best cure for a fever, and insisted that all their prescriptions should be applied. Fortunately, however, no consideration could prevail upon her to superintend the application. To approach the infected chamber, she would have thought nothing less than *felo de se*; – therefore the poor little sufferer was spared many unnecessary torments.

Mrs Boswell carried her dread of infection so far, that she would hold no direct communication with any one who entered the sick room; and she positively forbade her husband to approach his suffering child. But to this interdiction the father could not submit. His visits were stolen, indeed, but they were frequent; and he evinced on these occasions a sensibility which could scarcely have been expected from the easy indifference of his general temper. Often, while others were at rest, did the father hang over the sick bed of his child; offer the draught to her parched lips; and shed upon her altered face the tear of him who trembles for his only hope.

To his kindness and his sorrow she was alike insensible. Her fondness for me seemed the only recollection which her delirium had spared. She would accept of no sustenance except from my hand. If I was withdrawn from her sight, her eye wandered in restless search of something desired; though when I appeared, it often fixed on me with a heart-breaking vacancy of gaze. Thus circumstanced, I could no longer think of deserting her. Indeed I never quitted her even for an hour; and when wearied out I sunk to sleep, it was only to start again at her slightest summons. These attentions, which I must have been a savage to withhold, extorted from Mr Boswell the warmest expressions of gratitude; – gratitude, which springs so readily in every human heart, yet so rarely takes root there, and so very rarely becomes fruitful.

'God, reward thee, blessed creature!' said he once, when late in the night we were separating at the door of the sick-room, where he had been sharing the vigils of the nurse and me. 'My child's own mother forsakes her, while you! – God reward you.' As he spoke, he clasped my hand between his, and fervently pressed his lips to my forehead. But I started with a confusion like that of detected guilt, when I perceived, at a little distance, the half-concealed face of Mrs Boswell, scowling malignity and detection. Whilst I stood for a moment in motionless expectation of what was to follow, she darted forward, undressed as she was; her lip quivering, her face void of all colour except a line of strong scarlet bordering her eyelids. 'Mighty well!' cried she, in accents half choked by something between a hysterical giggle and a sob. 'Mighty well, indeed! I knew how it was! I have seen it all well enough. But I'm not such a fool as you think! I won't endure it – that I won't.'

Provoked by the recollection that this degrading remonstrance was uttered within hearing of a domestic, I looked towards Mr Boswell for defence; but seeing him cower like a condemned culprit, I was obliged to answer for myself. 'What will you not endure, madam?' said I. 'Your own preposterous fancy? – I know of nothing else that you have to endure.'

Mrs Boswell's natural cowardice always took part against her with a resolute antagonist. 'I am sure,' said she, whimpering between fear and wrath, 'I don't want to have any words with you, Miss Percy – only I wish – I am sure it would be very obliging if you would go quietly out of this house – and not stay here enticing other people's husbands ——'

At this coarse accusation, the indignant blood rose to my forehead. But the provocation was great enough to remind me that this was a fit occasion of forbearance; and I subdued my voice and countenance into stern composure, while I said, 'Woman! I would answer you, were I sure of speaking only what a Christian ought to speak.' Then turning from her, I took refuge from further insult in the apartment which I knew she did not dare to approach.

There I sat down to consider what course I should pursue. I had been insolently forbidden the house; and every moment that I remained in it might subject me to new affront. The very attendants in the sick-room could, with difficulty, restrain the merriment excited by Mrs Boswell's ridiculous attack; and I felt as if the impertinence of their half-suppressed smiles was partly directed against me. They had heard my dismission; and every instant that I delayed to avail myself of it seemed a new degradation. The most rooted passion of my nature, therefore, urged my immediate departure; but I had now learned to lend a suspicious ear to its suggestions. 'I shall never be humble,' thought I, 'if I resist every occasion of humiliation;' and when I looked upon the altered countenance of my poor little charge, I could have endured any thing rather than have withdrawn its last comfort from her ebbing life. I resumed my place by her side, resolved never voluntarily to quit her while my cares could administer to her relief.

My task was now of short duration. The very next day the physician informed me that the crisis of the disorder was at hand; and that an hour which he named would either bring material amendment, or lasting release from suffering. I entreated that the anxiety of the parents might not be aggravated by a knowledge of this circumstance; and undertook myself to watch the event of the critical hour.

The day passed in silent suspense. Mrs Boswell did not dare to approach me; and she contrived, by what means I know not, to keep her husband away. I was truly thankful to be thus spared from contest; for I had begun to feel the consequences of breathing the polluted air of confinement. A heavy languor was upon me. My eyes turned pained from the light. I was restless; yet I moved uneasily, for my limbs seemed burdened beyond their strength. In vain I tried to struggle against these harbingers of disease. Infection had done its work, and my disorder increased every hour. The physician, at this evening visit, observing my haggard looks, desired that I should immediately endeavour to obtain some rest. But to sleep during the hour that was to decide poor Jessie's fate, I should at any time have found impossible. I watched her till the appointed time was past; saw her drop into the promised sleep; sat motionless beside her during the anxious hours of its continuance; and, with a joy which brightened even the progress of disease, beheld her lifting upon me once more the eye of intelligence, and beaming upon me once more the smile of ease.

Thinking only of the joyful news I had to tell, I ran to enquire for Mr Boswell. He was in his dressing-room; and thither I hastened to seek him. I entered; and told my tale, I know not how. 'Thank God!' the father tried to say, but could not. He burst into tears. The first words he spoke blessed me for having saved his child; the next expressed his eager wish to see her. We were leaving the dressing-room together, when we met Mrs Boswell. Her face growing livid with rage, and her voice sharpening to something like the scream of a Guinea fowl, she exclaimed, 'Well! if this is not beyond every thing! To go into his very room! You are a shameless, abominable man, Mr Boswell. But I will be revenged on you – that I will.'

'I went into Mr Boswell's room, madam,' interrupted I, calmly, 'to tell him that his daughter is out of immediate danger; and I was just going to convey the same news to you.'

'Oh! no doubt but you'll be clever enough to find some excuse. But I don't wish to have any thing to say to you, Miss Percy, – only I tell you civilly, go away out of my house. I'm sure the house is my own; and it is very hard if I can't – so go this moment, I tell you ——'

She had gone too far. The mildest spirits are, when roused, the most tremendous; and Mr Boswell's was, for the moment, completely roused. Seizing her with a grasp, which made me tremble, 'Speak that again at your peril, Mrs Boswell,' said he. 'Her stay depends upon herself, whilst I have a roof to shelter her.' Then, throwing her from him, he passed on, whilst I shuddered at perceiving that his grasp had wrung the blood-drops from her fingers. The poor creature, terrified by this first instance of violence, stood gazing after him in trembling silence. 'Compose yourself, Mrs Boswell,' said I, as soon as he was out of hearing; 'I will immediately begone. I staid only for the sake of poor Jessie; now, nothing would tempt me to remain here another hour.'

Spent with the exertion which I had made, I could scarcely reach my chamber. I immediately began to collect my little property for removal; but before my preparations, trifling as they were, could be finished, my strength failed, and I sunk upon my bed.

A strange confusion seemed now to seize me. Black shadows swam before my eyes, succeeded by glares of bloody light. The hideous phantoms crowded round me, till my very breathing was oppressed by their numbers; and one of them, more frightful than the rest, laid on my forehead the weight of his fiery hand. Then came a confused hope that all was but a frightful dream, from which I struggled to rouse myself. I spoke, as if my own voice could dispel the terrible illusion. I endeavoured to rise, that I might shake off this dreadful sleep. In an instant I was on the brink of a fearful precipice, from which I shrunk in vain. Hands invisible hurried me down the fathomless abyss.

Again I perceived that these horrors were illusory. I strove to convince myself, that I was indeed in my own chamber, surrounded by objects familiar to my sight. My mind rallied its last strength, to recall the remembrance of my situation. Along with this, a dark suspicion of the truth stole upon me.

'Merciful Heaven!' I cried, 'are my senses indeed wandering; and must I be driven forth homeless while fever is raging in my brain! Forbid it! Oh forbid it!'

By a violent effort I flung myself on my knees. With an earnestness which hastened the dreaded evil, I supplicated an escape from this worst calamity; and implored, that the body might perish before the spirit were darkened. But ere the melancholy petition was closed, its fervour had wandered into delirium.

A time passed which I have no means to measure; and I saw a female form approach me. She seemed alternately to wear the aspect of my mother and of Miss Mortimer; yet she rejected my embrace; and when I called her by their names, she answered not. She clothed me in what seemed the chill vestments of the grave; she hurried me through the air with the rapidity of light; then consigned me to two dark and fearful shapes; and again I was hurried on.

At last the breath of heaven for a moment cooled my throbbing brow. I looked up and saw that I was in the hands of two persons of unknown and rugged countenance. They lifted me into a carriage. It drove off with distracting speed.

The succeeding days are a blank in my being.

CHAPTER XXIV

For he has wings which neither sickness, pain,
Nor penury can cripple or confine.
No nook so narrow, but he spreads them there
With ease, and is at large. The oppressor holds
His body bound; but knows not what a range
His spirit takes, unconscious of a chain.

Cowper.

I WAS awakened as from the deepest sleep, by a cry wild and horrible. It was followed by shouts of dissonant laughter, unlike the cheering sounds of human mirth. They seemed but the body's convulsion, in which the spirit had no part. I started and listened; – a ceaseless hum of voices wearied my ear.

A recollection of the past came upon me, mixed with a strange uncertainty of my present state. The darkness of midnight was around me; why then was its stillness broken by more than the discords of day? I spoke, in hopes that some attendant might be watching my sick-bed; – no one answered to my call. I half-raised my feeble frame to try what objects I could discern through the gloom. High above my reach, a small lattice poured in the chill night wind; but gave no light that could show aught beyond its own form and position. As I looked fixedly towards it, I perceived that it was grated. 'Am I then a prisoner?' thought I. 'But it matters not. A narrower cell will soon contain all of poor Ellen that a prison can confine.' And, worn out with my effort, I laid myself down with that sense of approaching dissolution, which sinks all human situations to equality.

I closed my eyes, and my thoughts now flew unbidden to that

unknown world from which, in these days of levity, they had shrunk affrighted; and to which, even in better times they had often been turned with effort.

Presently a female voice, as if from the adjoining chamber, began a plaintive song; which now died away, now swelled in mournful caprice, till, as it approached the final cadence, it wandered with pathetic wildness into speech. I listened to the hopeless lamentation; – heard it quicken into rapid utterance, sink into the low inward voice, then burst into causeless energy; – and I felt that I was near the haunt of madness. The shuddering of horror came over me for a moment. But one thought alone has power to darken the departing spirit with abiding gloom. The worst earthly sorrows play over her as a passing shadow, and are gone. 'Poor maniac!' thought I, 'thou and the genius which now guides and delights mankind will soon alike be as I am.'

But why record the feeble disjointed efforts of a soul struggling with her clog of earth? Oh, had my strivings to enter the strait gate been *then* to begin, where should I, humanly speaking, have found strength for the endeavour? My mind, weakened with my body, could feel, indeed, but could no longer reason; it could keenly hope and fear, but it could no longer exercise over thought that guidance which makes thinking a rational act. Worn out at last with feelings too strong for my frame, I sunk to sleep; and, in spite of the dreariest sounds which rise from human misery, slept quietly till morning.

Then the daylight gave a full view of my melancholy abode. Its extent was little more than sufficient to contain the low flock-bed on which I lay. The naked walls were carved with many a quaint device; and one name was written on them in every possible direction, and joined with every epithet of endearment. Well may I remember them; for often, often, after having studied them all, have I turned wearily to study them again.

As I lay contemplating my prison, a step approached the door; the key grated in the lock; and a man of a severe and swarthy countenance stood before me. He came near, and offered me some food of the coarsest kind, from which my sickly appetite turned with disgust; but when he held a draught of milk and water to my lips, I eagerly swallowed it, making a faint gesture of thanks for the relief. The stern countenance relaxed a little! 'You are better this morning,' said the man.

'I soon shall be so,' answered I, with a languid smile.

Without farther conference he was turning to depart; when, recollecting that I should soon need other cares, and shrinking with womanly reluctance from owing the last offices to any but a woman, I detained him by a sign. 'I have a favour to beg of you,' said I. 'I shall not want many.'

'Well!' said the man, lingering with a look of idle curiosity.

'When I am gone,' said I, 'will you persuade some charitable woman to do whatever must be done for me; for I was once a gentlewoman, and have never known indignity.'

The man promised without hesitation to grant my request. Encouraged by my success, I proceeded. 'I have a friend, too; perhaps you would write to him.'

'Oh yes – who is he?' said the man, looking inquisitively.

'Mr Maitland, the great West India merchant. Tell him that Ellen Percy died here; and dying, remembered him with respect and gratitude.'

The man looked at me with a strong expression of surprise, which quickly gave place to an incredulous smile; then turned away, saying carelessly, 'Oh, yes, I'll be sure to tell him;' and quitted the cell.

During that day, my trembling hopes, my solemn anticipations, were interrupted only by the return of the keeper, to bring my food at stated hours. But on the following day, I became sensible of such amendment, that the natural love of life began to struggle with the hopes and the fears of 'untried being.'

With the prospect of prolonged existence, however, returned those anxieties which, in one form or another, beset every heart that turns a thought earthward. The idea of confinement in such a place of imprisonment, perhaps perpetual, mingled the expectations of recovery with horror. To live only to be sensible to the death of all my affections, of all my hopes, of all my enjoyments! – To retain a living consciousness in that place where was no 'knowledge, nor work, nor device.' – To look back upon a dreary blank of time, and forward to one unvaried waste! – To pine for the fair face of nature! perhaps to live till it was remembered but as a dream! Gracious Heaven! what strength supported me under such thoughts of horror? Language cannot express the fearful anxiety with which I awaited the return of the only person who could relieve my apprehensions.

The moment he appeared, I eagerly accosted him. 'Tell me,' I cried, 'why I am here: surely I am no object for such an institution as this. Mr and Mrs Boswell know that my fever was caught in attending their own child.'

'To be sure they do,' said the man soothingly.

'Why then have they sent me to such a place as this?'

The man was silent for a moment, and then answered, 'Why, what sort of a place do you take it for? You don't think this is a madhouse, do you?' Seeing that I looked at him with surprise and doubt, he added, 'This is only an asylum, a sort of infirmary for people who have your kind of fever.'

I now perceived that he thought it necessary to humour me as a lunatic. 'For mercy's sake,' I cried, 'do not trifle with me. You may easily convince yourself that I am in perfect possession of my reason; do so then, and let me be gone. This place is overpowering to my spirits.'

'The moment you get well,' returned the man coolly, 'you shall go. We would not keep you after that, though you would give us ever so much. But I could not be answerable to let you out just now, for fear of bringing back your fever.'

With this assurance I was obliged for the present to be contented. Yet a horrible fear sometimes returned, that he would only beguile me with false hope from day to day; and when he next brought my homely repast, I again urged him to fix a time for my release. 'I am recovering strength so rapidly,' said I, 'that I am sure in a few days I may remove.'

'Oh yes!' answered he; 'I think in a fortnight at farthest you will be quite well; provided you keep quiet, and don't fret yourself about fancies.'

While he spoke, I fixed my eyes earnestly upon him, to see whether I could discover any sign of mental reservation; but he spoke with all the appearance of good faith, and I was satisfied.

My spirits now reviving with my health and my hopes I endeavoured to view my condition with something more than resignation. 'Surely,' said I to myself, 'it should even be my choice to dwell for a time amidst scenes of humiliation, if here I can find the weapons of my warfare against the stubborn pride of nature and of habit. And whatever be *my* choice, this place has been selected for me by Him whose will is my improvement. Let me not then frustrate his gracious purpose. Let me consider what advantage he intends me in my present state. Alas! why have I so often deferred to seasons of rare occurrence the lessons which the events of the most ordinary life might have taught me?'

Carefully I now reviewed my actions, my sentiments, and my purposes, as they had lately appeared to me in the anticipation of a righteous sentence. What tremendous importance did each then assume! The work perhaps of a moment seemed to extend its influence beyond the duration of worlds. The idle word, uttered with scarcely an effort of the will, indicated perhaps a temper which might colour the fate of eternity. In a few days, I learnt more of myself than nineteen years had before taught me; for the light which gleamed upon me, as it were from another world, was of power to show all things in their true form and colour. I saw the insidious nature, the gigantic strength, the universal despotism of my bosom sin. I saw its power even in actions which had veiled its form; its stamp was upon sentiments which bore not its name; its impression had often made even 'the fine gold become dim.' Its baleful influence had begun in my cradle, had increased through my childhood, had dictated alike the enmities and the friendships of my youth. It had rejected the counsels of Miss Mortimer; trifled with the affections of Maitland; spurned the authority of my father; and hurried me to the brink of a connection in which neither heart nor understanding had part. It had embittered the cup of misfortune; poisoned the wounds of treachery; and dashed from me the cordial of human sympathy. It had withheld gratitude in my prosperity; it had robbed my adversity of resignation. It had mingled even with the tears of repentance, while the proud heart unwillingly felt its own vileness; it had urged, I fear, even the labours of virtue, with the hope of earning other than unmerited favour. It had eluded my pursuit, resisted my struggles, betrayed my watchfulness. It had driven me from an imaginary degradation among 'mine own people,' to desolation, want, and dependence, among strangers. When were greater sacrifices extorted by self-denial, that 'lion in the way' which has scared so many from the paths of peace? Even the employment, which, by an undeserved good fortune, I had obtained, was degraded into slavery by the temper which represented my employer as alike below my gratitude and my indignation; while the pleasure with which pride contemplates its own eminence had blinded me to the awful danger denounced against those who cherish habitual contempt for the meanest of their brethren.

I now saw that, even with the despised Mrs Boswell, I had need to exchange forgiveness; since, against the evils which she had inflicted on me, I had to balance a scorn even more galling than injury. Of the injustice of this scorn I became sensible, when I considered that it was directed less against her faults than her understanding; less against the baseness of her means than the insignificance of her ends; since what was at once the excuse and the mitigation of her vices formed the only reason why they were less endurable to me than the craft and the cruelty of politicians and conquerors. When I remembered that a few hours of sickness had sufficed to reduce me in intellect far below even the despised Mrs Boswell; that a derangement of the animal frame, so minute as to baffle human search, might blot the rarest genius from the scale of moral being; while I shrunk from the harrowing ravings of creatures who could once reason and reflect like myself, I felt the force of the warning which forbids the wise to 'glory in his wisdom.' I admitted as a principle what I had formerly owned as an opinion, that the true glory of man consists not in the ingenuity by which he builds systems, or unlocks the secrets of nature, or guides the opinions of a wondering world; but in that capacity of knowing, loving, and serving God, of which all are by nature equally destitute, and which all are equally and freely invited to receive.

The reflections of those few days it would require months to record. They furnished indeed my sole business, devotion my sole pleasure. My cell contained no object to divert my attention; and the stated returns of the keeper were the only varieties of my condition. My strength, however, gradually returned. I was able to rise from my bed, and to walk, if the size of my apartment had admitted of walking.*

It may well be believed that I counted the hours of my captivity, and I did not fail to remind the keeper daily of his promise. It was not till the day preceding that which he had fixed for my liberation, that I discovered any sign of an intention to retract.

'To-morrow I shall breathe the air of freedom,' said I to him exultingly, while I was taking my humble repast.

'I am sure you have air enough where you are,' returned the man.

'Oh but you may well imagine how a prisoner longs for liberty!'

'You are no more a prisoner than any body else that is not well. I am sure, though I were to let you out, you are not fit to go about yet.'

* Miss Percy's description is far, indeed, from exaggerating the horrors of some lunatic asylums in Edinburgh, as they existed twenty years ago. One of these, which was even more recently the disgrace of Scotland and of human nature, is now managed with great attention to the health and cleanliness of its miserable inmates.

'Though you were to —— Oh Heaven! you do not mean to detain me still! You will keep your promise with me!'

'Oh yes,' said the man, with that voice of horrible soothing which made my blood run cold; 'never fear, you shall get out to-morrow;' and, regardless of my endeavours to detain him, he instantly left me.

'You shall get out to-morrow,' I repeated a thousand times, in distressful attempt to convince myself that a promise so explicit could not be broken. Yet the horrible doubt returned again and again. Drops of agony stood upon my forehead as I looked distractedly upon those narrow walls, and thought they might inclose me for ever. 'God of mercy,' I cried, casting myself wildly on my knees, 'wilt thou permit this? Hast thou supported me hitherto only to forsake me in my extremity of need? Oh no! I wrong thy goodness by the very thought.'

Well may our religion be called the religion of hope; for who can remember that 'unspeakable gift' which every address to Heaven must recall to the Christian's view, without feeling a trust which outweighs all causes of fear? By degrees I recovered composure, then hope, then cheerfulness; and when, at the keeper's evening visit, I had extorted from him another renewal of his promise, I was so far satisfied as to prepare myself by a quiet sleep for the trials which awaited my waking.

The next morning a bright sun was gleaming through my grated window; and anxiously I watched the lingering progress of its shadow along the wall. Long, long, I listened for the heavy tread of the keeper; thought myself sure that his hour of coming was past; and dreaded that his stay was ominous of evil. When at last I heard the welcome sounds of his approach, and felt that at last the moment of certainty was come, a faintness seized me, and I remained motionless, unable to enquire my doom.

The man looked keenly at the fixed eye which wanted power to turn from him. 'I thought as much,' said he triumphantly. 'I'll lay a crown you don't wish to go out to-day.'

'Oh yes, indeed!' I cried, starting up with sudden hope and animation: 'I would go this instant!'

The man again examined my face inquisitively. 'Eat your breakfast then,' said he, 'and put on these clothes I have brought you. I shall come back for you presently.'

Language cannot express the rapture with which I heard this promise. Overpowered with emotions of joy and gratitude, I sunk at the feet of the keeper; pouring forth, in the fulness of my heart, blessings made inarticulate by tears. Then recollecting how my suspicions had wronged him, 'Pardon me,' I cried, 'oh pardon me, that ever I doubted your word. I ought to have known that you were too good to deceive me.'

'Hush! quiet!' said the man knitting his brow, with a frown which forced the blood back chill upon the throbbing heart; and in a moment he was gone.

It was some time before I became composed enough to remember or to execute the command which I had received; but my mysterious apprehensions, my tumults of delight giving way to sober certainty, I changed my dress, and sat down to await the return of my liberator. Then while I recollected the horrible dread from which I was delivered, the fate from which I seemed to have escaped, gratitude which could not be restrained burst into a song of thanksgiving.

It was interrupted by the return of the keeper, who, without speaking, threw open the door of my cell, and then proceeded to that of the one adjoining. I sprung from my prison, and hurried along a passage which terminated in the open air.

I presently found myself in a small square court, surrounded by high walls, and occupied by twenty or thirty squalid beings of both sexes. Concluding that I had mistaken the way, I returned to beg the directions of the keeper. 'I am busy just now,' said he, 'so amuse yourself there for a little; the people are all quite harmless.'

'Amuse myself!' thought I. 'What strange perversion must have taken place in the mind which could associate such a scene and such objects with an idea of amusement!' I had no choice, however; and I returned to the court. I was instantly accosted by several unfortunate beings of my own sex, all at once talking without coherence and without pause. In some alarm I was going to retreat, when a little ugly affected-looking man approached; and, with a bow which in any other place would have provoked a smile, desired that he might be allowed the honour of attending me. Little relieved by this politeness, I was again looking towards retreat, when the party was joined by a person of very different appearance from the rest. Large waves of silver hair adorned a face of green old age, and the lines of deep thought on his brow were relieved by a smile of perfect benignity; while his air, figure, and attire were so much those of a gentleman, that I instantly concluded he must be the visiter, not the inhabitant of such a dwelling.

Reproving the intrusion of the rest with an authority from which they all seemed to shrink, he politely offered to attend me; and I accepted of the escort with a feeling of perfect security.

While we walked round the court, my companion conversed as if he believed me also to be a visiter. 'I sometimes indulge in a melancholy smile,' said he, 'on observing how well the characteristics of the sexes are preserved even here. The men, you see, are commonly silent and contemplative, the women talkative and restless. Here, just as in that larger mad-house, the world, pride makes the men surly and quarrelsome, while the ladies must be indulged in a little harmless vanity. Now and then, however, we encroach on your prerogative. The little man, for instance, who spoke to you just now, fancies that every woman is in love with him; and that he is detained here by a conspiracy of jealous husbands.' He proceeded to comment upon the more remarkable cases; showing such acquaintance with each, that I concluded him to be the medical attendant of the establishment. This belief inspired me with a very embarrassing desire to convince him of my sanity; and I endured the toil of being laboriously wise, while we moralised together on the various illusions which possessed the people round us, and on the curious analogy of their freaks to those of the more sober madmen who are left at large. Some strutted in mock majesty, expecting that all should do them homage. Some decked themselves with rags, and then fancied themselves fair. Some made hoards of straws and pebbles, then called the worthless mass a treasure. Some sported in unmeaning mirth; while a few ingenious spirits toiled to form baubles, which the rest quickly demolished; and a few miserable beings sat apart, shrinking from companions whom they imagined only evil spirits clothed in human form. In one respect, however, all were agreed. Each scorned or pitied every form of madness but his own. 'Let us then,' said I, 'be of those who pity; since we too have probably our points of sanity, though where they lie we may never know till we reach the land of perfection.'

'Perfection!' exclaimed my companion; 'is not its dawn arisen on the earth! Are not the splendours of day at hand? That glorious light! in which man shall see that his true honour is peace, his true interest benevolence! Yes, it is advancing; and though the perverseness of the ignorant and the base have for a time concealed me here, soon shall the gratitude of a regenerated world call me to rejoice in my own work!'

'Sir!' said I, startled by this speech, which was pronounced with the utmost vehemence of voice and manner.

'Yes!' proceeded he; 'the labours of twenty years shall be repaid! Punishment and pain shall be banished from the world. A patriarchal reign of love shall assemble my renovated children around their father and their friend. All government shall cease. All ——'

'Silence!' cried a voice of tremendous power; and immediately the keeper stood beside us. He rudely seized the old man's arm, and the flush of animation was instantly blanched by fear. I saw the reverend form of age thus bow before brute violence, and I forgot for a moment that I was powerless to defend. 'Inhuman!' I exclaimed; 'will you not reverence grey hairs and misfortune?'

Without deigning me a look, the keeper led his captive away; while I followed him with eyes in which the tears of alarm now mingled with those of pity. He presently returned, and sternly commanded me to go with him. Eager as I was for my dismission, I yet trembled while I obeyed. We reached the door of my cell; and though I expected to pass it, I involuntarily recoiled. 'Go in!' said the keeper, in a voice of terrible authority.

'Here!' I exclaimed, with a start of agony. 'Oh, Heaven! did you not say – did you not promise ——'

'Ay, ay,' interrupted the man; 'but I must see you a little quieter first. Get in, get in!'

'No, no! I will not! Though I perish, I will not!'

'A withering smile crossing that dark countenance, he seized me with a force which reduced me to the helplessness of infancy; and regardless of the shriek wrung from me by hopeless anguish, he bore me into the cell, shook off my imploring hold, and departed. I heard the dreary creaking of the bolt; and I heard no more. I fell down senseless.

When I revived, I found myself supported by the arm of a person who was administering restoratives to me. The first accents to which I were sensible were those of the keeper; who said, as if in answer to some question, 'She has been almost as high this morning ever.'

'So, so!' returned the other. 'Well! she'll do for the present, so I must be gone. Keep an eye on her, and tell me how she comes on. And harkye, give her a better place – if they don't pay for it, I will. I am sure she is a gentlewoman.'

In the hope that I might now effectually appeal to justice or to pity, I made a strong effort to rouse myself; but my compassionate attendant was gone. The keeper, however, who perhaps was severe only from a mistaken sense of duty, had been alarmed into treating me with more caution. He watched me till I was completely revived; and as soon as I could make the necessary exertion, removed me to a different part of the building.

My new place of confinement, though somewhat larger and better furnished than the first, was equally contrived to prevent all chance of escape. But I quickly discovered that I had, by the change, gained a treasure, which, whoever would estimate, must like me be cut off from the sympathies of living being. A swallow had built her nest in my window. I saw her feed her nurslings day by day. I watched her leaving her nest, and longed for her return. Her twittering awoke me every morning; and I knew the chirp which invited her young to the food she had brought. Their first flight was an event in my life as well as in theirs; for the interests of kindred are scarcely stronger than those which we take in the single living thing, however mean, whose feelings we can make our own.

Meanwhile I learnt from the keeper that the person to whose humanity I owed the improvement in my situation was the surgeon who attended the institution; and I looked forward to his next visit with all the eagerness of hope. Remembering, however, the dependence he had shown on the keeper's information, I became doubly anxious to remove the impression which I saw was entertained against the soundness of my mind. Alas! I forgot that it is not for the prejudiced eye to detect the almost imperceptible bound which separates soundness of mind from insanity.

'You assure me,' said I, one day, to my inexorable gaoler, 'that you have no instructions to detain me here, and you promise that I shall be dismissed the moment I am well: tell me how you propose to ascertain my recovery.'

'Oh, no fear but I shall know that before you know it yourself.'

'But what reason have you to doubt that I am already in perfect possession of my senses? I speak rationally enough.'

'Oh ay, I can't say but you have spoken rationally enough these three or four days. They all do that, at times.'

'What other proof of my recovery can you expect? Here I have no means of proving it by my actions.'

'Well, well. We'll see one of these days.'

'But if it be true that you have no wish to detain me, why must I linger on in this place of horror? Put me to any proof you will.

Propose, for instance, the most complicated question in arithmetic to me; and see whether I do not answer it like a rational creature.'

'I make no doubt. We have a gentleman here these fourteen years, that works at the counting from morning to night.'

'Fourteen years! Good Heavens! – Oh try me for mercy's sake in any way you please. Think of any experiment that will satisfy yourself; – let it only be made quickly.'

The man promised; for he always promised. He thought it a part of his duty. It is not to be told with what horror I at last heard that 'Oh yes,' which always began the heart-breaking assents addressed to me as to one whom it were needless and cruel to contradict.

All my anxieties were aggravated by the dread that his promises of release were deceitful like the rest; and that even, though he had no longer doubted of my recovery, the jealousy of Mrs Boswell might have bribed him to detain me. I balanced in my mind the improbability of so daring an outrage with the stories which I had heard of elder brothers removed, and wives concealed for ever. Where much is felt and nothing can be done, it is difficult indeed to fix the judgment.

To relieve my doubts, I enquired whether Mr Boswell knew of my confinement. The keeper could not tell. He only knew that the petition for my admission and the bond for my expenses were signed by Mrs Boswell alone. This circumstance was quite sufficient to convince me that Mr Boswell was ignorant of my fate; and I thought if I could find means to make him acquainted with my situation, he would undoubtedly accomplish my release. I implored of the keeper to inform him where I was; and he promised, but with that ominous 'Oh yes,' which assured me the promise was void.

By degrees, however, I had learnt to bear my disappointments with composure. I must not venture to say that I was becoming reconciled to my condition; I must not even assert that I endured its continuance with resignation, – for how often did my impatience for release virtually retract the submissions which I breathed to Heaven! But I had experienced that there are pleasures which no walls can exclude, and hopes which no disappointments can destroy; pleasures which flourish in solitude and in adversity; hopes, which fear no wreck but from the storms of passion. I had believed that religion could bring comfort to the dreariest dwelling. I now experienced that comfort. The friend whom we trust may be dear; the friend whom we have tried is inestimable. Religion, perhaps, best shows her strength when she rules the prosperous, but her full value is felt by the unfortunate alone.

Among my other requests to the keeper, I had entreated that he would allow me the use of that precious book, which has diffused more wisdom, peace, and truth, than all the works of men. He promised, as he was wont to promise; but weary of a request which was repeated every time he appeared, he at last yielded to my importunity. From that hour an inexhaustible source of enjoyment was opened to me. Devotion had before sometimes gladdened my prison with the visits of a friend; now his written language spoke to my heart, answering every feeling. How different was this solitude from the self-inflicted desolation which I had once endured? Nay, did not the blank of all earthly interests leave me a blessed animation compared with that dread insensibility which had once left me without God in the world.

'This is to be alone! This, this is solitude!'

But while I bore my disappointments with more fortitude, I did not, it will easily be imagined, relax my endeavours after liberty. On certain days, the institution was open to the inspection of strangers. On these days I was always furnished with a change of dress, and led out to make part of the show; and my spirit was for the time so thoroughly subdued, that I submitted to this exhibition without a murmur, almost without a pang. Circumstances had so far overcome my natural temper, that I more than once appealed to the humanity of those whom a strange curiosity led to this dreariest scene of human woe. But prejudice always confounded my story with those which most of my companions in confinement were eager to tell. I addressed it to an old man; he heard me in silence; then turning to the keeper, remarked, that it was odd that one fancy possessed us all, the desire to leave our present dwelling. 'Ay,' said the keeper, 'that is always the burden of the song;' and they turned to listen to the ravings of some other object. I told my tale to a youth, and thought I had prevailed, for tears filled his eyes. 'Good God!' cried he, instantly flying from a painful compassion, 'to see so lovely a creature lost to herself and to the world!'

The ladies had courage to bear a sight which might shake the strongest nerves, but not to venture upon close conference with me. They shrunk behind their guards, whispering something about the unnatural brightness of my eyes.

My only hope, therefore, rested upon the return of the humane surgeon, and upon the chance that he might find leisure to examine me himself, instead of trusting to the representation of the keeper. Yet, even there, might not prejudice operate against me? I had felt its effects, and had reason to tremble.

The day came which preceded his periodical visit to the department whither I had been removed. It was a stormy one, and heavy rain beat against my grated window. My swallows, who had tried their first flight only the day before, cowered close in their nest; or peeped from its little round opening, as if to watch the return of their mother. They had grown so accustomed to me, that the sight of me never disturbed them. In the pride of my heart I showed them to the keeper when he brought my morning repast. 'Who knows,' said I, 'if the doctor come to-morrow, but they and I may take our departure together.' As I spoke, a gust of the storm loosened the little fabric from its hold. I sprung in consternation to the window. The ruin was complete; my treasure was dashed to the ground. Let those smile who can, when I own that I uttered a cry of sorrow; and, renouncing my unfinished meal, threw myself on my bed and wept.

'Help the girl!' exclaimed the keeper. 'A woman almost as big as I am, crying for a swallow's nest. Well, as I shall answer, I thought you had got quite well almost.'

Aware too late of the impression which my ill-timed weakness had given, I did my utmost, at his subsequent visits, to repair my error; but prejudice, even in its last stage of decay, is more easily revived than destroyed, and I saw that he remained at best sceptical.

The day came which was to decide my fate. No lover waiting the sentence of a cautious mistress, – no gamester pausing in dread to look at the decisive die, – no British mother trembling with the Gazette in her hand, – ever felt such anxiety as I did, at the approach of my medical judge. With as much coherence, however, as I could command, I related to him the circumstances to which I attributed my confinement. He heard me with attention, questioned, and cross-examined me. 'Have you any objection,' said he, 'to my making enquiries of Mr Boswell?'

'None, certainly,' said I, 'if you cannot otherwise convince yourself that I ought to be set at liberty; else I should be unwilling to add to his domestic discomfort. I am persuaded that he has no part in this cruelty.'

The surgeon remained with me long; talking on various subjects, and ingeniously contriving to withdraw my attention from the ordeal which I was undergoing. The keeper, to justify his own sagacity, detailed with exaggeration every instance he had witnessed of my supposed eccentricity. 'To this good day,' said he, 'she'll be crying one minute, and singing the next.'

'Mr Smith,' said the doctor, shaking his head gravely, 'if you shut up all the women who change their humour every minute, who will make our shirts and puddings?'

He related the transports of my premature gratitude. 'By the time you are a little older, Miss Percy,' said the doctor, 'you will guess better how far sympathy will go; and then you will not run the risk of being thought crazy, by showing more sensibility than other people.'

Other instances of my extravagance were not more successful; for the doctor's prejudice had fortunately taken the other side. 'You know, Mr Smith,' said he, 'that I always suspected this was not a case for your management; and that if I had been in the way when admission was asked for this lady, she would never have been here.' My departure was therefore authorised; and, at my earnest request, it was fixed for that day.

And who shall paint the rapture of the prisoner, who tells himself, what yet he scarcely dares believe, 'This day I shall be free?' Who shall utter the gratitude which swells the heart of him whom this day has made free? That I was to go I knew not whither, – to subsist I knew not how, – could not damp the joys of deliverance. The wide world was indeed before me; but even that of itself was happiness. The free air, – the open face of heaven, – the unfettered grace of nature, – the joyous sport of animals, – the cheerful tools of man, – sounds of intelligence, and sights of bliss were there; and the wide world was to me, the native land of the exile, lovely with every delightful recollection, and populous with brethren and friends.

CHAPTER XXV

Oh! grief has changed me since you saw me last;
And careful hours, and time's deforming hand
Have written strange defeatures in my face.

Shakspeare.

THOUGH I resisted all idea of returning, even for an hour, to the control of Mrs Boswell, it was thought necessary, since I had been confined upon her authority and at her expense, that, before my departure, she should be informed of my recovery, and consequent dismission. After waiting impatiently the return of a message despatched for this purpose; I learnt that Mr Boswell's house was shut up; the whole family having removed to the country. My kind friend, Dr ——, however, would not permit this to retard my departure. He undertook for Mrs Boswell's performance of her engagement; which, he said, he could easily compel, by threatening to expose her conduct. For my part, I had no doubt that she had fled from the fear of detection, and with the design of preventing her husband from discovering the barbarity she had practised; for I knew that it was not the love of rural life, nor even of the fashion, which could have roused Mrs Boswell to the exertion of travelling fifty miles.

So far as I was concerned, however, her precaution was unnecessary; for she had injured me too seriously to have any return of injury to fear. Nothing short of necessity could have induced me to expose her, while I saw reason to dread that self-deceit might, under the name of justice, countenance the spirit of revenge. The only reason I had to regret her departure was, that I was thus prevented from receiving the money which Mr Boswell had acknowledged to be my right. Every thing else which could be called mine had been sent with me from the house, and was now faithfully restored to me. Feeble indeed must have been the honesty to which my possessions could have furnished a temptation! The whole consisted in a few shillings, and a scanty assortment of the plainest attire. And yet the heir of the noblest domain never looked round him with such elation as I did, when I once more found myself under the open canopy of heaven; nor did ever the 'harp and the viol' delight the ear like the sound of the heavy gate which closed upon my departing steps. I paused for a moment, to ask myself if all was not a dream; then leant my forehead against the threshold, and wept the thanksgiving I could not utter.

I was roused by an enquiry from the person who was carrying my portmanteau, 'whither I chose to have it conveyed?' The only residence which had occurred to me, the only place with which I seemed entitled to claim acquaintance, was my old abode at Mrs Milne's; and I desired the man to conduct me thither.

Though the gladness of my heart disposed me to good-humour with every living thing, I could not help observing that my landlady received me coolly. To my enquiry whether my former apartment was vacant, I could scarcely obtain an intelligible reply; and when I requested that, if she could not accommodate me, she would recommend another lodging-house to me, the flame burst forth. She told me 'that she had had enough of recommending people she knew nothing about. Mrs Boswell had very near turned away her sister for recommending me already.' I assured the woman that I should have sincerely regretted being the occasion of any misfortune to her sister; and declared that I was utterly unconscious of having ever done discredit to her recommendation. 'It might be so,' the landlady said, 'but she did not know; it seemed very odd that I had been sent away in a hurry from Mr Boswell's, and that I had never been heard of from that day to this. To be sure,' said she, 'it was no wonder that Mrs Boswell dismissed a person who had brought so much distress and trouble into the family, and almost been the death of both Mr Boswell and little miss.'

'Mr Boswell! did he catch the infection too?'

'To be sure he did; and so I dare say would the whole house, if you had not been sent away.'

I expressed my unfeigned sorrow for the mischief which I had innocently caused; for I was at this moment less disposed to resent impertinence than to sympathise in the joys and sorrows of all human kind.

My landlady's countenance at last relaxd a little; and either won by my good-humour, or prompted by her curiosity to discover my adventures during my mysterious disappearance, or by a desire to dispose of her lodging at a season when they were not very disposable, she told me that I might, if I chose, take possession of my former accommodation. With this ungracious permission I was obliged to comply; for the day was already closing, and my scarcely recovered strength was fast yielding to fatigue.

I was aware, however, that in those lodgings it was impossible for me, with only my present funds, to remain; for humble as were my accommodations, they were far too costly for my means of payment. Mr Boswell had, indeed, acknowledged himself my debtor for a sum, which, in my situation, appeared positive riches; but my prospect of receiving it was so small, or at least so distant, that I dared not include the disposal of it in any plan for the present. That I might not, however, lose it by my own neglect, I immediately wrote to remind Mr Boswell of his promise, and to acquaint him whither he might transmit the money. I had no very sanguine hopes that this letter would ever reach the person for whom it was intended; and was more sorry than surprised, when day after day passed, and brought no answer.

In the mean time, I made every exertion to obtain a new situation. I enquired for Mrs Murray; and found that she was still in England, where she had been joined by her son. I went unwittingly to the house of her repulsive sister; and found, to my great relief, that it was, like half the houses in its neighbourhood, deserted for the season. It was in vain that I endeavoured to procure employment as a teacher. The season was against my success. The town was literally empty; for though this is a mere figure of speech when applied to London, it becomes a matter of fact in Edinburgh. Besides, I had no introduction; and I believe there is no place under Heaven where an introduction is so indispensable. Without it, scarcely the humblest employment was to be obtained. Had I asked for alms, I should probably have been bountifully supplied; but the charity which in Scotland is bestowed upon a nameless stranger, is not of that kind which 'thinketh no evil.'

Observing one day in the window of a toy-shop some of those ingenious trifles, in the making of which I had once been accustomed to amuse myself, I offered to supply the shop with as many of them as I could manufacture. The shopman received my proposal coolly. Had I ordered the most expensive articles of his stock, they would probably have been intrusted to me without hesitation; but even he seemed to think that pin-cushions and work-baskets must be made only by persons of unequivocal repute. At last, though he would not intrust me with his materials, he permitted me to work with my own; promising that, if my baubles pleased him, he would purchase them. Even for this slender courtesy I was obliged to be thankful; for I had now during a week subsisted upon my miserable fund, and, in spite of the most rigid economy, it was exhausted. The price of my lodging too for that week was still undischarged; and it only remained to choose what part of my little wardrobe should be applied to the payment of this debt.

The choice was difficult; for nothing remained that could be spared without inconvenience; and when it was at length fixed, I was still doubtful how I should employ this last wreck of my possessions. I was strongly tempted to use it in the purchase of materials for the work I had undertaken; because I expected that in this way it might swell into a fund which might not only repay my landlady, but contribute to my future subsistence. But, fallen as I was, I could not condescend to hazard, without permission, what was now, in fact, the property of another: and, humbled as I had been, my heart revolted from owing the use of my little capital to the forbearance of one from whom I could scarcely extort respect. Once more, however, stubborn nature was forced to bow; for, between humiliation and manifest injustice, there was no room for hesitation; and I summoned my landlady to my apartment. 'Mrs Milne,' said I, 'I can this evening pay what I owe you; and I can do no more. I shall then have literally nothing.'

The woman stood staring at me with a face of curious surprise; for this was the first time that I had ever spoken to her of my circumstances or situation. 'If you choose to have your money,' I continued, 'it is yours. If you prefer letting it remain with me for a few days longer, it will procure to me the means of subsistence, and to you the continuance of a tenant for your apartment.'

After enquiring into my plan with a freedom which I could ill brook, Mrs Milne told me, 'that she had no wish to be severe upon any body; and therefore would, for the present, be content with half her demand.' This arrangmement made, nothing remained except to procure the money; and, for this purpose, I hasted to the place which I had formerly visited on a similar errand.

It was a shop little larger than a closet, dark, dirty, and confused; and yet, I believe, Edinburgh, at that time, contained none more respectable in its particular line. Some women, apparently of the lowest rank, were searching for bargains among the trash which lay upon the counter; while others seemed waiting to add to the heap. All bore the brand of vice and wretchedness. Their squalid attire, their querulous or broken voices, their haggard and bloated countenances, filled me with dread and loathing.

Having despatched my business, I was hastening to depart, when I was arrested by a voice less ungentle than the others. It spoke in a melancholy importunate half whisper; but it spoke in the accents of my native land, and I started as if at the voice of a friend. The face of the speaker was turned away from me. Her figure, too, was partly concealed by a cloak, tawdry with shreds of what had once been lace. An arm, on which the deathy skin clung to the bones, dragged rather than supported a languid infant. She seemed making a last effort to renew a melancholy pleading. 'If it were but the smallest trifle, sir,' said she.

'I tell you woman, I cannot afford it,' was the answer. 'You have had more than the gown is worth already.'

'God help me then,' said the woman, 'for I must perish;' and she turned to be gone. The light rested upon her features. Altered as they were, they could not be forgotten. 'Juliet! Miss Arnold!' I exclaimed; and the long tale of credulity and ingratitude passed across my mind in an instant. I stood gazing upon her for a moment. Sickness, want and sorrow, were written in her face. I remembered it bright with all the sportive graces of youth and gaiety. The contrast overcame me. 'Juliet! dear Juliet!' I cried, and fell upon her neck.

Strong emotion long kept me silent; while she seemed over-powered by surprise. At length she recovered utterance. 'Ah, Ellen!' said she, 'you are avenged on me now.'

'Avenged! oh, Juliet!'

It was then that I remembered the vengeance which I had imprecated upon her head; and it was she who was avenged!

When I again raised my eyes to her face, it was crossed by a faint flush; and she looked down as if with shame upon her wretched attire. 'I am sadly changed since you saw me last, Miss Percy,' said she.

I could not bear to own the horrible truth of her words. 'Let us leave this place,' said I. 'Come where you may tell me what has caused this wreck.'

I offered her my arm, and, with a look of surprise, she accepted it. 'Sure,' said she, 'you must be ashamed to be seen with a person of my appearance.

'Can you imagine,' said I, 'that appearance is in my thoughts at such a moment as this?' and vexed and chilled by this cold attention to trifles, I silently conducted her towards my home.

It was at a considerable distance from the place of our meeting; and the strength of my companion was scarcely equal to the journey. We had not gone far before she stopped, arrested by the breathlessness of consumption. Alarmed, I held out my arms to relieve her from the burden of the infant. Then first a painful suspicion struck a sickness to my heart. I looked at her, then at the child, and feared to ask if it was her own. She seemed to interpret the look, for a blush deepened the hectic upon her cheek. 'My boy is not the child of shame, Miss Percy,' said she. My breast was lightened of a load – I pressed her arm to me, and again we went on.

We at length reached my lodgings; and, regardless of the suspicious looks which were cast upon us by the people of the house, I led Miss Arnold to my apartment, and shared with her the last refreshment I could command. During our repast, I could not help observing that the change in Miss Arnold's appearance had but partially extended to her manners. She was no sooner a little revived than she began to find occasions of flattering me upon my improved beauty, which she hinted had become only more interesting by losing the glow of health.

'In one respect, Juliet,' said I coldly, 'you will find me changed. I have lost my taste for compliments.' Then fearing I had spoken with severity, I added more gaily, 'Besides, you can talk of me at any time. Now tell me rather why I find you here so far from home, so much – tell me every thing that it will not pain you to tell.'

Miss Arnold showed no disinclination to enter on her tale. She told me that, in consequence of her intimacy with Lady St Edmunds, she had, after leaving me, *necessarily* improved her acquaintance with her Ladyship's niece, Lady Maria de Burgh. A smile of self-complacency crossed her wasted face as she told me that a very few interviews had served to dispel all Lady Maria's prejudices against her. 'But to be sure,' added she, 'Lady Maria is such a fool, that I had no great glory in changing her opinion.' I remembered with a sigh the time when this comment would have given me pleasure; but I did not answer; and Miss Arnold went on to relate, that Lady Maria soon pressed her, with such unwearied importunity to become her guest, that the invitation was absolutely not to be resisted without incivility.

Lord Glendower was at that time Lady Maria's suitor; or rather, Miss Arnold said, he talked and trifled in such a way, that her Ladyship was in anxious expectation of his becoming so. 'However,' continued she, 'I soon saw that, had our situations been equal, he might have preferred me to his would-be bride.'

She stopped, but I waited in silence the continuation of her story. 'You know, Ellen,' said she, 'it was not to be supposed that I would neglect so splendid a prospect. I had no obligation to Lady Maria which bound me to sacrifice my happiness.'

'Happiness!' repeated I involuntarily, while I recollected my humble estimate of Lord Glendower's talents for bestowing it.

'Any thing, you know, was happiness,' said Miss Arnold, 'compared with the life of dependence and subjection which I must have endured with my brother.' She went on detailing innumerable circumstances which seemed to lay her under a kind of necessity to encourage Lord Glendower.

'Ay, ay, Juliet,' interrupted I, 'as Mr Maitland used to say, we ladies can always make up in the number of our reasons whatever they want in weight.'

Miss Arnold seemed to feel some difficulty in proceeding to the next step of her narrative. 'At last,' said she, hesitating, 'it was agreed; – I consented to – to go with Glendower to Scotland.'

'To Scotland! Was not Lord Glendower his own master? Could he not marry where he pleased?'

'It was his wish,' said Miss Arnold, blushing and hesitating; 'and – and you know, Ellen, when a woman is attached – you know ——'

'Don't appeal to my knowledge, Juliet, for I never was attached, and never shall be.'

A pause followed; and it was only at my request that Miss Arnold went on with her story. 'When we arrived here,' said she, 'I found Glendower's attentions were not what I expected. You may judge of my despair! I knew, though I was innocent, nobody would believe my innocence; – I saw that I was as much undone as if I had been really guilty.'

'Oh no, Juliet!' cried I, 'there is, indeed, only one step between imprudence and guilt; but that one is the passage from uneasiness to misery, abiding misery. But what did you resolve upon?'

'What could I do, Ellen? A little dexterity is the only means of defence which we poor women possess.'

'Any means of defence was lawful,' said I rashly, 'where all that is valuable in this world or the next was to be defended.'

'Certainly,' said Miss Arnold. 'Therefore, what I did cannot be blamed. I had heard something of the Scotch laws in regard to marriage; and I refused to see Glendower, unless he would at least persuade the people of the lodging-house that I was his wife. Afterwards, I contrived to make him send me a note, addressed to Lady Glendower. The note itself was of no consequence, but it answered the purpose, and I have preserved it. I took care, too, to ascertain that the people about us observed him address me as his wife; and in Scotland this is as good as a thousand ceremonies. Besides, you know, Ellen, a ceremony is nothing. Whatever joins people irrevocably, is a marriage in the sight of God and man.'

'Yes,' answered I, 'provided that both parties understand themselves to be irrevocably bound.'

Miss Arnold averted her eye for a moment; then looked up more steadily, and went on with her story. 'After this, I had no hesitation to accompany him to a shooting lodge, which he had hired, in the Highlands. We were there some months: I am sure I was heartily sick of it. In winter last we came here, and Glendower talked of going to town; but I was not able, nor indeed much inclined to go with him; he has got into such a shocking habit of drinking. So he left me here, promising to come back after I was confined; but he had not been gone above two months, when I saw in a newspaper an account of his marriage with Lady Maria. It came upon me like a thunder-stroke. The shock brought on a premature confinement, and I was long in extreme danger. However, I dictated letters both to Glendower and Lady Maria, asserting my claims, and declaring that, if they were resisted, the law should do me justice. I wrote often before I could obtain an answer; and at last Glendower had the effrontery to write, denying that I had any right over him. He had even the cruelty to allege, that the time of my poor little boy's birth in part refuted my story.' Juliet, who had hitherto told her tale with astonishing self-posssession, now burst into tears. 'As I hope for mercy, Ellen,' said she, folding her infant to her breast with all the natural fondness of a mother, – 'as I hope for mercy, this boy is Glendower's; and, as I truly believe, is his only lawful heir. If I could see him once restored to his rights, I should ask no more.'

She soon composed herself, and resumed her disastrous story. Lord Glendower, incensed by her claim, refused to remit her money. She wrote to her brother an account of her situation. He answered, that he had already spent upon her education a sum sufficient, if she had acted prudently, to have made her fortune; that he was not such a fool as to spend more in publishing her disgrace in a court of law, where he was sure no judge would award her five shillings of damages; – that he sent her thirty pounds to furnish a shop of small wares, and desired he might never hear of her more. The money came in time to rescue her from a prison; but the payment of her debts left her penniless. She had subsisted for some time by the sale of her trinkets and clothes. Lower and lower her resources had fallen; narrower and more narrow had become the circle of her comforts, till she was now completely a beggar.

She had also long struggled with ill health. 'This exhausting cough,' said she, 'and this weakness that makes every thing a burden to me, are very disheartening, though I know they are not dangerous.' I looked at her, and shuddered. If ever consumption had set its deadly seal upon any face, hers bore the impression.

'What is the matter, Ellen?' said she. 'I assure you I am not so ill as I look.'

'I hope not,' said I, trying to smile.

Evening was now closing; and as I knew that the place which Juliet had for some days called her home was at a considerable distance, I was about to propose sharing my apartment with her for the night; when my landlady opening my door, desired, in a very surly tone, that I would speak with her. Half guessing the subject of our conference, I followed her out of hearing of my unfortunate companion. In terms which I must rather attempt to translate than record, she enquired what right I had to fill her house with vagrants. With some warmth I resisted the application of the phrase, telling her that the misfortunes of a gentlewoman gave no one a right to load her with suspicion or abuse. 'Troth, as for gentility,' said the landlady, 'I believe you are both much about it. I might have my notion; but I never knew rightly what you were, till I saw the company you keep. A creature painted to the eyes!'

'Painted! The painting of death!'

'Well, well, painted or not painted, send her out of this house; for here she shall stay no longer!'

'Mrs Milne,' said I, scorning the altercation in which I was engaged, 'while that apartment is called mine, it shall receive or exclude whomsoever I please.' I turned from her, determined to use the right which I had asserted.

'Yours, indeed!' cried the enraged landlady, following me. 'It shall not be called yours long then. Either pay for the week you have had it, or else leave it this moment; and don't stay here bringing disgrace upon creditable people that never bore but a good character till now.'

I am ashamed to own that the insolence of this low woman overcame my frail temper. 'Disgrace!' I began in the tone of strong indignation; but recollecting that I could only degrade myself by the contest, I again turned away in silence.

She now forced herself into my apartment; and, addressing Miss Arnold, commanded her to leave the house instantly. Miss Arnold cast a supplicating look upon me. 'I shall never reach home alone,' said she.

'There is no need for your attempting it,' returned I; 'for if you go, I will accompany you.'

To this proposal, however, Miss Arnold appeared averse. She showed a strong inclination to remain where she was, and even condescended to remonstrate with the insolent landlady. Had I guessed the reason of this condescension, I might have been saved one of the most horrible moments of my existence. It had no other effect than to increase the impertience it was meant to disarm; for the 'soft answer which turns away wrath' must at least seem disinterested. Disgusted with this scene of vulgar oppression and spiritless endurance, 'Come, Juliet,' said I, 'if I cannot protect you from insolence here, I will attend you home; and since you cannot share my apartment, let me take part of yours.'

Miss Arnold still lingered, however, and again made a fruitless appeal to the compassion of Mrs Milne; but finding her inexorable, she consented to depart.

I threw my purse upon the table. 'Mrs Milne,' said I, 'after what you have obliged me to hear, I will not put it in your power to insult me by farther suspicion. There is the money I owe you.'

The landlady, now somewhat softened, followed us to the door, assuring me that it was not to me she made objections. I left her without reply; and giving Juliet my arm, supported her during a long and melancholy walk.

It was almost dark; and the thoughts of passing unprotected through the streets of a great city filled me with alarm. I breathed painfully, and scarcely dared to speak even in a whisper. Every time that my exhausted companion stopped to gather strength, I shook with the dread that we should attract observation; and when we proceeded, I shrunk from every passenger, as if from an assassin. Without molestation, however, we reached Miss Arnold's abode.

It was in the attic story of a building, of which each floor seemed inhabited by two separate families; and in this respect alone it seemed superior to the dwelling of my poor friend Cecil, who shared her habitation with a whole community. Miss Arnold knocked; and a dirty, wretched-looking woman cautiously opened the door. Presenting me, Miss Arnold began, 'I have brought you a lady who wishes to take ——' But the moment the woman perceived us, her eyes flashed fury; and she interrupted Miss Arnold with a torrent of invective; from which I could only learn, that my companion, being her debtor, had deceived her as to her means of payment, and that she was resolved to admit her no more. Having talked herself out of breath, she shut the door with a violence which made the house shake.

I turned to the ghastly figure of my companion, and grew sick with consternation. Half bent to the earth, she was leaning against the threshold, as if unable to support herself. 'Plead for me, Ellen,' said she faintly. 'I can go no farther.' In compliance with this piteous request, I knocked again and again; but no answer was returned.

I now addressed myself to Juliet; entreating her to exert herself, and assuring her of my persuasion, that if she could once more reach my lodgings, even the inexorable Mrs Milne would not permit her to pass the night without a shelter. But the weakness of the disease had extended to the mind. Miss Arnold sunk upon the ground. 'Oh, I can go no farther!' she cried; wringing her hands, and weeping like an infant. 'Go – go home, and leave me, Ellen. I left you in your extremity, and now judgment has overtaken me! Go, and leave me.'

It was in vain that I entreated her to have mercy on herself, and on her child; imploring that she would not, by despair, create the evil she dreaded. 'Oh, I cannot go, I cannot go,' said she; and she continued to repeat, weeping, the same hopeless reply to all that I could urge to rouse her.

The expectation which I had tried to awaken in her was but feeble in my own breast; and I at last desisted from my fruitless importunity.

But what course remained for me? Even the poorest shelter I had not the means to procure. We were in a land of strangers; and many a heart open to human sympathies was closed against us. To solicit pity was to provoke suspicion, perhaps to encounter scorn. I myself might return to my inhospitable home, but what would then become of the unfortunate Juliet? While I gazed upon the dying figure before me, and weighed the horrible alternative of leaving her perhaps to perish alone, or remaining with her exposed to all from which the nature of woman most recoils, my spirits failed; and the bitter tears of anguish burst from my eyes. But there are thoughts of comfort which ever hover near the soul, like the good spirits that walk the earth unseen. There is a hope that presses for admission into the heart from which all other hope is fled. 'Juliet,' said I, 'let us commend ourselves to God. It is His will that we should this night have no protection but His own. Be the consequence what it may, I will not leave you.'

My unhappy companion answered only by a continuance of that feeble wailing which was now more the effect of weakness than of grief; while I, turning from her, addressed myself to Heaven, with a confidence which they only know who have none other confidence.

CHAPTER XXVI

It is too late. The life of all her *blood*
Is touched corruptibly; and her *poor brain*
(*Which some suppose the soul's frail dwelling-*
house)
Doth, by the idle comments which it makes,
Foretell the ending of mortality.

Shakspeare.

I WAS startled by the approach of a heavy footstep. Trembling, I whispered to Miss Arnold an earnest entreaty that she would command herself, and not invite curiosity, perhaps insult, to our last retreat. But I asked an impossibility; poor Juliet could not restrain her sobbing. The step continued to ascend the stair. Though now hopeless of concealment, I instinctively shrunk aside. But I breathed more freely, when I perceived through the dusk that the cause of my alarm was a woman.

Crossing the landing, she knocked at the door adjacent to that which had been closed against us; then approaching my companion, she enquired into the cause of her distress. 'She is a stranger, sick, and unfortunate,' said I, now coming forward. 'The only place where she could this night find shelter is so distant, that she is quite unable to reach it.'

A youthful voice now calling from within was answered by the woman; and presently the door was opened by a girl carrying a lamp. Several joyous faces crowded to welcome a mother's return; and beyond, the light of a cheerful fire danced on the roof of a clean though humble dwelling. I turned an eye almost of envy towards the woman. The lamp threw a strong gleam upon her features; they were familiar to my recollection. She was the widow of the poor gardener who died in my presence at Greenwich.

She had turned to address some words of compassion to Miss Arnold; when the little girl pulled her by the apron, and, casting a sidelong look at me, said in a half whisper, 'Mother, *she* is like the good English lady.' The widow turned towards me, and uttered an exclamation of surprise; then doubting the evidence of her senses, 'No,' said she, 'it is not possible.'

'It is but too possible, Mrs Campbell,' said I; 'the changes of this restless world have made me the stranger now.'

'And its yoursel', miss! exclaimed the widow, looking at me with a glad smile. 'God bless you! ye shall never be strange to me. Please just to come in, and rest you a little.' Then recollecting Juliet, she added, 'If ye be concerned for this poor body, just bid her come in too.'

The wanderer, who, benighted in the enemy's land, has been welcomed to the abode of charity and peace, will imagine the gladness with which I accepted this invitation. I raised my dejected companion from the ground, led her to her new asylum, and fervently thanked Heaven for the joyful sense of her safety and my own.

We presently found ourselves in an apartment which served in the double capacity of kitchen and parlour; and our hostess placing a large stuffed elbow-chair close to the fire, cordially invited me to sit. She looked back towards my companion, as if doubtful whether she were entitled to similar courtesy. 'Lady Glendower,' said I, offering to her the place of honour. It was the first time I had called Juliet by her new name. After all my impressive lessons of humility, I fear I was not entirely disinterested in asserting the disparity between the rank of my companion and her appearance; but I fancied for the moment, that I was merely claiming respect and compassion for the unfortunate. I had, however, some difficulty in conveying the desired impression of my friend's dignity; and it was not until I had succeeded, that I enquired whether Mrs Campbell could give her the accommodation which she so much needed. The good woman seemed delighted to have an opportunity of serving me; and her little girl, who, with the awkward bashfulness common to the children of her country, had resisted all the advances of her old acquaintance, now whispered to her mother an offer to resign her bed to the stranger. This was, however, unnecessary. Mrs Campbell informed me, that since I had enabled her to return to her own connections, she had never known want, having obtained constant employment as a laundress; that her brother, a thriving tradesman, having lately become a widower, had invited her to superintend his family; and his business having for the present carried him from home, she offered Juliet the use of his apartment.

My companion thus provided with a decent shelter, I began to indulge some anxiety on my own account. It was near midnight; and I was almost a mile from home, if I could indeed be said to have a home. I had never traversed a city by night without all the protections of equipage and retinue. Now, without defence from outrage, except in the neglect of the passers by, I was to steal timidly to a threshold where my admission was at best doubtful. The only alternative was to request that the widow would extend to me the kindness which she had just shown to my friend; and this request required an effort which I found almost impracticable.

I hesitated in my choice of evils till the hour almost decided the question; then half resolved to utter my proposal, I began to speak; but the favour which I had petitioned for another, I found it impossible to ask for myself; and I was obliged to conclude my hesitating preface by a request, that Mrs Campbell would accompany me home.

Juliet no sooner saw me about to depart, than she was seized with the idea that I was going to forsake her for ever; and reduced by illness and fatigue to the weakness of infancy, she again began to weep. In vain did I promise to return in the morning. 'Oh no,' said she, 'I cannot expect it. I cannot expect you to visit me – me, forlorn and wretched.'

'These very circumstances, Juliet,' said I, 'would of themselves ensure my return. But if you will not rely on my friendship, at least trust my word. That you have never had reason to doubt.'

Miss Arnold did not venture to offend me by expressing her suspicions of a promise so formally given; but when I offered to go, she clung to me, entreating with an earnestness which betrayed her fears, that I would not leave her to want and desolation.

Overcome by her tears, or glad perhaps of a pretext for yielding decently, I now offered to remain with her, and proposed to share her apartment. Our grateful hostess willingly consented to this arrangement; and, with a hundred apologies for the poorness of my accommodations, conducted us to our chamber. She little guessed how sumptuous it was, compared with others which I had occupied!

It was to be sure of no modern date; it shook at every step; and the dark lining of wainscot gave it a gloomy appearance; but its size and furniture were handsome, compared with what I had been accustomed to find in the dwellings of labour. An excellent bed was rendered luxurious by linens which, in purity and texture, might have suited a palace; and here I had soon the satisfaction of seeing my exhausted companion and her infant sink into profound repose.

For my part, I felt no inclination to sleep. My mind was occupied in considering the difficulties of my situation. While I had scarcely any apparent provision for my real wants, I was in a manner called to supply those of another; for Juliet was even more destitute than myself. Health, spirits, and activity still remained to me; blessings compared with which all that I had lost were as nothing; while the disease which was dragging her to the grave had already left her neither power to struggle, nor courage to endure. To desert her was an obduracy of selfishness which never entered my contemplation. But it remained for me to consider whether I should first provide for my own indispensable wants, and bestow upon her all else that constant diligence could supply; or whether we should share in common our scanty support, and when it failed, endure together.

'Were I to supply her occasionally,' thought I, 'every trifling gift would be dearly paid by the recollection that she forsook me in my extremity. If we live together, nothing will remind her that she owes any thing to me, and in time she may forget it. And shall not I indeed be the debtor? What shall I not owe her for the occasion to testify my sense of the great, the overwhelming forgiveness which has been heaped upon me? O Author of peace and pardon! enable me joyfully to toil, and to suffer for her, that I may at last trace, in this dark soul, a dawning of thine own brightness!'

My resolution was taken, and I lost no time in carrying it into effect. Understanding that our present apartment was to be unoccupied for some weeks, I hired it upon terms almost suitable to the state of my finances. I explained to Juliet my situation and my intentions; telling her gaily, that I appointed her my task-mistress, and expected she would look well to her duty. I next proposed to go and settle the demands of my former landlady, and to remove my small possessions to my new abode. Juliet made no resistance to this proposal; though I could read suspicion in the eye which scrutinised my face as I spoke. When I was ready to depart, she suddenly requested me to carry her little boy with me, under pretence that she herself was unable to give him exercise. I was instantly sensible of this palpable contrivance to secure my return. To feel myself suspected of treachery at the very moment when I was impatient to make every sacrifice, assailed my temper, where, alas! it has ever been most assailable. 'What right have you to insult me?' – I indignantly began; but when my eye rested on the faded countenance, the neglected form, the spiritless air of my once playful companion, my anger vanished. 'Oh, Juliet!' said I, 'do not add to all your other distresses the pain of suspecting your friend. Thoughtless, selfish, you may have found me; but why should you think me treacherous?' Miss Arnold protested immutable confidence, and unbounded gratitude; but I was no longer the credulous child of self-conceit and prosperity; and pained and disgusted, I turned away. Common discretion, however, required that I should not, by dwelling upon her unworthiness, render the task of befriending her more burdensome. I had indeed neither time nor spirits to spare for any disagreeable subject of contemplation.

After settling my accounts with Mrs Milne, I expended the miserable remainder of my money, partly on indispensable supply for the wants of the day, – partly on materials for the work which I hoped to earn subsistence for the morrow. Of these I was obliged to be content with a very humble assortment. I remembered that, in our better days, Juliet, as well as myself, had shown inexhaustible ingenuity in the creation of toys; and I fancied that we might again, with pleasure, share these light labours together. But no one who has not made the experiment can imagine how deadly compulsion is to pleasure; – how wearisome the very sport becomes which must of necessity be continued the livelong day; – how inviting is every gleam of sunshine, every glimpse of the open face of Heaven, to one who dares not spare a moment to enjoy them! Oppressed by the listlessness of disease, Juliet could scarcely make this experiment; or rather perhaps her early habits could not give way to a sense of duty, or even of necessity. Her work was taken up and relinquished a hundred times a day. The trifle which was begun one hour, was the next deserted for another, to be in its turn forsaken. But what was worse, a series of efforts defeated, – the sense of a fault which she had not courage to amend, had an unfortunate effect upon her temper; and the once playful and caressing Juliet became discontented and peevish.

These humours indeed she seldom directly vented upon me; but her ill health, her misfortunes, her privations, the treachery of her husband, the cruelty of her brother, and the ill qualities of mankind in general, furnished her with sufficient subjects of impatience. Once indeed, for a moment, her self-command forsook her so far, that she turned her displeasure on a trifling occasion against me. I kept my temper, however; and she instantly recovered hers. But the cowardly fear of alienating me, the most provoking of all her weaknesses, prompted her soon after to overwhelm me with promises which were to be performed when she should be restored to her rights and dignities. I had resolved never to wound her by one severe expression, and even now I kept my purpose, though I wept with indignation.

But in spite of my forbearance, and Juliet's caution, I was often sensible that I had involuntairly given her pain. I could see that she often mistook the most casual expressions for subtle reproach, or insinuated threat. Though I forgave, I found it impossible to convince her of my forgiveness. However suppressed, the latent impression of her mind certainly was, that I must, in some sort, avenge myself for her former desertion; nor could she always conceal the mingled sentiment of fear and anger which this impression inspired.

But no expression of impatience, nor even of suspicion, was so tormenting to me as the abject entreaties for forgiveness, which were reiterated after the most solemn assurances that they were needless. 'For Heaven's sake, Juliet,' I would say to her, 'let this subject be dropped for ever. I beseech you to let me forget that I have any thing to forgive you. If ever you see me fail in kindness, if ever I seem to prefer my own comfort or advantage to yours, then – then remind me that you once did me wrong, that you may rouse me by the strongest of motives to love and benefit you.' But all I could say, did only, at best, impress her with momentary conviction. More frequently her efforts failed to conceal from me that she thought me more capable of inventing Christian sentiments than of feeling them.

In the mean time, her feeble frame declined from day to day; yet, while she was thus a prey to groundless apprehensions, the melancholy security, which is so frequent a symptom of her disease, blinded her to the approach of inevitable fate. It was heart-breaking to see her spending her last breath in devising schemes of vanity or revenge; fixing, with suspicious dread, her dying eye upon a fellow-worm, regardless of all that the Creator could threaten or bestow. Often did I resolve to awaken her to her danger; but so profound seemed her security, that my courage was unequal to the task. I did not, indeed, deceive her with the language of hope, but I forbore, explicitly, to express my fears; and with this concealment, so cowardly, so unfriendly, so cruel, I shall never cease to reproach myself.

It was, perhaps, for want of this very act of resolution, that I found it impossible to rouse her to any serious examination of her own mind, any alarming impressions of her condition as an accountable creature. Having once settled it that I had been converted to methodism by Miss Mortimer, she was as impenetrable to all that I could urge, as if the name she gave to the speaker could have affected the nature and importance of the truth spoken.

My desertion was the sole object of her serious fears; her hopes all centered in her little boy, or rather in the honours which she expected him to attain. She was constantly urging me to find out some lawyer, whom the love of justice, or the hope of future recompense, might induce to undertake her cause. The ruin which her success was to bring upon one whom I had once regarded as an enemy made me unwilling to take any part in Miss Arnold's scheme; and my extreme dislike to asking favours rendered me particularly averse to make the application she desired. At last, weary of my delays, she herself undertook the business.

As she was no longer able to walk abroad, the earnings of two entire days were spent in conveying her to and from the chambers of an eminent lawyer; but we forgot our wants and our toils together, when she received a written opinion, that her claims were at least tenable.

The exertion she had made was death to the unfortunate Juliet. Her cough and fever increased to an alarming degree. Her sickly appetite revolted from our homely meals; and every thing which I had the means to procure was in turn rejected with loathing. That which at times she fancied might be less distasteful was no sooner procured, sometimes with difficulty enough, than it became offensive. The most unremitting diligence, the most rigid self-denial, could not provide for the caprices of the distempered palate; while the habits of indulgence, uniting with the feebleness of disease, rendered even the trivial disappointments of appetite important to poor Juliet. She would fret like an infant over the want of that which I had not to give; and would repeat again and again the wish which she knew could not be gratified. I cannot boast that my temper was always proof against this chiding. Sometimes I found safety in flight, – sometimes in the remembrance of Miss Mortimer's patient suffering, – and in a heartfelt prayer, that my life and my death might want every other comfort, rather than those which had to the last supported the spirit of my friend.

To all our other difficulties, a new cause of perplexity was suddenly added. The toyman who purchased my work one evening informed me, that he had an overstock of my baubles; and that unless I would greatly lower their price, he could for the present employ me no more. I was thunderstruck at this disaster. My earnings were already barely adequate to our wants, therefore, to reduce my wretched gains, was to incur at once all the real miseries of poverty. After my former experience in the difficulty of procuring employment, the loss of my present one seemed the sentence of ruin; and I, who should once have felt intolerable hardship in one day of labour, could now foresee no greater misfortune than idleness.

I wandered home irresolute and disconsolate. I seemed burdened beyond my strength, and felt the listless patience which succeeds a last vain struggle. I entered my home with the heavy careless step of one who has lost hope. My companion had sunk into a slumber; and as I watched her peaceful insensibility, I almost wished that she might awaken no more.

In such dark hours our departed sins ever return to haunt us. I remembered the thoughtless profusion with which I had wasted the gifts of fortune. I remembered that, with respect to every valuable purpose, they had been bestowed upon me in vain. It was strictly just, that the trust so abused should be entirely withdrawn; and, forgetful of all my better prospects, I sunk into the despondence of one who feels the grasp of inflexible, merciless justice. 'I will struggle with my fate no more,' said I. 'I have deserved and will endure it patiently.' Patiently! did I call it? Were my feelings those of one invited in a course of steady endeavours to hope for a blessing, but forewarned that this blessing might not wear the form of success? Did they not rather resemble the sullen resignation of him who is thwarted by a resistless adversary?

A sentiment like this could not harbour long in a mind accustomed to dwell upon the proofs of goodness unspeakable, – accustomed to commit its cares to a Father's wisdom, to expect all its joys from a Father's love. The hour came, the solemn hour, appointed perhaps to teach us at once our dependence and our security, when, by the very constitution of our frame, all mortal being resigns itself into the hands of the Guardian who slumbereth not; – when all mortal being is forced to commit its possessions, its powers, to His care, in order to receive them renovated from His bounty again. I know not how it is with others, but I cannot help considering the helplessness of sleep as an invitation to cast myself implicitly upon His protection; nor can I feel the healthful vivacity of the waking hour, without receiving in it a pledge of His patience and His love. The morning found me in peace and in hope, although I was as little as ever able to devise the means of my escape from penury.

One scheme at last occurred to me, which nothing but dire necessity could have suggested; and which, in spite of the bitter medicine I had received, still gave me pain enough to indicate the original disease of my mind. This scheme was, to request that our landlady would endeavour to dispose of my work among the families by whom she was employed. Though she must have guessed at my situation, it could only be partially known to her; for I had always taken care to discharge her claims with scrupulous punctuality; submitting to many a privation, rather than fail to lay aside daily the pittance necessary to answer her weekly demand. To tell her of my wants, – to commit the story of them to her discretion, – to claim her aid in a traffic which I myself had been accustomed to consider as only a more modest kind of begging, – was so revolting to my feelings, that, had my own wants alone been in question, the effort would never have been made, while they were any thing less than intolerable. But I did not *dare* to resist the wants of Juliet, for Juliet had wronged me. I could not resist them; for a series of kindnesses, begun in a sense of duty, had awakened in my heart something of its early affection towards her; and her melancholy decay of body and of mind touched all that was compassionate in my nature.

Yet I gladly recollected, that Mrs Campbell's absence would afford me some hours of reprieve; and in the evening, the sound of her return made my breath come short. Coldly and concisely I made my request, striving the while for a look of unconcern. The request was cordially granted; and the good woman proceeded to ask a hundred questions and instructions; for she had none of that quick observation and instinctive politeness which would have made my Highland friend instantly perceive and avoid a painful subject. The only directions, however, which I was inclined to give her, were to spare my name, and to use no solicitation. Having prepared some toys, of which the workmanship constituted almost the sole value, I committed them to her charge.

The first day, she brought back my poor merchandise undiminished; and, in consequence, I was obliged to let the toyman take it at little more than the price of the materials. The second, however, she was more fortunate. She sold a little painted basket for more than the sum I had expected it to bring; and conveyed to me, besides, a message from the purchaser, desiring that I would undertake to paint a set of ornaments for a chimney-piece. My satisfaction was somewhat damped by the lady's making it a condition of her employing me, that I should receive her directions in person. There was no room for hesitation, however, and I was obliged to consent.

Poor Juliet was childishly delighted with our good fortune. 'Now,' cried she, 'I may have the glass of Burgundy and water that you have been refusing me these two days.' For two days she had almost entirely rejected the simple fare which I could offer, though day and night she ceased not to complain that she was pining for the support which her languid frame required; and this same glass of Burgundy and water was constantly declared to be the only endurable form of sustenance, the panacea which was instantly to cure all her ailments.

'Indeed, Juliet,' said I, 'we must endeavour to think of something else that you can take. All the money we have, excepting what must be paid Mrs Campbell to-morrow, would not buy the smallest quantity of Burgundy that is sold.'

'I am sure Mrs Campbell would wait,' returned Juliet: 'she does not want the money.'

'But we have no right to make her wait, Juliet. The money is not ours but hers. Besides, you know, we find it difficult to meet even our regular expense, so that to recover from debt, would, I am sure, be impossible.'

'Oh, from such a small debt as that, – but I cannot expect that you should inconvenience yourself for me. I have not deserved it from you. I have no right to hope that you should care for my wants or my sufferings, – only from pity to the poor infant at my breast.'

Juliet shed tears, and continued to weep and to complain, till, unable to resist, yet determined not to make a concession which I knew by experience would be as useless as ruinous, I started up and quitted her without reply. I left her for some time alone, in hopes that she would recollet the folly of her perseverance, or that her inclination might wander to something more attainable. But when I again opened the door, her hand was upon the lock. 'Oh!' cried she, 'I thought you would never come! Where is it?'

'Dear Juliet,' said I, sickened with her obstinacy, 'you know you ask impossibilities.'

She had persuaded herself that she had prevailed; and the disappointment, however trivial, was more than she could bear. She burst into violent sobs, which by degrees increased into a sort of asthmatic fit, seeming to threaten immediate dissolution. Fortunately the family were not yet in bed; and medical assistance, though of the humblest kind, was almost immediately procured. As soon as the fit was removed, the apothecary's apprentice, or as Mrs Campbell called him, 'the doctor,' administered to his patient an opiate, which was so effectual, that she was still in a quiet sleep when the hour came for visiting my new employer.

My reluctance to this visit was almost forgotten in the anxiety occasioned by the situation of poor Juliet. All night as I watched by her bed-side, I had half doubted the virtue of my resistance to her wishes, and thought I would sacrifice any thing rather than again exercise such hazardous fortitude. My blood ran cold at the thought that I had nearly been in some sort the means of hurrying her to her great account; an account for which she seemed, alas! so miserably unprepared. The danger she had just escaped increased the anxiety which I had long felt to obtain medical advice for her; and seemed to make it a moral duty that I should no longer trust to my own unskilful management, that which was so unspeakably important, and so lamentably frail. But the means of purchasing advice were beyond my reach; and the thought of procuring it in a manner more suitable to my condition had been often dismissed as too humbling to bear consideration.

My new employment now offered hopes of obtaining the assistance so much desired. But the accomplishments of these hopes must of necessity be distant, while Juliet's situation was no longer such as to admit of delay. The only way of escaping from this perplexity was one to which I felt extreme repugnance. This was, to request that the lady for whom I was to paint the ornaments would advance part of the price of my work.

I know not why I was so averse to make this request. Surely I was not so silly as to be ashamed of poverty, nor weak enough to feel my self-estimation lessened by the absence of that which could never be considered as part of myself, but only of my outward situation!

Besides, whatever disgrace might rest upon a petition for charity, no shame could reasonably attach to a fair demand upon the price voluntarily offered for my labour. Though in spite of these, and many other reasonable considerations, my averseness to this request remained in full force, I never exactly discovered the grounds of it; because experience had taught me, that when duty is ascertained to lie on one side, it is better to omit all consideration of what might be said on the other. Now, as it was certainly my duty, however painful, to procure assistance for poor Juliet, it would have been imprudent to pry into the reasons which might disincline me to the task.

All this, with a hundred anticipations of success and of disappointment, passed through my mind as I proceeded towards the place of my destination. I was shown into the presence of an elderly lady of very prepossessing appearance. The consistent, unaffected gravity of her dress, air, and demeanour, claimed the respect due to her age, while her benevolent countenance and gracious manner seemed to offer the indulgence which youth requires. She received me with more than courtesy; and entered into conversation with an ease which quickly made me forget what was embarrassing in my visit. I soon perceived that our favourable impressions were mutual; and was at no loss to account for this good fortune on my part, when the lady hinted that she had borrowed her sentiments from the grateful Mrs Campbell.

It was not until near the close of a long interview that she contrived, with a delicacy which spared the jealous sensibility of dependence, to give directions for the work which she expected me to do; and to make me understand that she would willingly proportion the recompense to the labour bestowed. But the more her politeness invited me to respect myself, the more painful became the thought of sinking at once from an equal to a suppliant; and as the moment approached when the effort must be made, my spirits forsook me. I became absent and embarrassed. I hesitated; and half persuaded myself, that I had no right to tax the kindness of a stranger. Then I remembered Juliet's extreme danger, the scene which was still before my eyes, her frightful struggles for breath, the deadly exhaustion which followed; and it seemed as if my humiliation would scarcely cost me an effort. 'There is a favour,' – I began; but when I met the enquiring eye, I hastily withdrew mine; the scorching blood rushed to my cheeks; and I stood abashed and silent.

'You were going to say something,' said the lady. I stammered I know not what. She took my hand with the kind familiarity of a friend. 'I wish,' said she, in a voice of gentle solicitude, 'that I could make you forget the shortness of our acquaintance. It is hard that you should think of me as a stranger, while I feel as if I had known you from your cradle.'

The voice of kindness has ever found instant access to my heart; yet it was not gratitude alone which filled my eyes with tears as I uttered my confused reply. 'Oh, you are good – I see that you are good,' said I; 'and I know I ought not to feel – I ought not to give way to – but not even extreme necessity could have ——'

I stopped; but the lady's purse was already in her hand. 'If I dared,' said she, 'I could chide you well; for I fear you are one of those who will scarcely accept the bounty of Providence if He administer it by any hand but his own. Try to receive this trifle as if it came directly from Himself.'

I now quickly recovered my powers of speech, while I assured the lady that she had mistaken my meaning, and explained to her the favour which I had really intended to ask. Then, recollecting the justice of her reproof, 'Yes, chide me as you will,' said I; 'I have not deserved so gentle a monitor. I deserve to be severely reminded of the humility with which every gift of Heaven ought to be received by one who has so often forfeited them all.'

The lady, who seemed perfectly to understand the character with which she had to do, now frankly bestowed the assistance asked, and delicately offered no more. As I was taking my leave, she enquired my address; adding, that she believed Mrs Campbell had neglected to mention my name. Again I felt my face glow; but I had seen my error, and would not persist in it. 'No, madam,' said I, 'a blamable weakness made me desirous to conceal my name; but you are not one of those who will think the worse of Ellen Percy because she contributes to her own support.'

'Percy!' repeated the lady, as if struck with some sudden recollection. 'But I think Mrs Campbell mentioned that you had no connections in Scotland.'

'None, madam; scarcely even an acquaintance.'

'Then,' said the lady, 'it must be another person for whom my friend is enquiring so assiduously.'

I would fain have asked who this friend was; but the lady did not explain herself, and I was obliged to depart without gratifying my curiosity. That curiosity, however, presently gave way to stronger interests. It was now in my power to obtain a real benefit for poor Juliet. As for the morbid inclination which had cost her so dear, I found it fixed upon a new trifle, which was soon procured, and as soon rejected. But I could now obtain medical advice for her, and I did not delay to use the advantage; though she was herself so insensible to her danger that she was with difficulty brought to consent that a physician should be called. Recollecting the person to whom I owed my escape from the most horrible of confinements, and naturally preferring his attendance to that of a stranger, I sent to request his presence; and he immediately obeyed the summons.

I watched his countenance and manner as he interrogated his poor patient, and could easily perceive that he judged the case hopeless; while she evidently tried to mislead him, as she had deceived herself, retracting or qualifying the statement of every symptom which he appeared to think unfavourable. At the close of his visit, I quitted the room with him. He had written no prescription; and I enquired whether he had no directions to give. 'None,' said he, hastening to be gone, 'except to let her do as she pleases.' I offered him the customary fee. 'No, no, child,' said he; 'it is needless to throw away both my time and your money; either of them is enough to lose.'

Strong as had been my conviction of the danger, I was shocked at this unequivocal opinion. 'Oh, sir!' cried I, 'can nothing be done?'

'Nothing in the world, my dear,' said he, carelessly: 'all the physicians in Europe could not keep her alive a week.'

Our melancholy dialogue was interrupted by a noise as of somebody falling to the ground. I sprung back into the passage, and found Juliet lying senseless on the floor. Some apprehension excited by Dr ——'s manner had induced her to steal from her apartment, and listen to our conversation. The intelligence thus obtained she had not fortitude to bear. She recovered from her insensibility, only to give way to the most pitiable anguish. She wept aloud, and wrung her wasted hands in agony. 'Oh, I shall die! I shall die!' she cried; and she continued to repeat this mournful cry, as if all the energies of her mind could furnish only one frightful thought. In vain did I attempt to console her; in vain endeavour to lead towards a better world the hope which was driven from its rest below. To all sights and sounds she was already dead. At last exhausted nature could struggle with its burden no more; and the cries of despair, and the sobs of weakness, sunk by degrees into the moanings of an unquiet slumber.

CHAPTER XXVII

A chieftain's daughter seemed the maid.
– – – – – – –
And seldom o'er a breast so fair
Mantled a plaid with modest care;
And never brooch the folds confined
Above a heart more good and kind.

Walter Scott.

In the morning, when I opened my eyes, Juliet was so peacefully still, that I listened doubtfully for her breathing; and felt myself relieved by the certainty that she was alive. I was astonished to find that she was awake, though so composed; and was wondering at this unaccountable change, when she suddenly asked me whether Dr —— was reckoned a man of any skill in his profession? 'for,' said she, 'he seemed to know nothing at all of my disorder, except what he learnt from myself; so most likely he mistakes it altogether.' Shocked to see her thus obstinately cling to the broken reed, yet wanting courage to wrest it from her hold, I entreated her to consider that it would not add to the justice of Dr ——'s fears, if she should act as though they were well founded; nor shorten her life, if she should hasten to accomplish whatever she would wish to perform ere its close. She was silent for a little; then, with a deep sigh, 'You are right,' said she. 'Sit down, and I will dictate a letter, which you shall write, to my brother.'

I obeyed; and she began to dictate with wonderful precision a letter, in which she detailed the opinion of her counsel; named the persons who could evidence her claims; and dexterously appealed to the ruling passion of Mr Arnold, by reminding him, that if he could establish the legitimacy of his nephew, he must, in case of Lord Glendower's death, become the natural guardian of a youth possessed of five-and-twenty thousand pounds a year. Who could observe without a sigh, that, while with a sort of instinctive tact she addressed herself to the faults of others, she remained in melancholy blindness to her own; and that the transient strength which the morning restored to her mind, could not reach her more than childish improvidence in regard to her most important concerns? But her powers were soon exhausted; before the letter was finished, her thoughts wandered, and she lay for some hours as if in a sort of waking dream.

How little do they know of a death-bed who have seen it only in the graceful pictures of fiction! How little do they guess the ghastly horrors of sudden dissolution, the humiliating weakness of slow decay! Paint them even from the life, and much remains to tell which no spectator can record, much which no language can unfold. 'Oh, who that could see thee thus,' thought I, as I looked upon the languid, inexpressive countenance of the once playful Juliet, – 'who that could see thee thus, would defer to an hour like this, the hard task of learning to die with decency?'

I was sitting by the bed-side of my companion, supporting with one hand her poor deserted baby, and making with the other an awkward attempt to sketch designs for the ornaments which I had undertaken to paint, when the door was gently opened; and the lady for whom I was employed entered, followed by another, whose appearance instantly fixed my attention. Her stature was majestic; her figure of exquisite proportion. Her complexion, though brunette, was admirably transparent; and her colour, though perhaps too florid for a sentimental eye, glowed with the finest tints of health. Her black eyebrows, straight but flexible, approached close to a pair of eyes so dark and sparkling, that their colour was undistinguishable. No simile in oriental poetry could exaggerate the regularity and whiteness of her teeth; nor painter's dream of Euphrosyne exceed the arch vivacity of her smile. Perhaps a critic might have said that her figure was too large, and too angular for feminine beauty; that it was finely, but not delicately formed. Even I could have wished the cheek-bones depressed, the contour somewhat rounded, and the lines made more soft and flowing. But Charlotte Graham had none of that ostentation of beauty which provokes the gazer to criticise.

Her face, though too handsome to be a common one, struck me at first sight as one not foreign to my acquaintance. When her companion named her, I recollected my friend Cecil; and there certainly was a family likeness between these relations, although the latter was a short square-built personage, with no great pretensions to beauty. The expressions of the two countenances were more dissimilar than the features. Cecil's was grave, penetrating, and, considering her age and sex, severe; Miss Graham's was arch, frank, and animated. Yet there was in the eye of both a keen sagacity, which seemed accustomed to look beyond the words of the speaker to his motive.

The deep mourning which Miss Graham wore accounted to me for the cast of sorrow which often crossed a face formed by nature to far different expression. Her manners had sufficient freedom to banish restraint, and sufficient polish to make that freedom graceful; yet for me they possessed an interesting originality. They were polite, but not fashionable; they were courtly, but not artificial. They were perfectly affable, and as free from arrogance as those of a doubting lover; yet in her mien, in her gait, in every motion, in every word, Miss Graham showed the unsubdued majesty of one who had never felt the presence of a superior; of one much accustomed to grant, but not to solicit indulgence.

Such were the impressions which I had received, almost as soon as Miss Graham's companion, with a polite apology for their intrusion, had introduced her to me by name. I was able to make the necessary compliment without any breach of sincerity; for feebler attractions would have interested me in the person with whom Cecil had already made me so well acquainted. But when Miss Graham spoke, her voice alone must have won any hearer.

'If Miss Percy excuses us,' said she in tones, which, in spite of the lively imperative accents of her country, were sweetness itself, 'my conscience will be quite at rest, for I am persuaded it is with her that my business lies. No two persons could answer the description.'

'You may remember,' said her companion, smiling at my surprised and inquisitive look, 'I yesterday mentioned a friend who was in search of a young lady of your name. We are now in hopes that her search ends in you; and this must be our apology for a great many impertinent questions.'

'Oh no,' said Miss Graham, 'one will be sufficient. Suffer me only to ask who were your parents.'

I answered the question readily and distinctly. 'Then,' said Miss

Graham, with a smile, which at once made its passage to my heart, 'I have the happiness to bring you a pleasant little surprise. My brother has been so fortunate as to recover a debt due to Mr Percy. He has transmitted it hither; and Sir William Forbes will honour your draft for 1500*l*.'

There are persons who will scarcely believe that I at first heard this intelligence with little joy. 'Alas!' thought I, looking at poor Juliet, 'it has come too late.' But recollecting that I was not the less indebted to the kindness of my benefactors, I turned to Miss Graham, and offered, as I could, my warm acknowledgments. Miss Graham assured me, with looks which evinced sincerity, that she was already more than repaid for the service she had rendered me; and prevented further thanks, by proceeding in her explanation.

'My brother,' said she, 'traced you to the house of a Miss Mortimer and from thence to Edinburgh; but here he lost you; and being himself at a distance, he commissioned me to search for you. I received some assistance from a very grateful *protegée* of yours and mine, whom I dare say you recollect by the name of Cecil Graham. She directed me to the Boswells; but they pretended to know nothing of you: so I came to town a few days ago, very much at a loss how to proceed, though determined not to see Glen Eredine again till I found you.'

'And is it possible,' exclaimed I, 'that I have indeed excited such generous interest in strangers?'

'Call me stranger, if you will', said Miss Graham, 'provided you allow that the name gives me a right to a kind reception. But do you include my brother under that title? I am sure the description he has given of you shows that he is, at least, well acquainted with your appearance.'

'The dimple and the black eye-lashes tally exactly,' said her companion. 'And I could swear to the smile,' returned Miss Graham. 'Nevertheless,' said I, 'it is only from the praises of his admirer, Cecil, that I know Mr Kenneth Graham, to whom I presume I am so much indebted.'

The playful smile, the bright hues of health, vanished from Charlotte's face; and her eyes filled with tears. 'No,' said she, 'it is not to ——' She paused, as if to utter the name had been an effort beyond her fortitude. 'It is Mr Henry Graham,' said her companion, as if to spare her the pain of explanation, 'who has been so fortunate as to do you this service.'

I know not exactly why, but my heart beat quicker at this intelligence. I had listened so often to Cecil's prophecies, and omens, and good wishes, that I believe I felt a foolish kind of consciousness at the name of this Henry Graham, and the mention of my obligation to him.

'Have you no recollection then of ever having met with Henry?' enquired Miss Graham, recovering herself.

I rubbed my forehead and did my very utmost; but was obliged to confess that it was all in vain. The rich Miss Percy had been so accustomed to crowds of attending beaux, that my eye might have been familiar with his appearance, while his name was unknown to me.

'Well,' said Miss Graham, 'I can vouch for the possibility of remembering you for ever after a very transient interview; and when you know Henry better, I dare say you will not forget him.'

We now talked of our mutual acquaintance, Cecil; which led Miss Graham to comment upon the peculiar manners of her countrymen, and upon the contrast which they offered to those of the Lowland Scotch. Though her conversation upon this, and other subjects, betrayed no marks of extraordinary culture, it discovered a native sagacity, a quickness and accuracy of observation, which I have seldom found surpassed. Her visit was over before I guessed that it had lasted nearly two hours; and so great were her attractions, so delightful seemed the long untasted pleasures of equal and friendly converse, that I thought less of the unexpected news which she had brought me, than of the hour which she fixed for her return.

My thoughts, indeed, no sooner turned towards my newly acquired riches, than I perceived that they could not, with any shadow of justice, be called mine; and that they in truth belonged to those who had suffered by the misfortunes of my father. I therefore resolved to forget that the money was within my reach; and to labour as I should have done, had no kind friend intended my relief. Still this did not lessen my sense of obligation; and gratitude enlivened the curiosity which often turned my speculations towards Henry Graham. Once as I kept my solitary watch over Juliet's heavy unrefreshing slumbers, I thought I recollected hearing her, and some of our mutual acquaintance, descant upon the graces of an Adonis, who, for one night, had shone the meteor of the fashionable hemisphere, and then been seen no more. I had been present at his appearance, but too much occupied with Lord Frederick to observe the wonder. I afterwards endeavoured to make Juliet assist my recollection; but her memory no longer served even for much more important affairs; and all my efforts ended at last in retouching the pictures which I had accustomed myself to embody of this same Henry Graham. I imaged him with more than his sister's dignity of form and gesture, – with all her regularity of feature, and somewhat of her national squareness of contour; – with all the vivacity and intelligence of her countenance, strengthened into masculine spirit and sagacity; – with the eye which Cecil had described, as able to quell even the sallies of frenzy; – with the smile which his sister could send direct to the heart. At Charlotte's next visit, I obliged her to describe her brother; and I had guessed so well, that she only improved my picture, by adding some minuter strokes to the likeness.

At the same time she removed all my scruples in regard to appropriating the sum which he had obtained for me, by assuring me, that he had undertaken the recovery of the debt only upon this express condition, that half the amount should belong to me; and that to this condition the creditors had readily consented.

The possession of this little fortune soon became a real blessing; for Juliet's increasing helplessness loaded my time with a burden which almost precluded other labour. She was emaciated to a degree which made stillness and motion alike painful to her; a restless desire of change seemed the only human feeling which the hand of death had not already palsied; and a childish sense of her dependence upon me was the sole wreck of human affection which her decay had spared. Even the fear of death subsided into the listless acquiescence of necessity. Yet no nobler solicitudes seemed to replace the waning interests of this life. Feeble as it was, her mind yet retained the inexplicable power to exclude thoughts of overwhelming force.

I had seen the inanity of her life; I had alas! shared in her mad neglect of all the serious duties, of all the best hopes of man; and I did not dare to see her die in this portentous lethargy of soul. At every short revival of her strength, or transient clearness of her intellect, I spoke to her of all which I most desired to impress upon her mind. At first she answered me by tears and complainings, then by a listless silence; nor did better success attend the efforts of persons more skilled in rousing the sleeping conscience. The eloquence of friend and pastor was alike unavailing to extort one tear of genuine penitence; for the energy was wanting, without which a prophet might have smitten the rock in vain.

I must have been more or less than human, could my spirits have resisted the influence of a scene so dreary as a death-chamber without hope; yet when I saw my companion sinking to an untimely grave, closing a life without honour in a death without consolation; when I remembered that we had begun our career of folly together, – that, from equal wanderings, I had alone been restored, – from equal shipwrecks, I had alone escaped, – I felt that I had reason to mingle strong gratitude for what I was, with deep humiliation for what I might have been!

It was not that I became sensible of the treasure which I had found in Charlotte Graham. Taught by experience, I had at first yielded with caution to the attraction of her manners; and often (though in her absence only I must own) remembered with a sigh how many other qualities must conspire to fit the companion for the friend. But now, when she daily forsook admiration, and gaiety, and elegance, to share with me the cares of a sick-chamber, I daily felt the benefits of her piety, discretion, and sweetness of temper; and a friendship began, which, I trust, will outlast our lives.

Although she had too much of the politeness of good feeling to hint an expectation that I should forsake my unhappy charge, she constantly spoke of my visiting Castle Eredine, as of a pleasure which she could not bear to leave in uncertainty; and she detailed plans for our employments, for our studies, for our excursions among her native hills, with a minuteness which showed how much the subject occupied her mind. All her plans bore a constant reference to Glen Eredine. They were incapable of completion elsewhere. My lessons on the harp were to be given under the rock of echoes, – in a certain cave she was to teach me the songs of Selma, – we were to climb Benarde together, – from Dorch'thalla we were to sketch the lake beyond, with all its mountain shadows on its breast; while the rocks, which a nameless torrent had severed from the cliff, and the roots which, with emblematic constancy, had still clung to them in their fall, were to furnish fore-grounds unequalled in the tameness of Lowland scenery.

To all the objects round her native vale, Charlotte's imagination seemed to lend a kind of vitality. She loved them as I should have loved an animated being; and the more characteristic, or, as I should then have expressed it, the more savage they were, the stronger seemed their hold on her affection. I like a little innocent prejudice, so long as it does not thwart my own. I verily believe, that Charlotte would have thought Glen Eredine insulted by a comparison to the vale of Tempe. She often spoke with enthusiastic respect of her father, whom she had left at Castle Eredine; and with so much solicitude of the blank which her absence would occasion to him, that I could not help wondering why she delayed her return. She never mentioned any business that might detain her; and amusement could not be her bribe, for her time was chiefly spent in my melancholy dwelling.

Our cheerless task, however, at length was closed. By a change scarcely perceptible to us, Juliet passed from the lethargy of exhausted life to deeper and more solemn repose. I felt the intermitting pulse, – I watched the failing breath; yet so gradual and so complete was her decay, that I knew not the moment of her departure. All suffering she was spared; for suffering would, to human apprehension, have been useless to her. I did not commit her remains to the cares of a stranger. The hand of a friend composed her for her last repose; the tears of a friend dropped upon her clay; but they were not the tears of sorrow. Poor Juliet! Less ingenuity than that which led thee through a degraded life to an unlamented grave would have procured for thee the best which this world has to give, an unmolested passage to a better.

Two days after her death, I received from her brother a promise of protection to the heir of Lord Glendower, and permission, in case of that event, to send the boy to his uncle, together with the pledges of legitimacy, which constituted his sole hold upon the justice or compassion of Mr Arnold. Fortunately for the poor infant, the question upon which depended the tender cares of his uncle was decided in his favour. Juliet's marriage was sanctioned; and though her death left Lord Glendower at liberty to repair, in some sort, the injury which he had done to Lady Maria, the rights of his first-born son could not be transferred to the children of his more regular marriage.

When my cares were no longer necessary to my ill-fated companion, I yielded to the kind persuasions of Miss Graham; and suffered her to introduce me to whatever was most worthy of observation in a city which I had as yet so imperfectly seen. Our mornings were generally spent in examining the town or its environs; our evenings in a kind of society which I had till now known only in detached specimens; a society in which there was every thing to delight, though nothing to astonish, – much good manners, and therefore little singularity, – general information, and therefore little pedantry, – much good taste, and therefore little notoriety. I could no longer complain that the ladies were inaccessible. Introduced by Miss Graham, I was every where received with more than courtesy; and I, who a few weeks before could scarcely obtain permission to earn a humble subsistence, was now overwhelmed with a hospitality which scarcely left me the command of an hour.

And now I was again assailed by the temptation which had formerly triumphed unresisted. There is no place on earth where beauty is more surely made dangerous to its possessor; and Charlotte and I could scarcely have attracted more attention, had we appeared mounted upon elephants. But I had lost my taste for admiration. I disliked the constant watchfulness which it imposed upon me; and its pleasures poorly compensated the pain of upbraiding myself the next moment with my folly in being so pleased. As to open compliment, it cost me an effort to answer it with good humour. 'The man suspects that I am vain,' thought I, as often as I was so addressed; and the suspicion was too near truth to be forgiven. The only real satisfaction which I derived from the preposterous homage paid to me, arose from the new light in which it displayed the generous nature of Charlotte Graham. Yes; trifles serve to display a great mind; and there was true generosity in the graceful willingness with which Charlotte, at a time of life when the precariousness of attentions begin to give them value, withdrew from competition with a rival inferior to her in every charm which is not affected by seven years difference of age.

Upon the whole, nothing could be more agreeably amusing, than my residence in Edinburgh; and the contrast of my late confinement heightened pleasure to delight. From the time of Lady Glendower's death, it had been settled that I was to accompany Charlotte to Glen Eredine; but I must own that I felt no inclination to hasten our departure. Without once uttering a word, which could place the delay to my account, Miss Graham deferred our departure from day to day. Yet some involuntary look or expression constantly betrayed to me, that her heart was in Glen Eredine.

'Ah, that very sun is setting behind Benarde!' said she with a sigh, one evening when, from a promenade such as no other city can present, we were contemplating a gorgeous sunset.

'One would imagine by that sigh, Charlotte,' said I smiling, 'that you and some dear friend not far from Benarde had made an appointment to watch the setting sun together.'

'There's a flight!' cried she laughing. 'No am I sure, that such a fancy would never have entered your mind, if you had not been in love. Come; look me in the face, and let me catechise you.'

'Not guilty, upon my honour.'

'Humph! This does look very like a face of innocence, I confess. But stay till you know Henry. Let me see how you will stand examination then.'

'Just as I do now, I promise you. I ought to have been in love long ago, if the thing had been possible.'

'Ought? Pray what might impose the duty upon you?'

'The regard of one of the best and wisest of mankind, Charlotte. It was once my fate to draw the attention of your countryman, – the generous, the eloquent Mr Maitland.'

I saw Miss Graham start; but she remained silent. 'You must have heard of him?' continued I; but at that moment, casting my eyes upon Charlotte, I saw her blush painfully. 'You know him then,' said I.

'Yes I – I do,' answered she hesitatingly; and walked on, in a profound reverie.

A long silence followed; for Charlotte's blushes and abstraction had told me a tale in which I could not be uninterested. I perceived that her acquaintance with Maitland, however, slight, had been sufficient to fix her affections on a spirit so congenial to her own. 'Well, well,' thought I, 'they will meet one day or other; and he will find out that she likes him, and the discovery will cost him trouble enough to make it worth something. She will devote herself willingly to love and solitude, which is just what he wishes, and I dare say they will be very happy. Men can be happy with any body. And yet Maitland hates beauties; and Miss Graham certainly is a beauty.' However, when I threw a glance upon Charlotte, I thought I had never seen her look so little handsome; for it must be confessed that the lover must be more than indifferent, whom his old mistress can willingly resign to a new one.

I soon, however, began to reproach myself with the uneasiness to which I was subjecting the generous friend to whom I owed such varied forms of kindness. But the difficulty was, how I should return to the subject which we had quitted; for, in spite of the frankness of Charlotte's manners, my freedom with her had limits which were impassable. When she had once indicated the point upon which she would not be touched, I dared not even to approach it. The silence, therefore, continued till she interrupted it by saying, 'You are offended with me, Ellen, and you have reason to be so; for I put a question which no friend has a right to ask.'

'Dear Charlotte,' returned I, 'surely you have a right to expect from me any confidence that you will accept; and I shall most readily ——'

'No,' interrupted Miss Graham, 'such questions as mine ought neither to be asked nor answered. If an attachment is fortunate, it is to be supposed that the event will soon publish it; if not, the confession is a degradation to which no human being has a right to subject another.'

'Well,' thought I, 'this is very intelligible, and I shall take care not to trespass. But I will not keep thy generous heart in pain. Cost what it will, thou shalt know that thou hast nothing to fear from me.' It was more easy to resolve than to execute; and I felt my cheek glow with blushes, more, I fear, of pride than modesty, while I struggled to relieve the anxiety of my friend. 'Nay, Charlotte,' said I, 'you must listen to a confession, which is humbling enough, though not exactly of the kind you allude to. I must do Mr Maitland the justice to say, that he never put it in my power to reject him. He saw that I was no fit wife for him; and, at the very moment of confessing his weakness, he renounced it for ever. Do not look incredulous. It is not a pretty face, nor even the noble fortune I then expected, that could bribe Maitland to marry a heartless, unprincipled ——. Thanks be to Heaven that I am changed – greatly changed. But I assure you, Charlotte, I have not now the slightest reason to believe myself any bar to your – to Mr Maitland's happiness with some – some – with somebody who has not my unlucky incapacity for being in love.'

To this confession, Miss Graham answered only by affectionately pressing my hand; and then escaped from the subject, by turning from me to speak to a passing acquaintance. From that time Charlotte, though in other points perfectly confiding, spoke no more of Maitland; and I must own, that my respect for her was increased by her reserve upon a topic prohibited alike by delicacy and discretion. We had indeed no need of boarding-school confidences to enliven our intercourse. Each eager for improvement and for information, we had been so differently educated, that each had much to communicate and to learn. Our views of common subjects were different enough to keep conversation from stagnating; while our accordance upon more important points formed a lasting bond of union. Whoever understands the delights of a kitten and a cork, may imagine that I was at times no bad companion: and Charlotte was peculiarly fitted for a friend; for she had sound principles, unconquerable sweetness of temper, sleepless discretion, and a politeness which followed her into the homeliest scenes of domestic privacy.

How often, as her character unfolded itself, did I wonder what strange fatality had forbidden Maitland to return the affection of a woman so formed to satisfy his fastidious judgment. But I was forced to wonder in silence. Charlotte, open as day on every other theme, was here as impenetrable, as unapproachable, as virgin dignity could make her. Notwithstanding the recency of our friendship, it was already strong enough to render every other interest mutual; and Charlotte easily drew from me the little story of my life and sentiments, while I listened with insatiable curiosity, to the accounts she gave me of her home, of her family, and, above all, of her brother Henry.

This was a theme in which she seemed very willing to indulge me. She spoke of him frequently; and the passages which she read to me from his letters often made me remember with a sigh that I had no brother. He seemed to address her as a friend, as an equal; and yet with the tenderness which difference of sex imposes upon a man of right feeling. She was his almoner. Through her he transmitted many a humble comfort to his native valley; and though he had been so many years an alien, he was astonishingly minute and skilful in the direction of his benevolence. He appeared to be acquainted with the character and situation of an incredible number of his clansmen; and the interest and authority with which he wrote of them seemed little less than patriarchal. Though I must own that his commands were not always consonant to English ideas of liberty, they seemed uniformly dictated by the spirit of disinterested justice and humanity; and Graham, in exercising almost the control of an absolute prince, was guided by the feelings of a father.

Though Glen Eredine seemed the passion of his soul, – though every letter was full of the concerns of his clansmen, – there was nothing theatrical in his plans for their interest or improvement. They were minute and practicable, rather than magnificent. No whole communities were to be hurried into civilisation, nor districts depopulated by way of improvement; but some encouragement was to be given to the schoolmaster; Bibles were to be distributed to his best scholars; or Henry would account to his father for the rent of a tenant, who, with his own hands, had reclaimed a field from rock and broom; or, at his expense, the new cottages were to be plastered, and furnished with doors and sashed windows. The execution of these humble plans was, for the present, committed to Charlotte; and the details which she gave me concerning them described a mode of life so oddly compounded of refinement and simplicity, that curiosity somewhat balanced my regret in leaving Edinburgh.

On a fine morning in September we began our journey; and though I was accompanied by all on earth I had to love, and though I was leaving what had been to me the scene of severe suffering, I could not help looking back with watery eyes upon a place which perhaps no traveller, uncertain of return, ever quitted without a sigh.

CHAPTER XXVIII

—— Every good his native wilds impart
Imprints the patriot passion on his heart;
And even those hills that round his mansion rise
Enhance the bliss his scanty fund supplies.
Dear is that shed to which his soul conforms;
And dear that hill which lifts him to the storms.
And as a babe, when scaring sounds molest,
Clings close and closer to the mother's breast,
So the loud torrent, and the whirlwind's roar,
But bind him to his native mountains more.

Goldsmith.

DURING our first day's journey, the road lay through a country so rich and so level, that but for the deep indenting of the horizon, I could have fancied myself in England. 'That would be thought a fine park even in my country,' said I, as we were passing a princely place. 'Ah, stay till you see the parks of Eredine!' said Charlotte.* It is not to be told what superb conceptions I formed of these same parks of Eredine; for my companion did not enter on the description. I thought Blenheim was to be a paddock compared with them!

* 'Near adjoining are the parks; that is, one large tract of ground, surrounded with a low wall of loose stones, and divided into several parts by partitions of the same. The surface of the ground is all over heath, or, as they call it, *heather*, without any trees; but some of it has lately been sown with a seed of firs, which are now grown about a foot and a half high, but are hardly to be seen for the heath.

'An English captain, the afternoon of the day following his arrival here, desired me to ride out with him and show him the parks of Culloden, without telling me the reason of his curiosity. Accordingly we set out; and when we were pretty near the

Towards evening, the mountains which had once seemed as soft in the distance as the clouds which rested on them, began to be marked by the grey lights on the rock, and the deep shadows of the ravine. The morning brought a complete change of scene. Corn fields and massive foliage had given place to dull heath, varied only by streaks of verdure, which betrayed a sheep-track or the path of a nameless rill; while here and there, a solitary birch 'shivered in silvery brightness.' The hill, climbed long and painfully, rewarded us with no change of prospect; and the short descent was immediately succeeded by a more tedious climb.

At last, in a narrow valley, which by contrast looked rich and inviting, we beheld traces of human habitation; and the change of garb, of countenance, and of accommodation, announced that we were now, as Charlotte said, in her 'unconquered country.' – 'The Roman,' said she, 'when he had bowed "the sons of little men" to the dust, was forced to shrink behind his ramparts from the valour of *out* fathers.'

I own that I was somewhat confused between my own perceptions and the enthusiasm of my companion. Her eyes flashing through tears of joy, she shook me triumphantly by the hand. 'You are welcome to the Highlands!' cried she; 'to the land where never friend found a traitor, nor enemy a coward!'

In spite of this burst of *amor partiæ*, we were still almost a day's journey from Charlotte's native place. The mountains had become more precipitous, and the valleys more clothed, when my companion pointed out the spot where we were to dine; and intimated, that we must there exchange our carriage for a mode of conveyance better suited to the way which lay before us.

The exterior of our inn was certainly none of the most inviting. The walls, composed of turf and loose stones, were too low to prevent me from plucking the hare-bells which grew on the top of them; and the thatch, varied with every hue of moss and lichen, was more to be admired for picturesque effect, than for any more useful

place, he asked me, "Where are these parks? for," says he, "there is nothing near in view but heath, and at a distance rocks and mountains." I pointed to the enclosures; and, being a little way before him, heard him cursing in soliloquy; which occasioned my making a halt, and asking if any thing displeased him? Then he told me, that, at a coffee-house in London, he was one day commending the park of Studley in Yorkshire, and those of several gentlemen in other parts of England, when a Scots Captain who was by, cried out, "Ah, sir, but if you were to see the parks of Culloden in Scotland!" ' – *Letters from a Gentleman in the North of Scotland to his Friend in London*, vol. i, p. 297.

quality of a roof. The chimney-crag seemed composed of the wreck of what had once been a tub; the hoops of which, having yielded to the influence of time and the seasons, were rather imperfectly supplied by bands of twisted heath. The hut was, however, distinguished from its fellow hovels, by a sashed window on one side of the door, a most incondite picture of a bottle and glass on the other, and a stone lintel, bearing, in characters of no modern shape, the following inscription: –

16 . . W. M. T. Pilgrims we be ilk ane, M. M. B. . . 07.
That passen and are gane;
Then here sall pilgrim be
Welcom'd wi' courtesie.

Before we could draw up to the door of this superb hotel*, it poured forth a swarm of children, more numerous than I could have thought it possible for such a place to contain. I was prepared to expect the savage nakedness of legs and feet, which was universal among these little barbarians. For the rest, their attire was rather ludicrous than mean. The boys, even though still in their infancy, were helmed in the martial bonnet of their countrymen; and their short tartan petticoats were appended to a certain scarlet or blue *juste au corps*, laced up the back, as if to prevent these children of nature from asserting a primeval contempt of clothing. With the girls, however, this point seemed intrusted to feminine sense of propriety; for their upper garment consisted either of a loose jacket, or a square piece of woollen cloth thrown round the shoulders, and fastened under the chin only by a huge brass pin, or a wooden skewer. The absurdity of their appearance was heightened by the premature gravity of their countenances; which were more like the grimvisaged babes in an old family picture, than the animation of youthful life. In profound silence they stood courtesying as we passed; while the boys

* Whoever recollects the inns at C——i——gh and B——rr——le, and no doubt many others, as they stood two-and-twenty years ago, will be at no loss for the prototypes of Miss Percy's house of entertainment. Later travellers in the Highlands may not find her description agree with their experience. The 'land of the mountain and the flood' has of late been the fashionable resort of the lovers of the picturesque, and of grouse-shooting; the refuge of those who wish to skulk or to economise; of fine gentlemen and fine ladies, who find the world not quite bad enough for them. The accommodations for travellers are of course improved. It were devoutly to be wished that this had been the only change effected by such visitants.

remained cap in hand till we entered the hut.

It consisted of two apartments; one of which I dimly discerned through the smoke to be occupied by a group of peasants, collected round some embers which lay in the middle of the floor. Into the other, which was the state-chamber, Miss Graham and I made our way. It appeared to have been hastily cleared for our reception; for the earthen floor, as well as an oaken table, which stood in the middle of it, was covered with *debris* of cheese, oat-cakes, and raw onions, intermixed with slops of whisky. The good woman, however, who was doing the honours, rectified the disorder seemingly to her own satisfaction, by taking up the corner of her apron, and sweeping the rubbish from the table to the floor. Meanwhile she entered into a conversation with Miss Graham, in which every possible question was directly or indirectly asked, except the only one which on such occasions I was accustomed to hear, namely, what we chose to have for dinner. But as it proved, this question would have been the most unnecessary of all; for, upon enquiry, we learnt that our choice was limited to a fowl, or, as the landlady termed it, 'a hen.'

While this point was settling, the head waiter and chambermaid appeared in the person of a square built wench, naked up to the middle of a scarlet leg, and without any head-dress except a bandeau of blue worsted tape. Having tossed a lapfull of brushwood into the chimney (for the state-chamber had a chimney), she next brought, upon a piece of slate, some embers which she added to the heap; then squatting herself upon the hearth, she took hold of her petticoat with both hands at the hem, tightening it by her elbows; and moving her arms quickly up and down, she soon fanned the fire into a blaze.

Next came our landlord in the full garb of his country; and great was my astonishment to see him hold out his hand to Miss Graham as to a familiar acquaintance. Nor was my surprise at all lessened, when he coolly took his seat between us, and began to favour us with his opinions upon continental politics. Provoked by this impertinence, and by the courtesy with which Miss Graham received it, I interrupted his remarks, by desiring he would get me a glass of water. Without moving from his position, he communicated my demand to the maid; and went on with his conversation. I took the first opportunity of reproving Charlotte's tame endurance of all this. 'What would you have had me do?' said she: 'he is a discreet, sensible man, and a gentleman.'

'A gentleman!' repeated I.

'Yes,' returned Charlotte, 'I assure you he is my father's third cousin; and can count kindred, besides, with the best in Perthshire.'

It was plain that Miss Graham and I affixed somewhat different ideas to the word 'gentleman;' however, upon the claims of his ancestors, I was obliged to admit this *gentleman* to our dinner-table; when, after a violent commotion among the poultry had announced mortal preparation for our repast, it at last appeared. Our unhappy 'hen,' whose dying limbs no civilised hand had composed, was reinforced by a dish of salmon (large enough to satisfy ten dragoons), which Miss Graham with some difficulty, persuaded the landlady that the stranger might condescend to taste.

Towards the close of our meal, our attendant pushed aside the panel of a large wooden bed, which occupied one side of our apartment; and, from a shelf within, produced a large cheese, and an earthen pitcher full of butter, which she placed upon the table. Then, from the coverlet, where they had been arranged to cool, she brought us a large supply of oat-cakes. I fear I was not polite enough to suppress some natural signs of loathing; for the girl, with the quick observation of her countrymen, instantly apologised for the cause of my disgust. 'It is just for sake of keeping them clean, with your leave,' said she; 'there's so many soot-drops fall through this house.' In spite of this apology, however, I was so thoroughly disgusted, that I heard with great joy the trampling of our horses at the door; and immediately ran out to survey the cavalcade which had been despatched from Castle Eredine for our accommodation.

It consisted of three horses of very diminutive size; two of which were intended to carry Miss Graham and myself, and the third to transport our baggage. This last was caparisoned somewhat like a gipsy's ass, with two panniers slung across his back by means of a rope that seemed composed of his own hair. Into one of these panniers the *gille trushannich** pushed Miss Graham's portmanteau; and finding that mine was too light to balance it on the other side, he added a few turfs to make up the difference. Besides this domestic, we were each provided with a sort of running footman†, whose office it was to keep pace with our horses and to lead them at any difficult or dangerous step; and our equipage was completed by six or seven sturdy Highlanders, who, in mere courtesy to their chieftain's

* A packer.

† Gille cumsrian.

daughter, had walked fifteen or twenty miles to escort her home.

Thus guarded, we set out; our attendants, seemingly without effort, keeping pace with the horses. With all of them Miss Graham occasionally conversed in their native tongue; and I could perceive that they answered her with perfect readiness and self-possession; but none of them ever accosted her until he was addressed, nor could she prevail with any of them to wear his bonnet while she spoke.

Henry's name was so often repeated by them all, that I felt no small curiosity to learn more minutely the subject of their conversation. But though I had resumed my Gaelic studies under Charlotte's tuition, I was not yet sufficiently initiated to follow the utterance of a native; and my friend had already begun to smile so slily at my questions concerning her brother, that the very circumstance which awakened my curiosity made me half afraid to gratify it. At last, looking as unconscious as I could, I asked Charlotte on what subject her servant was speaking with such ardour. 'My *friend* Kenneth,' answered she emphatically, 'is reminding me of an expedition of Henry's to extricate his nurse's sheep from the snow. But talk to him yourself; he speaks English. – Kenneth, poor Miss Percy cannot speak Gaelic; so tell her that story in English. I know you like to speak a good word for your friend Henry.' – 'If he were here,' said Kenneth, making a gesture of courtesy, which did not absolutely amount to a bow, 'he would need nobody to speak a good word for him to a pretty lady.' He then related very minutely how Henry and he had climbed the rocky side of Benarde; and, from a crag midway in the precipice, had rescued the whole wealth of a Highland cottager.

'And do you in the Highlands think nothing of risking your lives for a few sheep?' said I.

'Do you not think, lady,' said Kenneth, 'that I had a good right to risk my life for my own mother's beasts? And you know the young gentleman was not to be forbidden by the like of me. His life! I would not have ventured a hair of his head for all the sheep in Argyll.' Then speaking to my special attendant, he uttered, with great emphasis, a Gaelic phrase, which obliged him to translate, signifying, that 'a man's friend may be dear, but his foster-brother is a piece of his heart.'

'My mother,' continued Kenneth, 'would have lost the *best-beloved lamb of her fold*, if Mr Henry had not followed me that day; for the frost had seized me; and I would have laid me down to sleep for a far-off waking; but Mr Henry drew me, and carried me, and I do not know what he made of me, but the first sound I heard was my mother crying, "Och chone a rie, mo cuillean ghaolach." Blessings on his face for her sake! for had it not been for him, she would have had none but a fremd hand to lay the sod on her.' Kenneth had obeyed his lady's command; and he now modestly fell back, as if disclaiming further right to attention.

'Surely Charlotte,' cried I, 'you are the happiest sister in the world. How deep, how indelible, are the attachments which your brother seems to awaken! Though he has been so long a stranger among them, these people are absolutely enthusiastic in his praise. It is strange! I never saw any thing like affection in servants, except in a novel.'

Charlotte looked at me with an aspect of amazement; but she was too polite either to charge me with the true cause of my ill fortune, or to acquit me at the expense of my countrymen. 'Henry will not let his friends here forget him,' said she; 'for, however engaged, he never forgets them. He sends them advice, encouragement, reproof, and whatever else they most need. Poor Henry! I remember a letter which he wrote to acquaint me with one of the severest disappointments of his life – a letter written in the midst of toil and bustle. It contained an order for comfortable bedding for his bed-ridden nurse.'

'But how could your brother, – how could your parents allow a mere prejudice to banish him from such strong attachments? Surely he could have felt no self-reproach for giving evidence against a common thief, a miscreant who attempted his life!'

'I don't know,' said Charlotte, doubtingly. 'Neil Roy was a well-born gentleman; and in many respects a very honest man. Besides, where the punishment is so unjustly disproportioned to the offence, it is not very pleasant to be concerned in inflicting it. However, it was not that affair alone which first drove my brother from home. Cecil was partly right, and partly wrong, in the account she gave you. My mother, you know, was a stranger; and though she was one of the best and most respectable of women, yet it was natural that she should retain some of the prejudices of her country. My father intended settling Henry in a farm, or educating him for the church: but my mother, I believe, would have thought either little less than burying him alive. However, she must have submitted to necessity if the affair of Neil Roy had not assisted her in persuading my father to send Henry away. Her health, too, was so fast declining, that my father could refuse her nothing. So poor Henry was made a peace-offering to my mother's relations, who would never have any connection with her after her marriage with a Highland rebel – as they were pleased to call the best born and the most loyal in the land! Oh, Ellen! it sometimes goes to my heart to think he should owe so much as a shoe-latchet to those who dared to look down upon his father. But whatever may happen, Henry can never regret having obeyed a parent.'

This little narrative was given with as much freedom as if Charlotte and I had been alone; for our attendants no sooner observed us inclined to talk apart, than they retreated to such a distance as left us at perfect liberty. At last, however, they advanced, and the two *gillen comsrian* took our horses by the bridles, while the rest began to clear away the loose stones from the tract which was leading us round the brow of an abrupt mountain. My eyes were involuntarily fixed upon a dell which had no interest except what it gained from the certainty that a single false step would bring me a hundred fathoms nearer to it. The golden clouds that linger after sunset were still throwing strong light upon our path, while the dell lay in deep shade. I was so new to Highland travelling, that, in some alarm, I was consulting my attendant upon the expediency of dismounting, when my attention was diverted by Charlotte. 'Benarde!' cried she, with such a voice as, had my mother been on earth, I could have cried, 'My mother!' I looked up; and saw between me and the glowing west only a naked crag, towering above the vapour which was floating in the vale.

Presently our path wound round the brow of the mountain which we were descending; and, gorgeous in all the tints of autumn, harmonised by the sober shades of evening, Eredine burst on our sight. Charlotte uttered not a sound. She uncovered her head as if she had entered a temple; and raised her eyes as if in thanksgiving which words could not speak.

I myself was little more inclined to break the silence imposed by the scene. Far below our feet lay a lake, motionless, as if never breeze had ruffled its calm. All there was still as the yet unpeopled earth, except the gliding shadow of a solitary eagle sailing down the vale. A faint flush still tinged the silver towards the east; to the west, the huge Benarde threw upon the waters his own sober majesty of hue. But where the shade would have been the deepest, it was softened by the long lines of grey light that imaged the walls of Castle Eredine. Beyond, in a sheltered valley, the evening smokes floating among the copse-wood alone betrayed the hamlets, concealed by their own unobtrusive chastity of colouring.

We continued to descend; and the woods gradually closed the scene from our view. First, the birch drooped here and there its light sprays from the crag; then gigantic roots of oak, grappling with the rock, sent forth their dwarf stems in unprofitable abundance; lower, the vigorous beech and massy plane threw their strong shadows, and, by degrees, arranged themselves into a noble avenue. Yet this approach did not peculiarly belong to Castle Eredine; it led equally to many a more humble abode. Several of these were scattered by the way-side; and each, as we passed, poured forth a swarm to welcome Charlotte's return. Every eye shone with pleasure; yet all was calm and silence. No shouting, no tumult; none of the sounds which, in my native country, announce vulgar gladness, disturbed the quiet of the scene. The very children hung down their smiling sun-burnt faces, and waited with sidelong looks for the expected notice.

Issuing from the wood, the path now become a well beaten road, led us through a few small half-enclosed fields of corn and pasture, to a sort of natural bridge, or rather isthmus; the only access to the rock upon which Castle Eredine projected into the lake. I must own, that its lofty title, and Cecil's romantic tales of its ancient possessors, had ill-prepared me for the edifice which I now beheld. A square tower, with its narrow arched doorway, was the only trace which remained of warlike array; and a range of more modern building, with its steep roof, into which the walls rose in awkward triangles, and its clumsy windows, through which cross lights streamed from behind, gave me no exalted idea of the accommodations of Castle Eredine. It seemed, however, that others found no want of space within its walls; for at least thirty persons, of different ranks and ages, came forth to receive us.

The foremost of these must have attracted my attention and respect, even though Charlotte's gesture and joyful exclamation had not announced her father. Age had not impaired the firmness of his step, nor the erect majesty of a figure Herculean in all its proportions. His eye retained its fire; his cheek its ruddy brown; the snowy locks which waved from beneath his bonnet alone betokened that he had already passed the common age of man. The plumes by which these locks were shaded chiefly distinguished his attire; for the rest of his dress was entirely composed of the scarlet and blue tartan of his clan. Saluting me first on one cheek, and then on the other, he welcomed me to Eredine, with little more ceremony, and little less kindness than he received his own Charlotte; then giving an arm to each, he led us into the sitting-room.

It was a large apartment, panelled all round. Each panel seemed to open into either a cupboard or a closet, – the walls being thick enough to admit of either; while each side was a little enlivened by a row of windows sunk in recesses, every one of which might have contained a dozen persons. But the gloom of this apartment was completely dispelled by the blazing of a wood fire, proportioned in size to what more resembled an alcove than a chimney, and by the cordial looks and kind attentions which every one seemed disposed to exchange.

So little restraint did my presence occasion, – so easily and naturally did Eredine, Charlotte, and even the servants, admit me to the interchange of cordial courtesy, which seemed the established habit of the family, that, before our substantial supper was ended, I had almost forgotten that I was a stranger. Indeed, so well did they all understand and practise the delicacies of hospitality, that, in less than a week, I was as much at home as if I had been born in Glen Eredine.

In the spirit with which she constantly sought to impress me with feelings of equality and sisterhood, Charlotte offered to share her apartment with me, on pretence of its being the most modern in the Castle.

'Since I have dragged you to the land of ghosts,' said she, 'I am bound in honour to protect you as well as I can; and Henry has so modernised my room, that no true Highland ghost would condescend to show his face in it.'

This room was indeed furnished very differently from the rest, yet still so that nothing incongruous struck the eye. Many of the elegant conveniences of modern life found a place there; book-shelves, drawing-cases, cabinets, all that can be imagined necessary to the light employments of a gentlewoman, were supplied in abundance; but all were of such substantial form and materials, that they seemed no intruders among the more venerable heir-looms of Castle Eredine. A closet, opening from our bedchamber, and stored with a small but select collection of books, was appropriated solely to me.

When we had retired for the night, Charlotte, after a thoughtful silence, laid her arm on my shoulder, and said, 'Ellen, there is a caution I would give you; I should rather say a favour which I am going to ask.'

'A favour, dearest Charlotte! I thought it had been decreed that all the favours were to come from one side! Well! how can you hesitate so?'

'There is a gentleman whom you once mentioned to me, a – a mutual acquaintance.'

Charlotte's complexion explained her meaning. 'Mr Maitland?' said I.

'Oblige me so far, my dear Ellen, as never to mention his name to my father.'

'Certainly, since you desire it, I promise you that I never will. I am persuaded that the reasons must be strong and well weighed which induce you to use caution with a parent.'

'Yes, they are strong,' said Charlotte, thoughtfully; 'And one day perhaps you may be satisfied that they are so. It grieves me, my dear Ellen, to have even the appearance of a secret with you, but I am satisfied that I am acting as I ought – that the happiness of – of my life – that even your happiness ——'

'Stop, dear Charlotte!' interrupted I: – 'believe me I have no wish to listen to any subject which can give you pain. Continue to do what you think right. Only let me once more assure you, that I have no interest whatever in Mr Maitland, except as in the best of men, – the most disinterested of friends, – a friend whose kindness withstood all my unworthiness. Oh Charlotte, if Mr Graham knew him as I do, he would let no prejudice of birth, or of country, deprive his daughter of happiness, – the honour ——'

I was obliged to stop; for I had talked myself into a fit of enthusiasm, and tears filled my eyes. A pleased smile played round Charlotte's beautiful mouth; but she turned away without reply, as if unwilling to cherish a hope which might prove fallacious.

I had some curiosity to know whether the only obstacle to her wishes lay with her father; but I was deterred from asking questions, by recollecting her language on a former occasion. Besides, I was afraid that she might fancy I felt some interest in the disposal of Maitland's affections.

CHAPTER XXIX

Hail awful scenes that calm the troubled breast,
And woo the weary to profound repose;
Can passion's wildest uproar lay to rest,
And whisper comfort to the man of woes!
Here Innocence may wander safe from foes,
And Contemplation soar on seraph wings.

Beattie.

'No wonder that my countryman has celebrated the merits of a Scotch breakfast,' said I, upon seeing the splendour and abundance of the morning repast at Castle Eredine. The linen and china were exquisitely delicate; and the table, though loaded with a plenty approaching to profusion, was arranged with perfect order and neatness. Eredine, for so I found it was the custom to call Mr Graham, having placed me in a sturdy, square-built, elbow-chair, with a back lofty and solid enough to serve every purpose of a screen, began to heap before me all the variety of food within his reach. In vain did I remonstrate. The ceremonial of hospitality required that I should be urged even unto loathing. When I turned to supplicate my host for quarter, and hoped that he was inclined to relent, an old lady, who sat by me on the other side, assailed me in the unguarded moment with a new charge of ham and marmalade.

'Ah! if he had seen the breakfasts in my young days!' said Eredine, in answer to my comment. 'A Glen Eredine breakfast was something substantial then. It was not children's food that bred the fellows who fought at Prestonpans.'

'What could you possibly have, sir, that is wanting here?'

The chieftain smiled compassionately upon me, as on a representative of the sons of little men. 'Why, strong venison soup,' said he, 'and potted ptarmagans; or, if we were a hunting, a roasted salmon: – hunters are not nice, you know.'

As soon as we rose from table, Charlotte went to resume her office of housekeeper, which had, in her absence, been most zealously filled by one of her innumerable cousins. To associate me in this employment was one of the friendly arts by which Charlotte contrived to domesticate me at Eredine; and household affairs furnished some little occupation for us both, although the establishment at the Castle was then smaller than it had ever been from time immemorial.

Feudal habits were extinct; and the days were long since gone, when bands of kinsmen, united in one great family, repaid hospitality and protection with more than filial veneration and love. Eredine had outlived three elder sisters, who for the greater part of a century had resided under the roof where they were born; and two younger brothers, who, after expiating, by thirty years of exile, their adherence to their hereditary sovereign, had returned to lay their ashes with those of their fathers. His eldest son had, a few months before, fallen a sacrifice to a West Indian climate; his second was banished from home by circumstances which I have already mentioned. The family, therefore, consisted of Eredine, his daughter, and myself; four men and seven women servants; Charlotte's nurse; a blind woman, who, being fit for nothing else, was stocking-knitter-general to the family, and served, moreover, as a humble substitute for the bard of other times; two little girls, one humpbacked, the other sickly; and three boys, two of whom were maintained because they were orphans, and the third because his grandmother had been the laird's favourite, some sixty years before; and, finally, Roban Gorach, Cecil's deserted lover; who, as the humour served, tended Henry's old white pony, or wandered to all the sacraments administered within sixty miles round, or sat by his torn oak from morn to night unquestioned.

But these were by no means the only persons who daily shared in the good cheer of Castle Eredine. Besides several superannuated people of both sexes, who, for this very purpose, had been provided with cottages adjacent to the castle, we had stable-boys, and errand-boys, and cow-herds, and goose-herds; beggars and travellers by dozens; besides maintaining, for the day, every tradesman who executed the most trivial order for the family without doors or within. How was I surprised to learn, that this establishment was supported by an estate of little more than a thousand pounds a year!

This family party was, for the present, reinforced by visiters of all ranks, who came to congratulate Charlotte's return. Among the earliest of these was my old friend Cecil, who recognized me with tears of joy. Recovering herself, she began to applaud her own skill in prophecy. 'I told you,' cried she, 'that ye knew not where a blessing might light; and there, ye see, ye're in Castle Eredine. And now Mr Henry will be gathered to you, and that will be seen.'

In answer to my enquiries into her own situation, she informed me that her husband had returned home, having been disabled by sickness, and discharged from his regiment as unfit for service. She talked of his illness, however, without any alarm; for she had travelled on foot to Breadalbane to bring water from a certain consecrated spring*, on which she fully relied for his cure. 'What grieves us the most,' said she to me apart, 'is that he's no' fit to help at the laird's shearing this year; as he had a good right, as well as the rest. And ye see, I cannot speak to Miss Graham upon that to make his excuse, for she might think we were *reflecting*, because he got's trouble tending Mr Kenneth.'

The next day brought the harvest party of which Cecil had spoken. About four o'clock in the morning, I was awakened by the shrieking and groaning of a bag-pipe under my window; and starting out of bed to ascertain the occasion of this annoyance, saw about a couple of hundred men and women collected near the house. These I found were the tenantry of Glen Eredine, assembled to cut down the landlord's corn; a service which they were bound to perform without hire. Yet never, in scenes professedly devoted to amusement, had I

* The said Breadalbane spring once existed in Atholl; but its guardian Saint having been offended by some failure in respect, or in liberality, removed it to its present site. This neglect was the more unpardonable, because Highland saints have a very saint-like facility of propitiation. A halfpenny is considered as a profuse offering; a nail, a pin, or a rag, is all that the saints exact in return for the benefit of these healing waters. The saints' wells can generally be distinguished by the shreds of cloth hung upon the impending bushes; and other offerings of like value dropped into the basin.

Some of these springs are resorted to annually by way of preventative; others are visited as occasion requires. Some of the waters are taken as a medicine. Others – and these, I apprehend, the most useful – are externally applied. In this case, the ablutions must be repeated for three years successively; and if the patient die in the interim, a friend must complete this ceremony in his stead, bringing away at the same time a bottle of water, to be poured upon the grave of the deceased. Within these few years, an old woman, for this pious purpose, twice performed a journey of nearly a hundred miles.

witnessed such animating hilarity as cheered this unrewarded labour. The work was carried on all day, in measured time to the sound of the bagpipe, yet without causing any interruption to the jests of the young or the legends of the old. Mr Graham himself frequently joined in both, without incurring the slightest danger of forfeiting respect by condescension. Dinner for the whole party was, of course, despatched from the castle. Fortunately, the cookery was not very complex, for the old nurse and the blind stocking-knitter were the only persons left at home to assist Charlotte and myself in the preparation.

It was customary for the festivities of the day to conclude with a ball on the old bowling-green; and promising myself some amusement from the novelty, I repaired to the spot soon after the time when the dancers had been accustomed to assemble. But no dancers were there. Not a person was to be seen, except one sickly emaciated creature, wearing a faded regimental coat over his tartan waistcoat and philibeg, who stood leaning against a tree with an aspect of hopeless dejection.

Supposing that I had mistaken the place, I enquired of this person whither I must go to seek the dancers. 'Think ye, lady,' said the man, with a look somewhat indignant, 'that they would dance here this night? I hope they're no' so ill-mannered. It would be a fine story for them to be dancing, and the best blood in Eredine not well cold i' the grave yet!'

I perceived that he alluded to the recent death of Kenneth Graham; and, struck with such an instance of delicacy in persons whom I considered as little better than savages, I was going to enter into further conversation with the man, when seeing Charlotte at a distance, I hastened to meet her. I could not prevail upon her to express the slightest surprise at the sensibility of her countrymen. 'It is just as I expected,' said she; and she proceeded to inform me, that the person whom I had quitted was the husband of my old friend Cecil, and the foster-brother of Kenneth Graham. 'Poor James!' said she; 'I believe it would have broken his heart if that bowling-green had been profaned with the sounds of merriment. He visits it every evening at the same hour when he was wont to come five-and-twenty years ago to play with my brothers. That poor fellow has given the strongest proofs of the attachment to a superior which you think so uncommon. As soon as he heard that my brother was ordered abroad, he left his wife and children, and explored his way on foot to the south of Ireland, where the regiment was already embarked. He enlisted; watched his master in the dreadful disease which few could be found daring enough even to relieve; followed the remains of his foster-brother to the grave, when sickness had made him unable to return from the spot; and lay all night on the earth which covered the head he loved best. Alas! alas! it lies among stranger-dust, far from us all.'

Although, ever since we had been on confidential habits, Charlotte had spoken of her dead brother almost as much as of the living one, these were the only words of lamentation which I ever heard her utter.

On the contrary, the associations with which the remembrance of the dead was joined seemed to be pleasurable. She appeared to sympathise in the delight with which Lady Eredine and her son would meet; speaking of them exactly as she would of living persons possessed of all the sentiments and functions of mortality.

From these themes the transition was easy to the subject of Henry Graham, – a subject in which I took almost as much interest as she did herself; for what girl of one-and-twenty could be uninterested in an unknown lover? a lover described as handsome, brave, generous, good! and who had besides fallen in love at first sight; a compliment which, by the value some ladies put upon it, I suppose is estimated more by its rarity than its worth. Now, all this my imagination found in Henry Graham; for I was in the land of imagination. I was more than half persuaded of my conquest. There was no other way of accounting for his assiduous good offices; his flattering yet minute description of my appearance. But Charlotte never directly admitted this explanation of his conduct, and I durst not venture to show her how far vanity could lead me in conjecture; though curiosity often made me come as near to the subject as I dared. 'After all,' I would say to myself, 'what can it signify to me? I shall never like the man; and I would far rather earn my bread by labour than by marriage.'

In the mean time, I was as much domesticated at Eredine as if I had already been a daughter of the family. My kind friend soon found means to make me consider it as for the present my permanent abode. She knew me too well to expect, that this could ever take place so long as I felt myself a useless dependent; and this was, I am persuaded the real cause which inspired her with an enthusiastic desire to excel in music. There was no danger that this plea for my detention should soon be exhausted; for Charlotte's skill hitherto went no farther than jingling a strathspey upon an excruciating harpsichord. Precisely at the lucky moment, however, arrived a splendid harp, a present from her considerate brother; and our labours began with much zeal and some success.

In return, she exerted surprising patience in assisting my study of her native tongue; and the whole family, myself included, were delighted with my progress. We make rapid advances in a dialect which is the only medium of communication with three fourths of the persons around us; and, in justice to Highland politeness, I must assert, that there is no language which may be attempted with more perfect security from ridicule. This acquisition, together with my performance of some Gaelic songs, brought me into high estimation with my venerable host. He declared, 'that I could turn Chro challin or Oran gaoil almost as well as his mother, – *white be the place of her soul!*' and only regretted, that instead of 'that unhandy thing of a harp, which made trews where trews should not be, I had not the light lady-like Clarsach, that the d——d Hanoverians burnt when they ransacked Glen Eredine.'

There might have been danger that my favourite recreation, to which long abstinence gave all the charm of novelty, should make unreasonable encroachment on my time. But almost the earliest work of my renovated judgment had been to impress me with a solemn conviction of the value of time; and when I recollected that, of the few allotted years of man, seventeen had already been worse than squandered; that of the uncertain remainder, a third must be devoted to the harmless enjoyments, a part rifled by the idle fooleries of others, – an unknown portion laid waste of joy and usefulness, by sickness, by sorrow, or by that overpowering languor which palsies at times even the most active spirit; – when I remembered, that the whole is fugitive in its nature as the colours of the morning sky, irreversible in its consequence as the fixed decree of Heaven, I could no longer waste the treasure on the sports of children, or suffer the jewel to slip from the nerveless grasp of an idiot. I had formed a plan for the distribution of my time; to which I adhered so steadily, that I seldom spent an hour altogether unprofitably; that is, I seldom spent an hour of which the employment had no tendency to produce rational, benevolent, or devout habits in myself or in others.

Let it not, therefore, be imagined that my whole life and conversation were as solemn, and as wise, and as tiresome as possible. The flowers of the moral world were doubtless intended to scatter cheerfulness and pleasure there; and the woman who contributes nothing to the innocent amusement of mankind has renounced one purpose of her being. I am persuaded, that a happier party, or at times a merrier never met, than assembled round our fireside at Eredine.

Nor was it always confined to the members of our own family. Our neighbours – and all within twenty miles were our neighbours – often came with half-a-dozen of their sons and daughters, two or three servants, and a few horses, to spend some days at Castle Eredine. Uninvited and unexpected, they were always welcome. No preparation could be made; no bustle ensued. The guests were for the time members of the household, and partook in its business, its enjoyments, and its privations. The morning amusements of the gentlemen furnished us with game; those of the ladies, with lighter dainties; and our evenings were enlivened by music, more abundant, it must be confessed, than excellent.

But, though my hours were neither dull nor solitary, I must own, that my heart leaped light with the hope of something new, when, one morning, Charlotte, running into the room breathless with delight, exclaimed, 'He is coming, dearest Ellen! he is coming! He will give up all his habits, – his pursuits, – he will give back their trash, – he will return to his father, – to us all!'

'Henry! When, dear Charlotte?'

'Now! Soon! In a week! Oh, if that week were past!'

Charlotte was restless with joy. She left me almost immediately; and I followed her to her father. The good old man folded us both to his breast. 'God grant I live this week,' said he, 'and then ——' He paused a little, half ashamed of his emotion; 'I doubt,' said he, with a smile, 'my eyes are not so strong as they have been.' Then disengaging himself from us, he hurried out upon the road which led to Edinburgh, as if he had already hoped to meet his son; and repeated the same walk full twenty times that day. Next, he would count every stage of Henry's journey, and fix the very hour of his arrival, and order an infinity of preparations for his reception; and, when he had quite exhausted himself, he sunk into his great oak-chair ruminating, while a delighted smile at times crossed his face. 'The little curly-pated dog was his mother's darling,' cried he; 'and yet I never could find out how that happened, for there never was a Southron blood-drop in him. He was always a Graham to the heart's core.'

Had I before been wholly uninterested in Henry's arrival, – had I owed no obligation to him as the bestower of a secure though humble independence,– had all the suggestions of vanity been silenced, I must have sympathised in the joy expressed in every face I saw, in every voice I heard. The house-maids all claimed the honour of arranging his apartment; and as the division of labour, and all the distinctions between cook and chamber-maid, were quite unknown in Glen Eredine, the honour was bestowed according to seniority. The spinners celebrated their young master's return in the extemporary songs, so common among their countrywomen. The men brought home for him as many roes, black-cock, and ptarmagan, as would have satiated* courteous King Jamie's ravenous visiter. Charlotte's nurse told me endless anecdotes of his childhood; and I heard the blind knitter cry out in a tone of triumph, 'He led me up the loan with's *oun* hand, sirs; and that's what he never did to one o' ye all. And shame fa' me, if ever a man lead me by the right hand again, an it be no Eredine himsel'; and that's not to be thought.'

The only one who took no share in the cheerful bustle was poor Roban Gorach; yet he too could in his way, testify affection for his young master. I had strolled out; and taking my favourite station on a ledge of rock which overhung the lake, I had suffered my thoughts to shape, I know not what romantic dream, of Henry Graham, and friendship, and Charlotte, and Maitland, and Castle Eredine, and castles in the air; when I was roused by the approach of poor Roban, attended by the old white pony, which followed him like a dog. He accosted me with an earnest look, lowering his voice to a confidential tone. 'They say you're ordained for him,' said he; 'so blessings on your face! take him peaceably.'

Since I had become a favourite in Glen Eredine, so many dreams and prophecies had announced me its future mistress, that I had no difficulty in apprehending his meaning. 'Oh! you must let me refuse a little at first for decency-sake, Robert,' said I, laughing.

'Mysel' would fain you do's bidding before you be hindered,' said he; laying his fingers pleadingly upon my arm. 'What if he *would* see you going down the loan there, and through the wood, with another man's boy in bosom?' – he raised his arm, tracing as he spoke the path towards Cecil's dwelling; then letting it drop unconsciously, he proceeded in his native tongue, as if he had forgotten my presence.

*See Scott's Border Minstrelsy.

'He would care no more for his fine golden watch, and all the parks and *towns* of Eredine, than for the wind when *she* flies by him.' – 'But, Robert,' said I, interrupting his mournful reverie, 'how should you all like to have a Saxon mistress in the Castle?' – 'If it were so ordered,' answered Robert, 'who could say against? – and we might be very well, though it were so. Just you forget that you're a stepmother, with your leave; and we'll all forget it too.'

When I returned to the house, I learnt, what I had indeed inferred from Roban's language, that Cecil had been there. She came to ask medicine and advice for her dying husband; but when told the good news of the day, she retired without suffering Miss Graham's joy to be interrupted by her melancholy errand. Though, after having lived three months in Glen Eredine, I could no longer be surprised at this delicacy, it can never cease to please; and I immediately requested Charlotte to direct our evening walk toward Cecil's cottage.

We were received at the door by Cecil, who loaded us both with congratulations; and invited us, as she was accustomed to do, into her chamber of state, or as she phrased it, 'ben a house.' This apartment was at that time no unfavourable specimen of Glen Eredine parlours. It had to be sure an earthen floor not levelled with much nicety, but it was tolerably clean; it was ceiled with whitened boards, lighted by a sashed window, furnished with plane-tree chairs and tables, and ornamented with an open corner cupboard filled with gaudy stone-bowls, and jugs enriched with humble anacreontics. This was not, however, the family room; and, finding that poor James inhabited the other end of the building, we insisted upon adjourning thither.

The humbler apartment was separated from the other by a panelled closet or rather box, which served the double purpose of bed and partition. The remaining walls were imperfectly plastered with clay; and the rude frame-work of the roof was visible, where light enough to make it so was admitted by the aperture which served for a chimney, and by a window of four panes, one of which was boarded, and another stuffed with rags. Beneath the above-mentioned aperture, the bounds of the fire-place were marked only by a narrow piece of pavement, upon which a turf-fire smouldered unconfined against the wall. The smoke, thus left at large, had dyed the rafters of an ebon hue; and, mixing with the condensed vapour, distilled in inky drops from the roof. The floor was strewed with water-pails, iron-pots, wooden-ware, and broken crockery. Cecil's eldest child, a boy of about four years old, tartaned and capped as martially as any 'gallant Graham' of them all, sprawled contentedly in the middle of the litter, sharing his supper of barley-bread with an overgrown pet lamb; and the youngest attired with rather less ceremony, crouched by the side of a black pot, contesting with the cock the remains of a mess of oatmeal pottage.

From these postures of ease, however, Cecil instantly snatched them both. 'Up, ill manners!' cried she; 'think it your credit to stand when the gentles come to see you.' This maxim she enforced by example, for no entreaties could prevail upon her to be seated in our presence.

The sallow, haggard countenance of poor James appeared through the open panel of the bed; and Miss Graham approaching, enquired 'how he felt himself?'

'Ye're good that asks,' said Cecil, answering for him; 'but he'll never be better, and he has no worse to be.'

'These people are savages, after all!' thought I. 'Would any humanised being have pronounced such a sentence in the sick man's hearing?' I stole a glance towards the bed, half fearing to witness the effect of her barbarity.

'Trouble must have its time,' said the man cheerfully; 'but we must just hope it'll no be long now.'

This was so little like fear, that I was obliged to convert the words of encouragement into those of congratulation; and after Miss Graham had made some more particular enquiries, I expressed my satisfaction in observing such apparent resignation.

'Deed, ma'am,' said James, 'I cannot say but that I am willing enough to depart; I'm whiles feared, indeed; but then I'm whiles newfangled.'

'I'm sure, lady,' said Cecil, tears now streaming down her cheeks, 'he has no reason to be feared; for he's been a well-living Christian all's days, and a good husband he's been; – and he shall have no reason to reflect that he has no' as decent a burial as ever the ground was broken for in Eredine. And for that we're partly much beholden to you, Miss Percy, – a blessing on you for that, – and a decent departure might you have therefor! And thankful may we be, Jamie, that ye'll no lie in unkent ground, among strangers, and heathens, and all the offscourings of the earth!'

'No!' said Miss Graham; 'among strangers you shall not lie. You shall be laid by the place where your foster-brother should have lain; and your head-stone shall be my memorial of him, and of what you did for him.'

A flash of joy brightened the face of the dying man. He looked at Miss Graham as if he would fain have thanked her; but though his lips moved, they uttered no sound. Cecil was voluble in her thanks; and I verily believe was half reconciled to the prospect of her misfortune, by the honour which it was to procure for her husband.

'When you see my dear brother,' proceeded Miss Graham, 'tell him, James, that my only regret now is, that I should show neither love nor honour to his remains; and that they must rest so far from mine!'*

At this moment a casual change of posture made me observe, through the window, a human figure, partially hid by an old ash tree which grew within a few feet of the cottage wall. The figure advanced a step; and I perceived through the dusk of the evening that it was Roban Gorach. He was leaning against the tree, with his eyes fixed on the window; his head and arms hanging listlessly down, with that undefinable singularity of mien which betokens the wandering of the mind.

I was going to call Miss Graham's attention to the circumstance, when our strange conversation was interrupted by a scream from the youngest child, whom Cecil had hastily caught up in her arms. The scream was certainly the shriek of pain, perhaps partly of surprise; yet Cecil apologising for her child's temper, began to soothe him with the sounds which nurses apply to mere frowardness, mixing them at times with the hum of a song. Her remonstrances to the child were given in Gaelic, interrupted by apologies in English to Miss Graham and myself. More than once she pronounced the word† which signifies 'Go,' 'begone!' with strong emphasis; holding the child from her as if threatening to forsake him. He still continued to cry, and she to hush him with a song, which was at first irregular and indistinct; but which, by degrees, formed itself into regular rhythm, pronounced with such precision, that even my slender knowledge of her language was sufficient to render it intelligible to me; while its occasional interruptions gave me time to fix the meaning at least in my memory.

* Messages from the living to the dead are not uncommon in the Highlands. The Gael have such a ceaseless consciousness of immortality, that their departed friends are considered as merely absent for a time; and permitted to relieve the hours of separation by occasional intercourse with the objects of their earliest affection.

† Falbh bi falbh.

Of the plaintive simplicity of the original, – of the effect it derived from the wild and touching air to which it was sung, – my feeble translation can convey no idea; but I give the literal English of the whole*

Go to thy rest, oh beloved;
My soul is pained with thy wailing;
The wrath of a father is kindled by thy complaining:
Go to thy rest.

Choice of my heart thou hast been,
But now I lay thee from my bosom
That it may receive my betrothed:
Go to thy rest.

Oh cease thy lamentation;
Disquiet me no more.
Till the long night bring morning of pleasant meetings:
Go to thy rest.

Though I, having seen that Roban Gorach was one of Cecil's auditors, was at no loss to perceive the double meaning of the song, neither poor James nor Miss Graham could observe any thing peculiar in it. Cecil never appeared to cast a glance towards the real object of her address; and at every pause in the air she conversed with an appearance of perfect unconcern.

I own my esteem for my first Highland friend was far from being improved by this specimen of her dexterity in intrigue. As soon as Charlotte and I had taken our leave, I told her what I had observed;

* Extemporary songs are common among the Highlanders. With these they beguile their labours; often, of course, at small expense of taste or invention. The readiness with which they apply their verses to compliment, to banter, often to graver purposes, is, however, very remarkable; and Cecil is far from furnishing a rare or exalted specimen of the powers of Highland *improvisatori*.

I have been told, that an Argyllshire woman, one evening, while expecting her husband's return, was surprised by a visit from some persons whom she guessed to be officers of justice sent to apprehend him. Finding the man absent, they determined to wait his arrival in the hut; taking care, of course, that his wife should not go out to apprise him of his danger. She contrived, however, to hush her baby with an extemporary song, which, without alarming the vigilance of the guards, warned her husband from his perilous threshold, and he escaped. Other instances, somewhat of a similar kind, suggested the incident in the text.

Indeed, the only merit which the Highland scenes in Discipline presume to claim, is, that, however inartificially joined, they are all borrowed from fact.

but, unwilling to express a harsh opinion, I waited for her comments. The incident, however, made no unfavourable impression upon her. 'I know,' said she, 'that Cecil has a great deal of discretion and presence of mind.'

'Presence of mind, I allow; but really it seems to me, that if her husband had witnessed this piece of management, he would have been very pardonable for doubting her discretion.'

'How so? do you not think it was prudent to prevent her dying husband from being shocked by the sight of that poor creature?'

'To tell you the truth, Charlotte, I think such readiness in intrigue betokens Cecil's fidelity to be at least in danger.'

'Surely you do not suspect – you cannot suppose – setting aside all fear of God, think you she could make outcasts of her children! – transmit her name, black with the infamy of being the first unfatihful wife that ever disgraced Glen Eredine! No, no; Cecil would rather be buried under Benarde: ay, silly as he is, Robert would rather lay her head in the grave! No, no, Miss Percy; whatever may be the practice in other countries, we have reason to be thankful that such atrocities are unknown in Eredine.'*

Charlotte's warm defence was interrupted by the approach of poor Robert, who was following us home. 'Would ye just please to bid *her*,' said he, pointing towards Cecil's cottage, 'let me thrash two or three sheaves for her. She has nobody now to do for her; and if ye'll just allow me, it's as sure's death, I'll stay in barn, and never go near house to plague her.'

'I think, Robert,' answered Charlotte, 'it would be very foolish in you to take so much trouble for one who never even speaks to you.'

'Ay, but yoursel' knows I'm no very wise,' said Robert, with a feeble smile. Then, after a few moments' silence, he repeated his request. Miss Graham gave an evasive answer, and he again fell behind; but, during our walk, he came forward again and again to urge his petition, as if he had forgotten having offered it before.

'I beg pardon of Cecil and Glen Eredine, Charlotte,' said I. 'I had

* Although, in the remoter parts of Scotland, chastity is by no means the universal virtue of unmarried persons, instances of conjugal infidelity are still rare. Within the present generation they were almost unknown.

About twenty years ago, it happened, in a remote country town, that two persons of the lower rank were accused of adultery. The charge, whether true or false, had such an effect, that the man was driven like a wild beast from human converse. The very children pelted him with mud in the street; crying out, 'There goes the adulterer.'

forgotten the nature and constancy of this poor young man's attachment, when I suspected her of imprudence. I am sure that a virtuous man alone can feel, a woman of discretion alone can inspire, such disinterested, such unconquerable affection.'

'You are right, Ellen. Looseness of morals on the one side, or even a very venial degree of levity on the other, is fatal to all the loftier forms of passion. I believe even perfect frankness of manners is hostile to them: it leaves too little for the imagination.'

We both walked on musing, till my dream was broken by our arrival at the gate. 'Is your brother reserved?' said I, very consciously.

'I never found him so,' returned Charlotte, laughing; 'but you have so much imagination that I believe it will do, notwithstanding.'

The day approached when this object of universal interest was to arrive; and every stage of his journey, every hour of its duration, was counted a hundred times. 'Four whole days still!' – 'To-night he will sleep in Scotland!' – 'By this time to-morrow!' – In how many tones of impatience, of exultation, of delight, were these sentences uttered!

The father's joy was the least exclamatory. After the first emotion was past, he seemed to think much expression of his feelings unsuitable to his years; though every thing 'put him in mind what Henry said when he was last at home;' or, 'what Henry did when a boy;' and he every now and then shook Charlotte and me by the hand with such a look of congratulation!

He hinted some intention of riding as far as Aberfoyle to meet his son; though he seemed to doubt whether this were altogether consistent with his paternal dignity. 'It is not what one could do for every young man,' said he; 'but Henry was never a sort of boy that is easily spoiled.' So with this salvo, with which many a father has excused his self-indulgence, Eredine determined to meet Henry at Aberfoyle.

On the eventful morning the whole family arose with the dawn. Almost the first person I saw was Eredine, arrayed and accoutred in the perfect costume of his country, marching up and down in the court with even more than his usual elasticity of step. The good old gentleman prepared for his journey with all the alertness of five-and-twenty. 'Come, Charlotte,' said he, 'get me a breakfast fit for a man. Remember I have more than sixty miles to ride to day. Miss Percy, do you think any of your Lowland lads of seventy-six could do as much? Well, well, wait till nine o'clock at night; and, God willing, I'll show you a lad worth a fine woman's looking at.'

In spite of the entreaties of old Donald MacIan and the family piper, who would fain have led forth the whole clan, Eredine set out attended only by his household servants. But as soon as the laird was gone, Donald followed his own inclinations. The piper marched through every *baile** in the Glen, pouring forth a torrent of vigorous discords, which he called the '*Graham's Gathering*;' then took the road towards Aberfoyle, followed by the train whom he had assembled. By noon, scarcely a man was left in Glen Eredine.

On the other hand, the women came in crowds to the Castle, each bringing a cheese, a kid, a pullet, or whatever else her cabin could supply; and, having deposited these '*compliments*,' as they called them, they quietly returned to their homes. The servants ran idly bustling about the house, forgetting every part of their business which did not refer to Mr Henry. One began to air his linen as soon as day dawned. Another piled heap after heap of turf upon his fire. A third, at the expense of the state bed-chamber, embellished his apartment with a carpet not unlike, both in pattern and size, to a chess-board. I found a fourth busied in anointing his leather-bottomed chairs with a mixture of oil and soot; scrubbing this Hottentot embrocation into the grain with a shoe-brush. 'I'm just giving them a bit clean for him,' said she, in answer to my exclamation of amazement. 'He had always a cleanly turn, – God save him!'

At last all preparations perforce were finished; and the day then seemed endless to us all. Charlotte was silent and restless. She tried to work; but it would not do; she tried to read, and succeeded no better. She visited her brother's apartment again and again, and could never satisfy herself that all was ready for his reception. She began to fear that he might not arrive that night, yet she was half angry with me for admitting the possibility. Towards evening she stationed herself in a window to watch for him; turning away sometimes with tears of disappointment in her eyes, and then resuming her watch once more.

Twilight closed in the stillness of a frosty night. Charlotte drew me to the gate to listen. All was profoundly quiet. At last a dog bayed at a distance. 'I hear the pipe!' said Charlotte, grasping my arm. I listened. The sound was faintly heard, then lost, then heard again. By degrees it swelled into distinctness; the trampling of horses, – the tread of a multitude was heard, – voices mingled with the sound.

*Hamlet, – *Town.*

Charlotte ran forward, and then returned again. 'No! I cannot meet him before all these people,' said she; and we retreated to the house.

I saw through the dusk the stately figures of the chief and his son approaching on foot from the gate where they had dismounted; and I stole back into the parlour, unwilling that my presence should embarrass the expected meeting. Yet, with a fluttering heart, I listened eagerly to their quickened steps, – to the clasp of affection, – to the whisper of rapture. 'Brother!' – 'Charlotte!' pronounced in the scarcely articulate accents of ecstasy, were for some moments the only words uttered; the next that reached my ear, were those in which the traveller eagerly enquired for me. I sprang foward, for it was a well remembered voice that spoke; but the next moment I shrank before the flashing glance of Maitland!

CHAPTER XXX

Here have I found at last a home of peace,
To hide me from the world! far from its noise,
To feed that spirit which, though ——
—— linked to human beings by the bond
Of earthly love, hath yet a loftier aim
Than perishable joy! and through the calm
That sleeps amid this mountain solitude,
Can hear the billows of eternity,
And hear delighted!

John Wilson.

'But seriously, Charlotte,' said I, when at a late hour we found ourselves once more alone in our chamber, 'seriously, do you think it was quite right in you to use this concealment with me?'

'Seriously, I think it was. Long before I knew you, I could have guessed that you would dislike receiving even a trifling service from Mr ——. No, I never yet called Henry Graham by that upstart mercantile name, and I never will. To tell you the truth, Ellen, my brother had so far made me his confidant, that, judging of you by myself, I thought you would rather lose your money than owe it to his good offices.'

'I am sorry you thought it necessary to humour my pride at such an expense. Humbled and mortified I might have been by any kindness from Mr Maitland; but I have perhaps deserved the humiliation more than the kindness. He owes me a little mortification, for drawing him into the greatest folly he ever was guilty of.'

'Oh you must not imagine that all my discretion was exerted only to humour your saucy spirit. I had a purpose of my own to serve. I dare say we should never have slid into any real intimacy, if you had known me to be the sister of a quondam lover; watching, no doubt, with a little womanly jealousy, the character of one whom my favourite brother *once* loved better than me.'

'I am persuaded this could have made little difference; for my faults, unfortunately, will not be concealed; and my good qualities I shall always be willing enough to display.'

'Oh, to be sure, my dear humble Miss Percy would knowingly and wittingly have come here to ingratiate herself with us all! No doubt, you would have been much more at home with us, had you known our connection with your old admirer! and no doubt, you would have quietly waited his arrival here, that you might be courted in due form!'

'Pshaw, Charlotte, I am sure that it – I hope – I mean, I am quite certain that your brother has no such nonsense in his thoughts. And I am sure it is much better it should be so; for you know I have always told you that I have a natural indifference about me – Heigho!'

'What! even after you have seen that "it was your duty to be in love long ago!" Will you "deprive" yourself of "the honour," the "happiness" ——'

'Surely, Charlotte, you will never be so mischievous, so cruel, as to repeat these thoughtless, unmeaning expressions to your brother! You know they were spoken under entire misconception. And, besides, to be sensible of what I ought once to have done is a very different thing from being able to do it now.'

'Make yourself quite easy, my dear Ellen,' said Charlotte, with a provoking smile, 'I have more *esprit de corps* than to tell a lady's secret. Besides, even for my brother's own sake, I shall leave him to make discoveries for himself. But by the way, it is very good-natured in me to promise all this; for I have reason to be angry, that you think it necessary to warn me against repeating any thing uttered in the mere unguardedness of chit-chat.'

I made no apology; for I have such an abhorrence of trick and contrivance of every kind, that, to own the truth, I, at that moment, felt half-justified in withdrawing part of my confidence from Charlotte. 'How in the world did such a scheme occur to you?' said I, after a pause. 'Nothing like a plot ever enters my head.'

'It occurred to me in the simplest way possible, my dear. Henry writes to me remitting your money; describing you so as to prevent any chance of imposition; and charging me not to rest till I have found you. "It will distress her," says he, "to owe this little service to me, but perhaps there is no remedy." Now, was not the very spirit of contradiction enough to make one devise a remedy? Then he goes on – stay, here is the letter: –

' "If she be found, I do not ask you to receive her to your acquaintance, to your intimacy. There is something in Miss Percy which will irresistibly win you to both. But I do ask you to tell me, with perfect candour, the impression which her character makes upon your mind. Tell me, with minute exactness, of her temper, her sentiments, her employments, her pleasures. Describe even her looks and gestures. There is meaning in the least of them. Write fearlessly – I am no weak lover now. I know you ladies are all firm believers in the eternity of love; and one part of the passion is indeed immortal in a heart of ordinary warmth and delicacy. My interest in Miss Percy's welfare and improvement is not less strong than in yours, my own Charlotte. Perhaps the precariousness of her situation even turns my anxieties more strongly towards her. Of course, this will no longer be the case when I know that she is safe at Eredine; for you must prevail upon her to visit Eredine. She has a thousand little *womanlinesses* about her, which you could never observe in an ordinary acquaintance of calls and tea-drinkings; and you must be intimate with her before you can know or value that delightful warmth and singleness of heart, which cannot but attach you. I am sure she will bewitch my father. There is a gladness in her smile that will delight his very soul."

'Have not Henry and I shown a very decent portion of Highland second-sight and discretion, think you, Ellen? His prediction has been quite verified; and I am sure I have managed the plot incomparably.'

'Ah, but Charlotte, after all, I wonder how you found it practicable. It was a hundred to one that somebody should have let me into the secret.'

'Hum! I might have been in some danger while we were in Edinburgh, though few people there knew any thing of the matter. But, from the moment we reached Glen Eredine, I knew we were safe. Nobody here would mention to an inmate of our family the only shade that ever rested on its name. Thank Heaven, even this stain is effaced now; – if, indeed, it be a stain to submit to a temporary degradation in obedience to a mother. You need not smile, Ellen. I am not so prejudiced as you think me. I know that, if the name of those merchants had been mean as obscurity could make it, it would have become honourable when borne by Henry Graham. And to be sure, all professions are alike in the eye of reason; only there are some which I think a gentleman should leave to people who need money to distinguish them.'

'Well,' said I, laughing, 'now that you have convinced me that you have no prejudice, tell me how you could be sure that I only knew your brother by his "upstart mercantile name." If he had had the spirit of his sister, he could not have refrained from hinting his right to be called a Graham.'

'Oh, but Henry has nothing boastful in his disposition; and I knew that, having given up his name to please his uncle, he scorned to make the sacrifice by halves. The old gentleman hated us all as a clan of rebels; and, while he lived, my mother would never even allow us to address our letters to Henry under his real name; and I don't believe poor Henry himself ever mentioned it to a human being. So, before I saw you, I guessed that you might not be in the secret; and the moment I entered on the business with you, I found I had guessed right. But I dare say Henry will tell you his whole story now; for you must have many a confidential *tête-à-tête*.'

Confidential *tête-à-têtes* with Mr Maitland! The idea led me into such a reverie, that before I spoke again Charlotte was in bed, and asleep.

I rose early; and yet, in three months of country negligence, my clothes had all grown so troublesomely unbecoming, that, before I could make them look tolerable, the family were assembled at breakfast. Maitland took his place by me. 'I will sit between my sisters,' said he; and from that time he called me, 'Sister Ellen.' The kindness of his manner made me burn with shame at the recollection of my ungenerous purpose against his peace. I held down my head, and was ready to thank Heaven that I saw him well and happy. I was very glad, however, when I handed him his tea, that my hand and arm were quite as beautiful as ever. My embarrassment soon wore away. Maitland had evidently forgiven, he had almost, I thought, forgotten my misconduct. So respectful, so kind were his attentions, so equally divided between Charlotte and me, that I soon forgot my restraint; and caught myself chattering and playing the fool in my own natural manner.

The day was past before I was aware; and every day stole away I know not how. Their flight was marked only by our progress in the books which Maitland read with Charlotte and me; or by that of a large plantation which we all superintended together. Yet I protest, I have suffered more weariness in one party of pleasure, than I did in a whole winter in Glen Eredine. For, though the gentlemen always spent the mornings apart from us, Charlotte and I were at no loss to fill up the hours of their absence in the duties consequent upon being not only joint housewives in the Castle, but schoolmistresses, chamber-council, physicians, apothecaries, and listeners-general to all the female inhabitants of Glen Eredine. What endless, what innumerable stories did this latter office oblige me to hear? I am persuaded that I know not only the present circumstances and characters of every person in the Glen, but their family history from time immemorial, besides certain prophetic glimpses of their future fortunes.

I entirely escaped, however, the heavier labour of entertaining idle gentlemen; for the bitterest storm of winter never confined Eredine or Mr Graham to the fireside. Wrapped in their plaids, they braved the blast, as the sports or the employments of the field required; and returned prepared to be pleased with every thing at home. Our evenings were delightful; enlivened as they were by Eredine's cheerfulness, Charlotte's frank vivacity, and Henry's sly quiet humour.

How often in their course did I wonder that I could ever think Maitland cold and stately? His extensive information, his acquaintance with scenes and manners which were new to us all, did indeed render his conversation a source of instruction, as well as of amusement; but no man was ever more free from that tendency towards dogma and harangue, which is so apt to infect those who chiefly converse with inferiors. He joined his family circle, neither determined to be wise nor to be witty, but to give and receive pleasure. His was the true fire of conversation; the kindly warmth was essential to its nature, the brilliance was an accident. Maitland, indeed – but I must bid farewell to that name, the only subject on which I cannot sympathise with the friends whom I love the best. To me, though it be coupled with feeling of self-reproach and regret, it is associated too with all that is venerable in worth, and all that is splendid in eloquence. I exchange it for a noble name, – a name which has mingled with many a wild verse, and many a romantic tale, – a name which the historian and the poet shall celebrate when they blazon actions more dazzling, but not more virtuous than those which daily marked the life of Henry Graham!

Spring came; and never, since the first spring adorned Eden, did that season appear so lovely! So soft were its colours, so balmy its breezes, so pure, so peaceful its moonlight, – such repose, such blest seclusion, such confidential kindly home-breathing sweetness were in every scene! I shall never forget the delightful coolness of a shower that dimpled the calm lake, as Graham and I stood sheltered by an old fantastic fir-tree. No sound was heard but the hush of the rain drops, and now and then the distant wailing of the water-fowl. 'How often, both sleeping and awake, have I dreamt of this!' said Graham, in the low confiding tone which scarcely disturbed the stillness. 'And even now, I can scarcely believe that it is not all a dream. This profound repose! every shadow sleeping just where it lay, when I used to wonder what immeasurable depth of waters could so represent the vault of heaven! And after my weary exile, to be thus near to all that is dearest to me, – to feel their very touch, – their very breath on my cheek ——'

I know not how it happened, but at that moment, I breathed with some difficulty, and moved a little away. But then I suddenly recollected that Charlotte was standing at his other side; and I moved back again, lest he should think me very silly indeed. For Mr Graham was no lover of mine; that is, he never talked of love to me; but I had begun to feel an odd curiosity to know whether he ever would talk of it, and when.

I pondered this matter very deeply for some days; and, after sundry lonely rambles, and sederunts under the aforesaid fir-tree, I convinced myself that, if Mr Graham chose to make love, I could not, without abominable ingratitude, refuse to listen.

I had returned from one of these rambles, and was just going to enter the parlour, when, as I opened the door, I was arrested by the voice of Graham within, speaking in that impressive tone of suppressed emotion which he had already fixed irrevocably in my recollection. 'If it be so,' said he, 'I am gone to-morrow. This day se'nnight I shall be in London.'

I was thunderstruck. He was going then without a thought of me! My hand dropped from the lock; and I turned away, in a confused desire to escape from his sight and hearing.

'Bless me! Ellen! what is the matter with you?' cried Charlotte, whom I met on the stair. I hurried past her without speaking, and shut myself into my own apartment.

'What *is* the matter with me!' said I, throwing myself on a seat. The question was no sooner asked than answered; and, though I was alone, I could not help covering my face with my hands. The first distinct purpose which broke in upon my amazement and consternation was, to see Graham no more; to remain in my place of refuge till he was gone; and then – it did not signify what then! – all after-life must be a blank then!

However, I was obliged to yield to Charlotte's entreaties for admission; and, though all the interests of life were so soon to close, I was obliged to take my tea; and then I was half forced to try the open air, as a remedy for the headach, to which, like all heroines, I ascribed my agitation. I somewhat repented of this compliance, however, when I found that Graham was to be the companion of my walk; and, though I could not decently refuse to take his arm, I endeavoured to look as frozen and disagreeable as possible. He spoke to me, however, with such kind solicitude; such respectful tenderness, that I was soon a little reconciled to myself and him; and when Charlotte declared that she must stop to visit a sick cottager, and he would by no means allow me to breathe the close air of the cabin, I must own that I began to feel an instinctive desire to escape a *tête-à-tête*. But I had not presence of mind enough to defeat his purpose, and we pursued our walk together.

He led me towards a little woody dell; I talking laboriously without having any thing to say, he preserving an abstracted silence. But this could not long continue; and, by the time we had lost sight of human dwelling, our conversation was confined to short sentences, which, at intervals of some minutes, made the listener start. In mere escape from the awkwardness of my situation, I uttered some common-place on the beauty of the scenery; and desired Graham to look back towards the bright lake, seen through the vista formed by the shaggy rocks, which threw a twilight round us.

'Yes,' said he, with a faint smile; 'let us stand and look at it together for a few short moments. Perhaps one of us will never again see it with pleasure. Lean on me, dear Miss Percy, as you are used to do, and let me be happy while I dare.

He paused, but my eloquence was exhausted. I could not utter a word.

'This night, this very hour,' he went on, 'must make all these beauties a sickening blank to me, or perhaps heighten their interest a thousand fold! Before we part this night, Ellen, I must learn from you whether duty and pleasure are never to unite for me. You know how long I have loved you, but I fear you can scarcely guess how tenderly. Dearest Ellen! think what the affection must be, which withstood your errors, your indifference, your scorn; – which neither time nor absence, nor reason, could overcome. Think what it must be now, when I see thee all that man ought to love! To live without you now, to remember thy form in every scene, and know that thou art gone: – oh, Ellen! do not force me to bear this! Say that you will permit me to try what perseverance, what love unutterable, can do to win for me such affection as will satisfy your own sense of duty, your own innocent mind, in that blessed connection which would make us more than lovers or friends to each other.'

He paused in vain for a reply. If the fate of the universe had depended on my speaking, I could have uttered nothing intelligible. I suppose, however, the pleader began to conceive good hopes of his cause; for a certain degree of saucy exultation mingled with the tones of entreaty, as he said, 'Speak to me, dearest Ellen – only one word. Tell me that I may one day hope to hear you own, that friendship, or habit, or call it what you will, has made me necessary to your happiness.'

I would have given the world for some expression that should convey decent security to the worthy heart of Graham, without quite betraying the weakness of my own. 'I cannot promise,' said I, without daring to look up, 'that ever you will bring me to actual confession.'

'Nay, Ellen,' said the unreasonable creature, 'think you this little coquettish answer will content a man who asks his whole happiness from you?'

'I am sure I do not mean to coquet. Tell me what you wish me – what I ought to say, and I will say it, – if I can.'

'My own, my bewitching Ellen –' said Graham.

But hold! I will not tell what he said. If Henry Graham for once spoke nonsense, it would ill become me to record it. Nor will I relate my answer; because, in truth, I know not what it was. But Graham understood it to mean, that I was no longer the arrogant girl whose understanding, dazzled by prosperity, was blind to his merit; whose heart, hardened by vanity, was insensible to his love; no longer the thoughtless being whose hopes and wishes were engrossed by the most substantial of all the cheats that delude us in this world of shadows; – but a humbled creature, thankful to find, in his sound mind and steady principle, a support for her acknowledged weakness;

– a traveller to a better country, pleased to meet a fellow-pilgrim, who, animating her diligence, and checking her wanderings, might soothe the toils of her journey, and rejoice with her for ever in its blessed termination.

I have now been many years a wife; and, in all that time, have never left, nor wished to leave, Glen Eredine. Graham is still a kind of lover; and though I retain a little of the coquettish sauciness of Ellen Percy, I here confess that he is, if it be possible, dearer to me than when he first folded his bride to his heart, and whispered, 'Mine for ever.'

We are still the guests of our venerable father; and within this hour he told me, that his heart makes no difference between me and his own Charlotte. Some misses lately arrived from a boarding-school, have begun to call my sister an old maid; yet I do not perceive that this cabalistic term has produced any ill effect on Charlotte's temper, or on her happiness.

I am the mother of three hardy, generous boys, and two pretty, affectionate little girls. But far beyond my own walls extend the charities of kindred. Many a smoke, curling in the morning sun, guides my eye to the abode of true, though humble friends; for every one of this faithful romantic race is united to me by the ties of relationship. I am the mother of their future chieftain. Their interests, their joys, their sorrows, are become my own.

Having in my early days seized the enjoyments which selfish pleasure can bestow, I might now compare them with those of enlarged affections, of useful employment, of relaxations truly social, of lofty contemplation, of devout thankfulness, of glorious hope. I might compare them! – but the Lowland tongue wants energy for the contrast.

THE END